ISTHMUS of PANAMA

N
S

RIVER CHAGRES

CONTINENTAL DIVIDE

RIVER

Cruces

CRUCES

Gorgona

Bas Obispo

Gold Hill

Culebra
(Summit)

TRAIL

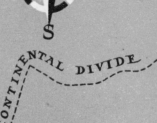

Cangri

PANAMA

La Boca

Pacific Ocean

TEN THOUSAND SHALL DIE

Few countries in the world have a bloodier, more dramatic or more erotic history than the Isthmus of Panama; save, perhaps, Haiti, the scene of Peter Bourne's best-selling novel, *Black Saga*. The narrow strip of mountainous jungle, which holds the Atlantic and Pacific apart by only thirty-five miles, forms the background of Peter Bourne's third novel.

Forced by the treachery of Al Simpson to flee from his home at Boston, Mass., Henry Stewart (only son of Duncan Stewart, hero of *Black Saga*) pursues the other man to Panama at the very time that the gold rush of '49 was attracting thousands of fortune hunters to California by way of the Isthmus. Henry reaches Panama only to find that his man has disappeared into the interior. Henry has sworn an oath not to return home until he has secured an admission of Simpson's guilt, so he determines to remain in this lawless, tropical country until he succeeds. Thanks to James McCollum, a surveyor, he is offered work with the firm of constructional engineers who have contracted to build a railroad across the Isthmus. Thus he becomes involved in one of the most spectacular feats of nineteenth-century engineering: a feat which cost ten thousand human lives before the last tie was laid.

Henry Stewart never loses sight of the reason which brought him to the country, the proof of his innocence. With implacable determination he maintains the hunt for his one-time friend, although three women dominate his life throughout that period: Abigail Vandusen, explorer and novelist, whom men accept on terms of equality because of her masterful personality; Maisie, a child of easy virtue from the House of All Nations, whose soft body and whimsical personality are in sharp contrast to Abigail's masculinity; and finally, Jean Martin, the girl he really loves.

PETER BOURNE

has also written:

BLACK SAGA

DUPE OF DESTINY

TEN THOUSAND SHALL DIE

by

Peter Bourne

HUTCHINSON & CO. (Publishers) LTD
London New York Melbourne Sydney Cape Town

First published 1951

Printed in Great Britain
by The Anchor Press, Ltd.,
Tiptree, Essex

CHAPTER ONE

"HEY there, Henry!"

Henry Stewart turned. The open swing-doors of Murphy's Saloon were framing the unsteady figure of Albert Simpson. His tail coat was wrinkled, the top buttons of his canary waistcoat undone, his tall hat was awry above his handsome, dissipated face. His smooth hand beckoned.

"C'mon in, Henry. C'mon in for a drink."

Henry shook his head. "Too early in the day, Al——"

"It's never too early for a beer on a hot day like this." Simpson lurched forward, and linked his arm with Henry's. "Be a sport, and c'mon in."

Henry tried to shake himself free from Simpson's clutch, but the other man held on with alcoholic obstinacy.

"Let go of my arm, Al," he urged in a mild voice. "I'm not a rich man's son, with nothing to do all day. I'm a business man." He patted the small leather case which he carried in his left hand, and which was secured to his wrist by a light, strong chain. "See!"

"Aw! Just one! I want someone intelligent to talk to for five minutes. I'm tired of those bums in there."

With Simpson still gripping his right arm, Henry realized that he would have difficulty in refusing the friendly invitation without attracting general attention.

Already, two women farther along the sidewalk were staring at him with reproving eyes instead of entering the brougham which awaited them. It really seemed as if the easier course would be to go in. Besides, it was a hot day, and five minutes more or less would not affect his mission.

"All right, Al. Just five minutes, no more."

Simpson roared approval. Giving one of the swing-doors a lusty kick he re-entered the saloon, dragging Henry in after him.

The saloon was practically empty. Apart from the pasty-faced bartender, who lounged against the bottle-filled shelf at his back and picked his teeth with a corkscrew, only two other men were present. They sat, side by side, on high stools at the far end of the bar, and gazed with maudlin eyes at their own reflection in the gilt-framed mirror which lined the wall behind the bartender. They were dressed in sailor's clothes, and had the appearance of foreigners.

"Sit down." Simpson pushed Henry on to a high stool near the door. "Joe," he called out. "Two beers."

With a weary air the bartender produced two tall glasses which he filled and placed before the two men. Simpson grabbed at his glass and half-drained it. His eyes were feverish; his manner nervous. Henry realized that his companion was tipsier than he had thought. He raised his own glass. The bitterness of the chilled liquid rasped his throat.

"Haven't seen you for some weeks, Henry. Your father again?"

Henry nodded. "He found out that I'm owing money to that damned Finklestein. You know what he's like on the subject of spending money on frivolous amusements!"

Simpson grimaced. "I haven't forgotten the lecture he gave me the other day. Told me I ought to be ashamed of myself, not working and spending my father's hard-earned money."

"Father's not one to mince his words."

"A dour Scotsman all right."

"American, Al, since he came to live in Boston. He's touchy on that subject. Proud as can be of being American."

"Was he proud enough to pay your debt to Finklestein?"

"Not he! Said it would do me more good to deduct ten dollars a week from my allowance until I had enough to pay the debt. Then he would give it to me in a lump sum."

"What about interest meanwhile?"

"That's what I pointed out. He said I must pay it out of what I earn at Evans and Talbot."

Henry gazed with self-commiseration at the rueful reflection which stared back at him from the mirror, and was startled by its blurred outline. He rubbed his eyes, but the reflection did not clear.

"Trouble is, Henry, your father married too old in life. He oughtn't to have had children."

"Too old . . ." Henry mumbled. What was the matter with the mirror? Everything in it was blurred. Al's face . . . the bartender's back . . . everything in the saloon . . . "Al——"

"What is it?"

"I don't think I'm feeling well—the place is swimming round."

"Think nothing of it, Henry. It's the effect of the heat, and the cold beer. Have another to cool you off."

"No——"

"Joe! Another beer for Mr. Stewart."

The taciturn bartender reached in leisurely fashion for two more glasses, but to Henry he was floating in the air. The pasty face, with its top of oiled-black hair, grew larger—still larger.

II

Then he saw that only the face was visible; that everything round about it was as black as the hair. He puzzled over this phenomenon; but in a casual manner, for he felt far too mentally lackadaisical to worry overmuch. But presently, as his brain slowly emerged from its torpor, other facts impressed themselves upon his consciousness. That he was lying on his back, for instance; that the blackness was studded with stars; and that the bartender's face had become a full moon.

At last the truth became a matter of concern; he realized that he was no longer in Murphy's Saloon, drinking a glass of chilled beer in the company of Al Simpson, but lying in a field some place, staring into the moon-lit night sky.

Alarmed, he sat up; but his left hand was firmly secured to the ground. He struggled to free it, and presently did so; to find that only his own weight had been holding it down. The coldness of loose chain at his wrist recalled to his memory the leather case to which it would have been attached.

"Oh God!" he muttered, for there had been ten thousand dollars in New England Bank bills in the bag. With growing anxiety he scrambled to his feet, and looked about him for the missing bag. The moonlight made everything near at hand clearly visible, but he struck match after match in the hope of detecting the small leather bag; and searched every yard of meadow within walking pace. The last of his matches burned out after it had scorched his fingers.

Even after that he prolonged his search, but was forced to realize that the case was gone and with it a week's wages for the staff of Evans and Talbot.

He was dazed with misery; but appreciating that quick action was necessary, he steadied himself and looked about him. He was some place far beyond the outskirts of the city, for he could see at least a mile in all directions; and nowhere could he see anything which remotely resembled a building. But nearby, in the direction of the Pole Star, he saw a line of trees which he hoped marked a road. He walked forward and presently was relieved to come across a rutted road which was running approximately east and west.

Which direction should he take for Boston? Without any means of knowing whether he was north, south or west of the city, he decided to travel east; at any rate until he reached a farm or other house where he could ask his way. So he turned his back on the Pole Star, and began walking. And thinking.

It was soon apparent that his memory was unlikely to help him bridge the gap between the moment when he became giddy in Murphy's Saloon and his regaining consciousness in the middle of a meadow. He could remember nothing of the intervening hours.

Nor could he think of any explanation to account for his being so far away from Boston. To begin with, why had Al, upon seeing him lose consciousness, not taken him home? Even if Al had been unwilling to face the accusing eyes, at least he could have paid the driver of a hackney to complete the final stage of the journey. Or, if he had fallen similarly ill—which Henry did not for one moment believe—surely the silent bartender would have called the watch to deal with the situation.

His thoughts went round in circles, never making sense, until they were disturbed by the echo of slow pounding hooves, and the rumble and creaking of wheels. Far ahead of him he saw the uncertain glow of a lamp. Later he was able to distinguish the outline of an approaching wagon, piled high with hay and the shadowy forms of three people; a man, a woman, and a child.

As the wagon approached, Henry halted beside the road and raised his hat.

"Whoa there!" the man called out. The wagon came to a creaking stop.

" 'Evening, wagoner. 'Evening, mam."

The man answered, "Evenin', mister. Want something?"

"Am I headed right for Boston?"

"No place else."

"How far off?"

"Nothing under three miles, I guess, though I ain't never been that far since I were so high."

"What would the time be?"

"Nigh on ten."

"Thanks." He raised his hat again. "Good night, mam."

"Good night, sir," she answered in a sweet, musical voice. The man echoed, " 'Night, mister," then "Gidup thar!" And the hooves of the two animals thudded on the hard road as they strained forward.

Henry strode on with growing anxiety. He had guessed that the hour could not be much less than ten, but now that he had received confirmation of the fact he thought of his parents, and shared their worry on his behalf. They would not normally have been alarmed by his absence from home at that hour, even without previous warning, for he had long since thrashed out with his father his determination to lead his own life within reasonable bounds. This night, he was miserably certain, would not be normal. Undoubtedly, Mr. Evans would have sent one of the staff round to the Stewart home to find out what had happened to his missing cashier. As soon as they learned that Henry had been carrying a large sum of money it was certain that his parents would conclude that some calamity had overtaken him.

So he hurried home as briskly as he could. He did not know whereabouts he was, or the names of the villages he passed through. He cared less. The more thought he gave to his situation the blacker it seemed. Unless the ten thousand dollars were found intact—a possibility that seemed less likely with every passing minute—it was certain that the tight-lipped, tight-fisted Aaron Evans would not be agreeable to standing its loss. The chances were that he would demand its immediate repayment on the grounds of Henry's carelessness; if not from Henry himself—which was an impossibility, Henry reflected bitterly—then he would try to obtain the amount, by fair means or foul, from Henry's father. And

Duncan Stewart, Henry knew, would pay, though he could ill afford to do so. For Duncan, in spite of his undeviating strictne with his two children, adored them both. For their sakes he would, if necessary, sacrifice his own comfort and that of his beloved wife. Besides, even if love did not urge the sacrifice, pride would. The Stewart pride and obstinacy; the dour pride and wilful obstinacy of Scots forbears.

At last, in the near distance, the lights of Boston. Henry's pace quickened, and soon he had moved out of the silver darkness of the countryside into the shadowed streets of the city, lighted by hissing gas-jets that were dull and yellow and ugly.

Then home. In total darkness. For some seconds his agitated hand was unable to guide his key into the lock: when he did so, still the door did not open: it had been bolted. He swallowed as he extracted the key, and tugged at the wrought-iron bell-pull. The jangle of the bell echoed loudly in the kitchen.

He looked up at the windows of the bedrooms above. The first room to show a light was his sister Peggy's; he saw her shadow on the curtains dance up and down as she lit the bedside candle, and slipped into a dressing-gown.

"Hurry up, Pegs," he whispered to himself, acutely anxious that she, and not his father, should let him into the house.

He was to be disappointed. Before Peggy had had time to hurry downstairs he heard the noise of the bolts being drawn. The door opened. He saw his father, clad in dressing-gown, night-cap and felt slippers, peering near-sightedly at him in the orange light of the brass lamp which the old man held up in his left hand. Because there was still no light in the bedroom he realized that his parents must have been waiting up for him in the back parlour.

"So ye are hame, at last, boy!" Duncan muttered, lapsing in the moment of stress into the accent of his youth. His voice grew stern, ominous. "Enter."

There was a glow of light in the back parlour; through the half-open door Henry could see his mother sitting in the rocker. Her eyes were red-rimmed, and she held a handkerchief to her pale, trembling lips.

Duncan led the way into the parlour, and sitting down, indicated that Henry should do the same.

"What have you to say for yourself?" Before there could be any reply he added, "Mr. Evans has been here. Where have you been all day? Where is the firm's money?"

"I—I don't know, sir."

"What?" Duncan's voice grew sharper.

"I don't know where I've been, nor where the money's gone. I've been unconscious——"

"Henry! Oh, Henry! You're ill." Jean half rose from her chair as if to hurry to her son's side.

"Sit down, Mother!" Duncan ordered; whereupon she obediently sank back into the rocker, but gazed at her son with a loving trust that no sternness on her husband's part would ever dispel. "He looks well enough to me."

Henry nodded. "I've been walking, sir. More than four miles." He continued hurriedly, "I'll tell you everything; what little there is to tell. On my way back from the bank, with the week's wages, I met Al Simpson——"

Duncan's mouth tightened. "That good-for-nothing rascal!"

"He had been drinking in Murphy's Saloon. He forced me to go back into the bar with him——"

"Forced!" The old man glared furiously at his son. "Did you say *forced*? You, a grown man, let that popinjay, that milk-and-water wastrel, *force* you——"

"Duncan, please, let Henry tell his story," Jean pleaded.

"I don't mean by physical means. I told you he had been drinking. He would have made a scene if I had refused."

"What if he had?"

"I—I don't care for scenes in public places," Henry nervously explained. "Inside the saloon wouldn't have mattered so much. I agreed to have one beer——"

"And then you took enough to become intoxicated!" the old man accused scornfully.

"That I did not," Henry retorted, spurred to anger by his father's manner. "I took only one—less than one. The room started going round in circles. That's all I know. When I came to I was lying in a meadow, four miles from the city."

"And the money. . . ?"

Henry shrugged. "Was gone."

A long silence followed his unhappy explanation. His mother's lips quivered so much that he feared she might sob, which would exasperate his father and increase the tension in the quiet room. But with courage she restrained her emotion, and gazed at her son with a loyalty and serene confidence in him which made his own eyes smart with the intensity of his gratitude.

Meanwhile, Duncan's stern face became drawn with uncertainty and distress as common sense derided both the story he had just heard and his instinctive belief in his son's probity. Something of the stiff, upright posture of which he was so inordinately proud deserted him. His shoulders bowed, and he fidgeted with his small white beard with fingers which were normally kept under strict control. For he was still a fine figure of a man, in spite of his years, and though his hair was as white as cumulus, it was as abundant and as unruly as it had been in his youth, when he had first landed in Saint Domingue.

Perhaps a memory of those far-off days stirred his emotions as his keen blue eyes regarded Henry in a steadying scrutiny; for there was in Henry so much of himself at the same age: the same untidy mop of red hair which no comb was ever able to subdue, the same deeply set eyes, the same rugged chin, obstinate, wilful, defiant. In one respect alone did the two faces vary, the past and the present: for in Henry's face a suggestion of recklessness, an expression of devil-may-care cynicism, was substituted for his father's dour, sombre prudence.

It was the existence of this headstrong streak in his son which worried Duncan; the fear that Henry might deliberately have spent the firm's wages in a wild spree; not in any spirit of dishonesty, but as a deliberate gesture of rebellion against the harsh rule of Aaron Evans. But Duncan also knew that, in the several tussles of will which he had had with his son since the boy was old enough to think for himself, Henry had never tried to excuse himself with a lie.

"I believe you, boy." Duncan straightened his back. "Have you any idea how you came to be in the country?"

"None, sir. I have tried to make sense of it."

"Did Simpson take you there?"

"Surely he would have brought me here, or seen that I was brought home."

"Unless he was too intoxicated to realize what he was doing. Perhaps he was seen to leave you there by some ill-disposed men who took advantage of your unconscious state to steal the money——"

His words were interrupted by the loud jangle of the front door-bell.

Hope brought comfort to Duncan. "Perhaps that's Al, with the money—or somebody else."

Lamp in hand he hurried to the door, opened it. The pale orange light revealed the burly figure of a night constable.

"Mr. Stewart—Mr. Henry Stewart?"

Henry nodded eagerly. "You have recovered the money——"

"Money!" The man laughed drily. " 'Tis not money I've brought ye, sor. 'Tis a warrant, me boy. A warrant of arrest. Will ye be coming wi' me now——"

CHAPTER TWO

"What is wrong, boy? Who is there?" Duncan called out as he walked towards the front door. "Has someone returned the money?"

"It's a police constable, sor," the man replied for himself in a respectful tone. "And it's bad, not good news, I'm bringing ye, to be sure."

"He says he has a warrant for my arrest, Father."

"Arrest! Nonsense——"

" 'Tis no nonsense. I've a proper sworn warrant for ye son's arrest in me pocket, if ye'll be whistful to see it."

"On what charge? Who's sworn a charge against him?"

"Mr. Aaron Evans, sor. He has charged Mr. Henry Stewart here with having absconded wi' the sum of ten thousand dollars, same being the property of the firm of Evans and Talbot of this city."

"Then Mr. Evans is a villain and a calumniator. My son is here, as you can see with your own eyes."

"Shure I can!" The constable slipped a hand under his hat and scratched his head in doubt. But his expression quickly turned obstinate. "What about the money? Can ye show me that, too?"

"I—I've lost it."

"Then ye must come wi' me to the gaol all the same, young sor."

"One moment," Duncan exclaimed sharply. "You can't lodge anyone in gaol because he's lost money. Losing money is not a crime."

"That's for him to tell his honour in the mornin', sor. Me own dooty now is plain. Having a warrant for his arrest it's me dooty to hand him over to the gaoler as soon as I can, after which it's no more of me business at all. So come along like a sinsible young gintleman; and don't be giving me any trouble, or it'll be the worse for you."

"The news that my son has spent a night in gaol, on a charge of theft, will ruin him, even when he is able to prove his innocence. Won't you wait until the morning?"

" 'Tis more than me job's worth, sor."

"I'm not a rich man, but what I could afford——"

The constable shook his head. " 'Tis no use, sor. I'll not be taking bribes from anyone. The young gintleman must come wi' me."

"One more moment, please," Duncan pleaded in desperation. "Suppose the money were to be found, and handed over to the magistrate for safe keeping?"

The constable appeared to weaken, so Duncan continued with vigour. "That my son has lost the money he is prepared to admit. If he should find it again no harm will have been done except to give you extra trouble."

" 'Tis not me that's complainin' of extra throuble; it's all in me line of dooty. But I'm a fair-minded man, and if the young gintleman can find the money within the next half-hour or so, well then I daresay Mr. Evans would agree to the warrant being withdrawn."

Henry shook his head. "It's no use, sir. Where could I hope to find it?"

"I don't know, but one can try." He turned to the police constable again. "Would you help look for the money? In my carriage, of course."

"Why not, sor, if it will help?"

"Thank you. Go, wake up James, Henry. Tell him to harness the horses and have the brougham on the road as soon as possible."

"Where should I go, sir? I searched the field——"

"To the home of your friend, Albert Simpson, of course," Duncan briskly answered. "He may know something of the money, God willing! And you're not going alone, boy. I'm going with you."

"You, Father?"

"Who else but your father, who believes in you, Henry."

"But at this time of night. It is late, well after eleven p.m.——"

"Would I rest easily while you were away? Will you step inside, Constable, and give me time to dress? I promise not to keep you waiting."

"Shure, an' I'll be glad to be of service to a gintleman like yourself." The man stepped into the house and removed his hat with a respectful gesture. "I'll drink to your success wi' finding the money, me young sor," he said to Henry.

II

Within twenty minutes the three men were on their way to the Simpson residence, not five minutes' drive distant. Upon arrival there Duncan's eyes were gladdened by observing that one of the windows of the ground floor was lighted.

The three men walked together to the main door of the old Colonial house, along a flagged path that was bordered on either side by a narrow strip of flower garden with lawn beyond. Farther off, also on either side, a row of handsome trees separated the property from the neighbouring grounds.

Their knock was answered by a white-haired Negro, whose large soft eyes smiled acknowledgment of Henry. He bowed his head with a courtly gesture.

"Good evening, gentlemen." He waited expectantly.

"Good evening, Moses." Henry's voice quickened with eagerness. "Has Mr. Albert retired to bed yet? I want to speak with him."

"Mr. Albert!" The Negro's eyes widened. "No, suh, Mr. Albert ain't done gone to bed yet."

"Good! Then let him know we are here, please."

Henry expected Moses to step aside, and invite the visitors to enter, but the man did nothing: he stood still and stared at Henry with white-rimmed eyes.

"Did you hear what I said, Moses? We want to speak with Mr. Albert."

"Yes, suh, I heared, but I jest kain't do what you say."

Overwrought by the events of the day Henry lost his temper. "You get along pronto, you woolly-haired dummy, and give Mr. Albert my message or I——"

Before he could put his threat into words a nearby door opened, and Albert's father stepped out into the hall.

"What does this noise mean, Moses? Who are these gentlemen?" Then he recognized Henry. "Mr. Henry Stewart, sir, what does this late visit signify?"

"Your pardon, sir, for disturbing you at this time, but I must see Al at once on an urgent matter, and Moses refuses——"

"With reason, Mr. Stewart. Albert is not at home."

"Can you tell me where he is, sir? I must find him tonight —now——"

"That is impossible, sir. Albert is on the high seas."

Henry gazed at Simpson with such dismay that the older man sternly explained.

"My son has gone to seek for gold in California, sir, where I hope that the rough life he will be forced to undergo will make a man of him instead of a dissolute young wastrel who was no good to himself or the company he kept. If you will forgive plain words, sir, you will be better for not having his friendship to tempt you into bad habits."

"But—but—I must speak with him, Mr. Simpson," Henry said wildly. "I must ask him what happened to me today, after we had met——"

"You had met!" Simpson frowned. "I do not understand, sir.

Albert sailed yesterday evening, aboard the *s.s. Monarch*, bound
for the port of Chagres in the Isthmus of Panama."

"He didn't go. I met him today. In Murphy's Saloon—I had a
drink with him——"

"I myself escorted Albert aboard the *Monarch*, saw him into his
cabin, and there handed him five hundred dollars; which is all he
has to live on until he finds gold or seeks employment," Simpson
stated in a cold voice.

Duncan touched Henry's arm. "Come, Henry." To the man
inside, "I am Henry's father, sir. Please accept my sincere apologies
for this untimely call."

Simpson bowed. "I trust you accept my explanation, sir?"

"Unfortunately, sir, I do," Duncan replied sadly.

III

"Ye'd best come to the gaol wi'out any further fairy stories,"
the constable said as the three men sat down in the brougham. "Will
ye tell your man to take us there, sor."

"No! No! No!" Henry exclaimed violently. "I won't go. You
believe me, Father?"

"You have never lied to me before, Henry——"

"I haven't now. I swear I haven't."

"Ye should have chosen a man not on the high seas," the constable interrupted. There was no longer warmth or sympathy in
his voice.

"But I saw him in the saloon. I had a drink with him. A beer—
served by a man he called Joe." He caught hold of his father's arm.
"Joe will remember, especially if I was ill there. Joe will speak for
me. Tell James to go to Murphy's Saloon, opposite the Albany line
railroad station."

"Are you sure you want us to go there?" Duncan asked
sadly.

"Of course I do. If Joe is still there he'll remember me, I tell
you. He'll prove that Al was there this afternoon. He knows Al
well."

"Very well!" Duncan leaned out of the brougham window.

B

"Go to Murphy's Saloon, which is opposite the Albany line railroad terminus."

"Yes, suh."

The men rode in unhappy silence. They still did not speak when the carriage stopped. The saloon was open; light streamed out above and below the short swing-doors. As they crossed the sidewalk they heard the loud hum of conversation. This ceased as the three men entered; partly in surprise at seeing a man of Duncan's age and station visiting a drinking saloon, but mostly at the sight of the constable. It was certain that something unusual was happening, so in the cause of curiosity the dozen or so occupants postponed their talk, and the only man who ignored the newcomers was a drunk who sat alone at one table, and held a mumbling, almost unintelligible conversation with a non-existent companion.

Joe was still behind the bar, but this time he had a mate to help him serve; a bland Chinese whose lips, in contrast with Joe's taciturn features, were parted in a perpetual smile.

They walked up to the bar. The constable said, "Hullo, Joe."

Joe nodded.

Henry leaned forward. "Joe, tell my father and the constable that Mr. Simpson was here earlier on today."

"Who?"

"Mr. Albert Simpson."

Joe reflected. His sallow face remained expressionless. At last, "No."

"What do ye mean, Joe?" the constable asked. "Ye won't tell?"

"He wasn't here."

"Oh God!" Henry stared at the bartender. "He was. You served him——"

"Leave this to me, sor," the constable ordered. "Ye know this here Mr. Al Simpson?"

"Sure."

"How well?"

"Better than I know you, Pat."

"Good enough. When did ye last see him?"

"Three days ago. Came in for good-bye drink. Said he were going to Calyforn-i-a."

Henry could not contain his fury. "Damn you! He was here today. You know he was. You served him and me with beer."

"You?" Joe eyed Henry with blank eyes.

"Yes, me! Mr. Simpson dragged me in. We sat on those two seats at the door end. There were two sailors at the other. He ordered two beers. I was ill. You must remember———"

Joe began to pare and clean his nails with a penknife. "Never seen you before."

"Henry!" Duncan nodded towards the door. "Come. Don't make matters worse."

"But I was here, Father," Henry desperately pleaded. "How else could I know about Joe being here?"

Duncan turned away. The constable touched Henry. "Come on, sor, if ye wouldn't be wanting me to take ye out the hard way," he warned in a low voice.

Henry turned, and stumblingly followed his father into the brougham. The constable followed.

"And now?" Duncan asked the man. He sounded weary and sad.

"Ye'll not be wanting to come wi' us to the gaol, sor?"

"Of course. It is the least I can do."

"No, Father. I'd rather you didn't. It's—it's bad enough, but knowing you to be there and see———" Henry choked. "Besides, mother———"

"He's right, sor," the constable nodded. "Let us be after taking ye home first; and then, if ye'd care to lend us the carriage———"

"Very well." Duncan called out of the window. "Home."

The booming echo of clattering hooves made the street noisy when James tickled the flanks of the horses with the end of the whip.

"You don't believe me, Father?"

"I don't know what to think, boy. You've been wild this past year, but you've never lied to me."

"I haven't now. I swear I haven't."

"If you haven't, then Mr. Simpson has, and his Negro, and the bartender. Why should they lie?"

"God knows! I don't understand———"

"Tomorrow perhaps I shall be able to think more clearly. Tonight I feel too tired. The shock—my son accused of theft———"

"Why should I steal money, sir? I am not in need of any—not in debt——" Henry faltered, remembering that he did owe money —to Finklestein.

"But ye do, sor," the constable drily interrupted. "To Mr. Finklestein."

"What do you know about my son's debts?" Duncan demanded.

"Mr. Finklestein set a receipt for two hundred and fifty dollars on account of repayment of your son's debts to the office of Evans and Talbot late this afternoon. That is what made Mr. Evans decide to prosecute. I had no meaning to tell ye this, thinkin' ye'd know soon enough. But ye may as well know the worst now."

"Henry!" the anguished father exclaimed as he turned away and gazed out of the window.

But Henry was not consciously aware of his father's heartbroken silence. For him the constable's last words had changed everything. Until that moment he had begun to doubt himself; believing that, in the light of the evidence against him, that he must be suffering from some form of hallucination: perhaps his illness had preceded his imaginary visit to Murphy's Saloon, and the rest he had dreamed. No doubt he had been robbed while unconscious, and subsequently taken to the country. That explanation would not make liars of Mr. Simpson, Moses, and Joe the bartender, and was therefore reasonable. For why otherwise should all three men deliberately lie, in order, presumably, to prove him a thief?

But the repayment of a portion of his debt to Finklestein was something that could be no part of an hallucination. The money must have been paid to the moneylender by the real thief—together with a request that the receipt be sent to the offices of Evans and Talbot!—with the deliberate purpose of averting suspicion from himself by directing it at Henry Stewart.

The vile trick had its compensations, since it restricted to four the people who could have conceived it—for the existence of the debt was known to only four, other than himself and Finklestein: of those, Duncan Stewart was one. Of the three remaining, only one could have executed it—Al Simpson! Simpson, the spendthrift, the playboy, the despair of his father. Simpson, who knew that Henry was in the habit of passing Murphy's Saloon at a particular hour every Friday. Simpson, who had dragged him into the saloon.

Simpson, who (Henry no longer doubted) had bribed the bartender to become his accomplice.

The evidence that Simpson was at sea ceased to worry Henry. A brain cunning enough to invent such a vile plot could easily overcome that difficulty. What if the elder Simpson had seen his son aboard the *Monarch*? No doubt it had been a simple matter for Al to land again as soon as his father had left the quayside—there were several small hotels in the city where he could have spent the night. And with the money his father had given him, together with the stolen money, he could continue his easy way of life—for a time— in some other city in the States; New York, for instance. As for the future, that was a word that never had appeared in Al's dictionary. He would not trouble to anticipate the day when the last of his dollars would be spent.

Al was the plotter, the thief. That fact Henry no longer doubted. But with dismay he realized that his story might never be believed. People—and most of all His Honour at the trial—would merely accuse him of adding to his offence by trying to save himself at the expense of vilefying a friend who was not present to deny the calumny. In the absence of substantiation he would merely harm himself by such a defence. And where was that proof to come from? Given time he might obtain evidence from crew and passengers that Al did not, after all, sail to Panama aboard the *Monarch*; but that might take months, and on its own the fact that Al had not travelled to Panama was not proof that he had robbed Henry Stewart.

Even this evidence might not be forthcoming. If the *Monarch* were calling in at New York on her way south, Al could possibly board her there, and maintain that he had never left her—a bribe here and there would secure willing evidence that he had been seen aboard at some time or other during her passage between the two ports.

He gulped as he stared through the brougham window at the deserted streets. Nothing, he believed, could save him from a prison sentence on the charge of appropriating money belonging to his employers. Prison—and a future ruined by the taint of imprisonment.

Prison! A sentence of six months—a year—even two years.

Two years of hell behind brick walls and iron bars. Two years of mental and physical degradation.

The suggestion of recklessness in his face, which often made women regard him with pensive longing, grew more marked; and had the constable been alert it would have given him warning to guard his prisoner with care: fortunately, the man was looking elsewhere and hoping that his wife had kept the soup hot on the stove. It did not occur to him that the young rip by his side had determined to escape.

Henry trembled with anxiety. Everything now depended upon the old coachman.

"Gid along there, Mary, gid along, Susie," the old man mumbled, giving the two mares an affectionate flick with his whip.

CHAPTER THREE

THE carriage drew up outside the Stewart house. Duncan alighted.

"Good night, boy," he said in a gentle voice. "Forgive me if I do not say much now. I shall visit you early tomorrow. We shall be able to discuss the situation with clearer minds."

"I understand, sir."

"Thank you, and God be with you. Good night, Constable."

"Good night, sor, and it's sorry I am, to be shure."

"I am sure of that." He indicated his thanks with a courteous gesture, then turned and marched stiffly forward to his house along the flower-bordered path. The front door closed behind him without his having once turned.

"A fine figure of a man," the constable muttered. "Ye should be proud of him, sor."

"I am."

"Then remember that, in the days to come. And now, sor, if ye'll give orders to the coachman. The sooner I get ye to the watch house, the sooner we'll both be in our beds."

Henry leaned out of the window. His heart was beating so

fiercely that breathing was difficult. He hoped that the constable could not hear its wild thumping.

"James?"

"Mas' Harry?"

"The city gaol."

A startled exclamation from the coachman. Then a loud giggle. "You always was one fer a lil' joke, Mas' Harry."

"It's no joke, James. The gentleman with me is a constable. I'm being arrested for stealing money."

"Mas' Harry! Jest let me speak to dat man. I'll done tell him that you couldn't steal no money nohow——"

"No, James, that would do no good. He hasn't known me so long as you have. You take me to the gaol, like you used to in the old days when Miss Peggy and I were children. Do you remember?"

A long pause, and then, "Yes, Mas' Henry. Old James doan' forgit nothin'." He flicked the mares' rumps. "Gid along ma ladies, gid along."

Henry leaned back against the padded seat. He was sure that the old coachman had understood the reference to childhood games, and remembered one that Mas' Harry and Miss Peggy had enjoyed most of all. How many scores of times had he solemnly driven them and the Martin children, Jean and Duncan, named after Jean and Duncan Stewart, round the block on their way to gaol, or the giant's castle, or the Red Injun camp; and had been solemnly unaware of the fact that one or the other, or sometimes all but one, had leaped from the carriage and, shrieking with excitement, had escaped into the vast forest that occupied one corner of their garden, while the carriage had ambled on, carrying away the cruel gaoler—or the wicked giant—or the red Injuns with their scalping knives——

The carriage rumbled on through streets lined with gardens and private houses; streets so quiet that the noise of the iron-shod wheels on the cobbles seemed to the taut senses of the prisoner louder than that made by the heavy drays that were to be seen in the neighbourhood of the docks; he wondered how any of the occupants were able to sleep through the thunderous roar. The streets were deserted, too; a young spark, homeward bound, a night watchman, and two men, discussing the coming election in loud contentious voices, were the only people he saw on the sidewalk until they entered a less exclusive quarter.

He held himself alert for the warning he hoped James would give him—the old familiar "Jump now, Mas' Harry" (or Miss Peggy or Mas' Duncan, or Miss Jean, when it was the turn of another to escape). He hoped, too, that the old coachman would choose a convenient spot where there were side-roads down which to dodge.

But James drove on, and Henry began to lose hope, believing that the old man hadn't after all understood the meaning behind the cryptic reference to the past. Another minute or two and the opportunity to escape would be gone, for they were nearing the watch house. In desperation he wondered whether to leap out notwithstanding, and take the risk of speed making him lose balance. His hand moved stealthily towards the handle of the door.

"Mas' Harry!" There was pleading in old James's voice; a choking order that he must not hesitate, must not fail, must escape.

Henry wrenched open the door and leaped out. Even before he had done so the coachman had savaged the flanks of the mares with his whip, and made them rear up, then bound forward with a jerk which flung the rising, unbalanced constable back against the seat. As Henry raced down a narrow side-road he heard the echo of pounding hooves dying quickly away in the distance, and knew that James had improved upon the old game.

"Thanks, old man," he whispered into the wind.

Farther down the road he turned left, and later right; then left again, then right. Soon he had no idea which street he was in, but he hoped that he was making for the general direction of the docks. There, more than anywhere in the city, he hoped to be able to hide for a few hours; in some dark corner between wharves, or in a railroad wagon, or perhaps beneath a dray.

So he hurried on, not running any more for fear of attracting attention, but walking as quickly as he dared. Presently he saw tall spars outlined against the silvered sky, and knew that he had reasonable hope of retaining his liberty.

Some minutes later he crawled beneath the tarpaulin of an empty six-wheeled wagon which stank of hides. He stretched himself out on some old sacking and relaxed, breathing heavily. August dawn was not many hours away, so he decided to make the best possible use of his time. Here, in safety and quietness, he could think, and decide what his next move should be.

Flight from Boston was the first essential. After that, what? What indeed? The future, now that he had a moment to consider it, assumed an ever blacker aspect. A criminal charge had been laid against him; so long as it remained on record he could not return to Massachusetts without incurring the risk of being arrested, and tried in open court.

He had no doubt about the verdict. What unprejudiced juryman with normal common sense was likely to believe him other than guilty, when even his father's faith in him had been shaken? It followed that he must consider himself exiled for life from his native State, from his family, and from his friends.

Determined not to dwell upon so gloomy a future, he considered his chances of escaping from the jurisdiction of the State, an essential first step to any future that wasn't connected with a prison cell. Of the three possible ways of escape open to him, by road, railroad, or by sea, the first he believed to be the most unlikely to succeed. Long before he could possibly hope to reach the State border his description would have been circulated by different means to most parts of the State, and every thief-taker in the State would be watching out for him. Nor did he see himself in the rôle of a hunted man, hiding by day and travelling by night; never daring to enter any public place for a meal, but existing as best he might on what he could beg from lonely farmhouses, or on raw vegetables pulled up out of isolated fields, and fruit picked from wayside orchards. And all this on the assumption that he could first reach the countryside.

The railroad might be less hazardous. It was certain that all passenger trains and stations would be kept under observation, but it might be possible to reach a freight train unseen, and hide away. That would not be without risk, of course, for the freight crews were notoriously unfriendly to uninvited guests. But once across the border it would be less a tragedy to be kicked off the train—the sheriffs would not be specifically looking out for him.

Lastly, the sea. This route was attractive. He had not the money to buy a passage, even to the port of Hartford, for he had had less than $5 in his pockets when he entered Murphy's Saloon. Besides, a watch would probably be kept on all passengers embarking on outward-bound ships—especially the Cunard ships bound for Liverpool, England. But surely it might be possible to stow away in one of the less conspicuous vessels? It would mean working his passage, of course, once he was discovered; and he had no illusions as to the rough treatment he was likely to receive. But he was young, healthy, strong, and any hardship as a free man was better than a prison sentence, and a degenerating existence inside the walls of a penitentiary. Nor would he care much whither the ship's destination—Chile, Liverpool, Hamburg, Shanghai, Panama.

Panama! The fleeting, unconscious thought reminded him of Al Simpson. His face grew white with cold rage as he remembered the man whose treachery was responsible for his present straits. If ever he should catch up with Al . . .

He grew rigid with excitement. Al was the one man in the world who could clear the name of Henry Stewart from the accusation of theft. A confession, properly signed and witnessed. And Al was *en route* for Panama and California!

Henry's future became instantly plain to him.

II

Semi-daylight through a crack in the tarpaulin awakened him from sleep into which he had fallen, without intention, from exhaustion and nervous strain. He crawled out of the wagon.

"Damn me wooden stump! What's this? Now then, young feller, what you been doing asleep under there?" A heavy hand fell upon Henry's left shoulder from behind; vice-like fingers dug into his flesh and spun him round: he found himself facing a stocky man with immense breadth, but without corresponding height. He was dressed in a reefer jacket over a guernsey and neckerchief, and wore on his head a glazed, peak cap. His trousers were of heavy blue serge, but only one boot was to be seen. The second trouser flapped loosely round a wooden peg-leg.

Henry squirmed to free his shoulder from the fierce grip, but far from succeeding the effort caused the fingers to tighten still more on his shoulders, intensifying the pain. He had no wish to create a scene. On the contrary, he was anxious to avoid drawing attention to himself. But the indignity of being held fast by a strange man was not one he was willing to accept. He stiffened, in readiness for battle.

"All right! All right! All right!" the man exclaimed hastily, releasing his hold. "There's no need for rough stuff. I only wanted a sight of your face." His face was as round as a melon, with a flattened nose and double chin. He smiled amiably, and his expression grew jovial and ingenuous. "No offence?"

"No."

"That's Christian-like of you, young feller. Until I saw your face I thought you must be a bum, or some cheap crook on the run. Are you?" He took the sting from the words by smiling broadly.

"What are you——?"

He waved a disarming hand; a rough, calloused hand. "Nothing fer you to worry about. Just an ornery feller that minds his own business—sometimes! S'pose you was on the run, it wouldn't mean nothing to me. I'm jest wandering through the docks to waste time."

Henry felt suspicious of the other man. "At this time of early morning?"

"Sure. I'm not a good hand at sleeping, so I sometimes spend me time jest wandering. Sort of keeps me interested."

Henry felt inclined to believe the man, whose goodwill and good humour were written in every line of his plump face.

"Interested in what?"

"Jest life. Young feller, in me you sees one of life's natural-born philosophers." The twinkling eyes turned shrewd. "Nervous of something?"

"Nervous?"

"Your glance ain't never still, like you was looking for someone. In trouble?"

"What if I am? What of it?" Henry wished the other man to Hades: he must do something about getting away from Boston before full daylight brought more people around.

"No offence! No offence! But as a natural-born philosopher, it's me duty and pleasure to help people in trouble to get out of it. Now, if you was wanting to leave this here city hasty-like, now . . ." He paused suggestively.

"Suppose I were?" Henry questioned, in what he hoped was a non-committal manner.

"I've pals round about what are willing to help people get away when they wants to go travelling."

Henry glanced suspiciously at the man. It was hard to believe that the form of help he most wanted could come his way quite so soon or quite so easily; fate, he knew, was usually far too perverse to be so considerate. Perhaps the other man was merely trying to worm information from him so as subsequently to turn him over to the constables in the hope of reward. Or perhaps . . . yes, there were several explanations to account for such a convenient offer. Yet there was a frankness about the plump amiable face which made Henry feel inclined to trust his companion. After all, his situation was bad enough as it was. Surely it was worth-while taking a risk.

"Well?"

"Suppose now—just suppose, I say—you wanted to go some place foreign, where might you be wantin' to go, now? Rio— Montreal——"

"What about California?" Henry asked hoarsely.

The man started. "Damn me wooden stump! You didn't say California?"

"Yes."

"If that ain't jest the darndest thing! You ain't ribbing me, chum?"

"No. Why?"

"Why should you? I'll tell you. 'Cause in a hour's time I'll be on the way there meself in the *s.s. Maid of New York*. There she is, the beauty! You can see her bows just beyond them heap of barrels." He lowered his voice. "Gold?"

Henry nodded. As good a reason as any for wanting to leave Boston. Men in all the big American cities were looking California way with longing eyes. Gold was there for the finding! Red rich gold! A fortune for the lucky man! Wealth beyond reckoning, waiting to be dug up! All one had to do was to reach California by fair means or foul, and there register a claim. For the lucky, gold!

For the unlucky . . . But who knew what happened to the losers? Who cared?

The man went on: "Feller! Of all the god-damned luck——"

"You can get me aboard?"

The plump expression turned crestfallen. "That's jest what I can't do, feller. That ship's fuller nor a biscuit with weevils. If you was to offer a thousand dollars the agents wouldn't be able to sell you spitting room on that craft. I only got me own passage—well, that don't matter. No, feller, you won't get to California by way of the *Maid of New York*. Where else now?" He rubbed his two chins reflectively. "How much money you got?"

"Something less than five dollars."

"Five!" A scornful laugh. "That wouldn't buy you a rat's hole in the after hold. But I'm soft-hearted, feller. I'll see what I can do for you some place else. Show the colour of your money so I can know what can be done for you."

Henry pulled out his wallet and opened it.

The man laughed. "*Five* dollars! Tarnation take me wooden stump! You're smarter than I took you for, feller."

With unbelieving eyes Henry stared at the wad of notes which nestled in the folds of his wallet. He was sure that he had left home in the morning with no more than six, since when he had bought himself a meal before going on to the bank. Six dollars, not sixty! More than sixty! He automatically counted them. Sixty—seventy—eighty—ninety—one hundred—one hundred and four. The four dollars he knew he had, plus one hundred extra.

No need to ask how they were there, or why. His expression turned hard and bitter. Al Simpson had put them there. He had forgone the money in order to create still further evidence to prove Henry's apparent guilt. Suppose that he had been searched after admission into gaol! Only an archangel would be likely to believe his protestations that he knew nothing of the money. Lesser beings would conclude—probably with justification—that the money was some of that which he had earlier collected from the bank.

His companion chuckled, and bored Henry's ribs with a stumpy forefinger. "All right, feller. I don't blame you not trusting me. Why should you? We ain't never seen one another afore this morning. But I don't bear no malice. I like to see a young feller smart. They needs to be, with so many bums about ready to use it themselves."

"Yes." Henry spoke automatically. His score against Al Simpson was mounting up. If once they met . . .

The man took his finger away from Henry's ribs, and slapped his shoulder.

"Look a-here, feller. I likes you. You're smart, see, and I likes smart fellers. I'm not asking you where them dollars came from, or why you want to get away from Boston in a hurry. That's your affair, not mine. But I ain't in no hurry to get to California for a week, and I could use ten of them dollars right now if I had them." He burrowed deep in an inside pocket of his reefer jacket, and presently produced a large piece of paper folded several times. He held it before Henry's face. "See this? Know what it is?"

"No."

"It's me ticket to the port of Chagres, in Panama. Forty dollars I paid for it. Give me fifty, and it's yours. In fifteen minutes you can be aboard the *Maid of New York*. In five hours you'll be at sea, heading for Panama. Ain't that worth ten extra?"

Henry could not believe his luck, but he hesitated to take advantage of it. "It wouldn't be right by you, sir——"

The man laughed jovially. " 'Sir' he calls me. 'Sir!' That's the first time. Damn me wooden stump! I like you more and more, feller. Here, take the tarnation thing before I changes me mind." He thrust the yellow ticket into Henry's unresisting hand. "You're Mr. Jack Malley, see. That's me. Mr. Jack Malley. Nobody aboard won't know different when you says you're Mr. Jack Malley."

Henry gazed at his passport to liberty. He could scarcely realize that within a few minutes from now he could be aboard a Panama-bound ship—not even under his own name.

"Are you quite sure, sir?" he asked, fearful that Malley should snatch the ticket back.

" 'Course I'm sure. What's one more week to me? Afore you can say Jack Robinson I'll be following you in another ship. I has ways and means of getting another ticket."

"What about your baggage?"

"Not aboard yet, so you don't have nothing to worry about."

"Then—then thank you——"

"Don't thank me, feller. Just give me the fifty dollars, see." The money changed hands. Malley clapped Henry on the shoulder again, and winked broadly. "Now get aboard afore too many other people comes snooping around. So long, feller. Meet you in California."

"So long, Mr. Malley."

The two men parted. With carefree happiness Henry walked towards the tall spars of the *Maid of New York*. As he did so he became aware how, in the short time he had been talking with Malley, the dockside had begun to liven up. Other people, too, he saw, were making their way towards the same ship; many of them carrying enormous packs on their backs; unshaven, unkempt men whose drawn faces seemed all set in the same mould, tense, suspicious, avaricious.

He joined the throng, and presently arrived at the gangplank which connected the quayside with the gently swaying deck of a trim-looking clipper. Several men were in line, waiting to go aboard, but held up by the ship's agent who was examining all tickets before allowing their owners aboard. Henry took his place in the line, and soon others fell in behind him. But now, with escape so near at hand, he grew apprehensive that something might happen at the last minute to prevent his boarding the vessel. He grew frantically impatient, and presently his spine began to prickle with alarm. He had the feeling that people were closing in on him from behind; constables who had been given warning of his impending escape. He could scarcely restrain himself from turning round, but with an effort he maintained outward composure. But when he heard loud voices not far behind him he grew breathless with despair, and would have made a run for it could he have hoped to get clear away. Instead, he stood still, ice-cold and sick, and listlessly awaited the horrible grasp of hand on his arms and shoulders. Only by torturing degrees did he realize that the voices came from other travellers, but his relief was tempered by worsening fears. Surely the constables would not overlook the possibility of his trying to escape by ship. They must soon arrive, if only as a routine, precautionary measure.

Then, at last, it was his turn.

The agent held out a hand. "Ticket," he demanded in a bored voice.

Henry handed it over. The agent unfolded it. Then he chuckled, laughed, roared. . . . He turned his head, and shouted to someone on deck.

"What you know, Mr. Wilson! Malley's found another sucker."

Wilson laughed. "That hombré's sure gunpowder, Mr. Marelli."

The agent turned back to Henry. "Sorry, bud, you've been sold a pup."

"What do you mean?"

"Did you buy this bit of yellow paper from a broad-shouldered, round-faced bum with a peg-leg?"

Dry-mouthed, Henry nodded.

"Then do what you like with it, bud. It ain't no use on this ship."

"But why——?"

" 'Cause it's forged, that's what." The agent pushed Henry on one side. "Next man."

CHAPTER FOUR

HENRY'S first reaction to the forgery was to chase the ingenious trickster, and force him to return the $50. Then the sight of a distant constable reminded him that he dared not do that. No doubt Malley had guessed that he was a fugitive of sorts, and had selected his victim in the certainty that he would not dare to demand the return of the money. Besides, the bogus seaman was probably far away by now.

With apprehension he watched the constable, and sheltered as much as he could behind the ship's agent. But the constable presently went his way; so Henry watched the travellers file aboard instead, and envied them with a longing that was not wholly inspired by fear. The tang of the sea was in his nostrils, and it smelled good. He looked at the faces of the men who were off to search for gold, and the feverish glow in their eyes stirred him. Excitement was in the air, and infected him. He became more tolerant of the men who tramped heavily up the gangplank. Nobody could say they were handsome. But not one face was without character; not one was weak-chinned, vapid or pasty. Some were stamped with vice; some were callous, some brutal; some were disfigured; all were either defiant or challenging; all expressed either restlessness or recklessness in a lesser or greater degree. And, for the moment, like responded to like: because the seed of recklessness ran in his blood, too, he wanted to join the ranks of the hot-eyed, clammy-handed Argonauts.

Presently the line dwindled, until none waited to go aboard. The ship's agent lit himself a cigar. Henry stepped up to him.

"Ticket," the agent demanded automatically.

"Excuse me, sir."

Marelli looked at Henry's face, and began to grin. "Oh! it's you! What do you want?"

"Are you sure it was forged—that ticket——"

"The one Malley sold to you? Bud, that Malley has sold so many forged passages to California that we could paper a room with them."

"Why isn't he stopped?"

"Because no one won't lay a charge against him. Will you?" the agent drily added.

"I—I——"

Marelli shrugged. "It's all the same to me whether you do or not. Malley is a wise guy; he knows how to pick his suckers."

Henry swallowed. "Do you know where I could buy a passage?" He nodded towards the *Maid of New York*. "Could you——"

"Not a chance. The ship's overfull as it is. The gold-bug's sure gotten into folk. But if you're set on going——"

The agent's words gave Henry hope. "Yes?" he answered with eagerness.

"Go and have a word with Captain Wilson." He called out, "Captain Wilson?"

"Well?"

"Man here wants a word with you. The one who bought Malley's ticket."

"Send him aboard, Mr. Marelli. Words don't hurt nobody."

Henry went aboard, and as he felt the slight sway of the vessel dipping to a freshening wind, he knew that he wanted nothing better in the world than to sail in her; south to the port of Chagres and the Isthmus of Panama.

"Yes?" Wilson barked. He was, in a vague sort of way, a replica of Jack Malley. The same square shoulders, the same reefer jacket, the same glazed cap, the same flapping trousers. But a much taller replica, with two legs instead of one, and a rugged, hard face, instead of a plump ingenuous countenance. Perhaps Malley had been a sailor before he lost his leg, Henry reflected.

"Mr. Marelli said to speak to you, sir."

"What about?"

"I—I was hoping to leave today for Panama. That's why I bought Malley's ticket."

"More fool you. He plays that game on somebody every time a ship leaves Boston for Panama. Know for why? 'Cause gold turns men mad, see. Softens their brains; makes 'em so they can't think straight for wanting to strike gold before the other man does." His red-rimmed eyes stared into Henry's: he thrust his face forward, so that Henry saw that the chin was square and fleshless; hard as iron. "So what?"

"If there's any chance of my buying a passage——"

"There isn't. But if you're ready to work—the cook could do with a table steward."

Work! Why not? He had been ready to stow away, which would have meant work in plenty and rough treatment.

"It'll suit me, sir. Any work you say."

"Not so fast." A crafty smile spread across the rugged features. "There's the question of premium."

"Premium!"

"There are plenty of men willing to pay a premium to be taught a steward's job—as long as they can sign off at Chagres."

Henry believed he understood now why neither the captain nor the ship's agent was perturbed by the operation of the swindler Malley; no doubt they had played this same trick upon other men who had bought Malley's forged tickets in good faith: no doubt the agent received his cut from the 'premium' exacted by the captain. What gold-crazy prospector, once aboard the clipper, was likely to have the will to leave it for the sake of a few dollars?

"How much?" he asked bleakly.

"One hundred dollars."

One hundred dollars for the privilege of serving meals to a crowd of roughnecks! $100 to lead for a week or so a life worse than a dog's! The captain was surely joking.

"I haven't that much——" he began.

Wilson shrugged. "Then you'd best get off my ship. I am no charity man, to let you use this craft to learn a trade. There'll be somebody else asking for the job before we sail. Hang around on the wharf. You'll see." He laughed.

Henry glanced, agonized, over the gunwale. That way lay disgrace, sorrow, imprisonment.

"I've only fifty-four dollars in the world," he explained in desperation. He took out his wallet, and exposed the notes.

For a time the captain looked at them in silence, contemplatively. "All right," he agreed abruptly. "They'll do for once. Hand them over. You'll earn some tips, if you're any good, to take ashore." He stowed the money away in his own pocket, and handed back the wallet. "Where's your dunnage?"

"I haven't any, sir."

"On the run, eh?" He looked sore. "I'd have charged you more, if I'd been certain. An hombré can always find more if it's that or the pen." He spat overboard. "Anyway, I'm a man of my word, so you can stay aboard. Report to Fritz in the galley." He turned away.

"He'll do, Mr. Marelli," he shouted ashore.

Marelli showed his white teeth in a flashing smile. "Sure, Mr. Wilson. I thought he would," he called back.

II

Henry lay on the deck, with his back against a bollard, and watched the thin, purple line of coast off the starboard bow that was fast disappearing into the black shadows of dusk. He realized, poignantly, that he was probably looking at his native country for the last time for many months, even years; perhaps for ever. He was weary to the last muscle of him; more physically tired than he had ever been. He knew that more weary days lay ahead of him, and God know what trials and tribulations. For now he was no more than a penniless émigré; a wanderer with no family, no friends, no ties.

Even so, he felt amazingly happy. He had not been to sea before, but he found the rhythmic motion of the ship soothing and restful, and when he licked the salt spray from his lips it tasted good to him; and the soft creaking of the masts was music in his ears.

In his heart he felt that he should be sad to be leaving behind all those pleasant things which, until the previous day, had made up his life: a comfortable home, safe employment, friends, and the thousand and one amenities which comprised New England civilization. But, try as he might, he was unable to feel any genuine regret, except on one count. His flight and absence would, he knew, bring sadness to his parents, and to Peggy; but even that sorrow would, for his parents, be tempered by the knowledge that he had escaped from the tragedy of public disgrace and imprisonment. With trust and reflection they would come to realize his innocence; and when they received his first letter and learned the identity of the real thief, and their son's determination to obtain a confession, they would be proud of him and look forward with hope to his return. Besides, they were so much to each other, so happy in each other's company, they were armoured against extreme bitterness. As for Pegs, she was young, resilient; she had her beaux to occupy most of her thoughts.

He was excited, too, at the prospect of visiting another country; especially one in the tropics. For years he had wanted to travel south as an inevitable result of hearing his father relate stories of life in a tropical country. Duncan had lived nearly half his life in Haiti, where he had witnessed the long series of dramatic events which had begun with an insurrection of Negro slaves against their French masters, and ended with the suicide of the Negro King, Henry.

Indeed—and he was more conscious of the fact than ever before

—Henry Stewart was himself named after that same King, for Duncan had befriended the Negro stable lad who afterwards became Henry I of Haiti, and had acted as his physician until the day of his death. Many a story had Duncan told, during the past two decades, of the days when Haiti, known then as Saint Domingue, had been owned by the French—and Henry had never tired of them, though heard many times; they whetted his determination one day to visit the country, and see for himself the tremendous fortress which King Henry had built at the cost of hundreds of lives.

He had not carried out that boyish intention. No sooner had he graduated from college than he had been caught up in the pleasant but sedate existence of the normal town-dweller: together with his particular cronies he had occasionally visited gambling saloons, where he had wagered (and usually lost) modest sums; made the most of Thanksgiving, the Fourth of July, and all Election Days by perpetrating ingenious practical jokes; and similar pranks. Lastly he had embarked upon a commercial career, by joining the staff of Evans and Talbot. There in the well-regulated office he had found himself in an atmosphere that was far removed from the exotic life of the tropics; and his boyhood ambitions had slowly receded.

Now—now he was actually on his way, not to Haiti it was true, but to a country no less romantic, no less exciting; a country which had proved a magnet to the adventurous since Alonso de Ojeda had first sighted it. He thought of all the great men of the past who had sailed there in search of gold—the succession of conquistadores, many of whom had started, by a strange coincidence, from Santo Domingo, the then capital of the island: the lawyer, Martin Fernández de Enciso, the ill-fated Vasco Nuñez de Balboa, Francisco Pizarro, the conquerer of Peru, the butcher Don Pedrarias, and many others. And in later years, the great Francis Drake, plunderer of Spanish gold, scourge of proud Spain. Still later, the pirates: John Oxenham, who relieved the Spaniards of treasure worth a million pesos, only to lose it again, together with his head; the foul François l'Ollonois of Calais; the Dutchman Mansveldt; Batholomew Sharp of Liverpool; and the greatest of them all, Henry Morgan. Morgan who, with a handful of buccaneers, had captured seemingly impregnable fortresses, hacked a trail through jungle teeming with ambuscades, defeated the Spaniards outside the city of Panama, and then burned down the city after his men had occupied it for a while, raping, murdering, and despoiling.

The Isthmus of Panama! Once Castilla del Oro, Golden Castile; then part of Tierra Firme; subsequently part of the vice-royalty of New Granada; then part of Colombia, and now once again part of New Granada. Probably few other citizens in the world had had to change their allegiance to an overlord more often than the inhabitants of the Isthmus. Probably few other countries in the world had had, proportionate to their ages, a more dramatic history of blood and gold. And he was on his way to this land of intrigue and lust, Indian paganism and Spanish dogmatic Christianity, jungle and mountain, mystery and death.

"Hullo, there!"

Henry looked up at the man who stood by his side: a man of medium height, dressed in a long black coat and silver-grey waistcoat; stiff white collar and black bow tie. He wore no hat; but his hair and whiskers were oiled and immaculate, and the wind did not ruffle them. His moustache likewise was oiled, and neatly pointed. To Henry's astonishment he carried a scruffy cat in his arms, which he was fondling: the cat purred so loudly that Henry could hear it in spite of the distance between them.

"Hullo, sir."

The man glanced at the bollard to Henry's left. "Mind if I sit down?" He smiled. "Not much room elsewhere."

This was true enough. The decks were crowded with passengers to whom only the poop deck was forbidden. They had overflowed on to the fo'c's'le head, which Henry had been told was exclusive to the crew. They smoked cigars and pipes, which made the air aromatic although the wind swirled the blue smoke into nothingness almost as quickly as it left their mouths. They also made the evening noisy with blustery talk.

"The cat was frightened by so many clumsy feet," the stranger went on. "It was on the way up the mizzen-mast when I rescued it."

Henry listened with only half an ear to what was said; he was more interested in the voice, which was soft, gentle, and very musical; absurdly, he likened it to the *vox humana* of the organ in his parish church. He wondered whether the man was a pastor, until he realized that no pastor was likely to seek gold in California.

"Poor pussy," soothed the gentle voice. "If you had climbed the mast you would have been afraid to come down again. Cats are like that." Then, to Henry, "When they climb too high they lose their nerve. Like some human beings."

Henry searched for words. "Are you fond of cats, sir?"

"Of all animals." A pause, and then, "You are young, and well dressed, to join in the search for gold. Or are you going to California for the more sensible purpose? There will be vast openings there for workers of the right type."

"I'm one of the crew, sir. Dining-room steward."

"Ah! So that is why you are relaxed instead of being like the rest, excited and aggressive?"

"Yes, sir."

"You don't have to sir me all the time. My name's Fox. Zachary Fox."

"I'm . . ." Henry hesitated. "Henry Malley," he added on impulse. "Otherwise Red."

Fox stretched out a hand. "Nice meeting you, Mr. Malley."

As they shook hands Henry was impressed by the feel of Fox's hand; it was like touching a piece of cool velvet stretched over coiled springs. In the fading light he saw, as the hand was taken away, that it was long and slender, and extremely white; that the nails were spotless and trimmed. He was quite sure that hand had never done a day's manual labour.

His curiosity aroused, he glanced next at the face of the other man. It matched the hand, for it was without colour, without blemish and without a line. Nor was it an unhandsome face in its way. Except for the eyes. The face of a pastor, he thought. Funny he kept on comparing Fox with a pastor! The eyes were green-blue; so pale as to be almost colourless—and Henry realized how nearly they matched the eyes of the cat. Strange! But as both pairs of eyes were benign at that moment the comparison was no more than amusing.

"This is your first trip, isn't it?" Fox went on. He smiled—and Henry saw how gentle and pleasant the white face was when it smiled: it brought life to a complexion that was wax-like; and masculinity to features that were inclined to femininity. "Neither your clothes nor your hands suggest that you have done manual work before."

Henry grinned back. There was something likable about Fox. "No more than yours do, Mr. Fox."

"Check!" Fox tickled the cat under its chin. "I never have. What do you take me to be?" He saw Henry's hesitation. "Say what you think. No offence will be meant or taken."

"Twice you have made me think of a pastor, but, of course, you are not——"

"Ah!" The exclamation was sharp, but the gentle smile robbed it of any suggestion of anger. "You are not without insight. My father was a pastor in Texas. What makes you sure that I am not one?"

"You wouldn't be going to California."

"Why not? A new country needs pastors as much as men of trade. In fact——" he glanced quickly at a group of passengers whose talk was growing angry and blasphemous. "More!" he added. "But you are right. I'm no pastor. I'm a professional gambler." After a long pause, "Shocked?"

"I—I don't think so."

"You are not sure?" Fox shrugged. "Suppose I add that I always play straight—no marked cards, no cheating of any kind—am I any worse than the man who plays with me?"

"But a pastor's son——"

Fox laughed. A deep, musical laugh; resonant as a church organ. There was truthfulness in it which demanded trust.

"You are insular and ingenuous, my young friend, but I like you for it." He pulled a gold hunter from his waistcoat pocket. "Time I went downstairs to the saloon. I think I shall be welcomed. Shall we meet again?"

"I'd like to, Mr. Fox."

"Then the same time tomorrow night." He rose, and merged into the twilight as he made his way towards the companion-way.

CHAPTER FIVE

FAIR winds and a dappled sky escorted the *Maid of New York* as she ran down longitude 75° after following the coast as far as Cape Hatteras, where the usual lazy swell turned a few faces pale, or as pale as it was possible for weather-burned, blue-chinned faces to look.

The steady rate of progress was not fast enough for the impatient passengers. Twice, during the first few days, a black smudge on the horizon revealed the presence of a steamer travelling on a parallel route, and when they were told by the mischievous crew that the other vessel was probably one of the United States Mail Steam Line steamers, outward bound from New York and Southern ports to Chagres, their impatience turned to fury that others would reach California so many days before them. The second time this happened several of the bolder among them went in a body to Captain Wilson and demanded more sail. When he laughed and, having told them to get the hell out of it, turned his back on them, some of the men began to threaten and suggestively finger Colt revolvers. Whereupon the captain did a surprising thing. He invited the most prominent of the grumblers to step forward. When the man, a beetle-browed individual with a heavy jowl, uncombed beard and the bowed shoulders of a coalminer, did so, Wilson turned to the helmsman and announced that henceforward the ship had a new captain to give orders. Taking his cue from Wilson the helmsman asked solemnly what course to take, and whether top-gallants should be bent on the main-mast? The grumbler shuffled away, red-faced.

Henry was a witness to this scene, for he had just brought coffee up to the captain. He was scornful of the passengers request for more sail; even a landlubber's eyes could see that the ship was carrying every inch consistent with safety in the freshening wind. On the other hand, he sympathized with the demand for more knots. Not one soul aboard was more impatient than he for the end of the voyage. Work had grown steadily more arduous as more and more of the passengers found their sea legs. Almost every hour of the eighteen he was awake was one of dreary penance and back-aching labour. He had never realized that work could be so torturing to the body and mind alike; nor that one could become so desperately tired that one's limbs twisted with cramp, and one's mind grew insensible.

There were two other aspects of life aboard the clipper which did not help to make it easier for him. Hitherto, he had lived amid the quiet serenity of comfortable, urban surroundings. His parents' friends, and his own, were people of good standing and gentle manners; people of substance in varying degrees of wealth. He had never been in direct contact with the uncouth existence of the poverty-stricken: the few occasions he had looked at life outside his own narrow circle he had seen it through the wrong end of a spy-glass.

Now he had been pitch-forked, without warning, into the opposite extreme. The lure of gold had brought aboard the clipper men as new and strange to him as the many States from which they had originally come. And as diverse. Black-eyed fishermen from the ports of Maine; slow-thinking failures from the farming communities of Vermont; backwoodsmen from the forests of New Hampshire. Cheats, absconders, wastrels; bums, who had scraped the passage money from God knows what sources; weak-chinned work-shys from the cities of the Eastern seaboard; refugees from the old world; drunks, mobsters, veteran pan-handlers. . . .

At the beck and call of these roughnecks, most of whom had never been in a position to give an order to another human; men who cursed him with foul profanities, who vomited where they chose, who used any available space as a vast spittoon, whose voracious appetites were not satisfied by the parsimonious portions doled out by a cook who lined his pockets from the sale of unconsumed stores—these were the men who peopled Henry's nightmare. Only the Stewart pride and the Stewart obstinacy sustained him in the darkest hour—that, and the determination to seek Al Simpson —and meanwhile, the anticipation of spending the last hour before darkness with Zachary Fox.

For him that hour was the one bright spot in the day. The more he saw of Fox the more he liked the man—and the more he was mystified by the complex character which the pallid face belied. Sometimes he wondered whether the gentle manner of the gambler was no more than a hypocritical mask concealing a sordid and unscrupulous determination to profit by other people's weaknesses. If it were so, he found no evidence to support that theory. Although Fox had nothing in common with the roughnecks who composed ninety-five per cent of the passengers, he was so consistently friendly that none of them resented his gentle, courteous manner, and they lost money to him less grudgingly than they lost to others.

Finally, to make an ever worse hell of the voyage for Henry, was the memory of Jean.

II

"Thinking of her?" Zachary Fox asked one evening as he approached unheard.

"Her!"

Fox chuckled. "If there isn't a her in the life of a young fellow like yourself, then I'm not Zachary Fox." He studied Henry's face, which was turned towards the western horizon where the sun was spraying the sky with mauves and purples and reds, and spreading a carpet of gold on the swelling surface of the sea. "Tell, if it'll make things easier for you, Red. It does—sometimes—when one's still young . . ." His eyes turned bleak.

"I've never thought of Jean as my girl until—the last day or two——"

"Now you are beginning to realize that you like her plenty?"

"Yes."

"That probably means that you've known her a long time?"

"Ever since we were so high. Nathaniel Martin was an old friend of my father's. They met in Haiti, years before I was born. It was Mr. Martin who persuaded Father to settle in Boston."

"Then your trip won't be wasted. You'll know what to do when you go back."

Henry swallowed. "I—I may never go back."

"Oh!" Fox placed his hand on Henry's shoulder. "I'm sorry, Red." They stood thus so long in silence that the gambler began intuitively to feel something of the overwhelming misery that was torturing his younger companion. "As I said just now, if it'll make things easier—you can trust me——"

Henry stared at the fast-disappearing sun. Tell Zachary Fox of what had happened; of the future? Why not? He had nothing to be ashamed of; and for days he had longed for the opportunity of talking frankly to someone of his trouble. Trouble shared is trouble halved, his mother had repeatedly told him. Fox could be trusted to keep the secret. And, who knows? Maybe he would help by looking out for Al. Al had always been too fond of gambling.

So Henry told his companion of the events which had led to their first meeting aboard the *Maid of New York*. Finally, he revealed his real name.

"I didn't want to bring disgrace on the name of Stewart," he explained chokily. "Father was so proud of it——"

"Why not?" Fox lit a cigar. "But if I were you," he added presently, "I should stick to the name of Red Malley. It wouldn't help if Simpson were to hear that you were on his trail."

"How could he?"

Fox's comment was dry.

"News gets around."

III

The following night Henry showed Fox a daguerreotype of Jean Martin.

"Look," he said shyly, as he pushed it forward. "This is Jean. It's crumpled, through being in my pocket so long. It was Mr. Martin's birthday present to her, two months ago, the twenty-seventh of June."

Fox inspected the picture with grave sympathy. The likeness was spoiled by the careless treatment it had received in Henry's pocket, but it was still possible to distinguish something of the charm which underlined the fresh, young face.

Henry moved closer to the gambler. "She's really far nicer than she looks there. She's too serious in the picture, and you don't often see her serious. She's nearly always smiling."

"I think she's charming, Red."

"You do?" Henry was delighted. "Her eyes are brown. Not dark brown like the Latin races have, but like, like . . . chestnuts. And her complexion; well, you've never seen anything like it. Like alabaster, living alabaster, if you can imagine——"

"I can. But it's not the face I'm looking at, Red. That is not the most beautiful part of her."

"Not—not the face——"

"No. I am looking at the person behind, my boy. Behind those nice brown eyes of hers, the alabaster skin, and that sweet mouth I can see someone who, if she said she loved you, would love you to the end of her days. Someone who won't ever believe you guilty of being a thief."

"That's so," Henry agreed presently. "She knows me too well."

"Does she love you?"

"Of course she doesn't. We're just comrades, that's all. Always have been."

"But you love her?"

"I—I don't know. I've never thought about—about love, Mr. Fox, until a few days ago."

"But now? Do you think she's worth waiting for?"

Henry nodded.

"Then remember that when you reach the tropics. Don't ever forget her. One day you may be glad of the memory of her."

"I don't understand . . ."

Fox passed back the crumpled square of pasteboard. "You will, boy, you will."

IV

The spirits of the excited argonauts rose boisterously higher as each day saw them nearer the glittering prizes of their imagination. Each day saw them sprawling on the deck wherever there was room, arguing in loud voices; just dreaming; gambling. Each evening saw them clustered in the main saloon, like so many wasps on a honey-pot, and as correspondingly noisy and dangerous as they argued belligerently; or roared lusty songs to the accompaniment of an accordion which a German traveller had brought aboard with him; or gambled. Every night saw them sleeping in the same saloon; snoring, snorting, moaning, or just breathing heavily, for the air was blue with tobacco smoke, and stale with the odour of unwashed bodies.

Marelli had not exaggerated when claiming that accommodation on the ship was fully booked. It was over-booked, time and time again; but the few square feet grudgingly allowed each man was not accommodation. Men bunked down on floors, on tables, and on forms; they filled the few cabins to overflowing; they were stretched out along the poop-deck beneath sailcloths. They slept heels to head, cheek by jowl; and the crew had to cat-walk over or between them when it was necessary to move from one part of the ship to another.

For little more than five hours out of every twenty-four was it possible to relax; and those were the hours from eight bells midnight to two bells of the morning watch. At other times the mood of the travellers was one of hot tempers, frayed nerves and itching fingers. Scarcely one watch reached the end of its span without the sound of a hoarse roar breaking out in one place or another, and the thumping of heavy feet on the deck. Each time this happened there was an eager rush of travellers in that direction, for the familiar noises heralded a few minutes' diversion, watching two men batter each other into a bloody pulp, with maybe a bet to add zest to the spectacle. And sometimes one fight started several others; on account of elbows accidentally digging into neighbouring ribs, or toes being painfully crushed beneath the heavy heel of some other over-thrustful traveller.

One afternoon, in between meals, Henry leaned over the starboard bow and looked down into the sea. Fascinated by the way in which the bow cut and folded over the blue water, turning it into a white frothing trail, he wondered idly by what alchemy of nature colourless water could first look blue, and then pure white. Presently he saw some greeny-brown substance turning over in the creaming spume; then more, and more again. Then he noticed that little islands of the same stuff dotted the ocean as far as sight could reach, giving the silvered surface of the water the appearance of being sick with measles. At last he recognized the islands as clumps of seaweed. He was surprised to see so much about, until he recollected having the previous night heard a fleeting reference to the Sargasso Sea. He was vaguely aware that the present position of the ship was well to the south-west of the dread spot, but cheered himself with the reflection that the weed had probably drifted where he now saw it after breaking away from that large area which all ships carefully avoided, for fear of being embedded in the noisome weed. There were sailors in Boston who told strange stories of the Sargasso Sea. Even if one didn't believe every word the fact still remained that one or two ships, known to be sailing in the vicinity of the Sargasso, had never been heard of again after being bespoken.

A day or so later he saw his first flying fishes. At first he could not make out what was happening, for the surface of the sea was disturbed by streaks of silver lightning which flashed constantly in and out of the water, just as if a thunderstorm were raging in the depths of the ocean. As the ship and the moving area of disturbance converged he was able to recognize the shape of fish.

The knowledge that they were moving into tropical waters quickened the feeling of excitement which had begun to disturb him soon after the last sight of land had banished his lingering fear of being arrested before he could catch up with Al Simpson. Morning, noon and night, the chief topic of conversation was gold. Gold! Gold! Gold! Wherever he went he heard the wizened prospector telling an exciting story of the last occasion when he had struck gold; or the middle-aged man with a warty nose and a cast-eye telling what he would do as soon as he had made his strike (the answer was in the feminine gender); or the under-sized spluttering Welshman, who intended to use his first funds to send for the family he had left back home in Caerphilly; or the solemn-faced, flaxen German, whose English was scarcely intelligible to his fellow-travellers; he planned to build a chain of opera-houses across the United States.

Always gold! How they would find it. Where. How they would spend it. Not one among the hundreds looked at the other side of the picture, and foresaw the doom of failure. They were blinded by the brilliance of the magnet which inexorably attracted their restless spirits, and could not see that its glittering lustre was intensified by a black-shadowed backcloth.

Henry caught the fever, too, and began to dream dreams, and share the general feverish urgency for the first sight of Chagres. But first the clipper had to make the Windward Passage, and late one afternoon he saw purpling headlands off the port bow, and realized that they were passing that tragic graveyard of Negro Empire, Haiti.

The sight brought with it vivid memories of his father, whom gold had tended to make him forget. With a smouldering gaze he gazed upon the land where, as Ti Rouge, friend and familiar of Negro slaves, Duncan Stewart had made and lost and remade a fortune, had taken for his mistress the most voluptuous, the most beautiful of mulatto women; and finally, after their long and tragic separation, had met once more the girl who had never lost faith in him; Jean, Henry's mother.

Then, as daylight faded and the velvet of night covered the distant mountains in a mantle of black mystery, Henry saw Haiti as once his father had seen it for the first time; for the white stars above were matched by red stars below, and the fragrance of coffee and spices and burning wood, wafted out on the wings of the gentle wind which blew down from the mountains, smelled good in his nostrils; and in his imagination he heard the exciting, disturbing pulsation of Voodoo drums—and he knew that the red stars were fires to which the drums were summoning the votaries of Voodoo for strange dances and stranger rites. . . . Then he wondered whether he might witness a Voodoo dance at Panama. They were held there, too, he had been told. . . .

v

Land ahoy!

The deck of the *Maid of New York* was already crowded with passengers and luggage, although only a thin dark line rising just above the horizon was visible to the naked eye, and their destination was still several hours' sailing time away—more, if the favourable wind should drop. But the whisper "Land ahoy!" had travelled through the ship with the speed of a prairie fire, and promoted a feverish activity that had only ceased as the last of the cursing, sweating passengers elbowed a place for himself among the packed mass already established on deck.

Haste was now the predominating factor: the haste which should ensure that each man was among the first to land. For only the first to land could hope to begin before nightfall the arduous six-day journey across the Isthmus. The *Maid of New York* had already made two journeys to the Chagres, and the handful among the crew who had previously resisted the impulse to desert and join the gold rush knew the ropes, and were willing, even eager, to sell their knowledge to the highest bidders.

From a corner in the bows Zachary Fox watched with contemptuous eyes the antics of the restless, quarrelling crowd as each man tried to edge nearer to the bulwarks.

"Fools!" he ejaculated. "Why don't they look at the sky for once?"

Henry was almost too weary to speak. Since dawn, when the first waking passenger had recognized land and shouted the news aloud, he had been on the move, staggering beneath the weight of baggage which he had helped to carry on deck in the hope of increased tips. Wooden trunks, brass-bound with rounded tops; monstrous canvas packs, roped together and topped with the essential tools of a gold prospector, axes, picks, pots and pans in variety; duffle bags filled to bursting-point; wooden cases—anything which would hold the pitifully few bits and pieces of clothes and equipment with which the hot-eyed travellers hopefully expected to wrest a fortune from the rivers of California.

Now he was exhausted, and almost too tired to think. But Fox's remark puzzled him.

"The sky?" He looked up. The northern sky was hidden by a mass of filmy cirrus which stretched across the arc in a line from east to west, and looked as if its southern border had been cut with pinking shears.

"Wind," Fox replied laconically.

Henry saw that the crew were in the yards shortening sail, and concluded that Captain Wilson evidently shared Fox's forebodings.

"What does that mean?"

"That we shall probably toss about in the open sea for a day or so before the boats come out from shore to take us off."

"Can't we land direct?"

Fox shook his head. "Not according to Captain Wilson. There are no facilities yet, although Howland and Aspinwall are contemplating a wharf here. Passengers and cargo have to be taken off in cayucas." He laughed. "At the rate of two dollars per head for passengers."

The price dismayed Henry. The charge of two dollars merely to land would make a hole in his pitifully small capital. "And when they've landed?" he asked, huskily.

"The usual method is to hire a cayuca, which holds four to six passengers, and three or four native boatmen. In the rainy season the cayucas are able to reach Cruces, some forty-five miles up-river from Chagres. From there they go overland, by mule, the remaining eighteen miles to Panama City, then they go the rest of the way to California by steamship."

"And the—the cost?"

"About ten dollars a person to Cruces, and as much again for the mule to Panama."

"Twenty dollars!"

"If one is lucky! Captain Wilson says that prices rise with every new shipload of passengers. Then there's the fare from Panama to California, another hundred dollars——" Fox saw Henry's expression. "You haven't that much, Red?"

"I've barely enough to reach Panama City."

"You'll be able to ship aboard one of the Pacific Mail steamers, I don't doubt, if you're willing to work your passage. Until then, how about you and me sharing a cayuca? We'll look about for some nice guy to make a third."

"If I may——"

"If you may, be darned! There's nobody else I'd prefer." He stared down at the milling crowd on the main deck. "Not aboard this ship. I don't remember seeing a worse bunch of bums. . . ."

VI

The threatening wind caught up with the *Maid of New York* long before she reached an anchorage. Soon she was pitching and rolling alternately with a corkscrew motion which began to wreak havoc among the crowd on deck. One after another became sick; but there was no room to lie down, or even to vomit without spattering one's neighbours. Voices grew louder and more angry as the hardier men became victims of pale-faced sufferers. Blows were exchanged; fights broke out. Soon the deck was a seething mass of sick and well; few of whom could move much for the scattered baggage which had been overturned or kicked aside during the mêlée.

Driven forward by the freshening wind, the clipper drew steadily nearer the coast of the Isthmus. Details of the coastline became clearer. Temporarily forgetting his troubles, Henry gazed at the bold promontory for which they were heading. The first noticeable feature was the white snowy line, separating the bright green of thick vegetation from the blue-green of the broken seas, which he presently realized was caused by the spume of breakers which hurled themselves at the jagged rocks footing the bluff. A line of mountains towered up behind, and he warmed with appreciation at the wild beauty of the interior. Then, as his gaze travelled back towards the mouth of the river Chagres, he saw the battlemented ruins of San Lorenzo which stood out starkly from the vegetation high up on the western cliff—a picturesque and compelling reminder of past centuries when gold trains on their way to Spain had been the prey of buccaneers and English freebooters. Across the mouth of the river, nestling at the foot of cliffs, was the native village of Chagres. As the last sail was furled and the booming clank of the anchor-chain signified the end of the ship's voyage, he saw the dangerous reef which had once sunk four of Morgan's ships, and which was still a hazard sufficient to prevent ships coming any closer to the town save in ideal conditions.

In the excitement of arrival even the sick passengers (and by now they were in a majority) forgot to be ill; and as many as could get near enough to the bulwarks to lean over did so. They saw half a dozen canoes bouncing over the waves, and instantly a discordant clamour arose as the passengers tried to hire them.

After ten minutes' commotion, in which it was almost impossible for any individual voice to be heard above the angry yelling of others, some of the passengers secured satisfactory terms. In spite of the captain's warning to remain aboard, they managed to transfer themselves and their baggage into the canoe-like boat. Among them was the beetling-browed, bearded coalminer who had been the ringleader earlier in the voyage. Henry was glad to see him go, for the man had been a confirmed trouble-maker. Fascinated, he watched that particular cayuca bobbing crazily towards the bar which protected the estuary of the river. It seemed unlikely that the frail craft could capsize, for the boatmen would surely be too used to heavy seas to take undue risks even for the sake of the $4 per head which they had demanded and received.

But the cayuca did overturn. The bearded man disappeared beneath the frothing waves of the bar and did not reappear, although it was presently seen that the native boatmen were swimming strongly for the beach. Then a second cayuca overturned, and two more white men vanished from sight. The remaining four canoes succeeded in crossing the bar, and the passengers aboard the clipper next saw the white passengers running towards the collection of huts which made up the native village of Chagres.

"God-damned lucky swine!" yelled one of the passengers, shaking his fist at the shore. "Jest because you had two dollars more'n me. . . ."

Not a word of regret for the three who had drowned.

CHAPTER SIX

Fox's pale eyes were wise with experience.

"Your first death, Red?" he asked gently.

Henry nodded, and swallowed.

"You'll see others if you stay in California. Some of them far less pleasant——"

"Pleasant! God Almighty!"

"California is a wild country. And gold lust is a fever that turns men into animals. These men haven't even smelled gold yet.

When they do some of them won't die in their beds. Envy and greed will make them killers. They'll fight—with guns, knives, fists—and boots! I saw one man stamp another to death. Some will be hanged. Some will die from Indian arrows. Some will starve, or frizzle to death in the desert."

"But one moment he was so alive—the next——"

"Our late passenger? You mean, one moment he was happy in being one jump ahead of his rivals, and believing in his good luck. The next—nothing! Could anyone wish for a happier death?"

The quietly-spoken words soothed Henry's shocked emotions. Sensing this, Fox continued:

"Conditions out west are going to be tough on you, Red. Your life has been too easy to prepare you for it. You'll need all the spunk you have to stick it out."

"I've got to stick it out if I'm to return to Boston."

"Sure, you have. And I believe you will. Your hair isn't red for nothing. But first——"

"Well, now that I've seen my first death I'm blooded, aren't I. More deaths won't mean a thing to me." The crisp, defiant note in Henry's voice told Fox that his younger companion had not entirely recovered his composure.

"There will be hardships, too——"

"I can take them."

"And there will be women to reckon with. Not your kind of women. I mean those who sell five minutes' happiness to a man for a few dollars. Is your memory of Jean going to survive?"

"Why not?" Henry challenged.

"Because tropical and semi-tropical climates do something to a man. Not always women, but mostly. The sun heats the blood in your veins until you are crazy for the things only a woman can give you. If you resist, the fever grows worse until it reaches explosive point and then——"

"Why are you saying these things to me?"

"Because there's still time to turn back, my boy. You can return to Boston on this ship—by the time you get back there the constables may no longer be on the look-out for you. You might be able to slip across the State border, and start life afresh in some other New England town, among the type of people with whom you belong. Providence, perhaps. Or New London. Or Albany. Even New York. There are opportunities there—for the right kind of man. . . ."

Henry's smile was wistful. He had fought out this very problem so many times during the past few days that he did not have to consider Fox's suggestion. Every day aboard the *Maid of New York* had made sweeter the memory of Jean Martin, until he had reached a state of mind when it tortured him to realize that he was faced with the prospect of living a future in which she played no role. Why it had taken him so long to realize the fact he could not understand. The one thing of which he was certain was that if a miracle could transplant him back to Boston he would not wait five minutes before declaring his love for her.

But the day of miracles had long since passed. There could be no returning to Boston, and certainly no telling her of his love, until his innocence had been proved. His resolution to continue his journey to California hardened. The day on which he could face Boston with Al's confession would recompense him for any trials which might beset him in the meantime. Besides, adventure called —a month or two in California might prove to be an experience to last a lifetime. . . .

Fox smiled, and clapped Henry on the shoulder: he did not have a wait for a verbal reply.

"Good boy, Red! You're made of the right stuff. . . ."

II

No more canoes came out to the clipper that day, or the next. But the third day brought a cloudless dawn, a smooth sea, and a small fleet of cayucas. The grinning natives circled the ship, and let the passengers angrily bid one another up to $3, then $3.25, $3.50, then $4, at which price the bidding stopped. The cayucas transported more than forty people at that price, but when it was seen that the men on shore were bargaining for cayucas and crews to take them up the river, and a few minutes later were departing southwards, those on the ship recklessly bid anew. The price rose to $4.50, and there was fighting to be the first to go at the increased price.

"They'll come down to two dollars before the day's through," Fox commented, his colourless eyes gleaming with sardonic humour. "We can wait. There's no hurry for us. The longer we wait the more gold will be dug; and the more dug the more the fools will be anxious to gamble it away and the more of it will find its way into my pockets."

As usual, his shrewd forecast proved correct. Fox went ashore, the last passenger off the ship, for $1.50. Henry went with him. Very soon they had passed over the bar and were rounding the bluff on which the ancient castle stood sentinel; and for the first time caught a glimpse of New Chagres, an American town of frame buildings, which was growing overnight to cope with the rapidly increasing transisthmian traffic.

The cayuca made for the native village, which was situated on the edge of a shallow bay and consisted of a number of huts made of bamboo uprights lined with palmetto leaves, with high, steep roofs of thatch. The interiors of the huts were invisible from outside, for the only means of admitting light and air was by a single doorway; many were occupied by women dressed in one-piece cotton garments, who sat just inside the cool semi-darkness and worked at handicrafts destined ultimately to be sold to impatient travellers. Henry looked in vain for young men. Seemingly the only other occupants of the village were old men who smoked cigars and stared at the white men with expressionless eyes; and countless naked children of both sexes.

As they landed on the shore, Henry became aware of the fierce tropical heat which blazed at them from all directions. It beat against his skin like a blast from a furnace, and caused the sweat to well out of his flesh as though it were being forced out by the internal impact of the hot, humid air which he breathed into his lungs in spasmodic gasps. He had known hot days in Boston when sweltering August heat had almost incapacitated the inhabitants, but never such high humidity.

As he mopped the sweat from his forehead he and Fox were approached by a dark-skinned man dressed, European fashion, in a loose-fitting suit of white denim, and a Panama hat. Although dark, he was much lighter than the Indians; and had the flashing eyes of a Spaniard.

"Buenos dias, señores," he greeted in a soft, lisping voice. He went on in English, "Pedro Romanos, at your service, señores, agent for the hire of cayucas. You want one, pronto, no? I regret you are too late. There will not be one back for several days. But you want me keep for you, no? Most reliable, trustworthy."

The pale eyes surveyed the eager, handsome face. "Sure we want one, señor," he drawled, "but not necessarily pronto. We are in no hurry."

The agent looked as if he could scarcely believe that he had heard aright.

"Not pronto . . ." he gasped.

"That's what I said."

"But you are Yanqui, no? And all Yanquis in big hurry to reach California."

"Not us."

At last the vivacious face expressed belief. "Then I can promise you best boat on the Chagres, señores. Good strong Negroes; willing workers, twenty dollars each, no?"

"No," Fox emphatically echoed, as he turned to move off.

The agent laid an anxious hand on Fox's arm. "You not want cayuca, señor?"

"Not at twenty dollars each."

"But, señor, twenty dollars not dear——"

"Ten dollars too much."

"But, señor, for the best boatmen on the Chagres . . ." He hesitated, then added with regret, "Eighteen dollar, then, señor?"

"Twelve," Fox countered with decision.

Tears welled out of the dark eyes of Pedro Romanos. "The señor is a hard man," he whimpered. "Nobody will take you to Cruces for twelve dollar. I make concession at eighteen because you have a kind, handsome face——"

"Twelve."

"*Madre de Dios!*" he cried, swallowed, wrung his hands. "You do not realize, señor—even if I agreed twelve dollars, the men would not take you. There are many people over there——" he pointed to the American settlement on the other side of the river. "They have been waiting days for a cayuca——"

"Then offer yours to them," Fox told the man, as he moved away.

The agent ran after him. "Fifteen!" he agreed, whispering the price as if he dared not let the echo of his voice reach the huts. "Fifteen dollars each person."

"Done," said Fox, after a moment's reflection. "Thirty dollars for the two of us, for the journey to Cruces by first available cayuca."

"Not for two of you only, señor," Romanos corrected. "Two more must go with you to make up sixty dollar."

"Then we'll pay sixty dollars, and please ourselves whether we take other passengers or not."

"Done," the agent agreed, cheerful and vivacious now that bargaining was over. "I shall tell you when the cayuca is back. Maybe one day, maybe two. Where shall I find you, señores?"

"Any suggestions?"

"There are two hotels in Yanqui Chagres, señores. The Californian, and the Crescent City. I find you at one?"

"I don't doubt. How we get across? Canoe?"

Romanos nodded. "I find one take you there cheap."

Some minutes later a small cayuca crossed the estuary, and left the two men on the opposite bank.

"Damn my soul!" Fox exclaimed, staring before him.

It was the first oath Henry had heard on the gambler's lips. It startled Henry, so rare was it for Fox to express any feeling other than dry humour.

"Anything wrong?"

"That town? We might almost be in Texas."

Henry inspected the Yankee town of New Chagres, which was mushrooming round the wharf that was in the making. Having never travelled west, he had not seen the mining camps which were springing up, almost overnight, and advancing steadily westwards into and through the newly-ceded states. But he had heard descriptions of them; seen pencil sketches by artists from the East who had trodden on the heels of earlier settlers. He would have realized, even without Fox's confirmation, that he was looking at a typical frontier town of the Western States. Only the background was strange; instead of springing up like an oasis in the midst of open ranching country, New Chagres had been hewn from the jungle which still ringed it. Even a few hitching-posts were to be seen; but these, perhaps, had been erected by some wag or other, for there were no horses tied to them. Nor was it likely there ever would be any, for it was not horse country hereabouts: impenetrable jungle spread in all directions as far as the eye could see.

One road comprised the town—though Henry reflected wrily that one would have to be in generous mood to call either the twin rows of frame buildings a road, or the whole a town. For there were fewer than thirty buildings all told; and the road between was virgin soil beaten hard by the passage of feet. There were no sidewalks. There was not even an attempt to maintain a straight line anywhere. Buildings had been erected in haphazard fashion, at the whim of the builder.

All the characteristics of a Western mushroom township were visible, especially the two hotels of which the cayuca agent had spoken. Both were two storeys high and therefore more prominent than their one storeyed neighbours, but looked not uninviting on account of the piazza which surrounded them on both floors. Not far off was a squat building which called itself, in white letters on a board which was placed above the door and ran the length of the building, the Eagle Café and Restaurant; several saloons; a hardware store; a small building which housed the office of the Pacific Mail Line; an Emporium; a secretive-looking structure which was called the House of All Nations; an Express office; and other buildings, some crudely constructed from scrap lumber and junk, which straggled along the river front to the edge of the jungle.

Even more typical of a Western camp were its assorted inhabitants; familiar characters to Fox. Tall, slim figures with bowed legs and gangling arms, who wore sombreros on their heads, jingling spurs on their jack-boots, and gun-holsters which were strapped close to their thighs and suspended from silver-studded belts. Bland-faced Chinese traders. One or two black-coated, tall-hatted gamblers. A few women in tight-waisted muslin frocks, with a loose fichu over their shoulders and poke bonnets on their heads, their sunshades of gaily-coloured silk held jauntily aloft. Barefooted Indians, too, in single cotton garments. Lastly, a handful of coffee-coloured Panamanians, soft-eyed, black-haired, often with traces of mixed Spanish, Indian, and Negro blood.

"Kinda takes me back a little," Fox murmured, not moving.

Henry was convinced that he had detected a note of wistfulness in his companion's voice, which embarrassed him. For want of anything else to say:

"Except for the Panamanians."

Fox shook his head. "They're like enough to Mexicans." His voice changed to its normal soft drawl. "No use stopping here all day." He shouldered the small wooden trunk he carried about with him and made for the nearer of the two hotels, which happened to be the Californian. Henry accompanied him, empty-handed.

As they walked the short intervening distance the illusion persisted that they had landed nearer the 35th parallel than the 9th, for they heard snatches of conversation carried on by men whose accents betrayed their origins as Mississippi, Kentucky, Louisiana. But wherever they came from, their talk revolved about the one absorbing topic of conversation. Gold! What happened in the world outside California was of no interest to them. They lounged up against walls on the shady side of the road and expressed their fury at the enforced delay in loud, blustering voices, or else boasted of the methods they would use on the cayuca boys to make them catch up with the luckier ones who had got away from Chagres that day.

The largest number of impatient travellers congregated about the doors of the four saloons; but the noise from within suggested that as many again were on the other side of the door. Fox smiled grimly, and foresaw rowdy nights for Henry and himself as long as they remained in Chagres. Too many of the loungers were armed with derringers and bowie-knives; one or two exposed the new Colt revolvers: Walker .44's, and Wells Fargo .315's. It was inevitable that impetuous tempers would be stirred by drink and impatience. If he knew anything of human nature there would be quarrels that night, he told Henry, and probably shooting—as there had been on board the *Maid of New York*. To his knowledge two lifeless bodies had quietly disappeared overboard during the course of the voyage.

A scraggy-looking individual received them at the Californian.

He had a bald head, which a few oily grey hairs failed utterly to conceal, grey whiskers and moustache, tired eyes and a weary manner.

"Howdy," he greeted laconically. "You two from the *Maid?*"

"Yes. The last."

"Want a room?"

"Two."

The man laughed as if he were enjoying a most satisfying joke.

"Can't have even one, mister. Thisyere town is full to bursting. Four ships in eight days, one from Boston yesterday week, the reg-lar from New York two days later, yesterday one from New Orleans, and now yours, all filled with people ravin' to get across the Isthmus quicker nor a dollar's worth of ice melting in the sun. As there ain't anything like enough canoes to take them by water, or mules enough to take them along the trail, they just stays here, see."

"What have you to offer?"

"A hammock at two dollars a head, take it or leave it." Seeing Fox and Henry exchange questioning glances, he continued, "And it ain't no use you reckoning to try anywheres else, mister. I'll give you ten dollars for any bed you can find to sleep in tonight."

"Then we'd best take two hammocks. Where are they?"

The man grinned. "You mean, where will they be?" He pointed to the open doorway opposite: beyond were the long tables of a dining-room. "In there, when eating's finished tonight."

There being no choice, they reserved two hammocks and paid in advance for two nights. Fox's trunk was then taken into the dining-room, and stored away in one corner where several other pieces of baggage were already piled.

"That's that!" Fox exclaimed. "Now time's our own until tonight. Anything you want to do, Red?"

Henry nodded. "Begin my search right here and now." Together with Fox he returned to the lobby, and the scrawny-looking man at the desk.

"Did you say a steamer for Boston arrived a week ago?"

"Sure. The *Monarch.*"

"Any passengers from it stay here?"

" 'Bout fifty."

"Would you recognize the name of one of them?"

"Could do."

"Albert Simpson."

A moment's reflection brought a shake of the scrawny head. "Never heard the name, mister. Try the Crescent City."

"Thanks, I will."

The two men left the hotel, and stepped into the blazing sunshine. A few steps brought them to the welcome shade of the Crescent City piazza. This time they were received by a fat little man with the black hair and dark eyes of a Panamanian. He saluted them with a gracious gesture.

"Good morning, señores. If you are looking for rooms, I'm sorry. . . ."

Henry quickly explained his errand. The man nodded.

"Yes, señor. Señor Simpson booked at this hotel."

Henry swallowed. "Is he still here? I must speak with him, urgently——"

"I am sorry, señor. He left for Panama City three days ago."

In spite of the fact that he had expected such an answer, Henry turned away disappointed. Fox clapped him on the shoulder.

"Cheer up, Red. You know he got as far as here. He might never have returned to the steamer after your meeting with him. That's something, isn't it?"

Henry nodded grimly. Fox was right. That was something. Sooner or later he would catch up with Al. . . .

CHAPTER SEVEN

THERE was little to do until nightfall, so Henry and Fox returned to the Californian. Relaxed and sleepy they settled in two vacant chairs on the lower piazza, and surveyed the town and the Chagres River beyond, where it could be seen between the buildings on the far side of the road.

In spite of Henry's keen interest in the scene the novelty of it began to wear off, perhaps because he was too tired to keep his eyes open. All the hours of sleep he had gone without since the night of the theft were beginning to have their effect. That, and the glare of the sun on the white walls of the wooden buildings opposite. Before long he closed his eyes. . . .

"Be damned ef it ain't the old Fox himself."

He was vaguely aware of a booming voice which seemed to be directed towards him, and of the sound of tapping heels on the hard roadway, but he was too tired to care or to open his eyes. He relaxed and tried to close his ears to the loud, hearty voice; but it did not stop; it grew louder, and he was unable to ignore it.

"What are you doing in this off-shoot of Hades, you goddamned son of an Egyptian sphinx? Where you come from? Where you heading for?"

He opened his eyes at last. Through a mist of sleep he saw in front of him the short, stocky figure of a man dressed in the felt hat, red shirt and tight trousers of a typical cowman. The face above was burned brick-red, and formed an incongruous background for both the lank black hair and drooping moustache which reached down to the square chin, and seemed scarcely in keeping with the unwavering eyes of pale blue.

He had never seen the man before, and felt annoyed with the stranger for having awakened him from a very satisfying sleep. Just as he was on the point of protesting, he heard Fox speak and realized that the remarks had been addressed to his companion.

"Jim Braddock!" Fox welcomed in his unemotional voice. He added casually, "How's tricks?"

"Bad."

"They were good the last time we met."

"Not so good as yours, when that tarnation face of yourn took nearly a thousand off me with a pair of god-damned deuces," Braddock commented without rancour. "Sunset Town were almighty relieved when you pulled up your stakes and moved on. It's my guess we was worse off by ten thousand dollars that day."

"Thirteen thousand four hundred and sixty-three," Fox corrected.

Braddock whistled. "The hell we were!"

"Which I lost the first night at Rogers Creek. All but a hundred."

"Not to Clem Parker of Diamond P?"

"He had nearly eight thousand. Man by name of Davis had the rest."

"Shorty Davis of Bar S at Fleming?"

"Could be. He was shorter than you, Jim."

"The lucky bastards! 'Tain't many as kain 'say they has out-bluffed Zachary Fox."

Fox laughed. "Not out-bluffed, Jim. I had good cards that night, but they held better. Two straight flushes, fours three times, and full-houses ten a penny. I left Rogers Creek on the next coach, like a whipped cur."

Braddock laughed loudly, but his keen eyes raked the gambler's tight, well-fitting clothes.

"Still not packin' a gun, I see?"

"No."

"I like you, Fox. You got guts. 'Tain't many gamblers would take a chance on not packin' a gun. And still fond of dawgs, I see."

Dogs! Henry glanced sideways and saw that Fox was pulling the ears of a small bitch which was curled up on his lap and gazing up into his face with adoring eyes.

The movement, slight as it was, drew the dog's attention, and then Fox's almost as quickly.

"Awake at last, Red."

"I haven't been asleep . . ."

Fox chuckled. "Not more than an hour, you haven't! Jim, meet a friend of mine, Red Malley. Red, this is Jim Braddock, the unluckiest gambler this side of the Rockies."

"Howdy, Malley." Braddock held out a huge, corny hand. "Any friend of the old Fox here is a friend of mine, I guess."

"Thank you, Mr. Braddock."

"You're a Down-Easter, I guess."

"From Boston."

"Humph!" Doubt entered his eyes. "If you're going for gold, and I guess nobody here is heading anywhere else, you're soft and green——"

"Let the boy alone. He's spunk enough for two. Draw that chair over, and visit with us."

"Nothing I'd like better." Braddock drew the chair over and sat down: it creaked ominously beneath his weight. He began rolling a cigarette.

"So tricks are bad with you, Jim?"

He nodded. "First rustlers had their pickin's, then drought hit me hard. What was left of Circle B I staked at faro, and lost. Now I've enough to get me to California, and keep me for a month or two while I stake me a claim some place." His broad grin seemed to indicate that the loss of his ranch was a matter of complete indifference to him. "What about yourself? I guess you ain't reckoning on becoming no desert rat."

"I'm content to let other people do the hard work of producing gold." Fox turned the dog over on its back, and began to run the tips of his slender fingers up and down the thin stomach until the animal's legs quivered with enjoyment. "I'll take my share after it's been found."

"As long as you don't run into no Clem Parkers?"

Fox shrugged. "I might do. *Quién sabe?* When are you moving on?"

"As soon as some of the damned cayucas return from taking the Falcon crowd."

"Red and I have hired one. Care to join us, Jim, at twenty dollars?"

"Sure thing—as long as you don't suggest a game on the way." Braddock grinned good-naturedly. "I want to keep what I got left. But if you aim to keep the cayuca you've hired, jest you introduce me to the son-of-a-gun what's promised it. I'll sit over him with a gun. . . ."

There was something rugged and dependable about Jim Braddock which Henry liked. He was glad that the ex-rancher was to make a third in the cayuca. For a time he listened to his two companions exchanging reminiscences of Sunset Town but presently his attention wandered, and he began to reflect upon his own affairs. Now that he knew for certain that he was on Al's track he felt happier than for many days past. Until that morning there had been no certainty that Al had indeed returned to the steamer. But Al, it seemed, was on his way to California, and was now only a few days' journey ahead. With luck, Henry thought, he might even catch up with Al in Panama City, where he might be waiting the arrival of the ship for California.

He was impatient to begin the journey across the Isthmus. A day wasted now might just be enough time for the next steamer to sail before he could reach Panama City, and easily make a difference of weeks, months, possibly years, before he might again be so close to his quarry.

He gazed at the river that would shortly carry him on to Panama City, and saw two craft afloat on the swift-flowing current. Both were empty of white passengers, and were making for the native town opposite. Both these canoes, he concluded, were kept for ferrying people to and fro between old and new Chagres. There were three other craft visible, from where he sat, but these were drawn up on the shore, being re-thatched with split palm leaves. Why couldn't one of those be hired? he thought angrily. They looked sound enough from a distance. What if they had only just returned from Cruces while he had been asleep, for they had not been there earlier on—surely the offer of an extra dollar above the agreed sum of $15 would tempt their owners. . . .

He turned to point out the three cayucas to his companions. Some while elapsed before he could break into their conversation without rudeness. But at last:

"Do you see those three canoes over there, Mr. Fox? Mightn't they be available at once?"

Fox looked towards the river. "Three? There wasn't one this morning——"

Braddock laughed. "Sure there wasn't. They arrived back while you was booking your bunks in thisyere hotel. I'd just come from over thar when I sees you."

"Trying to hire one?"

"Me—and a dozen others! But they wasn't hiring out one of them dug-outs for all the tea in China."

"Why not?"

" 'Cause none of the boys ain't slept with his wife for a week, and they ain't leaving again till they've worked it out of their systems."

Henry broke in again. "But if we promised them a bonus?"

"You're in a heck of a hurry, young man, aren't you? Thisyere gold fever——"

"Red isn't after gold, Jim, but something more precious," Fox interrupted in a quiet voice.

"What's more precious than gold? Diamonds——"

"Perhaps Red will tell you later. But there's something in what he says——"

"That's jest what there ain't. There ain't one of them coloured fellows over thar what ain't rattling a pocketful of silver dollars already. Now they wants to enjoy themselves awhile, like you would now and again ef you had blood in your body, Fox, instead of ice-water." He snorted. "The goddam' fools ain't got hoss-sense enough to make all the money they can whilst the going's good."

Fox twitched his smooth eyebrows. "You think the gold-rush will peter out soon, Jim?"

"Sure hope it doesn't, not until I've found me a big strike. I wasn't meanin' the gold-rush, Fox, but the railroad. When that opens up the Isthmus theseyere dug-out boys will have to go chase themselves."

"Railroad!" Fox stared at the unbroken line of jungle all about them; then at the chain of mountains to the south, which towered steeply up into the dappled sky. "How would they get the railroad coaches over the Continental Divide? Fly them over?"

"A valley's been found, so I've heeared, with a summit of three hundred feet or so."

"Only three hundred!" Fox smoothed down his neat whiskers with a reflective air. "Could be done, I suppose, as far as the gradient is concerned. But how could anyone hope to lay a track through jungle——?"

"*Quien sabe!* 'Tain't my headache, thank God!" Braddock grunted.

"But some Colombian has vision——"

"Colombian nothing! Us Americans have taken up a concession from the Colombian Government. There's a group of surveyors from New York in thisyere town right now."

"An American railroad!" Fox softly muttered.

"That's what I said. What's the matter with you, Fox?"

"Just thinking."

"You always was a fellow for thinkin' too deep." Braddock laughed amiably, then spat into a nearby spittoon with expert aim. "Personally, it don't make sense jest buildin' a railroad for the sake of a few god-dam gold-seekers——"

"And the mail," Henry added.

Braddock snorted. "Who wants mail delivered any quicker than it is now? No letters ain't never brung me good noos."

"There's more to it than that."

Both men looked enquiringly at Henry.

"Well, young fellow? You seem mighty enthusiastic sudden-like."

"I haven't worked in a port town without getting to know a little about commerce, Mr. Braddock. How many people were aboard the ship that brought you here?"

"Seemed like half the population of the United States, but maybe it were only two or three hundred."

"Right! Multiply that number by all the ships that have been carrying gold-diggers to California for the past year, and all the ships that will be on their way here for many months to come——"

"Unless the gold peters out," Braddock interrupted grimly.

"Well, the total will still amount to something, won't it?"

"Sure will."

"Which means that most of those people will stay out west; most of the unsuccessful ones, at any rate. That will mean that new towns will have to be built to house them. New towns aren't much use without stores, and it's no use opening stores unless you stock them with dry goods. All such goods will have to come from the east for a long time to come. Until the west establishes its own industry."

"I'm beginning to see your meanin'."

"Go on, Red," Fox encouraged in his gentle voice.

"It's something less than fifty miles across the Isthmus from ocean to ocean. By sea the distance would be more than seven thousand miles. You can see what a saving of time there would be if passengers and goods could be shipped from eastern to western ports by way of the Isthmus."

Braddock looked impressed, "You Down-Easters can sure

spout figgers. But you can't build railroads for peanuts, son, and you can't tell me that thar would be enough cargo going to California and other west-coast ports to make it worth building fifty miles of railroad track through thisyere sort of country." He waved a hand at the distant mountains.

"We shouldn't only be shipping cargo to United States ports, Mr. Braddock. Goods could be landed more cheaply in Colombia, Ecuador, Peru and Chili, and help our trade to compete with the English."

The rancher did not attempt to hide his admiration. "See what edjication does for a man, Fox. To be able to reel off all them countries, just like that! If you'd asked me I'd have said that Colombia was in Canada. Lookee here, if I strike lucky and thisyere railroad wants money, doggone it ef I don't put money into it. Sounds a darned sight easier way of makin' money than punchin' cattle."

"But first you've got to get to California," Henry pointed out. "The sooner you do so, the quicker you're likely to make your strike. . . ."

II

Influenced by Henry's artful promptings, Braddock lost something of his philosophical disregard for time and grew suddenly impatient to get going. He persuaded Fox and Henry to cross the river again, in the hope of bribing one of the cayuca owners to leave that day for Cruces. But all his offers, his blandishments and his threats failed to move the boatmen. In somewhat direct language they pointed out to the Americans that they had married their women because it was against nature for men to be celibate, and as they had already been away from their wives for a week they had been celibate at least five nights too many.

So the Americans returned, defeated, to the new town, and decided to make the best of it while they were there. They had an indifferent meal at the Eagle Café and Restaurant, then returned to the Californian Hotel where Fox arranged to hire a table for the evening. While he was doing this, Henry was writing a long letter of explanation to his father, which he finished by promising to write again as soon as he had definite plans to report.

With the coming of darkness New Chagres awoke from its sun-drenched lethargy. Men began to drift into the big saloon of the hotel in numbers which made one feel that they must have materialized from thin air, for they had remained out of sight during most of the hot, moist daylight hours. Some of them sat down at the gambling tables where black-coated croupiers and professional gamblers were already seated; tables to suit all tastes in gambling: faro, monte bank, poker, casino, or trente-et-quarante for those who preferred losing their money at cards; also roulette and crap tables. But most of the men congregated about the long bar which ran the length of the room, and at which price-lists warned thirsty customers that even the meanest drink cost the minimum sum of $1.

Before long the men were followed by women whose painted faces and flamboyant dresses advertised their profession. Then a tired-eyed, white-faced pianist sat down before a liquor-stained piano, and three Panamanian musicians grouped themselves about him. The comparative peacefulness of the saloon was soon disturbed by the noisy strains of raucous music. Couples began clumsily to dance on the small portion of rough-boarded floor allotted to them. Men crowding round the bar became more cheerful; and spoke in louder voices to make themselves heard above the sound of the music. The atmosphere of the room grew steadily hotter. Probably it would have stunk of sweating bodies, but it was kept more or less fragrant by swirling clouds of tobacco smoke which almost hid one side of the room from the other.

Henry entered the saloon just before nine o'clock, after a few more hours' sleep, and gazed at the crowded room with fascinated eyes. In the past he had occasionally accompanied Al Simpson to gaming-rooms in Boston, but none had even remotely resembled the one in which he was now. In spite of its primitive crudity and its stark pandering to vice, there was something honest and unashamed in its appeal which made it compare favourably with the furtive atmosphere of the gilded establishments of New England. Up north, people drank, or sinned, or gambled in an unnatural quiet that was disturbed only by the monotonous murmur of a croupier; the subdued voices of the gamblers as they raised the ante in vicious bids; the soft tread of unstudded leather soles on pile carpets; the restless preliminaries of secret and profane seduction.

But at this American outpost of civilization men enjoyed themselves with uninhibited restraint. They drank until their speech was slurry and argumentative; they cursed loudly when the turn of a card robbed them of a large stake, but were vociferously jubilant when the roulette ball clicked into the right compartment. They danced without grace, but with colossal energy; slobbered kisses upon the receptive lips of their hired partners, and pushed dollar notes into loose bodices as an excuse to fumble with warm, yielding breasts.

As Henry threaded his way through the crowded room the noise of crashing glass and blasphemous voices brought other sounds to a sudden and strangely enquiring silence. A spitting, unforgivable epithet echoing round the room was succeeded by an expectant sigh. Between the taut figures of two intervening onlookers Henry saw the flash of a leathery hand moving downwards. Two guns roared as one, but one bullet scored the wooden ceiling.

The second bullet found its mark. The victim was caught before he could fall to the ground. Four men carried out the lifeless body as the band raggedly resumed the refrain it had been playing. The dancers began shuffling. Voices were raised in loud argument. "Make your bets," a banker ordered in a flat voice as he twirled the wheel. . . .

"Come and name your pizen, son," said Jim Braddock's voice in Henry's ear.

CHAPTER EIGHT

HENRY gulped down his rye, and stared at a hatchet-faced man who leaned nonchalantly against the bar and laughed at something that two other men were telling him. It was hard to believe that, a few moments previously, he had killed another human being as the result of a drunken quarrel. Just as astounding to Henry was the general indifference to a brutal crime; and the bravado of the murderer in remaining where he was. Surely by now he should be fleeing to avoid arrest . . .

He was unaware of having spoken aloud until he heard Braddock answering the question.

"Arrest!" Braddock chuckled. "He don't have to worry 'bout being arrested."

"But he's just killed a man. That's murder."

"Murder! That man ain't no murderer. He killed a man in fair fight, which ain't murder."

"Fight?"

"Sure. Both men reached for their guns, didn't they? But that man thar drawed his quicker. That's why he's alive and the other man ain't. Might just as easily been the other way round."

"Will the sheriff accept that excuse?"

"There ain't no sheriff; no law or order within hundreds of miles of thisyere place, Red. Bogotá is supposed to be responsible for what happens on the Isthmus, but as there ain't no Colombians worth speaking about living here, nobody in Bogotá cares a damn what happens here."

"You mean, men can commit crimes here without risking punishment?"

"I wouldn't say that. If you wants to rob or kill someone and they shoots first, that's punishment enough, ain't it?"

Henry nodded. Fox had warned him he would see death in many forms. . . .

"Where will they bury the body? Somebody might want to see the grave one day."

Braddock clapped Henry on the shoulder. "You sure have been wrapped in cotton-wool all your life, Red. Won't be any use anyone wantin' to visit *his* grave. He won't have none. All bodies are thrown in the Chagres. That gets rid of them quick and easy."

"Will California be something like this, do you think?"

"Shouldn't wonder." The bleak eyes surveyed Henry with a questioning glance. "Does that kinda worry you?"

"I shall get used to it," Henry stoutly maintained.

The rancher's eyes twinkled. "Good boy! You ain't afraid of

being thought skeered. The Fox said you had guts, and by Jupiter! I think he's right." He grew silent and reflective, and was so long before speaking that Henry began to think that his companion had fallen into a doze. He remained equally silent, for his attention was fixed on one of the women dancers.

In contrast with the other women—whose smiling carmined lips and bold expressions were somehow repellant in cold blood, whose belladonna'd eyes were hard and disillusioned—the tiny face of this other girl was neither beautiful, nor handsome, nor even pretty. But she had a pert little nose, and melting eyes, and a dimple in her right cheek, and an expression that was whimsical and ingenuous. The reflection that she was willing to sell her dainty little body to any drunken sot who was willing to pay the price made him feel sick, and he realized that if one of the coarse, calloused hands that was gripping hers in a dance were to be transferred into her young, swelling bosom, he would be unable to resist attacking the man, a square-faced, black-bearded giant with unkempt hair and salacious eyes.

Would he ever get used to *that*? he thought bitterly. So used to the sight of young women selling their charms to coarse brutes that it would offend him no more than it did all the other men who leaned against the bar and leered at the exhibition? Would the proof of his innocence be worth the sacrifice of his inherited idealism of womanhood?

He had sense enough to know that the answer to the first two questions must eventually and inexorably be Yes. Familiarity would breed contempt. Of the answer to the third question he felt less certain. To become a cynic where women were concerned would be, he felt, to rob life of its savour; to take meaning out of existence; deprive Christianity of virtue.

Then he became aghast at his own inconsistency. He had looked unmoved at the other women being pawed. Why, then, should he feel so concerned about a girl because her eyes were melting, and her smiles more sincere than her companions'? He knew why. A vague similarity in the eyes, the nose, the whimsical expression and the slim, rounded body reminded him of Jean Martin.

The discovery filled him with disgust. He felt that he hated the girl on the dance-floor for daring to resemble Jean, however vaguely. Dear Jean! whose innate modesty would have made her shrink from the mere touch of strange fingers. Dear Jean! the essence of sweet and lovely womanhood. But it explained the impulse which made him want to attack the bearded giant. If any man were ever to paw Jean in that way . . .

He became aware that Braddock was speaking. "Lookee here, Red, I've been thinking. You won't take no offence if I tell you you need someone to keep a friendly eye on you till you git hardened up. Wal, what say you and me team up as pardners?"

Partners with Jim Braddock! Henry warmed with friendliness to the ex-rancher, and pride in himself. He realized that no greater compliment could have been paid him than to be invited to become the partner of a man who had a lifetime's experience in weighing up character; who judged people by Western standards, which were ace-high where manliness and courage were concerned. For a few moments he felt almost tempted to accept the offer and go hunting for gold. Suppose Jim Braddock and he were to strike a rich pocket . . .

The girl who reminded him of Jean swung briefly into sight, between the heads of the intervening men; and Braddock's offer lost its attraction. He was not on his way to California to seek for gold, but to force a confession from Al so that the world of Boston might know that Henry Stewart was no thief: so that Jean might know it.

"I'm not going to California to look for gold, Mr. Braddock."

"You mean the Fox weren't stringin' me about you looking for something more precious than gold?"

"No, sir. I'm going there on a man-hunt."

"You!" Braddock chuckled, and his blunt scorn was far from flattering. "You don't look much like a man-hunter to me, son. Now, if you said a lady——"

"I can't return to New England till I've found him."

"You can't, eh?" Braddock's amusement subsided; his eyes turned bleaker. "What chance do you think you'll stand against one of them Californians? They're tough *hombres*, let me tell you. I've met a few. And you—meaning no offence, Red——"

"He's an Easterner. A thief, who worked to fix the blame on me."

"Ah! Now I'm cottonin' on. He's the only one can prove you innocent?"

"Yes, sir."

"More power to your elbow, son." Once more Braddock clapped Henry on the shoulder. "Maybe you ain't so soft as you look, which makes me kinda sorry you ain't going to be my pardner."

"Thank you, sir." Henry glanced at the two empty glasses. "Fill them up," he told the barkeeper in a husky voice.

As the man stretched out a hand for the glasses Braddock's sinewy wrist descended on it with a loud thump.

"Let be, buddy. We don't want no liquor."

"I'm serving him." The barkeep nodded a bullet head at Henry.

"I said neither of us don't want no more liquor," Braddock stated. The barkeep glanced into the bleak eyes, then down at the shining barrel of the rancher's Colt.

"That's right, boss, you don't." The barkeep shrugged, and pulled his hand loose.

"Let's go see what the old Fox is doing," Braddock suggested, putting an arm round Henry's shoulders.

To find Zachary Fox they had to thrust their way through the biggest crowd of all those clustered about the tables. As soon as they were near enough they saw why his table was attracting so much attention. Besides Fox, five other men sat round it, and it was only necessary to glance at their faces to see that play was high. All five were flushed and feverish, and all five pairs of gleaming eyes watched every movement of Fox's white, slender hands with unconcealed suspicion. Their own hands trembled as they fidgeted with their separate piles of money.

Further proof that play was running high was supplied by the much larger pile of money that rested on the table in front of the professional gambler. In addition to silver dollars, Spanish gold doubloons, and Mexican *pesos*, there were three small gold nuggets, half a dozen ounce bags of gold-dust, and two stamped bars of gold.

Braddock whistled softly. "Looks like the old Fox is makin'

a killing," he said in Henry's ear. "I guess that thar gold is liable to cause some excitement back home."

His words were overheard. "It don't have to go that afar, mister, to do that," interrupted a man at his shoulder. "That little fellow there, and Balding on his left, have struck it plenty good. When they landed up here a coupla hours ago, on their way back to Philly, and flashed that gold about, the town went crazy trying to rastle up some boats to git moving. And I wasn't left behind neither."

"Any of them lucky?" Braddock asked jealously.

"Nary a one," was the disgusted reply. "But it's set some of them off, just the same, hoofing their way across. But not me, mister. I can wait that long for a boat."

"Sure," Braddock agreed with feeling.

Henry heard nothing of this conversation, for he was contrasting Fox's face with those of the dozen or so men who pressed in upon the gambler from behind. Nearly all eyes were fixed upon the gold bars and nuggets with an unhealthy, avaricious stare; and one could almost read from their angry gestures that it would not take much to set off their explosive impatience. But he was more interested in the new Zachary Fox, whom he was seeing for the first time.

In the amber light of oil-lamps suspended from the ceiling, Fox's pallid face looked more wax-like than ever, an effect that was heightened rather than offset by his oiled hair; for in spite of the light reflected from the smooth scalp, its very immaculateness and the perfection of its parting made it resemble a wig set expertly upon the head of a wax figure. Even his eyes seemed like green beads, for they were inhumanly void of expression. Only his hands moved; but as the long, slender white fingers manipulated the cards their graceful movements seemed to epitomize the very poetry of motion. They fascinated Henry to such an extent that he could not move his gaze away from them, and he was painfully reminded of the occasion when he and his parents had accompanied the Martin family to a performance of ballet at the local theatre.

Fox shuffled the cards with a deftness that made them appear to dance about in the air of their own volition. The standing audience was delighted and chuckled their appreciation, but the scowling furrows in the foreheads of the five seated men grew deeper with angry suspicion with each new burst of juggling. But abruptly the fifty-two separate entities became a solid deck once again, which Fox placed before the bald-headed man on his left. Baldy cut the deck. Fox picked up the cards with his right hand, fingers spread wide to reveal what was happening. He dropped the deck into the palm of his left hand, which he held uppermost so that every watching eye could see that the cards were not tampered with. Then he took the topmost card and turned it face upwards on the table to his left: the four of diamonds. Then the next, a deuce of clubs, which he placed next to it. He slid off the third card, the queen of diamonds. This he placed in front of him. The fourth card, the ten of spades, he placed in the centre of the table.

Three hands moved almost as one: the little fellow, Baldy; and a third man, an American who wore the vivid red shirt of a Californian, each dropped a small stake on the card. Fox covered each one with a coin of equal value. After a slight pause to make sure that all stakes had been made, he took the next card from the deck, the five of diamonds, which he placed next to the queen.

A hiss from Red Shirt greeted the card. "My lucky card!" he exclaimed hoarsely. With a trembling hand he pushed a large pile of dollars towards the card. "And there's twenty to prove it." His optimism was infectious. Others reached forward to stake on the five. Several of the men standing round the table backed the minimum stake of $2. The little fellow put five on it. So did the man on Fox's right, an unpleasant-looking customer, whose ugly face was worsened by a purple-blue birthmark which disfigured his right cheek, and the black eyeshade which concealed his left eye. His hair looked as if it might be ginger in colour if ever it should be washed.

As soon as Fox had matched all stakes he exposed another card, which he placed, face uppermost as usual, next to the five. This was the seven of hearts. This time the man opposite Fox was the largest backer: he had a swarthy, handsome face, of Spanish cast, and wore the clothes of a native Californian. He pulled a small bag from his pocket and from it produced a large gold nugget which he placed on the seven.

"One pound, two ounces, señor," he said to Fox, in lisping English. There was a note of enquiry in his voice.

There was immediately commotion round the table as the inflamed onlookers shouted with excitement and pressed closer to stare at the nugget. As the nugget's weight was passed on from mouth to mouth the Californian's words were repeated again and again in every shade of emotion, from incredulity to vicious envy. The hubbub grew louder as a series of agitated questions, all based on the vital "Where?" were fired at the Californian. He ignored them all, his face not less impassive than Fox's, and waited for the gambler's acceptance of the stake.

Fox nodded agreement, and waited for other stakes to be laid on the seven of hearts. But for some unfathomable reason no more stakes were offered.

"What's wrong with that thar card?" Braddock asked the man who had already spoken to him.

"Nothin', but the Californian has lost heavily all night. Ain't won a single bet yet. I guess that's 'bout all he's got left. P'raps they reckon that card's as good as lost now he's backed it."

"Wal, I ain't superstitious," Braddock grunted. He leaned forward, and dropped two dollars on the card. "Another two dollars for you, Fox," he called out, and grinned. But Fox's Sphinx-like face registered no gleam of interest or acknowledgment.

He turned up the next card. The seven of clubs.

The pandemonium which had barely subsided from the previous moments broke out anew. The Californian had won.

"Of all the bloody luck!" shouted One Eye in anger.

Baldy was scarcely more amiable. "Can't lose to one of us Americans fer a change, can you, mister?" he snarled at Fox.

Apparently oblivious to the milling, noisy scene about him, the imperturbable Fox pushed over to the equally impassive Californian a selection of smaller nuggets, bags of gold-dust, and a pile of silver dollars to make up the difference. Meanwhile, with a loud chuckle Braddock picked up the two dollars he had won.

"My luck's changed, son," he announced jubilantly. "Now watch me make a killin'."

Braddock's optimistic mood had evidently communicated itself to the players sitting at the table, for when Fox next turned up the three of clubs all five staked heavily upon it. The next card was the ace of spades. This, too, was heavily backed. Then the king of clubs, followed by the four of diamonds, the deuce of diamonds and the six of hearts. Excitement mounted; more and heavier sums were staked.

In hoarse, spasmodic whispers Braddock explained the game to Henry. "It's a variation of an old French game, son—as soon as Fox turns up a card matching any of those already on the table he pays out—except on his own card; that's the queen—then the game stops, and he takes all stakes left—any moment now he'll be paying out—they ain't many more numbers to come up, only eight, nine and knave. . . ."

Even as Braddock mentioned the knave, Fox laid down the knave of clubs. This was followed by the nine of hearts.

"Only eight and queen left," Braddock said, swallowing. "Look at them there stakes!"

It was almost impossible to see the cards now for the stakes which covered them. There was little left of the piles of money which had previously stood on the table before the players. Even Fox's money had dwindled to a dangerous minimum, for, as banker, he had had to match every stake placed on the cards.

"Ef a queen don't soon turn up the old Fox 'ull be through," Braddock chuckled. "I never thought to live to see him up agin it."

Fox turned up the next card. The eight of spades. A hiss of excitement travelled round the table. This was quickly followed by a silence that was all the more dramatic in contrast with the noise which had existed until then; also by the fact that it was an oasis in a desert of uproar, for elsewhere in the room the din continued unabated: the shuffling of heavy boots on the dance-floor, the monotonous music of the four-piece band, the clink of bottles and glasses, the discordant singing of drunken voices, excited conversation. . . .

Now everyone was anxious to back the cards still on the table. Every number save the queen was represented there: if the next card were not a queen (and the chances were certainly not less than thirty-nine to one against another turning up), then someone must win.

Convinced that the professional gambler had struck an unlucky streak, the five players at the table plunged heavily. By the time they had finished very few dollars were left on the table except in the middle. Henry anxiously counted Fox's money, and was sure that he had less than $100 before him.

Fox turned up the next card. The deuce of spades! There was a muttered oath from Baldy. Because of the two cards on Fox's left, the deuce and the four were the lightest backed cards of the thirteen already on the table—the odds on the third deuce's turning up having been considerably more against than any other card. The few lucky backers collected their winnings. The little fellow at the table, apparently inspired by a hunch that the fourth deuce would quickly turn up, backed five dollars on the deuce of spades. Nobody else followed his example, however.

The slender fingers slid the next card off the pack; turned it. The queen of clubs!

Zachary Fox had cleared the board.

A buzz of angry disappointment travelled round the table: some of the backers scowled their fury. One Eye showed his chipped, tobacco-stained teeth in a snarl.

"By God!" he exploded. "You won with that card last time you was banker."

"Meaning what?" Fox drawled.

One Eye's hands stiffened. "Meaning you'd best reach for 'em, mister. No damned sharper ain't going to have my money."

Fox smiled carelessly, but before he could move or speak a Colt had sprung into Braddock's hand.

"Hold it, stranger," he warned. "Fox here don't pack no irons. But I do."

In accordance with the code of the West, Braddock replaced his Colt in its holster, and with tensed muscles waited for the first, challenging movement.

One Eye glared into the bleak eyes of the interrupter. Round about the immediate vicinity of the two men there was no movement, no sound: the swirl of noise and movement beyond the circle of silent, motionless onlookers presented a contrast of incongruity that made Henry, stiffly apprehensive, want to laugh.

For five vital seconds the tiny world about the table stood still. Then One Eye relaxed.

"If he don't carry irons——" he mumbled.

"And he don't rig the deck neither."

One Eye swallowed. "If you say so, mister———"

"My gun says so. I've known Fox fer many years, stranger. You can take it from me he's straight, see."

A moment's hesitation. "I take it," One Eye muttered, as he rose from his seat and thrust his way towards the bar.

Fox picked up the cards and began shuffling.

CHAPTER NINE

HENRY did not easily fall asleep that night. Three images haunted his imagination: the winsome face of the young dancer, the inhuman impassiveness of Fox's waxen face, and the uncanny speed with which Jim Braddock's Colt had been transferred from holster to hand. He had been standing sideways on to Braddock at the time, therefore the weapon must have been drawn in the direct line of his vision: nevertheless, he had not been conscious of seeing any movement on the part of the rancher. One moment Braddock's hands had been hanging loosely by his side; the next his Colt was menacing One Eye's stomach.

The mental picture fascinated Henry. What power it must give a man, he reflected, to know that he could draw his weapon a fractional instant quicker than most other men. The power of life and death. The power of authority and command. Moreover, the power was, in a sense, cumulative: the mere knowledge that he had nothing to fear seemed to give its possessor an hypnotic power over others which often made it unnecessary even to use his material power. Twice that evening he had seen men cowered by something they had seen in Braddock's eyes: first the barkeep, then One Eye. Neither man had seen Braddock before, or knew anything about him; yet both had realized, One Eye particularly, that it might mean death to challenge Braddock to the draw.

Henry envied the rancher that power. What might such power not mean to him, in his pursuit of Al Simpson? Because (if he possessed the power) he inspired fear he would automatically obtain attention and obedience. And when at last he confronted Al, he might need no more than that power to force a confession from the other man.

This dream-like possibility dominated his reflections for a long time: he gave himself up to the enthralling but ingenuous pastime of imagining the scene as it might be when he came face to face with Al. He pictured the contemptuous sneer which would pass across the handsome, dissipated face at the mere suggestion of a confession. He heard the mocking laughter that would answer his first, restrained threats. Then he felt his hand flashing for the gun, and saw the incredulous look of amazement which would surely displace the previous contempt. Then would come fear—and finally panic-stricken willingness to do anything in preference to being shot. . . .

He came out of his day-dream with a start. With growing excitement he realized that the idea might not be the fantastic dream it had seemed. Suppose Jim Braddock were agreeable to teaching him the tricks of a quick draw! Suppose he were to practise day after day until he became efficient! It was unlikely he would ever become expert enough to match a born Westerner, or a true gunman, but for all practical purposes he might acquire sufficient skill to achieve the object of his journey to California. . . .

II

"Could I teach you to draw a gun, son? Sure, I could. But I won't." There was no hint of laughter in the bleak eyes. Nor annoyance, when Braddock saw the angry disappointment which settled on Henry's open face.

"Lookee here, Red," he went on in a quiet, amiable drawl. "Don't you go feeling hurt, but jest you listen to me. I don't aim to be doing what you ask 'cause I like you too much, see. You ain't got that red hair of yourn for nothin'. You've got spunk, and you've got temper. If you start totin' a gun the first thing you knows of you'll go looking for trouble to test your skill, an' be invitin' someone to draw jest because you don't like the way he looks at you. That means you'll have to kill him to stop him killin' you. Do you want to go about killin' men 'cause you don't like their faces?"

"I'm not likely to do that . . ."

Braddock smiled dryly. "That's what you think. But you're an Easterner. You're not born to pack a gun, and don't know what it does to a man what ain't born to one. It's like alcohol, son, wearing a gun is: it gives you too much confidence, and makes you too damned ready to see the other man in hell first. It ain't many who can hold their hosses when they pack a gun. And once you've tasted blood——"

Henry made one last effort. "I've a reason for asking you, Mr. Braddock."

"What reason?"

"I told you last night about Al Simpson."

The bleak eyes held Henry's: he had to exercise will-power not to look away. No wonder men grew afraid of Braddock, he thought. There was some force in the light blue eyes that kind of shrivelled one up. . . .

"Is that the only reason you want to pack a gun?"

"There's a girl back in New England whom I can't ask to marry me with a charge of embezzlement hanging over my head."

"That's a good enough reason for me, son. Let's get movin'."

"Moving?"

"Sure. You kaint pack a gun unless you buys one first."

III

Later that day Henry had his first lesson. From the Emporium down the street Braddock purchased a pair of second-hand Colts which a disillusioned, homeward-bound old prospector had sold to help buy a passage to Charleston. Then he took Henry out of the town towards the jungle, where they would be less likely to be overlooked. Here Braddock first filed off the front sights, to prevent their catching in the holsters, and possibly slowing up the draw. Next he showed Henry the flick of the finger by which the quick draw was achieved. For the next hour Henry practised drawing the guns, until his shirt was soaked with sweat, the tips of his fingers bruised and raw, and the muscles of his wrists and arms stiff. At the end of that time he had scarcely mastered even the rudimentary movements, but the rancher was not dissatisfied. As he explained, Henry had plenty of time before him in which to practise.

That evening passed much as the previous one had done. Early on Fox took his seat at one of the tables and announced that he was opening a bank for Lansquenet. Before long every vacant seat was filled with punters. Henry watched the game for some time, but having no money to stake he soon became bored with the game and went over to watch the faro table. Later he wandered across to the crap and roulette tables. Lastly he went over to watch the dancing.

"Want a dance, mister?"

He glanced sideways, and started. He had been thinking about the girl with the winsome face, wondering why she was not on the floor. He had thought about her several times that day. Indeed, he realized with annoyance that his only reason for not going to bed earlier had been a desire to see her again.

"No."

She laughed into his face. "What's the matter with you? Too shy?"

"No."

"Oh! come on, mister, don't be so standoffish." She took hold of his arm with her tiny hand. "You know you like the looks of me. I saw the way your eyes followed me about last night."

He was startled, and a little flattered, to think that she had noticed him among the hundred odd men who had filled the hotel saloon. But he could not forget that she had looked into the faces of other men with whom she had danced much as she was smiling at him at that moment. Nor could he overlook the fact that she reminded him of Jean Martin, and that he hated her for that reason. He freed himself from her arm.

She pouted with anger, and seemed inclined to walk away. Then she looked at his face before glancing at the other men who were hanging about waiting to pounce upon her for a dance. The quick expression of contempt indicated that she preferred Henry.

"Come on, mister," she urged, trying to push him on to the

dance-floor. "Two dollars a dance, and I'll give you an encore 'cause I like the look of you."

"I don't want to dance," he answered roughly.

"Then buy me a drink instead."

He hesitated long enough for her to sense that she could probably wheedle him. She caught hold of his hand, and this time turned towards the bar. The warmth of her hand was irresistible. He followed meekly as she pushed a way through the crowd of men standing before the bar.

"Blue Moon, Jimmy," she told the barkeep. "What you having?"

"Rye."

Jimmy pushed the two drinks over. "Two dollars."

Henry sighed as he regretfully paid over two of his precious dollars. Why hadn't he been man enough to resist her puckish smile? he miserably asked himself. Wasting two dollars—for he wasn't interested in the rye—on a girl he despised, just because she had soft hands and a pair of melting eyes!

"My name's Lucy. What's yours?"

"Red."

She stretched up on tiptoe and combed his hair with her fingers. "Ought to have guessed, oughtn't I? My! you've got nice hair, Red. Wish mine were as springy. On your way to the goldfields?"

"To California. Not the goldfields."

She seemed a little astonished; but quickly supplied her own solution to the mystery as her gaze travelled up and down his clothes, which still bore evidence of first-class tailoring.

"Guess you don't have to look for gold." She hastily swallowed her drink. "Buy me another, Red. Same as before."

"Please—no—I'm sorry . . ."

The concern in his voice was noticeable. She looked at him with contempt. "Purse-strings too tight even for a drink?"

"No purse, Lucy," he answered bitterly.

She inspected his face, and presently believed him. "Is that why you wouldn't dance with me?"

"That, and . . ." he began unthinkingly.

"And what?" she asked, when he came to an abrupt stop.

"Nothing."

"Tell me, Red."

"There's nothing to tell."

"Last night you stared at me as if you wanted to dance."

"That wasn't why."

"Then why?"

Her persistent questioning got on his nerves. "You reminded me of someone back home, that's all."

"Someone you're sweet on?" She guessed the truth from his wincing expression. "So that's it! You don't want to dance with me because you can't bear to think of your sweetheart being a tart?" She was bitter and scornful. "Bet she'd be a tart, too, if she had had my life."

"I'm sorry, Lucy . . ." he began, sorry for the pain he was causing her. "I didn't mean——"

Relenting, she smiled wistfully. "Guess you didn't, Red. Come and dance."

He resisted her pull. "I've told you——"

"I know. You haven't got two dollars. Forget it. I've made fifty cents out of you already." She laughed at his surprise. "My share of the drink. Coloured water. Come on. Once round the floor."

He had always loved dancing. He resolutely turned his back upon the past; and as his arm encircled her soft, yielding body he regretted that he had not a pocketful of dollars to enable him to dance with her for the rest of the night. She was as light as thistle-down, and danced better than he had anticipated. Reflecting upon how much of her life was taken up with partnering clumsy-footed, lumbering, and often drunken transients, he felt immensely sorry for her.

IV

Pedro Romanos was a man of his word. Towards late afternoon the following day he stood before Zachary Fox and with a flash of white teeth announced that a cayuca would be ready to leave Chagres for Cruces at noon the day after.

Of course, it was not ready. When the three men, accompanied by Romanos and two porters carrying their baggage, arrived at the edge of the river five minutes before the appointed time, there was no canoe anywhere along the west bank, nor one on the water.

After a wait of nearly fifteen minutes Braddock asked impatiently, "When is thisyere boat going to show up, mister? It's nearly ten after, and there ain't movement of craft or men t'other side."

"Don't worry, señor, Carlos Piérola will appear at any moment. I promised the other señor the best boatman and the best boat on the river, and Pedro Romanos is a man of his word."

"But is thisyere Piérola?" Braddock growled. "It's almighty hot on the open shore. I don't aim to melt into a grease spot this side of Monterey."

"He will be here in ten minute, twenty minute . . ." Romanos shrugged. "Time is not of so much consequence to us Panamanians as it is to you Yanquis."

"Huh!" Braddock growled. "You wouldn't think so if you was wanting to dig gold."

"By the grace of God, we Panamanians have no love of gold," the Panamanian stated, with a careless gesture. "Gold has been the curse of this country since the Spaniards first set foot on it."

"Wal! Maybe gold is a curse, but it's a mighty useful one."

"For what, señor? As long as one has the sun to warm one, food within reach to keep one's belly full, and a woman to share one's bed, what more can gold give? More sun? We have too much. More food? Who wants more when one's belly is full? More women?" Both his smile and the flash of his dark eyes were mischievous; he stroked his moustache with a self-satisfied air. "Panamanian women do not have to be bought, señores, and gold will not buy the extra virility to satisfy them. Otherwise, I should be in California."

"Why in California, Señor Romanos?" Fox asked quietly. "Isn't there still plenty of gold in New Grenada?"

"There is?" Braddock demanded.

The Panamanian nodded. "It is said so, señores. But the Indians, who know where it is, will not reveal the secret."

"Why not?"

"I have told you why, señor. Because gold has brought so much unhappiness and death to this country."

Another twenty minutes passed, but Romanos' imperturbability was not disturbed by Braddock's growing impatience.

"Piérola will come," he confidently stated.

"Not before we're all fried," the rancher objected.

The dark, handsome face flashed another of its mischievous smiles. "It will be much hotter in the interior, señor," he encouraged. At that moment three men came out of one of the huts opposite and walked slowly towards a cayuca that was drawn up on the shore. "There's Piérola now."

After the boatmen had loaded the canoe with their own requirements they pushed it into the water, and jumped in. As they paddled across the river the Americans inspected the craft that was to take them two-thirds of the way across the Isthmus, and liked the look of it. Romanos seemed to sense their approval.

"A trim-looking boat; no, señores? It is longer than most of the cayucas, being thirty feet. It has a beam of nearly three feet, and a draft of nearly ten inches, so you won't have to fear that it may turn over and give you a bath." He laughed at his own humour. "And newly thatched this morning," he went on, referring to the canopy of thatched palm leaves which covered the boat. "No insects, señores."

"Looks like the canoe's made all of one piece," Braddock grunted.

"All cayucas are made of one piece, señor; from the trunk of an espevé tree, which is hollowed by fire then shaped with a machete." He went on, "Piérola is sitting in the bows. He is a mestizo; of Spanish and Indian extraction, like most of us. He is chief boatman, and will be in charge. You will pay him at the end of the journey."

"The other two men look like Negroes."

Romanos nodded. "Descendants of African slaves, brought here by the Spaniards after they had massacred so many Indians that almost none was left to do manual labour. Those two men are brothers, señor. There is a touch of Indian blood in them from their great-grandfather."

They steered the canoe straight for the beach until its flaring prow was projecting well beyond the water-line. Piérola and one of the Negroes jumped out and at once began transferring the baggage into the back of the cayuca. The third man remained seated on the stern, which, like the prow, was solid.

"Anyone fancy any special place?" Fox asked.

Before his companions could reply, a voice behind them broke in, "You have room for a fourth passenger, gentlemen. May I not occupy it?"

All swung round. Henry gasped. Braddock muttered something unintelligible deep down in his throat. Fox alone acted normally. He swept off his hat with a graceful flourish, and bowed.

"Your servant, m'am."

Henry and Braddock hastily followed their companion's example, then stared curiously at the newcomer.

The first and most astounding fact was that her attire was masculine. She was dressed in a pair of baggy pantaloons, and a long, loosely-belted jacket of russet home-spun over a cotton shirt and knotted yellow neckerchief. On her feet she wore a pair of high-heeled riding-boots, reaching half-way up the calf, of soft, fine leather of a rich yellow exactly matching the shade of her neckerchief. Her hair was concealed beneath a wide-brimmed sombrero, which had a narrow band of yellow leather round its brim.

She was as tall as Zachary Fox, but even allowing for the extra inches afforded by the high heels, she remained taller than the average woman. Her shoulders were square, and she held herself upright with the stiffness of a trooper. The shape of her bosom was hidden by her jacket, which was buttoned up, but there was a sufficient swell in the tightness of the coat to·suggest that she was well fashioned there.

Lastly, the men glanced at her face. It was a strong face, and held no hint of frail womanliness. Her complexion was as brown as a berry; her chin, square; her eyebrows, strikingly thick and black; her firm lips, colourless. All three men varied in the estimate of her age: Fox's thirty-six was the nearest, for she was thirty-four.

Although surprise had made Braddock slow to recollect his manners, he was quick enough to answer her question. Perhaps, as the eldest of the three, he took it upon himself to act as spokesman.

"Why, m'am, there ain't nothing would give us more pleasure than to have you go with us," he said, gallantly. "As long as you ain't expectin' party manners——"

"I'm used to men's company," she crisply interrupted. "How much is the fare?"

"Nothing to you, m'am, being a lady——"

"Nonsense, sir. I insist upon paying my share." There was a note of authority in her voice which brought a wry smile to Fox's lips. "Come, come," she urged, when nobody spoke. "I refuse to be in anyone's debt. Unless you agree to accept my share of all expenses I shall have to find room elsewhere."

"In that case, m'am, we kaint do nothin' else but agree. The boat is costing us sixty dollars to Cruces."

"Then my share will make it fifteen dollars each. Thank you, gentlemen. May I put my baggage in the dug-out?" She indicated the small pack on the shore by her side.

In answer Fox stepped forward to pick it up. Before he could do so she waved him aside and picked it up herself with an ease which testified to her strength. "I'm your partner, for the time being, not a woman," she stated brusquely. "I am well used to caring for myself." With that she handed the pack to the Negro boatmen, then surveyed each of the Americans in turn.

"Humph!" she exclaimed. "You, sir, being the heaviest, will no doubt sit in the stern." This to Braddock. "Then you next, sir," she continued, looking at Fox. "I will sit in the next place, and you"—indicating Henry—"had better sit forward. Are we all ready to take our places?"

The speechless men nodded, and tamely obeyed her commands.

As soon as all the passengers were settled the Negro took his place in the middle of the cayuca; and Piérola, in the prow. With a broad grin and a wave of his brown hand, Romanos pushed the canoe off the shore. A few minutes later the town of Chagres had disappeared from sight round a bend, and with it the last contact with American civilization. Only the unbroken sweep of jungle was to be seen and the swift-moving surface of the Chagres River.

CHAPTER TEN

FOR a time nobody spoke. The only sound in the vicinity of the canoe was the rhythmic splash of the three paddles as they were dipped into the water. Perhaps the Americans were not easily able to recover from the surprise of having a fourth passenger thrust upon them so unexpectedly; more especially that she was a woman, that she was travelling alone, and that she was dressed in male attire.

On this last count Henry was the most affected. The two other men were accustomed to seeing Western women wearing breeches, but he had never seen a woman in trousers before; and both the idea and the fact vaguely shocked him. Nor did he appreciate the manner in which she had coolly ordered the three men into the canoe. It was her place, he thought, to remain discreetly quiet, both as a woman and an uninvited member of the party. Back in Boston he had always disliked Mrs. Sutter for having too masterful a character for a woman. He might easily begin to dislike their new companion for the same reason. At which thought he recollected that she had not even introduced herself, nor expressed any desire to know the names of her companions.

Then, as the primeval beauty of the scene that was unfolding before his eyes attracted his attention, he forgot the woman sitting behind him, and revelled in the fact that he was at last really entering tropical country. For the jungle had closed in upon them: the massive, dense walls of jungle which lined either bank of the river rose up like the walls of a canyon to heights of thirty feet and more. Sometimes even the canyon in its turn closed in upon them, where massive mango, mahogany and sycamore trees stretched across the water from either bank, and, almost meeting in a green ceiling, transformed the canyon into a mysterious, shadowed tunnel.

Colour, against the pervading background of green, was rampant. Large clusters of purple and yellow blossom sprinkled the jungle in all directions, reminding Henry of the Japanese paper lanterns which used to delight his young heart on celebration nights. Butterflies as large as the palm of one's hand fluttered across the water like fragments of a rainbow. Paroquets of brilliant plumage scolded them from upper branches. Spikes of dazzling scarlet and crimson stuck out from the heart of the ubiquitous orchid like tongues of fire, sometimes two to three feet in length. Large clusters of scarlet nuts hung below the foliage of the palm-trees. Thick curtains of parasitic creepers, dotted with convolvulus-like blooms of many colours, cloaked the rottenness that was sustaining them. Giant lilies carpeted the bogland below. Clusters of blue-tinted water hyacinths drifted downstream.

For most of the time the vision of the travellers was restricted by the rank tangle of bamboo grass which lined the water-side; but where the river widened or twisted in a broad sweep vistas of long distances were opened up, and they were able to see the mountains which on both sides paralleled the course of the river. Because these, too, were covered with dense vegetation up to their peaks, the intervening countryside lost its contours and made them look no more than round-headed hummocks in an unbroken green-topped plateau.

Progress was slow, for they were moving against a fast current. The gentle motion, allied to the regular swishing noise of the paddles and the burning heat of the day, presently made Henry sleepy. His heavy-lidded eyes closed, and his chin drooped forward on to his chest. . . .

"Perhaps now is a convenient moment to introduce myself to you, gentlemen. My name is Abigail Vandusen, of Washington, D.C."

"Pleased to know you, m'am. Mine's Jim Braddock, of Sunset Town, Texas, late boss of the Circle B, and now off to dig for gold in California."

"Zachary Fox, m'am, of somewhere south of the Mason-Dixon Line." There was dry humour in his voice, as if he guessed what construction she would place upon the deliberate concealment of his hometown. "I don't have to tell you my reason for going to California?"

"You're a gambler?"

"I am, m'am."

"The honestest gambler in the Union, m'am," Braddock added challengingly.

"You don't have to tell me that, sir," she said crisply. "I pride myself on reading faces. That's why I selected you three gentlemen two days ago as the most likely travellers to offer help to an unaccompanied woman."

"Two days ago, m'am!" Braddock repeated. "How did you know we was leavin' town jest when we did?"

"Because I've been keeping watch on you."

"Wal, I'll be doggoned, beggin' your pardon, m'am."

"No need to apologize, Mr. Braddock. It is my wish that you should all carry on as if no woman were accompanying you. You will not embarrass me. I am inured to travelling as the only woman in men's company." After a slight pause she added, speaking to Henry, "And you, sir, do you not wish me to know your name?"

Henry had his back to her, for the occupants of the dug-out all faced forward. He was, therefore, not aware that the question was addressed to him, for he had not paid attention from the moment she had mentioned the name of Abigail Vandusen. It was vaguely familiar, and he had concentrated on trying to recollect how and why; if they had met she might know him and be suspicious of his presence in Panama. Unfortunately, the memory of any such meeting eluded him.

"Red!" Fox called out. "Hey, Red!"

The sound of the gentle voice at last secured Henry's attention. He turned.

"Miss Vandusen wishes you to introduce yourself."

"I'm sorry," he stammered. "My thoughts were far away. I'm Hen——" He paused in confusion at having thoughtlessly pronounced half of his Christian name, then decided that he must finish the name in order not to raise suspicion in her, or Braddock's, mind. "Henry Malley, otherwise Red, of—of Boston." He hurried on, anxious to find out the worst as soon as possible. "Your name is familiar to me, m'am. Perhaps we've met——"

"Not in Boston. It's one of the few towns in the Union I have not yet visited. You probably recognize my name from having seen it in print. Perhaps you've read one of my books."

"Books, m'am?"

"I am an explorer. I have published several books about my travels."

He nodded. "Of course! Didn't you travel across India, from Bombay to Calcutta? Was it your book I read about two years ago?"

"Yes. Now I'm going to explore California."

Braddock chuckled. "You going to mention us, in your new book, ma'am?"

"Do you want me to, Mr. Braddock?"

"Sure, m'am. It would give something fer the grandchildren to be proud of their old grandpap about."

"How many grandchildren have you?"

The rancher laughed uproariously. "Doggone it, m'am, I haven't any children yet, for I ain't never married. But I aim to afore I'm many years older."

"And you, Mr. Fox, are you married?"

"No, m'am, nor am I ever likely to."

"A rash statement."

"I prefer to gamble on cards, not women, m'am. There's more chance of winning."

Silence followed the chuckle of male appreciation at this sally. Before turning to face forward again Henry glanced at the two Negro boatmen. Each man's only articles of clothing consisted of a battered straw hat, and a pair of white denim trousers which were rolled up above their knees; but their glistening bodies seemed as impervious to the fierce heat of the sun as their rippling muscles were to the hard labour of paddling the canoe. He envied them their fine figures, for their chests were broad; their backs square; and their long, clean-cut limbs hadn't an ounce of superfluous fat.

Piérola resembled his assistants in no particular. His body was of slighter build; he wore his trousers down to his slippered feet, and a white cotton shirt over. The hair beneath his hat was lank; the colour of his flesh light chocolate. But what he lacked in strength, apparently he made up in sinew and muscle. His paddle, giving time to the men behind, worked tirelessly. Henry noticed that he kept a sharp look-out ahead, and wondered why; for the man in the stern was steersman, and one who knew the route well, it seemed, for the tide was always slackest where the cayuca was.

Later, in the afternoon, the Americans learned the reason for Piérola's watchfulness. As they swung round a bend into a long straight stretch of water they saw some distance ahead of them another cayuca, bound upstream.

"*Vamos!*" the Panamanian called out in excitement. Simultaneously, the speed and length of his paddle strokes increased. The canoe moved perceptibly faster.

"Hey! What's happening there?" Braddock shouted, but nobody answered his question. The three paddles went in and out of the water with exciting precision.

"It's a race," Abigail Vandusen calmly announced.

"Is it, by thunder!" The rancher chuckled with pleasure. "Offering any odds, Fox?"

Fox laughed, and spoke to the Negro who sat in the middle of the boat between Vandusen and himself. "Why are we trying to race the canoe ahead?"

"*No hablo Inglés,*" he grunted.

So Fox called out to Henry to question the chief boatman.

"We race other cayuca because all Yanqui señores in hurry to get to Panama before anyone else," Piérola announced with pride. "You give extra tip if we race other cayucas?"

Henry passed the message on back to the others.

"Sure, we'll give the critters an extra tip," Braddock gleefully agreed. "I was gettin' sore eyes jest looking at nothin' but trees. Two to one on us, Fox," he added, squinting ahead. "We've catched them up several yards already."

"No takers, Jim. Wait until the people ahead see us."

The distance between the two canoes steadily decreased. Beads of sweat began to roll down the flesh of the Negro boatmen, but their stroke never faltered. Except for the wild gleam in their eyes as they stared fixedly ahead they might have been black automatons.

Their progress was too good to continue. There was a shout from the canoe ahead as the occupants realized that they were being overtaken; and the paddles of the boatmen began to move more quickly in response to the exhortations of the passengers.

For a while the foremost cayuca was able to hold its position, but not for long. The rear craft began to close in, though not quite so speedily as before. Nevertheless, Henry was soon able to distinguished angry words from the other canoe.

"Get a move on thar in front," he heard. "If you let that there canoe ketch up with us I'll drill a hole through your stinkin' black carcase as sure as me name is Donahue."

Unfortunately, Braddock also heard.

"Hey, there, you by the name of Donahue!" he bellowed. "I've got ten dollars in my wallet that says you haven't a hope in hell."

"Why, you god-damned son of a spavined maverick!" Donahue shouted back, turning in his seat to peer at his challenger. "Make it twenty, and I'll consider taking it as chicken-feed."

"Done," Braddock agreed with a cheerful oath.

"What's the name, gambler?"

"Jim Braddock to you, friend, and if I don't see you this side of Monterey, I'll be waitin' for you on the dock to collect. At the same time I'll show you what real gold looks like, so as you can write home to your mammy that you've seen some."

This pleasantry was greeted with a stream of lurid oaths, the finish of which was drowned by the sound of Braddock's mocking laughter. This was followed by some equally forceful language addressed to the boatmen. "Paddle, you black-skinned sons of Satan! Paddle, you stinkin' swine! Damn your lousy hides, paddle!"

Inspired by the fury in Donahue's voice more than by his fierce and colourful threats, not a word of which they understood, the boatmen pulled harder for a time. But the moment they slackened Piérola's steadier stroke had its effect. Amid mounting excitement in both boats (save on the part of Abigail Vandusen) the rear canoe drew level; and the passengers were able to stare angrily at one another—at least the men in the other boat were able to, and did so: they were a tough-looking crowd, bearded and travel-stained. For them the challenge was no sporting event, but a genuine and grim race for the gold-fields of California.

Presently Piérola's canoe swung in towards the left bank. The men in the other craft jeered in triumph, believing that Piérola's crew were tiring. But the jeers died away as they saw their competitor suddenly move ahead with a spurt.

"Paddle, you yellow rats!" Donahue bellowed in fury. "Paddle . . ."

But they had lost the race. In the slack water Piérola's cayuca went steadily ahead, leaving the other craft struggling to maintain position against the racing current. . . .

II

Towards late afternoon, as the cayuca rounded a particularly wide bend in the river, its passengers observed the beginnings of a broad savanna which stretched from the right-hand bank of the river as far as the foothills a mile or more back. As the craft made towards this bank the Americans realized, by observing the exertions of the three boatmen, that the current was running even more swiftly at this point than elsewhere. Soon they knew why, for they saw ahead of them on the left the confluence of the Chagres with one of its tributaries—the Gatún River, they learned from Piérola.

At the same time they saw, on the opposite bank which they were hugging, a collection of some forty to fifty cane and palm huts, which stood close to the river. Piérola nodded his head towards the village.

"Town of Gatún," he went on. "We sleep there." He grinned at the canoes which lined the bank. "Many people already here. Glory to God we raced the other four boats. Soon there won't be no place to sleep."

The passengers alighted gratefully, for they were cramped with many hours of sitting. Abigail Vandusen turned to the head boatman.

"Where do we sleep?" she demanded, with a return of the authoritative air which earlier had annoyed Henry.

"I find gentlemen nice hut. Does señora want separate hut, please? Not easy to find; town so crowded."

"I've no objection to sharing their hut, if they haven't," she replied casually, glancing at Braddock for confirmation.

He looked embarrassed. "Wal, m'am, none of us being married I guess we ain't used to seeing women around, but if thisyere town is as full as Piérola says, maybe you'd best bunk along of us."

'This way, if you please," Piérola urged, pointing downstream. "Other boats soon arrive."

At a nod from Braddock he led the way forward, and as the two Negroes had already shouldered the baggage, the Americans followed him.

Like the frame-houses in New Chagres, the native huts had been built higgledy-piggledy in twin lines, but there the resemblance ceased. The ground between the huts was inches deep in soft mud, and was used not only by human beings as a road, but also by animals as a convenient farmyard. Flocks of poultry and geese fluttered from side to side; a few mangy dogs, several pigs and a couple of she-goats, rooted about for food. Mules were tied up at odd places.

Even so, the animals were in the minority. Naked children, with shaven heads and swollen bellies, played in and around the huts, or stared, bright-eyed, at the Americans; their mothers worked in the shaded entrances; weaving, grinding corn, or making preparations for a meal; and gossiping cheerfully among themselves by calling in shrill voices from one hut to the next. Their menfolk squatted outside in groups, talking, smoking native-made cigars, drinking, and playing some kind of a native gambling game.

Against this typical scene of Panamanian village life the many American travellers were conspicuous and inharmonious as they waited impatiently to continue their journey to the Pacific. They greeted the arrival of Henry and his companions with rude pleasantries that were not wholly good-natured. Each new traveller to the Californian gold-fields was a rival who might reduce the share of the precious metal available—optimistically, in the envious mind of each man, to himself. Abigail, particularly, came in for a share of comment, which left her completely unmoved.

Piérola turned into a hut situated about half-way along the row. Through the open doorway the others saw him talking to an ample-breasted woman whose light brown face was lined with the strain of frequent childbirth. Evidently the talk was satisfactory to a point, for he waved to them to enter. They did so to find that the interior of the hut consisted of one single room with a ceiling of cane slats covered with what appeared to be hides. This room, they saw, had to serve every household requirement from bedroom to kitchen.

"Señora says, no room left on ground floor, but you may sleep up there." Piérola indicated the ceiling.

"There's room above?" Fox questioned.

G

"Yes, señor. Plenty room for eight people, on floor."

"It's as good as anywhere else," Abigail Vandusen calmly announced. "We'll take it."

Fox's lips twitched at the imperious *we*, but otherwise his pale waxen face retained its normal detachment.

Thirty minutes later they—and three other Americans who had arrived earlier and had secured hammocks on the ground floor with the señora, her husband and five children—ate a supper of roast pork and coffee, by the light of a single candle-end stuck in the neck of an empty bottle. For this the woman charged each person $1. Nevertheless, the food was palatable, and all were hungry.

Towards the end of the meal the noise of champing jaws and sucking lips was drowned by a loud drumming noise from outside the hut.

"Jumping jackasses! What's that?" Braddock demanded, as his hands flashed to the butts of his guns—an example that was repeated, less quickly, by two of the strangers present: the third man pulled out a bowie-knife from his belt.

The woman laughed. "Have no fear," she said in Spanish. "It is only the drums calling the people to a fandango. We always dance on a Sunday night."

"What she say?" one of the strangers growled.

When none of the men answered, Abigail laughed shortly and translated.

"What's a fandango?" the same man asked.

"A dance."

"A dance, eh! Is that why the population's out in Sunday best? Reckon it might be worth going to. I saw a coupla of them native girls——" He glanced quickly at Vandusen, then abruptly closed his mouth in annoyance.

His companions nodded.

Abigail glanced at her escorts. "Well, gentlemen?" she enquired with contempt.

Fox answered casually. "As we hope to make an early start I suggest sleep."

"Sure," Braddock agreed.

The three strangers looked at them with angry, suspicious eyes as one by one Henry and his companions climbed the notched pole which led up to the sleeping space above.

"In a damned hurry to get there, ain't they?" asked one.

A second man spat. "Blast them!" he growled.

CHAPTER ELEVEN

THE second day's race across the Isthmus varied little from that of the previous day. In spite of all Fox's protestations the journey was a race rather than the leisurely progress he had anticipated. Piérola would not believe the gambler. All Americans were in a hurry to get to California, he stated categorically. Americans were always in a hurry wherever they went. Why, otherwise, should his previous passengers have been so anxious to get to Cruces that they had agreed to pay him an extra tip for each separate canoe he passed? This ingenuous suggestion in a most ingenuous voice! But he went on to admit with pride that he had a reputation for speed to maintain: it would not be good business to lose it!

Meanwhile, Henry discovered that Abigail Vandusen could be, when one got to know her better, a vastly entertaining companion; all the more so because one was able to ignore the fact that she was a woman, and talk to her without constraint. She had none of the affectations to which he had become accustomed in women: neither coquetry on the one hand; nor, on the other, the habitual alertness of one forever on the defensive. He soon found himself talking to her with the ease and frankness that characterized his friendship with Zachary Fox. Indeed, there was the same respect in his voice when he addressed her as "M'am" as there had been when, at first, he had addressed the gambler as "Sir".

She had been to many countries: India, Africa, West Indies, Brazil, Russia, Turkey, Chile, and her accounts of them fascinated not Henry alone, but all her companions. In unconscious recognition of her experience they found themselves overlooking her masculine mannerisms, and her automatic assumption of leadership, to the extent of asking her advice—which, from Fox on the one hand, and Braddock on the other, was indeed a compliment.

At one moment Haiti was mentioned: she had stayed there twice, the first time for a week or two on her way from New Orleans to Pernambuco, when Henry Christophe was king. . . .

"Then you may have met my father," Henry interrupted, unthinkingly. "He was a doctor there—Christophe's private physician—until the day the King shot himself."

Fox grimaced wryly at this ingenuous question, but Abigail seemed as unconcerned about her age as she was about her sex.

"Scarcely," she answered in her low-pitched, masculine voice. "I was only four years old at the time, accompanying my parents." She paused, reflectively. "The Haitians still speak of a Doctor Duncan Stewart, who founded a School of Medicine at the Cap——"

"That was he."

"I heard about him when I was there again some years ago. So that was your father? I thought you said your name was Malley."

"Yes, m'am, I did," Henry explained stiffly. "So long as I'm here, I'm Malley." He continued eagerly, "Father loved Haiti. On our way to Chagres we passed close enough to the island for me to see the fires glowing in the mountains. Remembering his stories I could almost see the Haitians sacrificing a white goat to Damballa, and working themselves into an orgiastic frenzy. . . ." That is why he liked talking with Vandusen. One didn't have to choose one's words. . . .

"And what's that mean, son?" interrupted Braddock from the other end of the cayuca. "I wish you wouldn't use them long words."

"A sort of free-for-all sex spree."

Braddock laughed. "Then it's time you stopped imagining things what ain't so."

"But they are so, Mr. Braddock," Abigail stated calmly. "I have witnessed a Petro sacrifice. The dancers drink a mixture of blood and tafia—native rum—until they are half-intoxicated, then dance to the beat of drums until their sexual passions are roused to an abnormal degree. When they can no longer contain themselves they seize the nearest woman and take her into the jungle."

"Filthy beasts!" Braddock exclaimed in disgust. "Worse'n cattle."

"Señora . . ."

Four pairs of eyes turned towards the prow. Piérola had turned round. They saw that his eyes were uneasy.

"Well?"

"Please excuse, señora, but it is not good to talk of such things in Panama. Not if Negroes are present."

"Are there Haitians in Panama?"

"Not Haitians, señora, but Cimarrones." He glanced nervously at the distant mountains, and lowered his voice as if afraid that the monkeys chattering among the jungle trees could overhear his words and carry them away. "There are still Cimarrones living in mountains who hold dances, and sacrifice the goat without horns." He swallowed, and wiped the perspiration from his forehead with the back of his hands. "There are witch-doctors living over there who would kill me if they knew what I was saying."

"Is this true?"

"I swear it, señora, and if I dared ask the Negroes, and they dared to speak, they would swear it, too. If they knew what I was telling you the witch-doctors would give me poison to make me zombie."

"What the heck are theseyere Cimarrones and zombies?" demanded Braddock.

"You tell, please, señora, I not dare to."

"The Cimarrones, Mr. Braddock, are the descendants of African Negroes, who were brought here by the Spaniards in the sixteenth century to act as porters in carrying gold and merchandize across the Isthmus. Many of them managed to escape into the jungle, where they formed themselves into bands and made war upon their late captors. They became known as los Cimarrones, which means the untamed. When Sir Francis Drake made his piratical raids on the country they became his allies."

"That was three hundred years ago," Braddock protested. "Don't tell me, ma'am, they're still making war."

"Señor Piérola will have to answer that, Mr. Braddock."

The Panamanian shook his head. "No, señor, they are peaceful now like my boatmen. But they still have witch-doctors who practise magic, and dance to the drums, and sacrifice to black gods."

"Black magic, eh!" The rancher bellowed with laughter. "You'll tell me there are fairies next."

"I shouldn't laugh if I were you, Mr. Braddock," Abigail warned him. "Strange things of which the white man knows nothing happen in Africa, wherever there are Negro bocors, or witch-doctors; in the West Indies; and here, too, it seems."

"Are you asking me to believe there's sich a thing as black magic, m'am?"

"You were asking about zombies."

"Sure."

"A zombie is a person who is dug up from the grave, and brought back to life to become the dumb slave of its master."

The rancher was too materialistic in his conception of life to believe this. He chuckled loudly, and leaned forward to dig Fox in the ribs.

But Fox did not respond to Braddock's playfulness. "Do *you* believe that a dead person can be brought back to life, Miss Vandusen?" he asked, in his gentle voice.

"I did not say a *dead* person, Mr. Fox. The Negroes believe that the man is dead when he is buried; but the probability is that the person is not dead but suffering from a catalepsy which so closely resembles death that all but the witch-doctors are deceived. It is not so strange, therefore, that man can be brought back to life, provided that he is taken out of the grave before he has suffocated."

The explanation silenced the rancher.

But Fox asked, "Why did you mention witch-doctors, m'am? And why should anyone recovering from a catalepsy be dumb, and become a slave?"

"Because it is probable that the cataleptic condition has been brought about by the administration of poison concocted by a witch-doctor. Don't you agree, Señor Piérola?"

He was too terrified to answer. Henry, from his position just behind the Panamanian, heard the sound of his uneasy, spasmodic breathing.

Abigail continued, "The poison does more than induce catalepsy: it destroys the tissue of the brain. That is why, when the man recovers, he is not only dumb but without intelligence; a body without a soul. His body lives on and is capable of working, but in all other respects he is dead. He becomes a slave because he has no brain to make him do otherwise."

"My God! If I thought all that was true, m'am——"

"It is true, Mr. Braddock," she informed him. "I have seen a zombie in Haiti. So——"

"How can you talk about sich things so doggoned cool, m'am? I ain't no plaster saint. I done things in my life I wouldn't want my Ma to know about. But digging up people out of their graves and making them work is more'n I kain stummick. Ef I had my way I'd blow them witch-doctors to hell wheres they belong."

She smiled indulgently at his indignation. "When one has travelled widely one realizes what strange forces of good and evil exist in the world. It would be easier to make the white man renounce Christianity than to stamp out Negro superstitions. I have become philosophic, and resigned to the axiom, What Is, Must Be." She glanced thoughtfully at the Panamanian. "We must discuss these matters again, Señor Piérola."

"No, no," he refused in a frightened whimper. "I am doggone fool. I say too much already. *No sé nada.*"

"You know nothing!" She smiled confidently. "We shall see. . . ."

II

Hour after hour they poled and paddled their way up-river. Not infrequently they had to shelter beneath the out-flung branches of trees from rain which came down with the torrential force of a cloudburst, and thunderstorms which scored the sky with meteoric trailers and shook the ground with its stupendous blasts. After these storms Henry was fascinated by the rapid rise of the river, and the skilful way in which the cayuca was edged past swirling whirlpools of mud or through rapids that boiled and bubbled with flood water. Remembering the talk of a railroad across the Isthmus, it seemed to him that some dreamer in New York could not have taken into account rainstorms which, in a matter of hours, could convert a normal, placid river into a tearing, destructive torrent.

Steady progress enabled the party to reach Cruces by evening of the third day.

Cruces was a somewhat larger place than the two at which they had previously slept. As an embarkation point for the transfer of river freight to pack-mules it had been a village of some slight importance ever since the earliest Spaniards had organized pack-trains to connect the two oceans. As they neared the town the travellers were able to see, in addition to the usual living-houses, a few storehouses and many stables.

Here the invaluable Piérola found them lodgings for the night in the Alcalde's house, which differed from the huts in which they had so far spent their nights by having two rooms instead of one; and a window let into the wall of each room. There was also a stable at the rear, and the unmistakable smell of dung.

The Alcalde was an ageing man, who had buried three wives and was now cared for by two daughters. The younger one was by his third wife, and was not yet twenty years of age. She had a flashing smile, and vivacious eyes which immediately captivated the three men.

As soon as Piérola had arranged for lodgings he spoke about mules.

At once an expression of guile flashed across the wrinkled, venerable old face.

"Mules, señores," he repeated with a shrug. "It is my pleasure to accommodate you with hammocks for the night; and a meal, to be cooked by my dutiful and clever daughters, that the King of Spain would not refuse. But mules . . ." Or so his eloquent gestures led the Americans to believe he said, though Piérola's translation was somewhat more to the point.

"The old fox is haggling," he said in an aside.

"Why not? I know you have mules in your stables, old man, for I have a nose that says the dung there is fresher than the eggs your daughters will cook for the señores' meal tonight."

"Your nose does not deceive you, my young cockerel; but the truth of it is that the mules have made too many journeys to Panama during the past few months. Like me, they are ageing and need rest." The Alcalde laughed. "They are Panamanian mules, not American."

"How many American dollars would the mules ask to forgo their rest?"

"Fifteen dollars a head for riding animals, and ten dollars for each hundred pounds' worth of freight."

"The señores are wishing to hire the animals, señor, not buy them."

"Very well, if you wish only the cheapest animals you should speak to Hosta, who lives next to the American store. His animals are old and spavined, and their bellies are caving inwards for want of food, but you might hire them for five dollars each and take a chance of their being wafted into the air with the first breath of wind."

The argument proceeded with the utmost cordiality until the parties reached an amicable agreement that the mules should carry the Americans to Panama at $10 the head, and $6 per each 100 lb. of freight.

As Piérola turned away, Henry said, "Would you ask him, señor, if he has heard of an American by the name of Al or Albert Simpson?"

The Alcalde nodded in reply when the boatman put the question to him.

"Yes, señor. He left for Panama yesterday morning, after staying the night here and eating a meal that the King of Spain would not have turned up his nose at. . . ."

III

Thanks to the speed they had made during the two days' journeying Al was now less than forty-eight hours ahead! The news brought a hot glow into Henry's eyes. When Abigail Vandusen observed this, a reflective, questioning expression settled in her eyes and she began to look at him as if she were discovering an unexpected characteristic.

Jim Braddock would probably have been equally thoughtful, some minutes later, had he followed Henry out into the darkness.

For Henry began to practise drawing his guns, as he had done each night; but this time with a cold and calculated determination that would have pained the rancher, who would have noted with an expert's eye not only that his pupil was already more adept than he expected, but also the fact that the young greenhorn from New England was developing the passion and fervour of a killer.

Henry continued the practice until his limbs were too weary to function efficiently. Then he went back to the hut where the travellers, and some of the family, were already in their hammocks. He climbed into his, and settled himself for sleep. Before he had dropped off the rest of the household had taken to their hammocks, after one of them had blown out the candle.

But he did not sleep, although he was physically tired, and—apart from the fleas that bit him in the few odd spots still left unbitten from previous nights—immensely comfortable. His brain was too active. Al was less than forty-eight hours ahead of him! Granted the luck that no vessel would leave Panama for California during the next two days, he might catch up with Al before another two days had passed. And when that moment arrived . . .

The mental picture of that meeting was too precious to waste. He savoured it to the full, gloating. He rubbed each wrist in turn; partly because they were stiff, and partly in subconscious appreciation of the part they were destined to play in ensuring his return to New England.

Unfortunately, having savoured that moment of delicious prospect until his thoughts were sated with it, he still did not sleep. He became gradually aware of the eerie stillness of the world about him; a stillness so profound that it was not disturbed even by the breathing of the sleepers about him, or a single restless movement. For the first time since his arrival in the country he was affected by its mood of brooding mystery. He didn't doubt the reason for this belated discovery: it was due to Abigail's reference that day to black magic, Haitian sacrifices, zombies—and to Piérola's undisguised fear. That, even more than Abigail's unemotional accounts of horrible and unsuspected events. Piérola had been genuinely afraid of the tribal witch-doctors who lived deep in the heart of the surrounding jungle. Afraid of being overheard, although he was probably scores of miles away, afraid of becoming a victim of their secret poisons. Piérola, who was not even Negro, but a mestizo of Spanish and Indian blood!

The night seemed filled with mystery that first obsessed then fascinated him. As he lay stiffly uneasy in his hammock, feeling that he did not dare to move and break the silence, he began to experience the backwash of the Panamanian's fears. There *was* something fearful about the jungle, he reflected uneasily. Its hundreds of square miles of virgin growth, uncharted, unmapped, uninhabited; probably untrod by mankind, because no man could hope to force a way through growth so thick even with the aid of machete and axe. Hundreds of square miles in which death from a dozen different causes could strike one down without warning. A jungle sparsely inhabited by tribes of hostile Indians who allowed no stranger within their territories. A jungle which vomited deadly diseases with monotonous regularity: malaria, yellow fever, cholera. . . .

Then the silence was broken in the far distance by the echoing roar of a cheated jaguar. The menace in the deep-throated anger chilled Henry. He added one more item to the list of deaths he had already compiled in his thoughts. The roaring ceased, but his straining ears detected a new sound, faint but unmistakable: the throbbing beat of distant drums. . . .

This rhythm was taken up, nearer, much nearer. . . . A slower pounding and more even beat. Many seconds passed before he realized that his heart was thumping wildly. . . .

He grinned mockingly at the enveloping darkness. Fancy anyone believing that it was possible to drive a railroad through the jungle that men called the Isthmus of Panama. . . .

CHAPTER TWELVE

THE Alcalde's elder daughter awakened the Americans before dawn the next morning.

"The guide is here to take you to Panama, señor," she told each one separately. "Coffee will be ready as soon as you are up."

She used the same words to Henry, but he did not move. She shook him, and still he did not move. Abigail, who had been occupying the next hammock, joined her.

"Wake up, Mr. Malley," she urged in a louder voice, and used far more energy in shaking him than the girl had used.

He blinked, and through a mist of sleep saw Abigail by his side. She held a candle in one hand, and its flickering flame caused shadows to play about her face.

"Thank God!" he gasped. "You've escaped."

"Escaped!" she repeated in a startled exclamation. Then she realized the reason for his relief. She smiled. It was the first time she had smiled, except contemptuously, since joining the party. For that brief moment she became a woman.

"You've been dreaming. What about?"

He wiped the sweat from his face. "It was ghastly. You were— you were——" But already the dream had slipped away from his consciousness. "I—I can't remember. You were in some sort of danger. But what——"

"It's time to get up. We have to start soon." Before she turned away she added, "Thanks for the compliment of dreaming about me, and not about—well," she added slowly, "the Alcalde's younger daughter, for instance."

While the Americans were breakfasting on coffee and fruit the Alcalde joined them to receive the hire of his animals and to bid them farewell. As the first light of day pinked the mountain peaks they set off to the echoing shouts of the old man. His words were dismal.

"The sky is bad, señores. Prepare for much rain."

The Indian guide turned his back on the river. Presently the Americans found themselves heading for the jungle along a narrow, paved trail.

"The old Cruces trail," Abigail announced, pointing ahead. "Unchanged in nearly three hundred years. One of the most important links between East and West, and look at it!"

There was nothing about the trail to suggest its bloody history. Barely wide enough, where it pursued its way through the jungle, to allow two men to pass or walk abreast, it resembled little more than a straggling pathway which thick walls of jungle forever threatened to reclaim and swallow up in spite of their being constantly brushed back. Underfoot, the trail was marked at intervals by flagstones which, more than three hundred years ago, gangs of chained African slaves had carried and laid there; groaning beneath the weight of their burdens and the lash of their white captors. In those days completion of the trail had seen it flagstoned from end to end, but centuries of tropical rainstorms had washed many away: others had been worn thin by the movement of booted feet and the hooves of pack-mules.

"The Camino del Oro!" she continued, reflectively. "The Golden Road! Along this route travelled much of the gold which was mined in Panama, and most of the fantastic treasure that Francisco Pizarro plundered from Peru. Probably no other road in the history of the world has ever seen so much wealth passing along it." She pointed a brown finger ahead. "History repeating itself. Gold is still flowing along the Camino del Oro."

Coming into sight was a mule-train, proceeding northwards. Henry counted fourteen mules, tied head-to-tail in single line, and carrying loads of merchandize piled up on their backs. Three Panamanians, mounted on mules, preceded the pack animals; and three, similarly mounted, followed in the rear. Spaced at even intervals along the line of mules walked three other men, there to keep an eye on the baggage and touch up lazy mules with their whips.

"Have you previously visited the Isthmus, Miss Vandusen?" Henry asked her. "You know it so well."

"Only through books." She laughed. "In between my own voyages to foreign lands and writing books about them I take a busman's holiday by reading other people's books of exploration and travel. There are not many places in the world I don't know something about."

"Why do you——" He stopped abruptly.

"Why do I what, Mr. Malley?"

"I was about to ask what might seem an impertinent question."

"Ask it. I can answer it or not as I choose."

"Please believe I had no wish to be impertinent. Why do you undertake the discomfort, danger and rigours of travel in primitive countries when you might be at home . . .?" He paused again.

This time she guessed the sequence of his thoughts. "Married and raising a family!" she added drily. She was a long time continuing. "I don't know," she said at length. "I sometimes used to ask myself that question."

"Used to?"

"When I was still young enough to be attractive to men. Now ——" She shrugged. "It's too late. Men look for wives among young women who are soft and yielding; creatures without will or character."

"More fools they," he exclaimed gallantly.

"Thank you. That was very nice of you." But her smile was ironic.

"I mean it," he protested. "Most men would much rather have a wife more intelligent and less good-looking." He was thinking of Jean, who was intelligent and pleasant without being pretty or beautiful or handsome. Still thinking of her, he went on wistfully, "Somebody who wouldn't want to talk all the time about baby's new tooth, or first piano lesson, but who could discuss books and music and art."

"And the Isthmus of Panama?" she mocked.

"Of course," he answered seriously. "It would be fun to share impressions." He looked at her with reproach. "Now you are laughing at me."

"Not really, Mr. Malley, but I have mixed with men too much to place undue reliance upon their idealism." She hurriedly changed the subject. "Listen—rain——"

II

Rain it was! They heard it sweeping towards them with a roaring sound that reminded them of heavy breakers pounding on a shingle beach. It fell from the sky in a sheet of water, and beat against the jungle vegetation with a force that wilted and bent over all but the strongest branches.

They made for the nearest available tree, and reached it as the fury of the rain began falling about it. Within a matter of seconds they were soaked to the skin. Meanwhile, the mule-train plodded on towards them, as if oblivious of the rain. The swirling water and the hooves of the animals churned the beaten earth into mud which made a squelching, sucking noise with every hoof movement.

The rain swept on, and left behind it a soothing silence, a river of mud, and hot baking sunshine. Within a matter of minutes everything was steaming.

"Chagres fever!" Braddock muttered, with an uneasy glance at spirals of mist arising from the surrounding jungle.

As soon as the last animal in the train had passed by they resumed their journey southwards. Their clothes quickly dried. Soon they were deep in the jungle, and ascending a gentle slope up to the foothills of the Continental Divide over which they had to pass before reaching Panama.

Their progress slowed up, for the trail grew even narrower as vast trees closed in upon them. Here the traffic of centuries had worn the trail away until it was little better than a narrow gully with steep walls of baked clay that spreading roots of trees had held intact. In consequence, the clay floor held the water, and filled the gully with a frothing stream that reached nearly up to the bellies of the mules.

They reached the peak of the first hill. Ahead they saw more and more mountains, each one seeming to rise higher than the one before. More immediately they saw a deep pass into which they would have to descend before rising again to the next height.

The guide looked up into the sky. Automatically, the Americans did the same. They saw a heavy bank of clouds blotting out the light blue arc, and travelling slowly in their direction.

"More rain coming," the guide announced unnecessarily.

Braddock shrugged. "We won't reach Panama today if we wait for every doggone storm to pass."

The others agreed with him. "Let's get going," suggested Fox.

The journey down into the pass proved a nightmare. The sure-footed mules slipped and slithered down the precipitous, muddy slopes, and apparently had no fear of placing a foot in the wrong spot. Their ease of mind was not shared by their riders—with the exception of the guide, perhaps—and there were few moments when they were not instinctively bracing themselves against the tumble that seemed imminent.

They were only half-way down when the rain caught up with them. Once more they heard its roar as it moved steadily in their direction. Once more they halted to take what shelter there was to be had; not so much this time in the scant hope of getting less wet, but because the solemn-faced guide told them in a shout that it might be dangerous to proceed.

It did not take them long to see why. The flooding rain, swirling down the trail with the force of a cataract, could easily have swept one of them off his feet in the event of a mischance unhorsing him, and perhaps have carried him on down the steep trail.

This time the storm was of longer duration, with its force scarcely slackening. The rain blotted out the landscape; they could barely see one another.

"I never knew there could be this much rain in the entire world," Henry shouted. But the sound of his voice was lost in the drumming sound of the rain about them, and nobody answered.

The rain stopped; the sun shone; and steam filled the air.

"Wait a time," the guide ordered, pointing to the trail. Another half-hour passed before he would let them resume their way down into the pass. There they were supposed to ford a narrow river, but when the guide looked at the water he shook his head.

"We shall have to go some miles west. Can't cross here."

"Why not?" Braddock demanded.

"The water's risen more than eight feet."

"We can swim our mules across."

"No, señor, current too strong, and too many other dangers. Look!" An uprooted tree was being carried downstream at a rapid rate; it was being tossed about from bank to bank, twisting and turning like a cork in a whirlpool. Not far behind was a second, and a third. A knock from any one could easily stun one or break a limb.

"Looks like he's right, Jim," Fox muttered. "This isn't our day."

They turned left, and followed the guide along a rock-strewn path that ran parallel with the course of the river. Progress was slow; for the path had not been used for a long time, and the jungle had already spread tentative arms across it. The guide had constantly to stop and clear a way through with his machete.

They forded the river, made their way back to the original trail, and started up the ascent. Half-way up they met a mule-train on the way down. There was not room for both parties to pass. The Americans had to huddle into the wall of green to let the others pass. No sooner had the train gone by than the rain came down again. A lighter storm, this time, which made them uncomfortable without halting them.

Two hours after the scheduled time they reached a palm-covered plateau. Here they stopped for a rest at one of the few lonely ranches to be seen along the route. It was occupied by Indians, who sold them goats' cheese and bread, a few bananas, a pineapple, and cups of treacly coffee. Long before they had finished eating the guide was worrying them to move on.

"Much more rain later," he warned them. "We no get to Panama before night not hurry."

So on again to the farther limit of the plateau, where they saw more mountainous country ahead of them.

"Is thisyere trail supposed to be the best going?" Braddock asked the guide.

The Indian nodded. "Yes, señor, many, many years ago, before white man come to this country, Indians find easiest routes to travel." He waved a brown-skinned hand, first to one side of them, then the other. "See, mountains much, much worse on either side. Mules not go up and down them. We have to walk, climb."

"Don't sound so different," the rancher grumbled. "Doggone it ef I'll sit down again this side of next Friday."

"Come," the guide impatiently urged. "If we waste time, night come quicker." He cast an anxious glance at the sky which was cloudless in all directions. The sun blazed down at them, making them feel listless and weary. Their underwear, which rain and sun had wet and dried alternately, was clammy again, this time with sweat.

They ascended the next ridge, slithered down the other side, and ascended another. All this time the jungle scolded them for their unwelcome intrusion: parrots, with piercing angry squawks, as they flew to and fro above the travellers heads; monkeys, with

H

chattering cries and grimacing expressions as they swung from tree to tree and kept pace with the party for a short distance; a disturbed peccary with alarmed grunts as it crashed its way through the undergrowth.

"Hurry! Hurry!" the guide worried as the sun began to dip towards the range of mountains on their right.

The Americans could see no cause for alarm. For several hours no cloud had been seen. The sky was still clear. There was a sharpness about its blue which made Henry wish he were a painter with the skill to capture it.

"How many hours from Panama are we?" Fox asked the guide.

"Still four, señor," the Indian replied.

"Four!" Fox glanced at the sun. "Then we can't make the place before dark."

"No, señor. But when we reach other side of mountains, darkness no matter. Me know all trails through swampland like back of my hand."

"Come on, then."

As they forded the Rio Grande the sun tipped the highest peak of the mountain range on their right. Simultaneously, the first warning cloud sailed into its spreading golden glow.

"Hurry," the Indian urged once more. "Much rain soon. And wind."

The cloud looked no bigger than a man's fist, but it was followed by larger, blacker clouds which in turn were followed by an unbroken mass that closed in over the quickly descending sun and hid its dying glory. The sky turned grey, and a soughing moan preceded the rippling rustle of leaves stirred in the wind. Swiftly the sough's moaning sound had developed into a rushing wail, and the tops of the trees were bending and creaking before the onrush of a tropical gale.

Then came the rain once more. It lashed them with fury, soaking their clothes within seconds, and smarting their flesh with its whipping sting. It filled their eyes, and blinded them to the precipitous slope down which they had just started. They held fast to their mules, leaving to them the responsibility of safely reaching the bottom of the ravine. The animals responded to this trust, each one placing its hooves in the track left by the one in front. By slow degrees they made their way down the trail.

An extra fierce gust of wind brought calamity. A sentinel tree, which had long been kept upright only by the parasitic vines which had robbed it of its vital juices, crashed behind the rearmost pack-mule. As its outflung branches struck the animal a sharp blow on its flank, the frightened mule leaped forward and cannoned against the animal in front of it, Braddock's. Side by side the two unbalanced beasts went slithering down the trail into the hindquarters of Henry's mule.

Before momentum had been halted, three mules had been thrown: they lay on the ground at intervals down the slope, helplessly pawing the air with three legs only. . . .

III

Every minute made the catastrophe increasingly fantastic. Thunder clouds overhead began to erupt lightning in incessant white flashes which compensated for the loss of daylight. Each tremendous clap of thunder was intensified by the high walls of the ravine in which they were, and its echo was hurled backwards and forwards so many times that its reverberating roar was not entirely lost in distance before it was succeeded by the next crash. They winced with each one, for it seemed to strike against their ears with the force of physical impact. The rain continued to lash them, and sometimes blot out the trail. To each one the bedraggled, colourless faces of the others made them look like phantoms from another world.

"Dante's Inferno," Fox shouted, in between roars. Both Abigail and Henry nodded agreement.

"Now what?" Braddock demanded, as his hands fell upon the butts of his Colts. "Them mules are only fit for killing."

"Wait, señor," the guide suggested. His wraith-like figure disappeared into the curtain of rain, and was lost to view. When he reappeared he was dolefully shaking his head.

"They all got broken leg, señor."

Braddock nodded, and moved towards the beasts. The others

heard the first crack of his gun, but after that no more, for all other sounds were drowned by thunder.

He returned. "That leaves us just three mules among five people and baggage."

"There's only one thing to do." Abigail turned to the guide. "Is there anywhere near where some of us could shelter?"

He thought for a time, then nodded. "We near cave I know of, big enough to shelter two."

"Good! Will it be possible to hire other mules in Panama?"

"At a price, señora."

"Would you bring mules here from Panama if we pay you well?"

"Yes, señora. Me good travel all night long if paid well."

"Then——" She had to wait for the thunder to die away before she could carry on. "There's no use all of us waiting for his return. Two of us can shelter in the cave until he comes back."

"Sure, m'am," Braddock agreed. "Me and Fox will wait——"

"Certainly not," she snapped. "As the mule I was riding is dead, it is my place to remain behind."

"But, m'am, we can't let you stay—you're a woman——"

"Mr. Braddock, if you dare to drag my sex into the discussion——"

"All right, m'am," he bellowed against the thunder. "If you say so."

"Who was riding the other mules?" she questioned as soon as she could make herself heard.

"I was," Henry told her.

"The baggage mule was the third, señora," the guide said.

"Then Mr. Malley will stop with me," she announced authoritatively. "Is that agreed, gentlemen?"

They had long since learned that one couldn't argue with Abigail Vandusen when she had made up her mind. So Fox spoke for them all.

"If you insist, m'am," he replied in a dry voice.

CHAPTER THIRTEEN

To call the place to which the Indian led Abigail and Henry a shelter was to pay it an undeserved compliment. In fact, it was little more than a fissure in part of the volcanic rock which made up one wall of the ravine; a fissure that was about seven feet high, nine feet long, and seven to eight feet wide. But as it had the advantage of being dry, it was a more than adequate resting-place for the intervening hours before the Indian could return with more mules.

They said good-bye to the guide, then sat down side by side at the back of the cave. By then the storm had travelled some distance, and the noise of the thunder resembled the resentful growling of some animal. The rain had lessened to a steady downpour.

Conscious of the weirdness of their surroundings, which the muffled sound of their voices did nothing to dispel, after a few enquiries directed towards the other's comfort they lapsed into silence. This lasted some time, and was eventually broken by Abigail.

"Sleeping?"

"No."

"Sleepy?"

"I don't think so. No, not one bit. Too wet, I think."

"Why not change into spare clothes?"

"Haven't any, m'am."

"Oh!" Then, "I hadn't realized——"

"Won't you change, m'am?"

After reflection, "I'll change my underclothes." She rose to her feet, and felt for her baggage. "It's not going to be easy, changing in this abysmal darkness. If I'm not careful I shall be putting things on back to front."

He heard rustling movements. "Pity the storm's moved away. You could have done with the lightning."

She laughed. "Yes."

After a time, "I've managed."

He felt her hand on his shoulder as she tried to locate his whereabouts. Then she sat down beside him again. "That's better. Give me your hand."

He moved his hand towards her, until it touched part of her. She caught hold of his hand in hers, then pushed something into it. "A spare shirt of mine. Change into it."

"But—I'm already drying——"

"You must," she ordered sharply. "Do you want to catch pneumonia or fever?" She added, more gently, "I have others."

He did as he was told, glad to do so, then sat down again in his turn.

Once more a long silence followed.

"Thinking?" she enquired.

"Yes. Of this cave. Being in it reminds me of my father. His whole life was influenced by a cave. Would you like to hear?"

"Of course."

"He was a Scot. Born in a valley that everybody for miles around called Deil's Glen, because there was a cave in it which the devil was supposed to inhabit. Father ran away from Deil's Glen when he was still a boy and was adopted by Doctor Anderson, who took him to London."

"That's why your father became a doctor?"

"Not really. He swore to become a doctor the day he heard that his mother died in giving birth to him. But he was never able to escape from the influence of the cave in Deil's Glen. Every now and again he dreamed of it. Every time he did so something happened the next day that affected his future life."

"Something good or bad?"

"Sometimes one, sometimes the other."

"So now you are wondering whether this cave is going to influence your life?"

There was an unusual note in her voice which was strange to him, and which he could not identify.

"You are laughing at me," he reproached.

"Certainly not. Why should you think that?"

"Your voice was somehow—different." He hurried on, "But I *was* wondering just that."

"How could it affect your life?" she asked presently. Her voice sounded constrained.

"I may miss the next ship for California by the few hours I spend here in this cave."

She exclaimed angrily. "Gold! Do you men never give a thought to anything else? What difference will missing a ship make? A few days at the most. But even if it were a few weeks, a few months, a few years, would that matter? You are young." She swallowed. "Ridiculously young. *You* can afford to wait."

He laughed. "Judging by the tens of thousands of men who are flocking into California, a few years could make all the difference between wealth and poverty. In that time they are likely to have dug up California from end to end." He sensed that she was again stiffening with anger. "But I'm not going there for gold," he added quickly.

"Oh! I'm sorry. For taking for granted that you were, I mean. Are you looking for work, then?"

"No. For a man." Then he told her everything. He believed that she would understand, and help him in his search.

"Thank you for telling me," she said, when he had finished. "Hearing it explains so much to me. You puzzled me from the first. I couldn't understand your wearing guns."

"Why not?"

"Easterners don't wear guns, and you couldn't possibly be mistaken for anything else." After a long pause, "I wonder if you will ever go back there again."

"To New England?"

"Yes."

"I'm determined to find Al if it takes me half my life. The only thing I pray is, that I find him before my parents—die." He gulped.

"I don't mean that. I'm sure you will prove your innocence. A spirit like yours is bound to achieve its objective. I mean—afterwards."

"Why shouldn't I go back once I've proved my innocence?"

"To a stool in the offices of Evans and Talbot—was that the name you said?" She laughed softly. "You've grown into manhood during the past few weeks. Do you think that keeping accounts is a job for a man?"

"But"—he paused. "But somebody has to keep accounts," he finished tamely.

"Of course, but not someone who has practised drawing guns and tasted life in the raw. There's a new empire being founded in California, Mr. Malley, and you're the stuff empire-builders are made of. If I were a man I'm sure I shouldn't be content adding up figures all day long. I should want to build, to construct, to create——"

Her abrupt stop startled him. Nor could he understand the strange distortion in her voice as she swallowed the last word. It was as if something had touched or alarmed her.

"Is anything wrong, m'am?"

"Only my—my conscience. I shouldn't have used that particular word. A case of the pot calling the kettle black."

He understood neither the inference nor the reason for her bitterness. "I don't follow you, m'am."

"I spoke of your creating, Mr. Malley. But that should be my job, too. Creating new lives to occupy your new empires."

He felt embarrassed. "Well, m'am——"

"Don't say something trite," she sharply warned him. "I've only myself to blame. As a young woman I refused two offers of marriage—and you're the first man I've ever made that admission to. But I had already seen too much of the world to settle down to a normal domestic life. I was more interested in exploring the primitive places in this world, and writing about them. At one time I would have sold my soul to the devil to have changed my sex." She laughed. "As the devil couldn't help me to do that, I helped myself. I became a man in every respect save having a man's body."

"Then you've had the best of both worlds, m'am. I don't see there's anything about a man's body that's worth having."

"Don't you?" she asked drily. "That's because you've not suffered from the ailments that a woman's body is subject to."

A long silence followed her words. He realized that the storm had completely passed on while they had been talking. Even the rain had ceased. All was quiet and still. He could not remember having ever experienced such complete and utter stillness. Nor quite such a Stygian darkness. The strange fancy affected him that

Abigail and he were in a little island world of their own that was
shut off from the great world outside. A rather fantastic world, at
that, for surely there was no stranger woman in the world than
Abigail Vandusen. The last woman one would voluntarily choose
as one's only companion in an isolated world of two.

And yet—he grinned at the trend of his rambling reflections—
on second thoughts, was this true? Was she the last woman he
would choose? If one thought of her only as a woman to share one's
bed, then undoubtedly she was. There was nothing womanly about
her. Not her hair, which she wore in a bun at the nape of her neck;
but drawn back so tightly from her forehead that, from the front,
it looked more like a man's than a woman's. Not her square face;
which was as brown as a berry, and untouched by cosmetics. Not
her square back. Not her legs; for in pantaloons and high boots they
looked no different from a man's. Not her hands; brown, un-
manicured and hard. Not her self-assured emancipation.

But as a companion—to use his original word—perhaps one
couldn't wish for better. As strong as a horse, capable, more than
willing to take her share of work, intelligent—yes, above all,
intelligent—she might prove ideal. Especially if she were able to
cook and sew and do other household chores! He grinned again.
Surely she could do those things even if she were more man than
woman? Plenty of men could: sailors, prospectors, desert rats and
the like. So, why not she?

Would he choose her, in preference to any other woman, to be
his companion on a desert isle? he dreamily asked himself—Lord!
he was beginning to feel drowsy, after all. He must rouse himself.
What was he trying to work out in his mind? Oh yes! Would he
choose her. He gulped. Choose her in preference to Jean Martin—
or even that melting-eyed little trollop, Lucy.

"Mr. Malley?"

"Yes?" he mumbled.

"Give me your hand again. I've something for you that might
help to pass the time."

He sleepily reached towards her. She caught hold of his hand,
and lifted it. His hand cupped itself round something that was
warm and round and as smooth as velvet. . . .

"Oh God!" he muttered.

II

His first instinctive action was to snatch his hand away in embarrassment, in the belief that it had accidentally brushed against her. But she pressed it more firmly against her breast, so that he could not move it. She was as strong as a horse. . . .

"Please . . . Red . . ." she breathed softly. He felt the warmth of her breath against his cheek, and felt her leaning against him. "Don't move—yet——"

"But—but . . ." he stammered. His mouth felt dry. "But——"

"Don't speak, please. I want to do the talking."

"But . . . m'am——"

"Feel, Red! I told you I was a man in every respect except one. I want *you* to know that I really am a woman in that particular respect. I'm tired of being a man all the time. I've been one too long."

"Tired!" he repeated stupidly.

"Most of the time I'm glad to be like a man. It makes travelling easier. It makes men look upon me as one of themselves; then they respect me, and leave me alone. I wanted it that way . . . until recently. Ever since then I've wanted . . . this." She pressed his hand so fiercely into her breast he feared he must be hurting her. He tried to relax the pressure.

"Shocked?"

"Yes," he admitted.

"Why?" she demanded. "Haven't you ever felt a woman's breast before?"

He felt his face flushing. "Yes. Once—twice."

"The same woman?"

"Girl. Yes. She was seventeen. I was twenty. She was a serving girl."

"Why did you?"

"Because—because——"

"Because you wanted to know what a woman's breast felt like?"

"Yes."

"So you went about finding out the usual way. In the fields, one summer's night, I suppose?"

"Yes."

"Then why are you shocked because I want to know what it feels like to have a man's hand fondling my breast?" Her voice grew bitter. "Or do you think that what's sauce for the gander isn't sauce for the goose?"

"I don't know."

"You men!" She choked. "You've grown to think that a woman hasn't any natural passion, but something that responds only to man's urgency. If women were free of conventions, do you think they wouldn't be as polygamous as the average man?"

"Haven't you been as free all these years?"

After a long pause, "Check!" she exclaimed in a bitter voice. "I've been as free as the wind. But I haven't dared. I've always wanted men's respect, wanted to be on an equality with men. I also knew that once I did—this—I should lose both respect and equality."

"No . . ." he vigorously protested.

Her laugh was wistful. "That's sweet of you, Red. But it's true. If I hadn't known that tomorrow we shall part company and never see each other again, do you think I should have dared reveal my—my weaknesses to you?"

"That isn't fair to me."

"I'm not trying to be unfair, Red dear. But you are a man, and cannot change your nature. You will no more be able to resist despising me on two counts than you will be able to stop growing older."

"Two counts?"

"One, for being the instigator—the worst sin of all, in the opinion of man—and the other, because I'm enjoying it as much as you—no, more—more—more! A man respects what he cannot obtain, and despises what comes easily to him. Like gold!" she added with scorn.

She released his hand. "There you are, Red. The spider sets you free."

He slowly withdrew his hand—then realized that he no longer wanted to. He half-turned, and caught hold of her with both hands.

As they glided over her warm flesh he realized that she had no clothes on above her pantaloons. The soft smoothness of her flesh inflamed his passions. He groped for her head, then forced it up towards his so that his lips could find hers. . . .

III

Later she felt for his cheek and stroked it.

"You will try not to despise me too much, won't you, Red?" she pleaded, in a voice so changed from her normal masterful tones that he could barely recognize it.

"I'll never do that, never," he maintained stoutly.

"I wish I could believe that. But you'll remember that it was I who seduced you, and you'll particularly resent that fact whenever you remember that I'm older than you."

He kissed her with grateful gentleness. "You've given me a lovely memory that will last all my life." After a pause, "How long have you waited for this?"

"Two, three years. I'd never given it a thought before then. If anything I was rather scornful."

He kissed her again. "Thank you."

"What for?"

"Choosing me." He added, jealously, "It was *me* you chose, and not circumstances?"

"Dear Red!" She pulled his hand to her lips and kissed it. "How am I to explain without hurting you?"

"Then it was circumstances," he accused. "If it hadn't been my mule which broke its leg, but Mr. Fox's, or Mr. Braddock's . . ." He choked with anger.

"Not Mr. Fox. I like him. I admire his honesty, his courage in going without guns—oh, many things! But not—this!" She shivered. "Never."

"Then Mr. Braddock?"

"I don't know, Red dear. He's clean, and rugged and wholesome. I think, if he had made the first suggestion—perhaps—my dear, I'm not making you understand. For three years now this thing has been stronger than I. I have all but prayed that some man

might penetrate my masculine disguise, and sense the woman
beneath. But no man ever did, and I never dared to let down my
protective armour until tonight. So you see, dear, dear Red, you
mustn't look upon yourself as merely a sexual guinea-pig."

At first he could not feel entirely satisfied, but when he pictured
her as she had been throughout the journey across the Isthmus, he
began to realize that this strong-minded, self-willed, proudly inde-
pendent woman would not easily have sacrificed so many things
she held dear for the sake of a physical urge unless she had been
genuinely drawn towards him, and trusted him. He resolved to
repay that trust.

"I do understand," he said unsteadily, "and to prove that I
mean what I say, this time I'll be the first. . . ."

IV

Some time later they heard the guide's voice hailing them from
a distance. By then they were ready for him.

The remainder of the journey to Panama City passed without
incident. Shortly after leaving the cave they began the descent
from the mountains, and smelled the salt air of the Pacific Ocean.
Overhead the clouds had vanished, and a waning moon lighted
the way for them. They saw miles of swamp lowlands on either side
of the road, now paved again, and presently huts.

Later, the huts gave way to the stone houses of old Spanish
colonial days, the first they had seen since their arrival in Panama,
and realized that they were looking at some of the first European
houses to be built in the New World.

So into Panama City itself, and the Hotel Americano, where
Zachary Fox had already engaged cots for them.

CHAPTER FOURTEEN

In spite of having had only a few hours' sleep Henry awoke early the following morning. His first thoughts were of semi-conscious regret at waking up from a marvellous dream, and in that same state he tried to will himself back into sleep. Bright sunshine in his eyes, and the noise of much movement about him, effectively defeated this attempt. As full consciousness slowly returned to him he smiled wistfully. Exciting as the real event of the night before had been, it lacked the exquisite ecstasy of a comparable dream. He wondered why.

He opened his eyes and found himself in a large room; a dozen cots were ranged, almost top to toe, lengthwise against whitewashed walls that were completely bare. That is, if one excepted the nails stuck in the wall above the foot of each bed, to hold hats, coats, and pieces of personal baggage. The cedar floor was similarly bare. The enormous windows were without casements. The only other articles of furniture in the room were three wash-hand basins on one side of the windows.

Two or three of the cots were still occupied: one by Zachary Fox, who was lying on his back, still fast asleep. In spite of having been in bed for several hours, his hair and whiskers were immaculate. But with closed eyelids concealing any visible sign of life, his waxen face appeared corpse-like. He looked, in fact, as if he had been laid out ready for burial.

Jim Braddock, on the other hand, was up. He was at one of the wash-hand basins, puffing and blowing and singing execrably in a cracked voice as he splashed water all over his face, neck and hands. Some of the other occupants of the room were similarly engaged, or moving about, or dressing. One way and another, the picture was one of activity.

For less than a minute Henry lay in relaxed contentment and contemplated the room. But no longer. He had a purpose in coming to Panama, and for all he knew every minute might be of importance. He threw off the sheet which covered him, and drew on his socks and trousers. Then he joined Braddock at the wash-hand basin.

"Good morning, Mr. Braddock."

The rancher rubbed the soap out of his eyes and looked round. His broad smile was disgustingly jovial for that time of morning.

"Ha! So you got here safely, son! That Indian sure travels fast. How you feeling?"

"Fine."

"Up early, eh!" The bleak eyes studied Henry's face. "Starting out after your man?"

"Yes."

"Wal, I've got one piece of news for you. No boat ain't left Panama for anywheres these past three days. So you kain be sure your man ain't far off. Maybe in thisyere very hotel."

"By God! If he is . . ."

The bleak eyes twinkled; the tousled head nodded approval. "Good luck to you, son. You won't ferget what I told you about that finger of yourn?"

Henry nodded, and set about the job of washing and shaving. Braddock moved off. "Be seeing you."

When Henry arrived downstairs in the entrance-hall, a spacious room that like the rest of the hotel was devoid of any form of decoration, the only person present was a Negro porter who gave Henry a broad, welcoming smile and asked, when he saw the visitor looking about him with an enquiring air, "You looking for someone, sar? Is there anything I can do?" He spoke with an accent that was strange to Henry's ear.

"You're not from the States, or Panama?"

"No, sar, I'se a Jamaican. I'm Thomas." He pronounced the name with such an air of pride that Henry was sure he was supposed to know the porter's name and all about the man.

"Ah!" he exclaimed, with what he hoped was convincing recognition. "I wanted to ask someone a few questions."

"There's only me here jus' now, sar," Thomas said in his soft, liquid voice, "but I'll be glad to help you, sar. There's nothing about Panama that I don' know. Do you want to make an excursion to old Panama——"

"Not for the moment. Have you a guest staying here by the name of Albert Simpson?"

The black head nodded. "Certainly we has, sar. He reached

here the night before las', and is staying until the *California* leaves
for San Francisco."

Henry tried to mask his excitement. "He's a friend of mine. I
want to meet him. Can you tell me where I'll find him?" His fingers
stiffened as his hands moved subconsciously towards his guns, but
fortunately the porter remained unaware of this.

"He's booked in room six, sar, sleeping in cot three. Leastwise,
that's where he slep' the firs' night."

"What do you mean, the first night?"

"He didn't sleep there las' night, sar. He went out about nine
o'clock, and hasn' come back yet."

"Do you know where he went?"

A broad grin stretched from ear to ear. "I know where most
gennelmen go, sar, that don' come back before mornings."

"Then he should be back soon?"

"I 'spec' so, sar. Shall I tell him you is asking for him?"

"No," Henry said sharply. He added, more calmly, "I want to
surprise him. Can I eat here?"

"No, sar."

"Will you watch out for him while I'm having breakfast?"

"Certainly, sar. You leave it to Thomas to watch out."

At Thomas's suggestion Henry went to Victor's for his meal,
for there was no restaurant attached to the hotel. There he found
Braddock in the dining-room, so he joined the rancher. "My bird
is staying here sure enough. But he went out last night and hasn't
returned yet."

The rancher loudly chuckled. "The ladies, eh, son?"

"That's what the porter hinted at. But he might be gambling.
He never could resist the gaming tables at Boston."

"What about me and you looking this burg over ef he ain't
back by the time we've finished eating?"

Henry nodded. He felt that he needed some form of exercise
to offset his increasing impatience to settle his account with Al.

When the two men later returned to the entrance-hall they
found Thomas there. Upon his report that Al had not yet returned
to the hotel they stepped out into the sun-drenched street and
began sight-seeing. For them both the experience was stimulating,
for they found themselves in a city different from any they had

hitherto encountered: a city that bridged the three thousand miles' gap between the Old and New Worlds; a city in which the sixteenth and nineteenth centuries merged; a city whose native inhabitants were descended from three continents and three colours: the white of Spain, the black of Africa, and the brown of America; a city whose every stone was redolent of rumbustious and bloody history.

They walked along a straggling street so narrow that two men on horseback would scarce have room to pass each other, and where the wooden balconies of the first storey were scarcely beyond the reach of a tall man; balconies where dusky-eyed señoritas lounged about in loose gowns and performed their household chores while they ogled the world passing below. They peeped into cobbled courtyards which reeked of the stables; and from which, as often as not, came snatches of melodies plucked from the strings of guitars.

They wandered along wider streets, where each stone house was enclosed by its own high wall, and whose patio was only to be reached by way of ornamental iron gates kept studiously closed: sometimes they heard the soothing music of plashing fountains or the cooing of doves.

They passed by churches so old and neglected that some of the plasterwork had crumbled away to expose the bare stone beneath; and the elements had smoothed the sculpted figures of saints into things without form or beauty; where the seeds of parasitical vegetation had rooted high up in the towers, and was covering the mouldering masonry with a curtain of green leaves and brilliant blooms. They entered these same churches, smelled interiors reeking with decay and stale incense and the pungent odour of hot candlegrease; saw young girls prostrate on the stone floors before golden, jewelled altars and yellow-ochred images; and heard the low murmuring of Ave Marias.

And coming out of one church they heard the loud clanking of chains, and saw a shuffling line of shackled prisoners being cursed to their place of labour by an armed mulatto.

So to the heart of Panama City, Plaza Independencia, where naked Negro children played up and down the stone stairs of the old Cathedral, or teased a tethered mule which was trying vainly to feed upon the parched grass which the recent rains had not yet turned green. From there they looked down a street of fine homes of heavy stone, and saw the burnished surface of the Pacific beyond the arched gate in the old wall.

Jim Braddock dropped his heavy hand on Henry's shoulder. "Ef thisyere city ain't somethin' to see then I'm a god-damned jackass."

Henry nodded. He was feeling much the same way.

"It's dying on its feet," the rancher went on. "It smells to high heaven, and most of the people look as if they don't know what it means to do a day's real work. But there's something about the place. . . . It's like looking at a history book 'stead of jest having a school-marm larn you about something you don't care a god-dam' about."

They strolled down the street towards the ocean. About half-way down they passed by a whitewashed building from which the Stars and Stripes was drooping in listless folds. This, they saw, announced the offices of the American Consul. With an affectionate glance at the flag as acknowledgment of the warm feeling which the sight of it inspired in their hearts, and then a quick turning away from nostalgia, they carried on down the street; presently to emerge on the broad ramparts of the fortress which a King of Spain had ordered to be built as a defence against buccaneers and other enemies.

Here was history, indeed, which even the strollers who turned the place into a promenade could not disguise. The decaying turrets with their significant loopholes and castellations; the richly-embossed brass cannon which lay on the ground, dismantled and neglected; the thickness of the decaying walls; these things hinted equally at the one-time magnificence which the King had been at such great cost to protect, and at the shadow of ever-threatening danger under which the sixteenth- and seventeenth-century Panamanians had lived.

"Wal, thar she is!" Braddock exclaimed, as he stared at the Pacific, which at that moment was at its bluest and gentlest. "What odds would you have given a few weeks ago on seeing her, son?"

"A million to one and up."

Perhaps there was a note of bitterness in his voice, for the rancher clapped him on the back. "Same here, son. Two months ago I hadn't a notion to leave Sunset Valley. Then, one night, Lefty Harrison says to me, 'Jim, old pal, they tells me people is striking plenty gold in California!' So I says, 'Lefty, ef that's so, then, by Jees! it's me for California.' So next morning I pulls up my stake, says adios to Sunset Valley, and starts off for Charlestown. And here I am, and feeling like a puppy-dawg sniffing a bitch fer the first time." He added, "Don't git feeling too hard about pulling up stakes, son. Sometimes it does a man good, and stops him turning into a cabbage."

Henry laughed. "I'm not sorry I'm here, if that's what you're thinking, Mr. Braddock. In fact, if it weren't for knowing what people at home are thinking of me, I'd be tickled to death."

"I thought so. I been watching your face. You kinda like it here, don't you?"

Henry nodded. "Yes, I do. Don't know why, but seeing these old buildings makes something inside of me bubble with pleasure. I guess it's because I'm only one generation removed from the Old World." He glanced back at the town. "Do you mind if we return to the hotel now?"

"You sure don't mean that man to get away from you, son. There ain't no ship within sight."

Henry's mouth hardened. "Haven't you ever wanted anything so bad you couldn't wait for it, Mr. Braddock?"

"I ain't never wanted anything bad, Red. Maybe I ain't got that sort of nature. But I'm all for dealing with that mean critter. Let's go, and when you've got what you want we'll find us a saloon and celebrate."

But when they returned to the Hotel Americano, Thomas shook his head. "He hasn't come back yet, sar."

"He hasn't moved some place else?"

"He's left his baggage here, sar."

"He'll be back sooner or later," Braddock joined in heartily. "Let's go see if the old Fox is up and ready for a drink."

They found Fox at Victor's, with Abigail. They had just finished eating.

"Morning, m'am. Morning, Fox." The rancher glanced back at Abigail. "Travelling sure suits you, m'am. You're looking bloom-ing this morning. Will you come and have a drink with us? There's a saloon across the street where we kain order a champagne cocktail, or ef you prefer hard liquor, iced brandy and water."

"A champagne cocktail sounds attractive, Mr. Braddock. We'll drink a toast."

"To what, m'am? Finding gold?"

"No. Mr. Fox is not searching for gold. Nor am I. Nor is Mr. Malley."

"We must drink a collective toast," Fox suggested. "To each one of us the attainment of his own particular desire."

"Too many long words," the rancher grumbled.

"I have a better," Abigail announced. Her glance rested fleetingly on Henry's sombre face. "To our continued association."

"Suits me plenty," Braddock agreed with enthusiasm.

II

They found the saloon too crowded for comfort, so they went on to a second, then a third; but only to find all alike. Panama City was overcrowded with the hundreds of travellers who were waiting for the next California-bound vessel to arrive; so, with nothing else to occupy their time, they filled the saloons where almost every type of drink was to be found, from Braddock's iced brandy and water to absinthe, from champagne cocktails to local chica, from French claret to Milwaukee beer.

At the fourth saloon they gave up their search for comfort, and pushed their way into the crowded bar. It was noisy with a babel of half a dozen different languages, in which native Spanish and American accents predominated. Amid all the uproar two Panamanians played billiards on a somewhat dilapidated table; two Frenchmen and two Germans played dominoes under the porch. Four red-shirted Californians played cards. Several Americans from Alabama and Virginia played crap.

After drinks they went on to Victor's for a meal. Then, in a group, back to the hotel, to make further enquiries. This time the worried proprietor answered Henry's enquiries. No, Señor Simpson had not returned, and if he should not arrive at the hotel before night to pay for his cot, it would be let to someone else. With dozens of newly-arrived Americans looking for sleeping accommodation it was not just that one cot should remain empty.

Thirty minutes before sundown the Americans, at Henry's insistence, made further enquiries at the hotel. Thomas's reply remained the same: Mr. Simpson had not returned. Nevertheless, he had some news for Henry. In his quaint English accent the Jamaican went on to say that he had made some enquiries among his friends, and had learned that Mr. Simpson had not, after all, visited the red light district, but had started off for the Louisiana saloon where gambling tables had lately been set up.

"Perhaps somebody there will be able to give you news of him, sar, if you go there," was Thomas's sensible suggestion.

Braddock glanced at the others. "Shall we all go? How about a busman's holiday, Fox? And you, m'am?"

Abigail answered promptly. "Certainly we'll all go," she said with a snap. "We all know how much it means to Mr. Malley to find this man Simpson."

The roads outside the hotel were more crowded than they had been all day, for approaching darkness was already bringing a welcome coolness to the streets. All Panama seemed abroad, and the city was noisy with clattering hooves and lively conversation. They saw water-carriers on mule-back, carrying kegs of fresh water destined to be tipped into the large earthenware tanks which were kept under the shade of every balcony; riders returning from an afternoon gallop, and mounted on lively little Peruvian stallions that were handsomely caparisoned with silver-mounted bridles and gay high-peaked saddles of Spanish design; Negro women dressed in low, loose dresses which revealed more of their prominent ebony breasts than they concealed; women of lighter hue, more colourfully clad in calico dresses, red satin slippers and beribboned Panama hats; Jamaican women selling cakes and fruit; and mashers of many colours and races, dressed in black Alpaca coats, white trousers, Panama hats and patent-leather boots.

They passed under the portico of the Louisiana saloon—where men were lounging about smoking local cigars, and exchanging pleasantries that produced constant bursts of ribald laughter—through the main bar, which was packed, and upstairs to the gaming-rooms.

Play had not started but several black-frocked professional gamblers were there, preparing their tables for the night's session. There was a short bar at the far end of the room; and behind the two lamps which stood upon it they could see a white-coated barkeep polishing glasses. Two waiters were gossiping nearby.

A light-skinned Panamanian approached them. His smile was ingratiating. He spoke in moderately good English.

"Señora. Señores. Play has not started, as you see. If you would care to drink meanwhile . . ." He waved an extraordinarily elegant hand in the direction of the bar.

"In one minute, señor," Abigail said, taking charge of the situation with her usual imperious gesture. "First, we have something to ask you."

A slightly surprised look passed across the man's face. "Yes, señora?"

"We are looking for an American who is supposed to have come here last night, but hasn't yet returned to his hotel. Describe him, Mr. Malley . . ."

Before Henry could do so the Panamanian lifted a protesting hand. His affability had vanished.

"The room was crowded last night with men from America," he said in a sulky voice. "I am sure it would not be possible to remember one particular person among so many."

"There ain't no harm in trying, is there?" Braddock asked, with his hands arched suggestively above his guns.

"No," the Panamanian agreed. "No, señor, as you say, there's no harm in trying. What was he like?"

"Well, son?" This to Henry.

"Tall, with light-coloured curly hair, waxed moustache of the same colour, blue eyes, well-dressed in a grey suit with green waistcoat and black bow tie. On the whole, rakish-looking. He was crazy on gambling."

"Well, now. . . ." The man reflected. After a time, "Señor Matthews?" he called out.

One of the gamblers looked up. "Yeah?"

"Do you know the name of the American señor who lost everything to you last night?"

"Sure, I do. His name was on an I.O.U. he wagered. It was Albert Simpson, of Boston."

"What time did he finish gambling?" Henry asked.

" 'Bout one a.m., when he'd lost every bloody cent he had in his wallet."

"What happened then? Did he leave?"

"Yeah. He left. And he ain't been back to repay the money like he said he would. It's my guess he done what he threatened to do if he didn't win something back."

"What was that?"

"Throw his god-damned self into the sea," the gambler replied with indifference.

CHAPTER FIFTEEN

FOUR sombre-faced people sat round a table under the portico of the St. Charles saloon, which was a stone's throw from the Hotel Americano. Two days had passed since their visit to the gaming-rooms. During that time there had been no further news of Al Simpson. His baggage was still at the hotel, unclaimed. Meanwhile, within the past hour they had received news from Zachrisson and Nelson, who were agents for the Pacific Mail Steamship Company: the *California* would be leaving for San Francisco the following day.

Braddock drained his glass, returned it to the table with a loud thump. "Wal, son, it looks as if thisyere is the moment. Ef you'd change your mind and come to California with us I reckon I kain persuade Mr. Nelson to pack you in some place."

"But Al Simpson——"

"Is probably giving bad digestion to some poor shark."

Henry shook his head. "I don't believe it."

"Looksee here, Red," the rancher began testily, "you kaint deny that that son of a gun has disappeared some place. There ain't a god-damned soul what has seen him since the night he lost all his money at the tables. Nobody at the saloon ain't seen him; nobody at the hotel ain't seen him; Mr. Nelson ain't seen him, and if anyone should have seen him, Mr. Nelson's the one. He kain't sail for California without seeing Mr. Nelson first."

Henry nodded. "I know, but——"

"But you still think the critter's alive?" the rancher exploded testily.

"Yes."

"Why? If he's alive he ain't living on air. He must eat sometimes. But he ain't been seen eating no place. Why not? Why hasn't he come back to the hotel?"

"Maybe he's hiding."

"Hiding! Who from?"

"Me, Mr. Braddock. He may have seen me the morning of my arrival, and guessed why I am here. So he's taken cover, in the hope that I shall be catching the next steamer for California."

"Quite a reasonable possibility, Mr. Braddock," Abigail said.

"They're right, Jim," Fox added. "It's just the sort of thing a man of his nature might do."

Henry's jaw set in an obstinate mould.

"Besides, I have a second reason for being sure. Al Simpson isn't the man to commit suicide, however desperate. He hasn't the courage."

"So he's still alive, Red! What are you going to do about it? Whether he's dead or alive, you can't return to Boston."

"The Isthmus is a small place. As long as he remains here I'm likely to find him sooner or later. And in the meantime . . ." His hands fell upon the butts of his guns. "Every day will allow more practice. At shooting as well as drawing."

"But you kaint live on air, son, no more'n Simpson kain."

"I'll find work. I'd have had to find it in California."

"What work? There ain't work fit for a white man to do in this country."

"Yes, there is, Mr. Braddock."

Surprised, the rancher turned to Abigail. "Wal, m'am?"

"There's a man here in Panama at this moment who would be glad to give Red work. His name is James McCollum. He's a surveyor working for the engineers who have contracted to build the railroad across the Isthmus."

Fox murmured his approval. "Bravo, m'am."

"I don't know the first thing about surveying," Henry pointed out.

"You could learn, and while you are learning you could act as assistant, or clerk."

Puzzled by her interest in his future, he looked, unthinkingly, into her eyes. It was the first time he had dared do so since the hours they had spent together in the cave; for though the memory of the episode still gave him a feeling of exquisite pleasure, it twisted his conscience and caused him embarrassment because he had convinced himself that the fault was his. The sudden impulse that had tempted her to offer herself to him would, he argued, have been resisted by a man of honour and integrity, whatever the cost.

Now, as he looked into her eyes—hazel-tinted, he realized for the first time—he became more than ever aware of her dominating personality. For some reason or other she was determined that he should work on the railroad, and meant to use every means she could to make him do so. Why? he wondered.

Evidently the question in his thoughts must have communicated itself to her, for her next words answered it.

"If I were a man it's the kind of work I'd be proud to help with."

Braddock shook his head. "They won't never succeed in building a railroad across the Isthmus, m'am. It would be a tarnation miracle. What with swamps and jungle, and rivers that rise God knows how many feet in a few hours, and mountain ranges, and fevers——"

"Haven't you faith in your countrymen, Mr. Braddock?"

"As much as the next man, m'am, but I don't aim to expect them to work miracles."

She smiled. "We shall see! And suppose it should be built, wouldn't you like to think, one day, that you had helped in building it? There's no pride to equal that of a hard job well done."

"Wal, ef you puts it thataway—and seeing, as Red says, that he has to do some sort of work——"

She turned to Fox. "You agree, too, don't you, Mr. Fox?"

"M'am, you almost tempt me to give up gambling and become a railroad builder myself. Almost . . ." he added drily. "Unfortunately, you can't teach an old Fox new tricks!" The mischievous gleam in his pale eyes was the only evidence that he shared the laughter of his companions. "But if I were Red's age, and looking for work, why yes, I should be proud to assist in that achievement. For it will be an achievement, if it is ever finished."

"Well, Red?" she enquired.

But Henry had already decided. Jim Braddock's catalogue of obstacles had brought about the abrupt decision. The idea of challenging nature was somehow inspiring. He nodded.

"It's an idea," he agreed in a sober voice.

"Then good luck to you, son. I sure won't forget my promise to invest money in the railroad when I make my strike." His confidence was sublime. "Well, m'am, the three of us had best get along to see Mr. Nelson."

She shook her head. "I've changed my mind, Mr. Braddock. I'm not going to California."

"Not going——"

"I'm going to let somebody else write about California. I've seen enough of Panama to realize that this is the place for me for the next twelve months at least. The country is so rich in material there are half a dozen books to be written about it. And a further one, maybe, about the building of the railroad."

The rancher turned a comical face towards Fox. "It only wants you, you old Fox, to say that you're not going to California, to complete my day."

"Then your day's complete, Jim."

"By all the god-damned sons of——" Braddock broke off, and grinned. "Just your little joke, Fox. You'll go where the gold is, or you ain't the man I think you are."

"The gold is here, Jim; in Panama and in Chagres. What's the first thing most men think of doing the moment they strike gold?"

"Spending it," Braddock answered promptly.

The gambler's bloodless lips parted in a dry smile. "Yes. Easy come, easy go. Much of it will be spent at the gaming tables in California, where, according to what Mr. Nelson said last night, half the gamblers in the States have already set up. But what about the second thoughts of the men who strike gold?"

Braddock reflected. "Making for home," he suggested.

"Exactly! And their way home will be through Panama and Chagres. Do you think they won't spend money freely at every place they stop at, to celebrate their good luck? Well, the gamblers here are penny-ante fellows for the most part. I'll give the returning gold seekers a chance of real play; a chance to double their fortune while their luck's still in. But a more important point is this: the railroad will bring trade to Panama. Trade will bring money. Well——"

"Money and gold, Fox: it has to be earned. But gold washed out of the river-beds for nothin' jest itches to be spent."

"Perhaps, but one day the gold will peter out in California. Trade, on the other hand, will increase with every year."

"You old Fox!" the rancher exclaimed, beaming with admiration at his old friend's perspicacity.

"Do you stay, too, Mr. Braddock?" Abigail asked him.

"Not me, m'am. If thisyere railroad's got to be financed, I've got to get me some gold nuggets in a hurry."

II

It was a sad moment for the four travellers as they stood together on the edge of the ocean, and waited for a canoe to take Jim Braddock to the steamer *California* that was anchored about two miles out. Four more diverse people would not easily have been found, yet they had enjoyed one another's companionship and were sorry to part.

There was little to say, however, so they talked in meaningless formalities until the expected canoe arrived just off-shore. Then Braddock gave each one a warm handclasp and signalled to the Negro boatman that he was ready. In spite of his weight the Negro lifted him easily, and carried him through the breakers to the canoe. Soon the little craft was skimming along the surface of the water in company with dozens of others engaged on the same errand.

When it was a mile or so out the watchers on the beach saw

Braddock turn and wave. They waved back. The rancher waved once more, then faced the steamer again.

"Shall we go back to the town?" Abigail suggested in her abrupt manner. "It's a miserable business, seeing people off."

They were all agreed on this, so they turned away from the shore and began walking back towards the city.

"A nice man," Abigail commented presently. "I like him."

"One of the best," Fox agreed in his quiet way.

Presently: "James McCollum will be at the hotel by the time we get back, Red. Do you still wish to see him?"

Henry nodded. "The sooner the better. I'm down to my last five dollars."

So they returned to the Hotel Americano, where they saw a man reading a copy of the *New York Herald*.

"That's Mr. McCollum," Abigail told Henry. "He's expecting you."

Henry chuckled. "Then he must be a thought-reader as well as a surveyor——"

"I told him to expect you," she explained.

He frowned. This was going too far, he reflected testily. It wasn't as if he were just out of high school, looking for a temporary job. . . .

Fox's hand rested lightly on his shoulder. "Good luck, Red," he murmured. But Henry realized that the gambler had divined his annoyance, and was really saying, "Don't be impatient with her: she means well by you."

So he nodded his understanding. As the other two made their way towards the stairs he crossed the hall in the direction of McCollum, inspecting the surveyor as he did so.

There was nothing particularly striking about McCollum. Rather the contrary, indeed. He was almost nondescript. He had a scarecrow figure, and stooping shoulders. His brown hair was long and dishevelled. So were his whiskers, his moustache, and the tuft of beard he wore. His nose was hooked, and he wore metal-rimmed glasses, which gave his face a permanent questioning look. But he looked up when he heard footsteps, and Henry noticed that he had a firm, reliable mouth, and humour in his intelligent eyes.

"Mr. James McCollum?"

"Himself."

"I'm Henry Malley."

McCollum stretched forth a bony hand. "Glad to meet you, Mr. Malley. Been hearing a lot about you."

"Such as?"

"Seems like you're interested in wanting to help build the Panama Railroad."

It sounded nice, put that way; so Henry lost his irascibility.

"I'd like to help, if there's anything I can do. Unfortunately, I've never done anything before in that line."

"If you're willing, that's something. Been here best part of two weeks, haven't you?"

"Yes."

"Long enough, then, to know some of the tricks this climate's capable of. It's poison for white men."

"Yes, I know. Malaria—yellow fever——"

"And cholera, Mr. Malley."

"I've found that out, too. It was raging here a month or two ago."

"And may rage again, anytime. So you're willing to take the risk?"

"I am."

"Why?" McCollum asked sharply. Then he added, "Not that it matters. You're hired."

"Just like that?" the surprised Henry queried.

"Just like that," the surveyor answered grimly. "Needs must, when the devil drives. I lost my assistant last week from cholera. I need another. When can you start?"

"I've five dollars left. When do you want me to start?"

The strong mouth parted in genuine humour. "That's language I like talking. Tomorrow?"

"Tomorrow it is."

"Good! You understand that the company will have officially to confirm your employment? But they will." McCollum was utterly assured on the point. His self-confidence was refreshing, even inspiring. "We shall be leaving for Chagres in three days' time." He glanced at Henry's suit. "Bring more suitable clothes with you. We shall be surveying the interior from time to time."

Henry smiled wryly. "Haven't any, sir. This is all I have."

"I'll be damned!" McCollum first fondled his untidy whiskers, then dived into his pocket. "Here's a hundred dollars on account. Buy what you need. . . ."

III

Later that day, after Henry had made all necessary purchases, he wrote his second letter to his parents. He told them of all that had happened to him; also of his determination to remain where he was until he had found, and forced, Al to sign a confession. He went on to beg them to write to him in the care of the shipping agents at Chagres. He finished with a postscript:

Please tell Jean and Duncan Martin how sorry I am to miss the usual Thanksgiving Party, and say that I often think of them. Please say to Jean, in particular, how often I have regretted not being able to be at the dance which Mr. Martin told me some time back he was going to hold in honour of her eighteenth birthday. I hope it was a wonderful success, and that she had an especially happy time. I am sure she did. She has so many beaux.

IV

The more Henry saw of McCollum, the more he liked the surveyor. In his case appearances were deceptive, for he possessed such determination and decision that it was impossible not to have confidence in him. He appeared to possess vast vitality, and never wasted more time than was necessary. Yet he was tolerant of the mistakes of others as long as the other person was not being maliciously stupid or obstructive.

Henry found his work easy; he had little to do but take notes. Time passed quickly, however, for he became greatly interested in watching the surveyor at work, and learning the rudiments of the science. Almost before he had time to realize what was happening he was having his last meal in the company of Abigail Vandusen and Zachary Fox.

"We're off to Chagres tomorrow," he told them. "I had almost forgotten, until Mr. McCollum reminded me an hour ago."

"What about Al Simpson?" Abigail asked.

"I'm not forgetting him, Miss Vandusen." Henry's expression revealed a more inflexible determination than his audience had hitherto believed he possessed. "I can make the work I'm doing help me to that end."

"How?"

"In several ways. During the next few months Mr. McCollum expects to travel quite a bit of the proposed route. As I shall be with him most of the time I shall be able to make extensive enquiries."

She nodded. "Of course. And——"

"I shall be earning my keep plus enough money to spare some as a reward for news of him."

Fox smiled. "You're learning," he murmured.

Abigail's eyes reflected her satisfaction. "Then you don't intend to give up your pursuit of him whatever happens?"

"Not unless one of us dies."

"And if he goes on to California?"

"I'll go too. As long as he leaves a trail, by Heaven, I'll follow it. What does worry me is that he might leave for California without my knowing."

"But if he should, to follow him you would have to give up your new work. Would you do that?"

Fox's eyes twinkled. He felt that Abigail Vandusen was deliberately testing Henry.

"If I have to, of course." Henry relaxed as he grew pensive. "But I should be sorry. The job's already beginning to mean something to me. More than I thought possible. It's like creating something out of nothing. As a writer, you create. You know what it means to a person."

"It's the greatest satisfaction in life, Red."

"That's what I feel, but I can't let my parents die believing me guilty of theft."

"I'm sure they don't believe you guilty."

"Perhaps that's not what I mean. Boston itself has already come to mean nothing to me. I no longer care what people think. But I do want to give my parents the satisfaction of proving to everyone that they are not the parents of a thief."

She rested her hand on his. "That's almost the nicest thing I've ever heard you say."

Fox's pale eyes surveyed the younger man. "Will it ease your mind, Red, if I promise to keep in touch with the shipping people here in Panama?"

"If you would do that for me——"

The gambler smiled at Henry's relief. "Of course." To avoid the threatened thanks he hastily changed the subject. "What is your future programme?"

"We are going back to Chagres for the time being, to meet Mr. Trautwine, of Messrs. George H. Totten and John C. Trautwine who have contracted to build the railroad. Mr. Trautwine is surveying the coast from Chagres to Porto Bello to locate the northern terminus——"

"Northern?" Abigail interrupted.

Henry chuckled. "I made the same query when I first heard Mr. McCollum speak of Chagres as the northern terminus, and Panama as the southern. I always looked upon them as being east and west respectively. As a matter of fact, Panama is slightly east of Chagres."

"And after you have seen Mr. Trautwine?" Fox prompted.

"I don't know. It depends upon where the terminus is to be. Anywhere and everywhere, I suppose. But we shall be coming to Panama fairly frequently, so I'll be able to keep in touch with you."

"Good! We'll be looking forward to those visits, eh, m'am?"

She shook her head. "I am not staying in Panama for the time being, Mr. Fox."

Henry felt suddenly chilled. "Then I shall not be seeing you——"

"But you will," she reassured him. "I'm returning to Chagres with you and Mr. McCollum. I want to see the first rail laid."

Warmth flowed round Henry's heart again as the significance of her decision made it thump with excitement.

As Fox gazed at each of his companions in turn Henry knew

that the gambler's eyes had been opened to the hitherto unsuspected developments of the journey to Panama. But no hint of this discovery betrayed itself in his pale eyes. As always, they were as unreadable as the eyes of the great Egyptian Sphinx.

CHAPTER SIXTEEN

"THERE," announced Mr. Trautwine, pointing with outstretched arm to the bay below them. "That is Manzanillo Island, where the railroad company proposes to establish the Atlantic terminus of the Panama Railroad."

They were standing on the headland of Toro Point, high up on the rocky promontory which formed the western arm of the Bay of Limon; or, as it was called by many, Navy Bay. Three other men made up the pure white section of the party: Trautwine's partner, Totten; James McCollum; and Henry. The climb had been a wearisome one, because of its gradient, the heat, and the rain. They had even passed through low-lying cloud to reach the height. But the climb was worth the effort, for the rugged coast stretched away on either side of them: westward, half-way to the old fortress of San Lorenzo; eastward, seemingly to infinity.

But the panorama eastward or westward held no interest for the people on the headland. Their eyes followed the direction of the engineer's arm; they saw the rigid forefinger pointing directly at a tiny islet that was situated off the opposite, eastern, shore of the bay, from which it was separated by a narrow channel. To Henry's eyes it looked microscopic and insignificant, but the trained eyes of Colonel Totten and McCollum were able to estimate that Manzanillo Island comprised an area of approximately one square mile.

Totten was the first to speak. "Where were you proposing to establish the first stop?"

"Probably Gatún, seven miles south. On the opposite bank, of course, from the present village."

"The distance from Chagres to Gatún is much less."

"Certainly it is, but there are two good reasons for the corporation's not establishing the terminus and docks at Chagres. The first is a natural obstacle; the bar which prevents big ships approaching the shore, and the absence of any headland to form a lee. Whereas, Navy Bay makes a fine anchorage, as you can see."

Totten nodded his head. "Quite, but mileage, Trautwine——"

"I am not overlooking the cost of the extra mileage, but in spite of that we shall save money by running from Manzanillo to Gatún."

"How?"

"Because of the second obstacle, Totten. An enterprising New Yorker by the name of George Law has bought most of the suitable land between Chagres and Gatún, and is asking a purchase price that would cost us a large proportion of our contract price."

"Damned money-grubbing son of a horn-tailed bitch!" angrily raved Totten, who could swear on equal terms with any man. He quietened down. "Hand me that spy-glass, McCollum."

The surveyor did so. Colonel Totten examined the island and the country behind it.

"Damn my eyes, Trautwine!" he exclaimed at length. "That's not an island, but a goddamned swamp. There isn't a bloody building on it. And no wonder. The only tree I can see through this glass is the mangrove. Are you proposing to fill the swamp?"

"It's the only possible alternative to Chagres."

"Then what about the country behind it? That looks like swampland, too."

Trautwine nodded. "It is. As far as Gatún. The natives call it the Black Swamp."

"Seven miles of swamp to be filled in before we can lay a tie——"

"And the River Mindi to be crossed en route," Trautwine added, in a dry voice.

"Jesus! How are we to keep to the contract price? Are you sure it wouldn't be cheaper to buy land from that blood-sucking Wall Street leech?"

The junior partner shrugged. "You can examine the figures for yourself. . . ."

Later the party descended to the shore of Navy Bay, and were paddled out to Manzanillo Island. There Henry was able to see for himself the obstacles that lay ahead of the engineers: obstacles that in previous years had daunted the engineers of Britain and France. Even in his abysmal ignorance of the rudiments of constructional engineering Henry realized that only men of vision, great courage, and incomparable efficiency would have dared undertake the contract. He was grateful to Abigail for having pointed the way to him to help in this tremendous undertaking, and regarded the engineers with humble reverence.

For Manzanillo Island and the Black Swamp were noisome and miasmatic, and more resembled the nightmarish invention of a warped, distorted genius than a place of living reality. Dense groves of mangrove trees, interlaced with vine and thorny shrub, had with the passing of centuries created natural barriers through which no animal could force its way. Seeping water had turned the soil into stinking, slimy mud which alligators and reptiles alone inhabited. Few birds rested among the trees; and the only sounds to disturb the eerie silence were the hum of mating mosquitoes, and an occasional explosive crack as a decayed branch broke away from its parent tree. The chirrup of monkeys would have been welcome music; but even they appeared to avoid the dismal spot, for none was to be seen or heard.

"Well?" Trautwine queried. "Do we agree to make a start here?"

"I don't know whether we're bloody optimists or god-damned fools," Totten replied. "But this is the place."

II

The days passed quickly for Henry. He had never worked so hard, or for such long hours; but nor had he ever been so happy at work. His flesh turned steadily more brown; and his body, leaner; for work and the heat combined to drain him of every ounce of surplus fat. On the other hand, exercise hardened his muscles, straightened his back, and gave lithe grace to his springing walk. Men from the cattle country no longer summed him up, with one glance, as an Easterner. They accepted him as a Middle-Westerner until he began to speak. His Boston accent continued to betray his origin.

Although Chagres was McCollum's headquarters, he and Henry, and two native assistants, were rarely there for more than two days in eight, for they had been ordered to survey Manzanillo Island, and there was no convenient trail between there and Chagres. They had to make the journey between the two places by sailing canoe, which took time. So they slept in the canoe as best they could, returning to Chagres in between times to rest and recuperate for their next visit.

Recuperation was vital for health's sake. Most of the time their thigh boots were not high enough for the depths of oozing mud and water in which they had to work, so for hours on end they were rarely dry from the waist downwards. Nearly as often they were as wet above; again and again drenching rains soaked them to their skins. The air they breathed seemed poisonous in their nostrils, for it hung about the trees in the form of vapour that stank like a death vault of rottenness and decay. Moreover, they had to remain constantly on the alert against the alligators and poisonous reptiles which they were liable to disturb.

One day, on his return to Chagres, the owner of the Californian Hotel shook his head when Henry asked for a cot.

"Howdy, mister; Miss Vandusen said as how I was to ask you to go along first to the end of the town afore you checked in here. You'll find her in the last house on this side, which ain't been up more'n a coupla days."

Wonderingly, Henry trudged down to the end of the road, which already had been several times extended farther into the jungle during the few weeks he had been in the country. Almost overnight, it seemed, new frame-buildings added to the length of the road, all made from timber imported from the United States.

The door of the last house stood invitingly open. As he approached a voice sang out, "Is that you, Henry? Come right in."

He could not see the speaker, but he recognized Abigail's voice. It sounded excited. He entered the house. The contrast between the glare of the sun outside and the cool shadows of the room made it difficult for him to distinguish anything clearly. As he stood still, bewildered, he felt a pair of arms turn him round, then cling round his neck. Warm lips pressed against his.

It was the first time they had kissed since the hours they had spent together in the cave, for they had never been alone. Perhaps this was his fault, for he had contrived not to be alone with her since he sincerely wished to spare her any embarrassment. Even so, the recollection of their first kiss was still fresh in his memory. He was able to compare it with her present embrace, and was aware of a subtle difference between the two occasions. The first time there had been a quality of passion in her kiss which had fired unsuspected desires, and made him powerless to resist the fierce urge which had quickly developed into a frenzy of restless undulations.

This time there was a possessive tenderness in the pressure of her lips which made his spirit glow with a responsive warmth. He slipped one arm round her waist, where it grew rigid with sub-conscious protection; but his free hand he raised to her head, and stroked her tight hair with trembling fingers.

What was the mystery behind her presence in the new house, and why was she clinging to him with an ever-deepening emotion, were questions to which he could think of no answer. His only conscious thought was that something solemn and wonderful was happening to him, which filled him with an ecstasy he had never experienced. So exquisite was the sensation that he had not the courage to break the spell. His arm grew rigid as he pressed her yielding body closer to him, and he kissed her tenderly but end-lessly on every part of her face. Soon she was weak, and moved with happiness; but at last, gasping for breath, she gently pushed him away from her.

"Henry!" she breathed. "Oh dear, dear, dear Henry!"

He gazed at her with glowing eyes, and slowly realized that for the first time he was seeing her dressed in women's clothes. He had become so accustomed to her in man's clothes that he was not sure he liked her in the proper attire of her sex. In contrast with the emerald green of her silk gown, her brown face looked unnaturally wealthy and out of place.

"Henry!" she exclaimed again. "Look!" A comprehensive wave of her arm indicated the room they were in, and by inference the house itself; which at first glance differed in no great extent from other frame-houses he had seen in Panama. A second glance corrected this snap judgment. Deft touches here and there made the room infinitely attractive; not so much with the materials used, which were restricted by climate, as by their arrangement. She had an artist's touch.

"Do you like it?"

"It's charming, but I don't understand——"

She laughed at his puzzled expression. "I've rented the house, Henry, and furnished it with the few things I could buy here. It's for *us*."

In spite of the emphasis, he did not hear the last word: he was thinking about the first part of the sentence.

"Are you going to stay in Chagres, Abigail? I thought you would be travelling all over the country—into the interior, sometimes——"

"So I shall be, but I must have a headquarters for writing and resting in. It isn't possible to do either at the hotel."

He nodded agreement. "You'll certainly be more comfortable here." A thought occurred to him, and he chuckled. "Now I shall have some place to visit."

"You don't understand," she explained patiently. "I've rented this house for us to live in, Henry dear. For you and me——"

In spite of the heat he turned cold. "Abigail, you don't know what you are suggesting."

"Why not?"

"I couldn't live here and remain—straight! Especially after what happened—in the—the cave. God! I'm not made of stone."

"I should hope not," she retorted coolly.

He stared at her. "You mean, live here as—as lovers——"

"Yes, my dear, as lovers—unless I've no longer any attraction for you——"

"Don't say that!" He moved to her side, and took her into his arms. "Please don't think that can happen—ever. . . . Promise?"

A sad expression passed across her face. "I'll try not. You'll come?"

"I didn't say so. How—how can I? People would find out, and talk. Your reputation——"

"Means less than nothing to me," she assured him with contempt. "If I had let my life be fettered by what other people thought of me I should never have become a traveller and writer."

He was quiet so long that she became impatient. "Now what are you thinking about?"

"Abigail . . ."

"Well?"

"We could be married."

"Marriage between you and me? . . . Don't be absurd, Henry."

He gestured his bewilderment. "But if you are willing to be my mistress——"

"We should both be free to break off the association any time either of us wanted to."

"But if we love each other, Abigail darling——"

"Love!" Her laughter was contemptuous. "You don't love me, nor ever will. You are in love with Jean Martin. If we live with each other it will be because you need a woman, and I wish to satisfy a want that could become an obsession if it is not soon satisfied."

"Sometimes I don't understand you . . ." he muttered unsteadily.

"Because I can face facts without distorting them with romantic nonsense." Taking pity on his obvious distress she took his hand and rubbed it against her cheek. "My dear, it is because I love you as much as my nature is capable of loving another that I won't marry you."

"Why not? Because of Jean?"

"Yes, but even if there were no Jean to come between us now, one day in the future there would be. One day, when the appetite of youth loses its violence, you will look about you for someone with a whiter, smoother complexion, someone with fewer wrinkles, someone with a younger body, someone more complacent towards masculine rule. If I were to be holding you then against your will you would hate me; which would turn to ashes the memory of everything preceding that moment."

He knew she was right, but the admission seemed disloyal to his sex. "There's not all that difference of age between us——"

"Not now, perhaps, my dear, but when I turn sour with the change of life, what then? You'll still be a young man, ardent and virile."

"You make men seem beasts . . ."

"I'm not trying to. It is natural for youth to cling to youth. To achieve and maintain real happiness, men and women must grow old together. Meanwhile——" She reached up and kissed each cheek in turn. "Until you find Al Simpson, and can go back to your Jean without fear, I'll be your mistress and preserve you from those trollops at the House of All Nations. . . ."

III

For a while Henry continued to resist Abigail's suggestion: partly because he automatically resented her having usurped a rôle which should, he felt, have been his; partly because he was embarrassed by the thought of what McCollum and Totten and Trautwine would think when they heard that he was keeping a mistress—as hear they were inevitably bound to, probably in a matter of hours! Indeed, McCollum might already be anticipating the news, for the mysterious drums of Africa could not spread news more quickly than the proprietor of the Californian Hotel.

Abigail brushed aside Henry's opposition with her usual imperiousness. Within an hour of his return to Chagres he had transferred his few belongings, which the hotel guarded between times, to the frame-house on the fringe of the jungle. Later, while Abigail prepared a meal, he relaxed in a comfortable chair and smoked a local cigar. Before long a sense of serene peace dispelled his remaining scruples. He began to feel grateful to Abigail for her vision and courage. This room was almost like home, he reflected. In fact it was a home: not someone else's home, but his! His and Abigail's—for, of course, he could insist upon bearing the expenses of it, now that he was earning good money. Here was something worth working for; something to think about, and look forward to, while he was away in the jungle. Here was a restful quietness, in sharp contrast to the overcrowded hurly-burly of the hotel lobbies and public rooms. Here, too, was comfort, which was conspicuously missing at the hotel. Above all, here was privacy, which was not to be found anywhere at the hotel; not even in the bathrooms and the toilets. Nowhere was it possible to escape from the scraping of booted feet, the sound of irritated or angry voices, the interminable discussions about gold. . . .

Then, as his lazy thoughts progressed, he realized that there were other privileges of home life which were now his to enjoy. The joy of a bedroom not filled to capacity with cots or hammocks; the joy of a hair mattress in place of a straw palliasse, or even bare boards; the joy of pillows. The joy of darkness and silence.

Lastly, so ingenuous was he at heart, he thought of the woman who was to share the bed with him. His face crinkled in a shy smile.

Dear Abigail Vandusen! he reflected. As if a few years really matter. . . .

CHAPTER SEVENTEEN

WHEN Henry and McCollum met on the landing-pier three days later, each was conscious of the air of constraint with which he imagined the other greeted him. After the usual "Good morning, Red," and "Good morning, Jimmy," an awkward silence followed. The boat which was to convey them to Manzanillo Island was as usual late, so both men pretended to occupy themselves scanning the opposite shore for signs of its coming.

"Later than usual," McCollum grunted. "The day they're punctual——"

"That won't ever happen." Henry couldn't think what else to say.

"Sure, but one can always hope." The surveyor turned and looked at the town behind him. "Two more buildings went up yesterday, I see. I didn't know towns could grow that fast."

"It needs to. Have you heard that three more steamers are due next week?"

"It won't take long to populate California at the rate emigrants are flocking through this place."

The dialogue continued, stilted and informal. After an embarrassing pause, Henry went on:

"Someone was telling me, yesterday, that Howland and Aspinwall are importing a small stern-wheeler to start a regular service up the Chagres from here to Gorgona."

"That's right, except that they're not starting one, but continuing the one they started last year."

Henry was unexpectedly interested. "I didn't know they had. I've never seen anything bigger than a canoe on the river."

"That's because you've been here during the dry season——"

"Dry!"

"The rainy season doesn't begin until next month. Then you'll see *real* rain."

Henry thought of the rainstorm that was the indirect cause of his present liaison with Abigail, and wondered what *real* rain would look like. He told McCollum of the storm.

The surveyor nodded. "I remember those few days. Anytime the trade wind stops blowing away the clouds which form over the Isthmus, down comes the rain. Even during the dry season."

"When is that? The first four months of the year?"

"Roughly. You've seen the best of the climate since you've been here, Red." McCollum indicated the river. "During the dry season anything drawing more than twelve inches of water scrapes her bottom. That's what happened to the *Orus* last year."

"The *Orus*!"

"A two-hundred-and-fifty-ton side-wheeler. Howland and Aspinwall aimed to compete with the cayucas, but they weren't able to use her till the rainy season started. Then they did so well with her that they ran a second steamer, especially designed for the Chagres service—until they ran into fresh trouble." McCollum chuckled. "The teredo worm mealed off the exposed hulls until they were leaking like a sieve."

"What about the new stern-wheeler? Won't the same thing happen?"

"I'm told it's to be iron hulled, and will carry four hundred and fifty passengers each trip."

The arrival of the canoe interrupted their discussion. After they had been afloat more than fifteen minutes Henry convinced himself that the surveyor was deliberately avoiding conversation, and sulkily resolved not to be the first to break the ice. But when the prolonged silence became intolerable—for normally they were good companions—he reversed his decision.

"Jimmy . . ."

McCollum looked round.

"You know I've moved from the hotel?"

"Pearson told me." Pearson was the scrawny proprietor of the Californian Hotel.

"He told you where I'd gone, of course?"

"He said something about you—you lodging with Miss Vandusen."

"Or did he say living?"

McCollum fidgeted with embarrassment. "That was his meaning, Red."

"Shocked?"

The surveyor laughed. "You're not thinking that of me, are you?"

"Well . . ."

"Then you're a tarnation fool, Red. To begin with, it's no business of mine; and besides, I don't blame you." His voice turned bitter. "A man can't remain virtuous for long in this god-damned climate without something going wrong. Not at our ages, at any rate. Maybe Mr. Trautwine and the Colonel——"

"But you, Jimmy—you haven't——"

"Not yet. You see, Red, being married makes that sort of thing different. Phyllis trusts me. Then there's Susan. I wouldn't want her to think that her father was a—was risking——" He came to a faltering pause. "Anyway, I'm doing my damnedest for their sakes, but it isn't easy. There's a girl at the hotel. When she looks at you with those soft eyes of hers——"

"Lucy?"

"Yes. You know her?"

"I danced with her one night. She's kind of—of cuddlesome, isn't she, Jimmy?"

"I wouldn't care to trust myself with her," the surveyor

admitted quietly. "But if I was single—like you. . . Anyway, good luck to you, Red."

"Thanks."

There was a long silence. Both men stared seawards with unseeing eyes.

At last McCollum stirred. "She's older than you, isn't she, Red?"

"Does that matter?" The question challenged in its sharpness.

"No. Of course not. It's better that way . . ." The surveyor tried to conceal his insincerity.

"She's a wonderful woman," Henry commented in a solemn, self-satisfied voice. "I shouldn't have thought the difference in ages could have made such a little difference."

"When a woman has both intelligence and charm . . ." McCollum gestured vaguely, not knowing what else to say.

Henry nodded sagely. "That's the answer, Jimmy. Intelligence and charm. Youth and good looks don't mean a thing in comparison. The average woman soon loses both, but the older an intelligent woman gets, the more charm she has."

The surveyor realized that Henry was really smitten with Abigail Vandusen, a fact which gave him some satisfaction because it seemed to lift the liaison above the usual run of such affairs.

"I envy you," he assured Henry, and meant every word. "Perhaps you'll ask me round one day?"

"You bet we will," Henry replied with genuine happiness. "I'll speak to Abigail. . . ."

II

When they returned to Chagres some days later they were called to a conference of all the contractors' engineers and surveyors who were stationed in Chagres or nearby. The conference was attended not only by Totten and Trautwine, but also by J. L. Baldwin, chief assistant engineer, who had recently discovered a summit gap thirty-seven feet lower than the lowest hitherto recorded.

Totten took charge of the meeting. "Gentlemen," he began,

"I have an important announcement to make. Mr. John L. Stephens, President of the Panama Railroad Company, has written to me from Bogotá, to say that he has been able to negotiate a favourable treaty with the New Granada Government for the construction and maintenance of a railroad across the Isthmus of Panama.

"There are eight principal provisions of the treaty, of which only the first two interest us as contractors. They are: first, that the company is allowed eight years for the completion of the railroad, with the southern terminal at Panama City, and the northern terminal wherever the company chooses to locate it.

"The second provision allows the company access to all public land on the Isthmus during construction; and later, permanent title to quarter of a million acres.

"In short, gentlemen, we're all set to go."

A murmured applause was quickly silenced by a flourish of Totten's impatient hand.

"We all know where that northern terminal is to be, and if any contractor has ever been faced with a worse nightmare of a job than converting a god-damned island swamp into an effective railroad terminal, I'll be happy to meet the almighty liar, shake him by the hand, and turn the contract over to him in return for a glass of Milwaukee beer."

His audience laughed. They could see the dynamic, hard-mouthed Colonel turning the contract over to a rival concern!

"I can think of a hundred better places in the world to be in than Manzanillo Island, but the choice of location wasn't our pigeon; and as the Railroad Company has driven a stake into the swamps there, that's where we make a start. And as soon as possible—which in my language means at once." The hard, blue eyes stared at McCollum. "Are you ready for work to begin, Mr. McCollum?"

"The line is located as far as Folks River, Colonel—that's the name of the strait which separates the island from the mainland."

Totten transferred his attention to Baldwin. "Have you begun initial clearing, Mr. Baldwin?"

"No, Colonel."

"What!" The exclamation sounded like the crack of a whip.

The assistant engineer had known the Colonel too long to be frightened by the other's peppery behaviour.

"No labour, Colonel. We've recruited exactly seven men, and three white Americans; bums who worked their way here and haven't the spunk to hoof it on to Panama."

The Colonel exploded. "What's the matter with the god-damned scum who lie about in the shade of their palms the blasted day long? Aren't they interested in good, hard money?"

"Sure they are, Colonel, but they can earn more with far less labour poling emigrants up-river to Gorgona and Chagres. As long as the gold-rush continues there's as much hope of recruiting labour on the spot as seeing pigs fly."

Totten never allowed his temperament to prejudice his sense of values. As his thin lips tightened in reflection he first swept his thin hair farther back off a domed forehead that already stretched far back towards his scalp, then smoothed the square, iron-grey beard that curled belligerently forward from a prominent chin.

"Hum! No labour, eh! That's almighty serious, sir. Our company contracted to build that railroad on the assumption that there would be an adequate supply of cheap labour to draw on." He stood for some moments in reflective silence, then swung round to his partner.

"There's only one way out of our immediate difficulty, Trautwine. I'll go to Carthagena by the next ship and recruit some of the labour we used for the canal."

Trautwine nodded agreement. "An admirable suggestion. While you are gone, we will continue with our efforts to recruit local labour. But I'm not hopeful."

"But we plan to make a beginning next month, whatever happens?"

"We must, Totten. We cannot afford to waste time."

The Colonel swung round to face his employees. "You hear, gentlemen? We will begin next month, as soon as I return from Carthagena with labour. Any questions?" he snapped.

"Yes, Colonel," McCollum spoke up. "Where do you propose to sleep your labour?"

"On the job, of course, as we usually do. We have a supply of tents, and timber for building."

The surveyor shook his head. "I've been over practically the whole island, Colonel, with Mr. Malley here. There isn't a square yard any place where you could pitch a tent without sleeping in mud."

"A coral reef surrounds the island. Isn't that a firm enough foundation? God save us, sir! Mr. Trautwine and I have slept often enough on coral."

"The reef is firm enough for a tent, Colonel, but it isn't dry. Every tide covers it."

"What about the mainland?"

"Worse, if anything. Unless you bring them back each night as far as Chagres——"

"Impossible! Waste of time."

Baldwin claimed attention. "I've been giving thought to the question of sleeping the labourers, Colonel. I've a suggestion to make."

"Well, sir?"

"There's an old hulk lying off-shore close to the landing-pier, a brigantine of about two hundred tons—you can see it from the window——"

"I've seen it, Mr. Baldwin. Go on."

"I've been over it. It's rotten and leaky, but it brought a load of emigrants here—God pity the poor devils!—before it was abandoned. If we were to patch it up, and anchor it off the island, it could be used as sleeping-quarters until better accommodation becomes available."

"An excellent idea. Excellent." Totten nodded briskly.

His partner voiced a doubt. "How do you propose we should get the hulk to Manzanillo? Its ropes and sails are so rotten an average wind would blow them to shreds."

"The *Orus* is due back here next week, sir, to resume her regular river service. We might be able to hire her for towing the hulk."

"Very well. I don't doubt that can be arranged. Who owns the hulk?"

Baldwin laughed. "Nobody, that I can find. The moment she got here captain and crew joined the passengers, and went on to California. Nobody knows either her name or nationality."

"Then we'll take it now and argue afterwards," Totten broke in with an impatient gesture.

III

As soon as the hulk had been repaired sufficiently to make it waterproof, and more or less habitable, Trautwine loaded it with provisions, tools, timber and other requisites for building; then ordered an early departure for Manzanillo. One dawn in May he, Baldwin, McCollum and Henry assembled on the shore and went aboard the hulk. They were shortly followed by the seven natives whom Baldwin had earlier recruited. But there was no sign of the three American bums who had volunteered to work for the contractors. The *Orus*, manœuvring for position to throw tow-ropes aboard the hulk, sounded her siren for action, so Baldwin hurried off in search of the men.

He returned without them. Two days previously they had unexpectedly left by cayuca for Cruces, en route for Panama and California. Where the money to pay their journeys had come from nobody knew; but another American had disappeared about the same time, after winning several hundred dollars at the gaming tables. A familiar story, in Yanqui Chagres. . . .

They soon reached the island, where they anchored off-shore. The *Orus* went on her way with a friendly hoot. The Indians unshipped a canoe they had brought with them, and went ashore. While two of them went back for the Americans, the other five used machetes to hack away the tangle of vines and undergrowth which faced them. Then the four Americans landed. Trautwine and Baldwin carried axes. As soon as the Indians had cleared enough space round the base of a tall coconut palm, the two white men lifted their axes. Soon the sharp edges were biting large chips out of the base of the trees. When the bite was deep enough they moved on to the next tree, while McCollum and Henry used a double-handed saw on the first. Presently they heard an ominous creaking sound.

"Timber!" McCollum sang out.

A few more thrusts with the saw—the tearing, rending, and

rather sad noise of breaking wood—a reluctant shiver—a crashing thud. . . .

Work on the Panama Railroad had begun.

IV

By nightfall the united efforts of the party had effected a clearing in the jungle large enough for the erection of a small storehouse on stilts. They went aboard more or less satisfied with their first day's work. They ate a satisfying meal which one of the Indians had prepared for them in the galley. Then they settled down for sleep.

Disillusion was soon forthcoming for the four white men. As soon as they had settled in their hammocks they were attacked by mosquitoes and sand-flies. In spite of their fatigue they were unable to sleep. They cursed and swore, slapped at every pinging hum within reach, turned and turned again, but without success. At last McCollum announced with bitterness, "Me for the deck. Suppose it does rain . . . no place could be more unpleasant than this." Henry chose to accompany McCollum up on deck, but the other two decided to remain below.

Not for long. In less than thirty minutes they had joined McCollum and Henry.

"At least, the rain will keep the damned insects away," Trautwine muttered, as he stretched out alongside Henry.

There was no rain that night. But the following night there was.

To ring the changes, on the third night a gentle swell developed. The hulk rolled monotonously from side to side. The slow, unceasing motion was more than most stomachs could stand. First Baldwin, then McCollum, and lastly Trautwine were sick. Henry was not sick, but the queasy feeling in his stomach was bad enough to make him decide that rain was preferable—which was paying the rain no compliment.

But the clearing grew; and a second storehouse on stilts was erected. More trees were felled, and sawn into timber for various purposes. The work was slow, in circumstances that could scarcely have been worse. They had to wear net veils over their faces;

L

otherwise they could have moved nowhere on the island without having to stare through a dark curtain of mosquitoes which would have swarmed about their sweat-impregnated flesh, clogging their eyes, ears, and nose. Their feet were never out of mud or water, or both. Showers of light rain fell often, a prelude to the coming rainy season. The four Americans spent much of their leisure time in arguing which was worse, day or night: sweltering sunshine, laborious work, and mosquitoes, or stifling nights, sea-sickness and mosquitoes. They were unable to reach any decision.

Then Colonel Totten arrived with forty labourers from Carthagena, and the Americans were no longer left in doubt as to which was worse. The unpleasant consequences of sea-sickness being multiplied forty times needs to be calculated by geometrical progression to arrive at its true misery!

CHAPTER EIGHTEEN

THEY were on their way back to Chagres.

"You're looking serious, Red," McCollum twitted. Then he turned bitter. "*You* ought to be bubbling over, having someone to welcome you——"

"So I am. But just then I was thinking about something that happened during the night."

"Such as somebody not being sick for a change?"

A cheerful grin puckered Henry's face, but it quickly vanished. "While I was lying awake I heard the sound of drums from the mainland."

"A fandango, some place——"

"No," Henry denied sharply. "These drums were quite different from those which call people together for a fandango."

"In what way?"

"It's hard to explain, Jimmy. There was something about the drums last night which sounded savage, primeval."

"You can't call the villagers here one hundred per cent civilized."

"I know, but the difference in the drums last night was what I imagine the difference between a fandango and a Petro sacrifice to be."

"A what! What in Pete's name are you talking about, Red? A sacrifice——"

"The Cimarrones in the interior practice the cult of Voodoo."

"What's that, anyway? What were they supposed to be sacrificing, and to what?"

Henry shrugged. "A monkey, maybe. Or perhaps a child." He almost added "Or a zombie" but checked himself: McCollum had too precise and realistic a nature to regard the possible existence of zombies with tolerance. Even the mention of a human sacrifice had made his lips twitch with disapproval at other people's credulity. Henry went on, "Roughly, a Petro sacrifice is a tribal dance which the presiding priest or priestess begins by sacrificing an animal to one of the African gods; often, a snake."

"You spoke of a child."

"Children have sometimes been sacrificed—and eaten!"

"Surely you don't really believe in such nonsense, Red?" McCollum looked testy.

"My father witnessed a Petro sacrifice in Haiti. Afterwards the Negro slaves rose in rebellion against their French owners."

McCollum tried to hide his scepticism. "That was nearly sixty years ago, and in Haiti."

"The Negro character doesn't change in half a century. Only last August the Haitians elected Soulouque as their Emperor, and Soulouque is a confirmed Voodooist. There are Negroes here, too, Jimmy; descendants of African slaves. If Petro dances are still held in Africa and in Haiti, why shouldn't they be held here, too?"

McCollum's only answer was a shrug.

Henry continued obstinately, "I'm sure those drums last night meant something. Whether they did or not, Jimmy, they kind of reminded me that this country isn't part of the civilized world as we know it."

"I don't see how you forgot that, the last few days. I wish I could have."

"I suppose because we're building something that's the last word in civilization and handling tools that are farther removed from the jungle than the North Pole. Railroads and jungles somehow don't seem to go together."

The surveyor nodded. "I'm beginning to get the drift of what you mean. Sort of romantic, aren't you?"

"Why?"

"Seems to me that you see the job through rose-coloured spectacles."

"Sort of! Don't you? Doesn't it mean anything to you to be making the world smaller?"

McCollum smiled drily. "To me a job's a job; to be well done within the specified time. The sooner it's over, the sooner I'll get home to the wife and family."

Wife and family! The words brought a warm, reflective smile to Henry's lips as they brought home to him the pleasure of returning, not to a wife and family, perhaps, but to a woman who was his wife in every sense save the legal one. This knowledge had given him comfort during the worst moments of his sleepless nights aboard the anchored brigantine. The pleasure had not palled with the passing days but had grown deeper; an intangible part of him, as it were, like a growing appreciation of Bach, or Thoreau.

How fuller, how much more rich life became, he reflected, when one had someone to go home to. It even gave added zest to work; for it was something to think about during periods of monotony or boredom; made one feel warm with anticipation. There was always something to look forward to. In another three days' time I'll be having supper with her in a small, cheerful room, by the warm light of a pink-shaded lamp, seated in a comfortable chair, eating well-cooked food served on china. . . .

How much more pleasing in prospect it all seemed, in contrast with the rough living conditions they had had to endure during the past few days. Just as a sunny morning is brighter and warmer for having followed a dismal day, so the meagre comforts of Abigail's house in Chagres seemed to transcend those of his father's home in Boston.

McCollum saw the contented smile which played about Henry's lips; and guessing the purport of his companion's reverie, checked what he was about to say. He was a sport in his own dry way, was McCollum. He was also human; and falling into a reverie on his own account, thought of the girls he had seen at the House of All Nations which he had visited one night out of curiosity. How much longer would he be able to resist temptation? he asked himself. It was almost too much to ask of a normal man—not everyone could be a Saint Anthony.

As the boat rounded the headland and the estuary of the Chagres became visible, the occupants saw that it was filled with shipping. Automatically their glances travelled landwards, to Yanqui Chagres.

Henry whistled. "Looks like the population's increased a few thousand since we left, Jimmy."

The surveyor nodded gloomily. "That'll mean hash again tonight unless they brought provisions with them."

"How much longer will the rush to California continue? They can't all hope to find gold."

"They can hope, Red. 'Hope springs eternal in the human breast.' But there isn't enough gold in the world for everyone who is going to California to have a picking. It's a pity the railroad isn't already built. Think of the revenue which would be coming in."

Henry chuckled. "Got shares in it?"

"No. Just interest in the job, I suppose."

"That's how I feel."

The town was even more crowded than it had appeared from a distance. Remembering his first view of it, Henry was sure that it was half as full again. Similarly the impatient discontent on the faces of the men who lounged about the street was twice as marked. It was evident that the town was absorbing newcomers more quickly than they could be moved on. So many of them wore pistol belts and bowie knives that the feel of his own weapons pressed against his thighs was a comforting one.

"There'll be a few more bodies floating out to sea before this lot is shifted," he muttered in a low voice to McCollum. "They look an ugly crowd, taken as a whole."

"And all raving to get to California by the quickest route. J. C. will be pleased!" John C. Trautwine was J. C. to his employees.

"Why J. C.?" Henry asked.

"How long do you think the new recruits from Carthagena will remain on the pay-roll after they find out they can make twice as much money by transporting these bums up-river? You'll see, come Monday."

Henry left McCollum at the Californian, and continued along the straggling street towards the house he was sharing with Abigail. Curious eyes watched him, as their owners wondered what was his job in life. Easy to see that he was no transient, for he was dressed in loose-fitting clothes of drill, of some colour already bleached and weathered beyond recognition; a low-crowned wide-brimmed hat; and thigh boots; and his face, although burned a deep, healthy bronze that was in sharp contrast to the gaunt skeleton-like faces of too many of the permanent white population, was mute witness of his having been in the tropics for many weeks. Nor were men alone interested in him. Some of the women from the House of All Nations were taking the air, and they ogled him with brazen eyes and sensuous smiles; for he had developed a husky body and a confident walk during the past weeks, and his face had firmed up and gained manliness at the expense of his previous soft, good looks.

Henry was unaware of the interest he was arousing. He was bubbling inwardly with excitement, for his thoughts were fixed upon the meeting with Abigail, now no more than a few minutes ahead of him. It was almost frightening, he thought, to realize how much a woman could mean to a man; and how unexpectedly and completely one could fall in love, even with a woman older than oneself. . . . For he was in love. That was undeniable. Only love could account for the quickening desire to see again the strong, intellectual face with its direct gaze, and cool, resolute mouth. Incredible that such a woman could have chosen to fall in love with him—she, who could have had her pick of older, more experienced men. He warmed again; this time with gratitude, and a deep sense of devotion.

She did not hear him enter the house for she was seated at a table, with her back to the door. On the table were some scattered sheets of notes, and some blank paper on which she was writing with a caligraphy as upright and finely made as her own figure.

It was the first time he had seen her at work. For a short while he watched her write with an unhurried, methodical speed that was so characteristic of her nature. But the even curve of her neck was, in his present mood, too tempting: it seemed positively to ask to be kissed.

He tiptoed across the room, and bent over her. Her first reaction, upon feeling his lips against her flesh, was one of unconscious irritation as she half-lifted her hand to brush a mosquito away. She recovered in time, and dropped her hand.

"Henry!" There was a hint of reproach in her voice. "When I'm at work!"

"Aren't you glad to see me?" he teased gaily.

"Of course I am, my dear. Always."

"Well, then——"

"But when I'm at work I mustn't be distracted. So get cleaned up and changed: by then I shall have finished this chapter."

As he left to do as she suggested he felt very proud to be the husband of a famous, clever woman. The word husband rose unbidden to his thoughts, and some part of his happiness dwindled as he recollected that he was a consort rather than husband; that she was free at any moment to leave him; that one day he might return to the house after a week's work to find it empty, deserted. The possibility was horrifying. He must make her agree to a legal marriage. . . .

She had not fulfilled her promise to be finished by the time he returned, so he sat himself down in a chair and watched her at work. He had never seen any writer on the job, and, without realizing what he would have expected to see, was vaguely surprised to see how apparently effortlessly the work proceeded. No pauses, no grimaces, no gestures of anger, no irritable tappings on the table. Her impassiveness reminded him in some respects of Zachary Fox.

She finished, and looked up. "How is work going?"

He grimaced. "If it weren't for sleepless nights, badly-cooked food, being bitten to death by mosquitoes, living in wet clothes most of the day, working in mud, avoiding alligators, and one or two more minor unpleasantnesses, everything would be dandy."

"Is it really so bad?"

"Every bit, darling."

"But you are enjoying the work?"

"Enjoying!" He grinned. "I could think of a thousand better jobs which I could really enjoy, but it interests me a lot and I'm glad to be helping."

"You'll carry on?"

"There's only one thing will stop me. News that Al has left Panama. If he goes, I go, too."

"Of course."

"But I'll come back. That I'll promise, Abigail. I'll come back to you, and the work."

"You make me very proud of you, Henry. I was sure you would not betray my faith in you when I promised Mr. McCollum that you would stick to the work as long as I had any influence with you."

"*You* promised . . ." His irritation quickly passed. "Skip it!" he murmured to himself. "And *your* work, darling?" he asked aloud.

A rare smile of enthusiasm spread across her face. "The book on Panama is going to be one of my best, Henry dear. I know that already. Panama has had a marvellous history. Strange to think that gold, which focussed the attention of the world on the country during the height of Spanish power, should bring it back into prominence after a decline lasting almost two centuries. The seventeenth-century Camino del Oro has once more become the Golden Road."

"Because of the emigrants to California?"

"No. Because of the gold which is flowing along the old highway, as it used to in the days of Pizarro. I'm told that gold trains organized by either Howland and Aspinwall, Zachrisson and Nelson, or Wells-Fargo, are crossing the Isthmus almost every day." She tidied her papers and stood up. "Hungry?"

He swallowed, jumped hurriedly to his feet, and took her into his arms. "For you I am."

She eluded his groping lips, and pushed his arms away. "There's a time and place for everything, and now is neither the time nor the place."

"It is when you've been away in the jungle for a week."

Her expression was serene. "You're not a barbarian, Henry. At least, make some effort at self-control. Your behaviour isn't gentlemanly."

II

McCollum's prophecy came true. Of the forty labourers whom Totten had brought from Carthagena, less than half reported for work the following Monday. Colonel Totten swore his longest and finest string of oaths; and for once Trautwine joined in. But as there was no immediate way out of the difficulty, it was decided to carry on as best one could. Baldwin, McCollum, and Henry went off to Manzanillo Island to continue work with what men were still available, leaving Trautwine behind to continue local recruitment while the Colonel returned to Carthagena to bring back yet more labour.

Conditions which had been bad enough in May grew steadily worse as the rainy season developed. Alternately wet and dry, the constant change began to effect not only the spirits of the white men, but also their physique. They began to flag in their work, and to look forward with ever-increasing desire to the next period of rest at Chagres. It was realized that a week's recuperation would have to alternate with a week's work, and arrangements were made to divide into working gangs under the leadership of Trautwine and Baldwin alternately.

Totten returned with another fifty volunteers from Carthagena. A few white Americans were also recruited in Panama, also some Indians and mestizo Panamanians. The number of workers gradually increased. By the end of July the contractors had one hundred names on their wages books. This was a small proportion of the total entries, for too many names were entered only to be struck out again as soon as there was an opportunity to desert. There were also some deaths. Men—especially foreign white men—collapsed from the physical strain of working in such adverse conditions. It was truly a case of the survival of the fittest. Even so, there were now too many men working at one time for them to be accommodated in the brigantine at night. Clearing and fitting on the island were slowly proceeding, but not yet to the extent of being able to sleep the men in dry quarters. To augment the brigantine, another hull was purchased, the condemned steamboat *Telegraph*, and sent to the island for use as a residence.

The contractors redoubled their efforts to increase the number of labourers, for they had not yet raised one-tenth of the required number. They increased their rates of pay. This move was, for a time, successful. Unfortunately, more and more emigrants to California arrived almost daily at Chagres, and the demand for trans-Isthmian transport increased in the same ratio. By then the *Raphael Rivas* was carrying 450 passengers to Gorgona every other day, but this number was only a fraction of those angrily clamouring for a passage across the Isthmus. The *Harry Gleason*, an old side-wheeler from the Mississippi, joined the *Rivas*; and then a sister ship, the *Swan*. Still the accommodation remained insufficient, so the more impatient travellers fell back on the cayucas, and labourers continued to desert the contractors.

"Mr. Trautwine's going to New York," McCollum told Henry one day. Behind the sunburn his face looked sickly and drawn: there was a strained look in his eyes. "God-damned lucky devil!"

Henry realized that the surveyor was thinking of the wife and family way back in the States. Falling into a similar mood he thought of his parents in Boston, and then of Jean . . . but with a sense of guilt. This feeling, allied to nostalgia, made him feel sombre. He had recently heard from Zachary Fox, in a letter which one of the muleteers in a gold train had brought to Chagres. Fox had written to say that although there was no definite news of Al Simpson, or his whereabouts, it was certain that he had not yet left the Isthmus; at any rate, by way of Panama City. That he had not left by way of Chagres, either, Henry was convinced: Pedro Romanos, anxious to earn the reward which Henry was offering for news of Simpson, had gladly agreed to keep a sharp look-out for the missing man.

Unwilling to dwell too long upon thoughts of Boston, Henry abruptly asked, "Why?"

"For one thing, to buy an old steamer for transporting materials up-river to Gatún and above, so that it can be already on the spot when the track reaches that far."

"When!" Henry commented drily. "It'll take us years to reach Gatún. What have we got to show for four months' work?"

"The first permanent building of the new terminal. And the route located for the first two miles. Railroad construction is slow work, Red, especially when labour is short."

"What could you do with more men, even if you had them? There's no room left on the two ships."

"Have you noticed where the island has been cleared that the insects are far less troublesome?"

"Yes."

"If we build shacks there for the men they would probably sleep more comfortably. Even that would help speed up progress."

"How about the tide?"

"If we build on stilts we shouldn't have to worry about the tide."

While Henry was still considering this suggestion he heard a shout.

"Señor Malley. If you please, señores . . ."

Turning, he recognized Pedro Romanos. The Panamanian was running towards them, his face vivacious with excitement, his teeth glistening whitely against his brown, puckish face.

"Looks like he's bursting with news," McCollum commented.

Henry's hopes soared. News—of Al, perhaps. . . .

"What do you think, señores?" He gasped. "A Howland and Aspinwall gold train—on he Cruces trail——" He stopped for want of breath.

"Well?" Henry urged with impatience. What was this news to do with Al?

Romanos gulped. "Attacked by masked robbers—thirty thousand dollars' worth of gold stolen. . . ." His trim slight figure trembled with excitement. "Isn't that something?" he claimed, with an air of satisfaction.

CHAPTER NINETEEN

HENRY'S life with Abigail had long since settled down to the peaceable routine of an otherwise normal marriage. If it lacked the exuberant passion of a more emotional union he was not particularly disappointed or surprised. He had known so many legal husbands forced to tolerate the same lack in their marriages that he accepted it as typical, and definitely preferable, to the more disturbing pendulum of ecstasy and temperamental estrangement.

Besides, his sense of justice reassured him that in her case there were compensations for the rhythm of desire which restricted physical union to bespoken occasions, and excluded the raptures of impulse. In the first case, when she gave she gave freely and gladly within the limits of an orderly and self-disciplined nature. In the second, provided that one did not challenge her leadership, she was agreeably even-tempered and dependable. Her companionship never lost its charm, nor its integrity, nor its interest. It never dulled; never irritated.

When Henry told her of the robbery of the gold train, an amused smile parted her lips.

"I've been expecting some such news for some weeks past."

He was startled. "Why?"

"For several reasons. There are far too many disillusioned 'tough hombres' about, as Mr. Braddock once described them to me, not to anticipate their trying to make easy money, especially in a country that is not policed. Why shouldn't they rob the trains? What is to stop them? Another reason is that history has an unfortunate habit of repeating itself; and I always look to it to do so."

"How do you mean, darling?"

"Even in the days of Pizarro the gold trains had to be heavily guarded against robbers, who, in those days, were called buccaneers."

"Morgan?"

"He was not the only one. There was the English Oxenham, the French François l'Ollonois, the Dutch Mansveldt, and many others. Before the buccaneers there were privateers, Francis Drake in particular. Before him Cimarrones plundered the gold trains. And before them, sometimes rival Spaniards plundered one another." Her eyes glowed with enthusiasm. "Every stone along the old trails could relate a history of greed and blood, if it could speak."

He loved her most of all when she talked to him. There seemed to be no limit to her knowledge of matters historical and geographical. He marvelled that one brain could absorb and retain such a compendious mass of information; and yet retail those facts not as a catalogue of statistics, but in conversation of absorbing interest. Each time he listened to her his pride in her deepened.

"Shall we have Jimmy McCollum along some time this week?" he asked abruptly.

"He was here not long ago. Do you like him that much?"

"I like him well enough, darling. There are not many men I'd get along with better. He's generous, too; in the time he gives me, teaching me surveying. But that's not the reason——"

"What is?"

"I'm sorry for him. He's a family man at heart, and missing his home like hell. I'm afraid that if he dwells too much on his loneliness he'll break out."

"Does he drink? I haven't noticed him drinking too much."

"I wasn't meaning drink, darling, but the House of All Nations."

"That place!" Her mouth registered distaste. "Surely he can wait until he gets back to his wife?"

He thought the remark unwarranted, coming from Abigail. Unfortunately his expression, too often revealing, and his mischievous, reminiscent smile, betrayed the rambling reflection.

"Henry!" she sharply reproved. "If you are comparing Mr. McCollum with me, please remember that I waited for many years before finally yielding to impulse." She spoke without embarrassment. "Is it too much to ask a man to wait so long?"

"Well——"

"I can see you think so." She paused, and in a rare moment of indecision a worried expression passed across her strong face. "Henry, I do make you happy?"

"Supremely. Without you——" He gazed starkly out of the window at the fringe of jungle that was already creeping back towards the house. "If I had to work in that damned swamp without knowing I had you to come back to . . . God! Let's not talk about such morbid ideas."

She sat on the arm of his chair and stroked the springy red hair which no brush or comb could ever subdue. "You don't regret that sometimes I'm not more—co-operative——"

"I wouldn't change one single thing about you, dear, dear Abigail," he claimed with stout loyalty.

She pressed her lips lightly on his forehead. "Thank you, my sweet." Then, in a matter-of-fact voice, "Of course, ask Mr. McCollum along, Henry. Tomorrow night. . . ."

II

He stared up into the darkness. Already he had been in bed for more than an hour, but he felt less sleepy than when he had blown out the candle. He listened anxiously for sounds from Abigail's bed; but beyond the whisper of her even breathing he heard nothing. From the moment of darkness in the bedroom there had been no sound; certainly not the sighing restlessness he would have given so much to have heard.

It often happened thus. She possessed the facility of falling into sound, serene sleep within seconds of settling comfortably in bed. As a general rule he shared that facility. But not always. Sometimes the restlessness of desire kept him awake, as now. Her tenderness earlier on had misled him, encouraged him to hope; but as he had bent over and kissed her good night she had rested one hand lightly on his shoulder, in readiness to push him gently away if he lingered too long—always her affectionate manner of conveying her answer to him—and he had realized that her rhythm was out of tune with his.

Sometimes physical tiredness helped him to overcome his disappointment fairly quickly, but not so on this occasion. Perhaps it was an unconscious feeling of sympathy for Jimmy McCollum, perhaps his own blood was more than usually feverish on account of the August heat, perhaps it was just the hot night itself. Whatever the reason, he was unable to calm his thoughts enough to fall asleep.

This business of separate beds now. . . . She had used as an excuse for each sleeping in a separate bed the heat of the nights, which the warmth of a second person in a double bed would make intolerable. Doubtless she was justified in using that argument, but he knew that it was a secondary rather than the main reason for her choice. It was her cursed sense of individuality, a rigid determination to remain mistress of her own body and her own soul, a damned obstinate pride in her own invulnerableness. In a shared bed she would be at the mercy of her companion; to be kissed, touched, stroked or petted when he desired, rather than when the desire was at her dictation or command.

Yet it was the moment of mood and impulse which he most missed; for no other reason than to enjoy the intimate but exquisite pleasure, before dropping off into contented sleep, of lightly resting a hand in subtle companionship on her soft thigh, or perhaps cupping one of her firm breasts. He asked no more than that; and perhaps an occasional glimpse of her shapely body.

But no. Such intimacies were beyond her comprehension, he reflected in bitterness. "There's a time and place for everything . . ." When *her* rhythm of desire dictated, then and only then would she willingly sacrifice her fierce, jealous ego and surrender to his embraces.

III

The rain fell pitilessly, hour after hour. But no sooner had the clouds passed away than the burning sun filled the swamp with a miasma that terrified the white labourers; for it was no secret to them that the steamy vapour was impregnated with fever which might strike anyone without warning.

But the work went on. As acre by acre of Manzanillo Island was cleared of jungle growth, its swamp water drained off, and its thick mud hidden beneath tons of filling materials, more and more shacks were erected to house the growing quantity of stores, and the increasing numbers of labourers recruited from many sources by indefatigable contractors.

There were more coloured men from Carthagena; and some from Jamaica; white men from the United States, and from Europe. Some of these were staioned at Gatún, seven miles on from the terminal at the far side of the Black Swamp. There a camp had been erected at the confluence of the Chagres and Gatún rivers; on the opposite bank from the old native town, which Henry and his companions had slept in on the first night of their journey across the Isthmus.

Here the gangs began the work of piling and grading backwards towards Manzanillo. Conditions for them were easier, for the contractors had imported an iron-hulled steamer which ran between Chagres and Gatún, and kept them supplied with tools and construction materials. Besides, there was the old town just across the river to visit when one wanted a change of faces, or female company. . . .

In spite of continued desertions, the number of employees rose from one hundred to two, from two hundred to three, from three hundred to four. The contractors began to feel more hopeful. Thanks to previous desertions, and unforeseeable difficulties, they were already many weeks behind schedule; but their organization was getting into stride, with cumulative effects. Labour was spared to erect more comfortable dwellings on Manzanillo, and hospitals were built. One was justified in anticipating that lost time would be made up later on.

This reckoning neglected to take into account the hours of torrential rain, and the hours of scorching sunshine.

IV

"What's the matter with Mr. Baldwin?"

McCollum and Henry were on the mainland shore opposite the island, where they were resting wearily after a two-mile trek through the Black Swamp, from the point where they were locating the line on its way to Gatún. Across the dividing neck of water they could see a stricken look on the face of the chief assistant engineer, and his dejected attitude.

Henry unwrapped the veil of protective gauze from his face.

"Something's gone wrong," he hazarded. "Wonder what?"

"We'll soon know." McCollum hailed the boatman whose duty it was to ferry people to and fro between the mainland and the island.

A few minutes later they joined Baldwin.

"Something wrong, Mr. Baldwin?"

"Plenty!" the other man replied with a grim nod. "Fever!"

"You?"

"Not yet, thank God! The labourers. They're going down like flies."

"You mean, fatally?"

"I do, McCollum. Sixteen new cases today taken ill: four deaths from previous cases."

McCollum and Henry glanced at each other. The surveyor sucked at his lips. Henry swallowed, suddenly aware that his throat was dry. . . .

"Not so good," McCollum croaked.

"Maybe a few isolated cases," Henry suggested.

"Maybe nothing!" Baldwin denied in a snapping voice. "Thirty-five went down the previous four days, with numbers increasing each day: seven, eight, nine, eleven and now a jump to sixteen. If it carries on at that rate——"

"And the—the deaths?"

"Six to date. Six out of forty-four cases."

"One in seven."

"The figures are worse than that. They live a few days after being taken ill. Of the earlier cases the number of deaths is one in five."

"Good God!"

"It isn't only deaths we're worried about."

"Desertion?"

"Sure. They're beginning to desert in large numbers. See here, you two! Want some good advice?"

"Yes, Mr. Baldwin?"

"Double your dosage of quinine for the next few weeks. It's bad enough to lose labourers and mechanics. We can't afford to lose members of the executive."

During the next few weeks both the number of new cases and the number of deaths rose. One day McCollum and Henry arrived at Manzanillo Island after their week's leave, to find that work had stopped.

They went along to Baldwin's office—some of the executive now had offices on the cleared section of the island. They found the engineer sitting idly at his table, staring gloomily at a mixture of blue-prints and specifications in front of him which he made no attempt to inspect.

M

"Why has work stopped?" they asked him.

"Why do you think? There's only a handful of men left to do any. Do you know how many employees we've sent to the hospitals since the outbreak? More than two hundred."

Henry whistled. "More than half the roster."

"Yes."

"But that still leaves the other half, Mr. Baldwin."

"Does it?" The engineer laughed grimly. "Then you find them, Mr. Malley. Most of the rest have deserted to the California Transit."

"But you've raised wages week after week for the past two months."

"Sure we have. We've been offering them the moon to keep them at work. Trouble is, they don't want the moon. They prefer the California Transit, and less risk of fever."

"What's to happen now?"

"Nothing."

Baldwin's companions were startled. "You're not giving up, Mr. Baldwin?" Henry asked quickly.

"That depends. I was about to tell you both, there's a second reason for the stoppage. Totten and Trautwine are through. Not enough money in the kitty."

"Not enough!" This time the speaker was McCollum. "But I understood that the contract price was a fair one."

"It was, in normal circumstances. But who could have foreseen that a chance discovery of gold in California would result in labour costs going sky high? As things are now, if Totten and Trautwine carried on they would become bankrupt before the line reaches Gatún."

"So——"

"J. C. has sailed for New York, to petition the Panama Railroad Company for a release. You can go back to Chagres, boys, and take it easy until the Colonel gets back here."

"Where's he gone to?"

Baldwin grinned. "You can't keep a good man down." There was a note of admiration in his voice. "On another recruiting expedition," he continued, answering the surveyor's question.

"But what about the release?"

"Until it comes through the firm is still responsible. Meanwhile, the hospitals are benefiting."

"Doing what?"

"According to the latest rumour, shipping corpses to medical schools in all parts of the world for good American dollars," he explained, with a macabre chuckle. " 'Cadavers Wholesale Company" . . ."

V

As soon as both partners had returned to Chagres, Colonel Totten assembled the executive for a conference. Characteristically, he wasted no time in preliminaries. Precisely on the hour for which the meeting had been called he rapped for attention and rose to his feet.

"Gentlemen, I'm quite sure that the reason for the journey to New York, and the stoppage of work, is no secret to any of you. On account of rising costs, which would soon have bankrupted us, Mr. Trautwine and I had to ask the Corporation for a release from the contract for building the railroad.

"I am glad to tell you that negotiations with the Corporation were carried on with cordiality and understanding. When the full circumstances were made known to the directors of the Corporation, a release was readily granted. The present position is that the firm of Totten and Trautwine are no longer responsible for constructing a railroad across the Isthmus of Panama."

A low buzz followed the Colonel's words, but the murmuring quickly ceased when he raised a hand for silence.

"In usual circumstances this release would have meant that another firm of contractors would move in, with their own executive staff, and we should all return to our own country, leaving the new people to finish the job we started. But the circumstances are unusual, and the usual course of events is not being followed. The Panama Railroad Company is itself undertaking the responsibility of constructing the railroad."

This time the buzz was louder, for the news surprised nearly everyone present. The buzz also continued longer, for the Colonel stood still and eyed the scene with an air of sardonic amusement. Presently the murmuring died away of its own volition, as the executive wondered what was to follow. They were not kept long in suspense.

"No doubt you are wondering, gentlemen, what knowledge a financial corporation can have of constructing a railroad. The answer is the obvious one. They have no such knowledge. For this reason . . ." The Colonel paused, while his mischievous eyes appeared to survey each man in turn. "For this reason," he continued, "the Corporation are retaining Mr. Trautwine and myself on a salary basis, to carry on construction, which will be financed out of its paid-up capital."

Having dramatized the news to his own satisfaction, the Colonel became too impatient to allow further interruptions. His crisp voice carried on.

"Those of you who are willing to carry on the work of construction will be granted temporary leave of absence from the firm so that you may enter the employment of the Panama Railroad Company. But before any of you take that step I want you to consider carefully the dangers it involves." His voice grew bitter. "Of the four hundred men we were employing two months ago, nearly eighty have died from sickness caused by the conditions in which we have been working. A few of those were members of the executive, friends of mine and yours. Those of you who sign on with the Corporation will be subject to the risk of following those friends to the grave. Those of you who, for any reason, do not want to sign on will be transported to the United States by the first available ship, at the expense of Totten and Trautwine.

"Gentlemen, the choice is yours. How many of you want to go back?"

After a long pause, four men indicated their desire to return to the States. One of them was James McCollum.

CHAPTER TWENTY

WHEN Henry told Abigail of McCollum's decision to go back to the States she was silent so long that he glanced searchingly in her direction. To his astonishment he saw that her eyes were unsteady with apprehension.

"Abigail!"

She seemed unaware of his exclamation. "Why is he going back, Henry? Is he afraid of the fever?"

"I suppose so. We all are. But I don't think that's the reason."

"Then what is?" she asked, in a voice that shook a little.

"Plain homesickness. He's afraid of himself; afraid that if he stays much longer in the tropics he'll be driven to the House of All Nations."

"No," she contradicted. "I can't believe that of Mr. McCollum, Henry. He had too strong and fine a character to allow himself to be influenced by mere physical desire into giving up vitally important work. Work of which he was immensely proud."

"Sure, he was proud of his work——"

"Wait! I think he probably used that excuse because it was one most likely to obtain sympathy from the other men." She was unable to conceal her scorn. "I think he was afraid of death, not on his own account, but for the sake of his wife and little Susan."

"Maybe that as well, but I know that he was more afraid of the results of his own passion than he was of losing his life."

"Mr. McCollum—passionate——"

"Just like I said, Abigail. He didn't look like a man of strong sexual passions, did he? But then, he didn't look like he really was in any respect. I've never known anyone look less like himself. You'd think he was an inoffensive sort of guy. Third invoice clerk at some two-bit exporter's office. Blackboneless, ineffectual . . . And all the time he was just the opposite. And he didn't look like a Don Juan, either."

She laughed scornfully. "Of course he didn't."

"But that's what he would have been," Henry obstinately maintained. "If he'd let himself be. But he had too much conscience to do that. I haven't worked with him all these months without getting to know him."

"If one can ever get to know a man," she commented. "Or should I say, understand him?" The bleak look returned to her eyes. "You—you don't ever feel like that, do you, Henry dear?"

He laughed loudly. Too loudly. "Afraid of my red hair, honey?" he mocked.

She winced, and diverted the conversation from such a dangerous subject.

"Had you been free to return to the States, Henry, would you have chosen to go?"

He considered the question for some time before answering, but resolutely banned all thoughts of Jean. "I don't know what to say. It's no picnic at the best of times, constructing a railroad. But in the existing conditions it's damn' near hell."

"But you will carry on when work is resumed?"

"That's tomorrow. Yes, Abigail. You see, it's a man's work, and that's come to mean something to me in the past year. It makes me feel sort of proud to know I'm challenging Nature, and doing something for the world at the same time."

Her eyes glowed. "I love to hear you say that, my sweet."

Sometimes her pride in him embarrassed him. He shifted restlessly. "Besides, there's another reason; a much more mundane one. I'm beginning to earn good money. That's a good enough reason for stopping on, isn't it?"

"Yes, of course." She seemed to go limp.

His eyes gleamed with mischief. "There's a third reason," he continued casually.

She was no longer interested. "Yes?" she prompted in a flat voice.

"You, my darling."

"Dear, dear Henry," she murmured, as her face reflected her happiness.

II

The indefatigable partners, aided directly and indirectly by Stephens, the President, and Center, the Vice-President of the

Railroad Company, went out into the highways and byeways of the Caribbean Sea, and scraped the bottom of the local labour markets. Men began to arrive at Chagres from all directions. The number of employees mounted daily. One day in December good news was passed on to the executive staff. The thousandth man had just had his name added to the pay-roll.

By this time the rainy season was slackening off. The charted line of sickness cases was falling in a steep curve. The rate of progress was quickening daily. Docks began to thrust out seaward from the coral reef which, countless centuries before, had been the beginning of Manzanillo Island. Steamers carrying cargoes destined for the construction of the railroad began to discharge there instead of at Chagres. A small township began to grow up around the docks—warehouses, living-quarters for the men, offices, a stores—and, of course, a saloon. . . .

One of the steamers to arrive at the island brought in its hold all the equipment for pile-driving. It was quickly unshipped, assembled and set in position to begin the work of driving in the foundations for the track. Nearby, another steamer was discharging ballast.

Baldwin spoke to the Irishman who was in charge of the gang.

"Soundings show solid earth at one hundred and eighty feet, Pat."

"One hundred and eighty! Begod now!" The foreman wiped his mouth with the back of his hand. " 'Tis a mountain ye'll have to be movin' here to occupy that space, sor. Ye wouldn't be askin' me to fill up the Atlantic Ocean while I'm on the job?"

The engineer grinned. "You'll have all the filling you need. Get busy."

"Ay, sor." The foreman whistled. "Get moving there, ye black-skinned limbs of Satan."

An endless stream of labourers began to wheel barrow-loads of discharged ballast from the dock to the piling machine. Load upon load was tipped into the oozing mud, and disappeared with an eerie squelch. Hour after hour the work continued monotonously, while the Irish foreman sucked a clay pipe and patiently waited for the first sign of a hardening surface.

By the time the steamer had finished discharging its cargo the pile of rock rubble on the dockside was mountainous; and the line of men who scooped microscopic nibblings from its base looked ant-like in comparison as they trundled their loads across the few intervening yards between the dock and the waiting pile-driver. But with the mountain visibly shrinking before the honeycombings of the human chain, the face of the foreman turned first bewildered and then desperate as the stinking mud still swallowed up the ballast.

"Hold it," he ordered, and the human chain came to an unquestioning stop. O'Connor took a sounding.

"Jees!" he ejaculated with naïve astonishment.

He checked his reading, gave the signal for the chain to resume work, then went in search of the chief assistant engineer.

"Begod, sor, and what sort of a job is this, that you're after having done?"

"Well?"

"Did me ears hear aright when ye told me your soundings showed solid at one hundred and eighty feet?"

"They did. That was the figure. Why?"

"Because we've already dumped three thousand tons of filling in the bog, and the sounding still reads one hundred and eighty."

Baldwin's exclamation was forceful but satisfying. "I'll check," he continued, snatching up his hat.

The check showed no error on the part of the foreman.

"Carry on," Baldwin ordered with resignation. "We'll fill this bloody island if it means importing the State of Connecticut to do so."

Day after day the work went on of creating a road bed, but the pile-driver moved forward by inches.

Meanwhile the stream of emigrants passing across the Isthmus did not lessen. Day by day ships of all sizes and descriptions reached Chagres from a score of different countries. They crowded the hotels, the saloons, the brothels, and even the stores and the offices, sleeping wherever there was enough space for them to lie down. Tormented by impatience, and affected by the trying weather conditions, quarrels were frequent and often bloody. Few were the nights which did not see a corpse flung into the estuary;

victim of a stab, or a bullet wound, or a broken bottle. The spirit of lawlessness and unrest spread even among the railroad labour gangs. An ill-chosen word, an accidental push, a petty theft—and another name had to be transferred from the pay-roll to one of the small wooden crosses at the new cemetery which was laid out at Mount Hope, an eminence two miles south of Manzanillo. There were no sheriffs to say nay. . . .

III

Christmas! Henry was shocked one morning, during his week's leave at Chagres, to realize the date. December 14th. . . .

"Christmas . . ." he began.

"I wondered when you would realize how near we are to Christmas."

He grimaced. "Christmas and Panama don't—well, mix." He gazed wistfully up at the wooden roof. It was black with mosquitoes and other insects which it was not possible to keep out of the buildings. " 'Way back in Boston it may be snowing. Or maybe it is one of those cold, crisp nights when every star in the sky seems to be trying to outshine the one next to it; and one's face pings with the cold wind."

"You'd like to be there, wouldn't you, Henry dear?"

"Yes," he admitted. "Just for the Christmas vacation." He thought of turkeys with cranberry sauce, of a lighted Christmas tree in the window, of children romping through the house, of his parents, of Jean. . . . "Yes, I would. And you, honey?"

"I used to feel like that. But I've been away too many Christmases."

A present for Abigail! Something superlative, to let her know how grateful he was. No, how much he loved her. He did love her, didn't he? His feeling for her was love. It had to be. . . . It was too deep, too sincere not to be.

A present! Such as? What could he buy in Chagres, suitable to express all he felt? Something different. Something local or Spanish. But Panama was the place to find such a present, not Chagres. Panama was one of the crossroads of the world. A link between the old and the new. There were many foreign merchants in Panama. His eagerness spurred his imagination.

"Can you do without me for a short time, honey?"

She looked startled. "Is that why you spoke of Boston, dear? But the risk! Suppose the constables——"

He laughed. "Not Boston, my dear. Panama. I'd like to see Zachary Fox again. Besides——" His expression turned grim. "I want to question him about Al. It's funny there's still no news. He must be somewhere."

"You can trust Mr. Fox."

"I do trust him. But——"

"No, Henry. I don't want you to go."

His mouth twitched. If only she would try to be less authoritative. But he answered gently. The words mattered more than the manner. She didn't want him to go. That was nice. Better than not caring a damn, or even being glad. . . .

"The trip is quicker than when we took it. The return journey can easily be done in a week. Overnight to Gorgona by one of the steamers——"

"I wasn't thinking of time. Haven't you heard the news?"

"What news?"

"The robbery two days ago."

"No. Bandits again?"

"Yes. A Zachrisson and Nelson train this time. The robbers got away with more than a hundred thousand dollars' worth of gold."

He whistled. "Somebody's going to get mad. One hundred thousand dollars, just like that!" He grew puzzled. "But what's that to do with my going to Panama?"

"It isn't safe for travellers——"

"Not ones with one hundred thousand dollars' worth of gold, maybe."

"I mean ordinary travellers. The day after the hold-up the bodies of three Americans were found along the trail. Their guides had stabbed and robbed them."

"Not so good. Poor devils!" Henry's expression hardened. "It's time Bogotá did something. The country is getting more lawless every day."

"As long as no New Grenadians are hurt, the Government isn't likely to interfere. The Panamanians are not complaining. They hate the Americans."

"But they don't hate American dollars." He relaxed. "My dear, the robbery isn't going to stop me going to Panama. I haven't practised using my guns this past year for nothing. I can take care of myself."

"I'd rather you didn't, Henry," she stated firmly, but with supreme confidence that he was unlikely to go contrary to her wishes.

His Stewart eyes turned obstinate. He did not resent her attitude. By now he knew her well enough to know that it was part and parcel of her nature; the unconscious arrogance of one who had lived by herself too long.

"Abigail . . ." he began.

IV

"Red!"

Fox's white face confirmed the warmth of his voice with no more than a flicker of emotion; but it expressed more than Henry had ever seen it express before. A soft ball of kitten purred on his lap; a fat-ribbed black dog of uncertain parentage contentedly thumped its long tail on the floor where it was stretched out; a gay-plumaged parrot screeched a welcome—or was it? The living creatures somehow made the bare room homely.

"What brings you here?"

"To see you, and——"

"Thanks, lad!" The voice was apparently the same old toneless voice, and yet Henry felt that it expressed more genuine pleasure than a score of adjectives from anyone else. "And——"

"To buy a Christmas present for Abigail." Henry realized that Fox couldn't possibly know about Abigail: in the letters which had been exchanged from time to time nothing had been said about sharing her home. "You see," he went on awkwardly "Abigail and I——"

Fox nodded his sleek, immaculate head. "I know, Red. You don't have to explain."

"But how——"

"People talk," he casually explained. "I knew when it started. The night you and she were left in the cave."

"How could you have known?" Henry burst out. "When?"

"The next morning. Her eyes were starry. And you exuded pride." Fox dismissed the subject with a wave of his white slender hand. "How is the railroad proceeding? Do you like the work?"

Henry talked for some time. At last Fox took pity on him. "You're mad to ask me for news, aren't you, Red?"

"Yes—no—I guess, not so much as you think. I know you'd have sent news if you had any."

"News, yes."

There was a reservation in the gambler's voice which puzzled Henry.

"There's something else?"

Fox pushed his forefinger into the ball of fluff on his lap. The kitten wriggled in ecstasy.

"I've one or two friends in Panama," he began. (Of course, thought Henry. He makes friends wherever he goes. And without trying.) "They've kept me well advised. As I've written to you from time to time, I'm as certain as I can be, in the circumstances, that Al Simpson hasn't left Panama by way of this city."

"Well?"

"Some time back I befriended a Negro. At least, I saved his life. A drunken emigrant wanted to shoot him as a thief. The real thief was a Kentucky man, but never mind about that. From that time on Juan, the Negro, became my man. You know about the Maroons or Cimarrones of this country?"

"Piérola told us——"

"Yes, of course. I should have remembered. Well, Juan is a Cimarrone. Lives way back in the interior, to the west. Probably no white man has been within miles of his country, since Spanish days. His people grow coffee and cocoa, which he and others bring to Panama for trade. An interesting man, Juan. Miss Vandusen would enjoy meeting him, if she could persuade him to talk."

"May I mention him to her?"

"Of course. But she won't get him to talk. Down, old boy,

down." This to the dog, who had decided that the human visitor
was occupying too much of the beloved master's attention. Fox
scratched the dog's head until it lay down again, with its head
poised upwards so that it could gaze adoringly with liquid brown
eyes at the gambler.

"One day I thought of asking Juan to scout around for information about Simpson. You know how the natives get to hear things
—there are mysteries about the black men which we whites are
never likely to solve." Fox paused.

Henry was too impatient to let the other man take his own
time. "What did he find out?" he questioned eagerly.

"That a man by the name of Simpson was living in Cruces up
to a few months ago."

"Doing what? Working? I can't imagine Al being content to
work. He wasn't the kind."

"No?" Fox dangled a piece of string for the kitten to play with.

"What happened then?"

"He disappeared from Cruces."

"And after that?"

"Ah! One can put two and two together, and make four—but
one might be adding the wrong twos together." The colourless
eyes surveyed his visitor. "Have you heard of La Pantera yet?"

"No. What is it, a village?"

"I suppose you speak Spanish by now, Red?"

"More or less."

"Then you know the English word for La Pantera?"

Henry puzzled for some seconds. "The Panther?" he suggested
at last.

"Yes. The Panther."

"Why should I have heard of a panther? I know there are
panthers in the jungle——"

"*The* Panther, Red, not any panther. The nickname of a man
whose name is on everyone's lips here in Panama."

Henry's thoughts became confused. Obviously, Fox hadn't
introduced The Panther into the conversation without meaning.

"Not Al?"

Fox shrugged. "It is not certain. Only a handful of men can be
sure. But——"

"Why should anyone call Al The Panther? Why talk about him?"

"Because, my dear chap, it is rumoured that The Panther is the man who is responsible for the gold-train robberies."

Henry recollected the handsome, dissolute face, its petulant wilfulness, its reckless defiance. And odd scraps of scandal, which had been whispered guardedly from time to time—a missing ring, a forged promissory note. . . .

"Could be," he agreed.

CHAPTER TWENTY-ONE

LA PANTERA—The Panther—Al Simpson. . . .

The more Henry considered the possible connection between the leader of the hold-up gang and the young rake he had known in Boston, the more likely it became that Al could well be La Pantera. The pattern fitted. Al's distaste for work, his lack of moral scruples, his recklessness. . . . Even so, the gap between Al and La Pantera still remained a large one.

"What makes you think that Al may be this La Pantera?"

"Circumstantial evidence. It is known that an American is connected with the leadership of the gang which held up the two gold trains. That's not particularly surprising, of course; for if one is to judge by clothes, colour of flesh, talk and so on, three or four of the gang are Americans. But the leader was heard to give orders in English—in a New England accent."

"Go on."

"That leader is tall, with curly blond hair. His shoulders droop as if they were too heavy for the rest of his body."

"That sounds like Al. He never exercised to straighten them. Did anyone spot a small mole about half the size of a dime beneath the right eye?"

"Nobody got a chance, Red. All the gang were masked."

"Ah! Anything else?"

Fox nodded. "Simpson left Cruces for the last time two days before the first hold-up."

"Where do the gang sleep? Some place in the interior?"

"Juan doesn't think so. His idea is that they split up and come back to Panama."

Henry stiffened. "Including Al?"

"Who can say? But he doesn't stay here in the name of Simpson."

"You haven't seen him—I mean, anyone who could be him?"

Fox shook his head. "I have kept a sharp look-out. And I haven't heard that anyone resembling him has visited tables in other establishments."

"Then he's not been sleeping in Panama. Nothing would keep him from gaming tables so long as he had money in his pockets. This man, Juan—will he keep on the look-out?"

"He will."

Henry was comforted. There was no suggestion of doubt in Fox's soft voice as he gave the assurance. But even had there been, Henry would not have been unduly disappointed. He was convinced that, sooner or later, Al would pay a visit to Panama City. He was too confirmed a spendthrift to be content with money rattling idly in his pocket. He would venture into the city. Once there, no power on earth would keep him away from the gaming tables.

"Anything different about the last robbery?" he questioned.

"Not that I've heard of. The bandits were on horse-back, and masked. They came out of the jungle without warning, threatened the muleteers and escort with their guns, drove off the mules which carried the gold, and disappeared as mysteriously as they had come."

"Were they followed?"

Fox shrugged. "Nobody thought of hiring Indians to follow the trail."

"The bandits must know the jungle well."

"They probably have some bad Indians with them."

"And some first-class spies here in Panama."

"Sure."

"Isn't anyone doing anything?"

"Yes. The express companies are sending to the States for weapons to arm their escorts. Tracy—he's the Wells-Fargo agent here—has written for a dozen Colt revolving rifles, two dozen pairs of revolvers, and two dozen Bowie knives. That display should make the bandits hesitate before attacking a convoy."

"How many are there?"

"More than forty held up the Zachrisson and Nelson train."

"Forty!" Henry whistled. "It needs a small army to convoy against as many as that."

"Sure—and they'll be needed next week."

Henry's interest sharpened. "Next week?"

"The *Northerner* is due about then, Nelson was telling me the other day, with more than two and a half million dollars in gold aboard, and a large number of returning prospectors who have struck rich." The bleak eyes observed Henry's face. "What is it, Red?"

"If the bandits don't try to ambush that shipment——"

"That's Nelson's conviction. He's worried."

Henry's eyes glowed. "I'm waiting for that convoy, Zachary. If La Pantera is there . . ."

II

The next week passed very pleasantly for Henry. He stayed with Zachary Fox, who had rented a spare bedroom in the upper floor of a small house near Plaza San Francisco.

The first two days Henry spent in looking for Abigail's Christmas present. His masculine eyes were tempted by a score of articles: exquisite silk shawls, of gold and silver thread from India; exotic négligés from China, many with a dragon motif; pieces of barbaric jewellery from the countries of South America. But each time he was deciding on a purchase the warning voice of common sense stopped him. Abigail, he reflected, was not a woman to appreciate feminine fripperies: she might even accuse him, in the dry voice she reserved for her deepest contempt, of regarding her as a woman of the brothels, to be seduced by the ostentatious display of gaudy and useless gew-gaws.

At the end of the second day he bought, for want of a better choice, a watch, an exquisitely-wrought piece with jewelled numerals and hands. It cost him several months' wages.

Each evening he spent at Fox's gaming-rooms, where he soon realized that the gambler's judgment had not been at fault in electing to remain behind at Panama. Fox had rented a floor above one of the innumerable saloons situated in the vicinity of Central Plaza; and during the comparatively few months he had been established there had attracted to the rooms as regular patrons the cream of Panamanian society. Night after night these people, prominent among the world's inveterate gamblers, played at one or another of the games of chance which he offered them, from poker and blackjack to faro and roulette. To these rooms came also, as he had foretold, transient Americans; more particularly returning prospectors, whose anxiety to follow a hunch that luck was with them was only equalled by that of the professional gamblers to meet the challenge. Play ran high at Zachary Fox's rooms. Many a small fortune changed hands overnight. And many a saddened, chastened man returned to California, humbly to seek a second chance at wresting wealth from the bosom of that generous, bounteous State.

One day the *Northerner* dropped anchor in the Bay. Within the hour a steady stream of cayucas was conveying its five hundred passengers ashore; five hundred heavy-pocketed, boisterous-mannered Californians, whose only thought was to spend and enjoy the golden harvest they had reaped from the rivers, the incredibly fertile plains, or the mushroom towns of California. They filled the hotels, the bars, and the brothels with their loud boasting, their rowdy songs, and their gold. All Panama City knew that great wealth had flowed into its streets that day, and all Panama did its best to see that some portion of it remained behind.

But in the offices of the express companies the local agents were gloomy. Theirs was the responsibility; to see that the two and a half million dollars' worth of gold, and five hundred prosperous travellers, safely reached their destination in the United States. To lessen the risk of a bandit raid it was decided among them to form a convoy of all the passengers, many of whom were armed with revolvers. Not only would this large number of armed men afford

N

one another mutual protection, but incidentally the gold also. Surely no sane bandits would attempt to hold up a caravan of such prodigious strength.

Every available animal was hired, whether horse or mule, to convey this small army of travellers to Gorgona. Muleteers were engaged. Early on the morning of departure for Chagres the convoy was assembled in some sort of formation—but nearly a mile separated the vanguard from the last man in the convoy.

"I don't like it, Red," Fox exclaimed. A heavy-eyed Fox, for he had risen at an unusually early hour to see Henry off. "There's more weakness than strength in a convoy of this length. If the bandits strike——"

"Will they dare? Men with guns are spaced regularly along the line." Henry laughed grimly. "And many of them are trigger-happy."

"I know, but look at the long line. What help will the people in the rear be able to give to those in the van if there is an attack? Half a dozen armed men could control the narrow track in both directions."

"The gold is in the middle. So are most of the hired guards."

"And you, Red?"

"I'll be near the gold, too, Zachary. If there's any attack on the convoy . . ."

Fox was not consciously aware of seeing Henry's hands move, but suddenly each was holding a six-shooter which was pointed with disconcerting directness at the pit of his stomach.

For once in a while the colourless eyes were startled into betraying their owner's thoughts. The gambler leaned forward and patted his companion's arm.

"That's the slickest draw I've seen, Red," he praised. "The pupil has outstripped his master."

"Incentive is a powerful aid."

"Yes," he muttered. "I can understand that." A shrill whistle echoed along the line of travellers. "Good luck, Red. Come and see me again as soon as you can."

The leading animals were whipped or heeled into action. Soon the whole long line of the convoy was lumbering along the old trail across the swampy lowlands which separated the city of

Panama from the interior. From the heights of the mountains for which they were heading the mile-long line of the convoy must have looked more like an undulating curtain of moving smoke; for a week's spell of hot weather had dried and powdered the surface of mud into a thick layer of fine dust, which the hooves of the pack-animals and the shuffling sandals of the muleteers stirred and tossed up into the air. So thick was the yellow cloud which hung over and about the convoy that it restricted visibility to a short distance in front and behind; and seeped into the noses and throats of the travellers, making them choke and swear.

But though the curtain of dust effectively concealed what was happening behind it, the noise of the convoy was revealing and travelled far afield: the thudding of hooves, the cracking of whips, and the shouts of the muleteers urging their animals onwards, combined to create a vast, muffled roar which made the distant jungle stir in uneasy alarm.

Progress was slow; and as the morning grew steadily hotter, and conditions worsened, the most hardened travellers fell into disconsolate silence and left the others to waste breath on cursing the necessity for such an unpleasant mode of travel. After a while even the grumblers turned quiet, for the word passed down the line that they were approaching the edge of the jungle; and among the strangers a feeling of tension was created and grew.

This feeling was not shared by Henry, whose knowledge of the country assured him that any attempt at robbing the convoy was unlikely to be made until they were on the far side of the snake-like pass in the mountains through which the railroad would ultimately run. Before that point the nature of the country made an ambush difficult in spite of deep ravines and narrow gorges. Besides, he reflected, the bandits would probably choose level ground for a hold-up because it would ensure easier escape routes for them. So, although he remained on the alert, he permitted himself the luxury of lazy meditation.

Now that, for the first time since leaving Boston, he was possibly within measurable distance of Al Simpson, he realized how much he hated the blackguard. He felt warmly jubilant at the prospect of first making Al metaphorically grovel at his feet, and then forcing the thief to write out a full confession. As soon as the

confession was safely in his pocket he would resign from his job
with the Railroad Company, and return to the United States.

What a moment that would be! So often during the past months
he had pictured the scene in his imagination, but it seemed more
real than ever before. His mother's face, tear-stained but so welcoming; so openly, so challengingly expressing her great love and trust.
. . . His father's, scored by Haitian years but softened by the crown
of hair, as thick and unruly in age as in early manhood, but now
snowy white—the two faces had never seemed clearer, but maybe
this was because the background of swirling yellow dust made them
as distinct as a daguerreotype.

At midday the convoy was halted for a two-hour siesta. Many
grumbled at the enforced delay, because they were in a hurry to
reach civilization. But the leader of the convoy was adamant. He
reclined in the shade of a palm, and watched the vegetation curl
and wilt beneath the sun's fiery caress.

The day grew hotter with cumulative heat; for the sky was
cloudless. The rising temperature silenced even the impatient
grumblers, and it was the leader who reluctantly had to spur the
others to rise. Like a giant sleepy snake the long train eased itself
into motion, and slithered forward into the jungle.

The hours passed. The convoy passed over the Continental
Divide, and thankfully began the descent into the Chagres valley.
By this time the majority of the travellers had grown contemptuous
of the threat of a hold-up; but for the remainder anxiety was just
beginning, for they were approaching that part of the trail where
previous hold-ups had been staged.

Here the green walls which bordered the trail were at their
thickest. Keen ears listened for warning sounds; keen eyes stared
anxiously into the mass of greenery in a hopeless endeavour to
pierce its depths. For all that could be seen, every trunk, or every
clump of ferns, or every full-leafed bough overhead might be
hiding a man. The guards moved like automatons, watching—
watching—waiting—waiting—watching.

Even so, they were taken by surprise.

A single shot . . .

Masked horsemen materialized from the green walls. They were
spaced at intervals along the length of the cumbersome, snake-like

convoy, some on one side, some on the other. Each brown or white hand held a cocked gun in it, which swung menacingly from side to side, covering many men within its arc.

"*Arriba!*" The command was barked by one who had appeared in the vicinity of the gold. He was the leader of the bandits, it seemed, for the word, in Spanish or English, rippled away from him, on either side, down to the man who blocked the way for the vanguard, and another who threatened the nethermost traveller.

"*Arriba!*" "Stand still!" "*Arriba!*" "Stay where you are!"

No other commands were necessary. No need to warn the members of the convoy not to move. The swinging muzzle of the guns did that more effectively than any voice.

The hold-up was a masterpiece of organization. The leader pointed to the gold-carrying mules with unerring instinct. Or pre-knowledge! Three of his followers whipped these mules into a twisting narrow cross-trail, where they soon disappeared from view. Two and a half million dollars' worth of gold disappearing from sight! And not one man dared move.

Another signal from the leader. The bandits moved towards the travellers from California. There were personal pickings to be had in addition to $2,500,000 worth of gold! Five hundred wealthy prospectors, every one with heavy pockets. Loot beyond the dreams of avarice!

One of the bandits made for a particularly prosperous-looking traveller. He crossed in front of Henry, concealing him for a fractional part of a second from the restless eyes of the leader. But time enough for Henry to draw. His gun flamed as the leader turned. The bullet made a loud thudding plonk as it struck human flesh. The brigand choked and fell, deaf to the gunfire which flared up all along the line. More bandits fell, for others of the travellers, also, were quick on the draw.

Then some of the bandits, having no stomach for lead, dropped their guns and raised their hands. Others spurred their animals into the green wall, and vanished.

"The gold . . ."

There was no need for the warning. A number of the travellers were already chasing along the cross-trail along which the gold had disappeared. They reached a clearing in time to see the gold being transferred from mule to horse-back. The brigands did not wait to complete their task. It was no use having gold in one's pocket if that meant a bullet in one's back! Discretion being the better part of wealth, they fled with one hundred thousand dollars' worth of gold and left the balance to be rounded up by the jubilant Americans.

All this Henry learned later, for he had left the pursuit of the gold to others. With shaky limbs he moved towards the dead leader of the bandits. He had not meant to kill, but only to cripple. A dead Al meant perpetual banishment from Massachusetts.

With unsteady fingers he pulled the concealing neckerchief away from the dead man's face. But it was completely strange to him.

CHAPTER TWENTY-TWO

NOR was the dead man The Panther.

"No, señor," admitted one of the captured bandits. "He is not La Pantera."

"This man was your leader, wasn't he?"

"Yes, señor."

"Who is he?"

"Tomas."

"Tomas who?"

The bandit shrugged. "Who knows? He came from Chile."

The leader of the convoy, who was the questioner, gazed at the face of the dead man. "I've seen him before."

"Probably, señor. He was a muleteer. Like me, and some of the others."

"If the Chilean isn't La Pantera, who is?"

The prisoner shrugged, and remained silent. The convoy leader kicked the prisoner in the ribs. "Answer, you dog. Who is La Pantera?" He swung his foot to and fro in a suggestive manner.

The muleteer swallowed. "I don't know, señor. None of us knows."

Henry broke in. "Is he an American?"

"Yes, señor."

"Has he a small mole under the right eye?"

The bandit looked surprised. "Yes, señor."

The convoy leader turned to Henry. "Do you know him?"

"Yes. Name of Albert Simpson."

"Ah!" To the prisoner again. "You said the Chilean was your leader."

"He was."

"But The Panther——"

"He, too, was our leader."

"Damn your lying, twisted tongue! How could you have two leaders?"

"La Pantera organized the hold-ups; Tomas led them."

"Didn't La Pantera take part in them?"

"Only from the rear. He says keeping in the rear is the art of good generalship."

"Yellow——"

"No, señor." There was a note of pride and respect in the bandit's denial. "A good general must keep in the rear to be in a position to see what is happening, and give commands."

"Sounds like one of Al's arguments," Henry commented.

"Yah!" jeered the convoy leader. "Was he in the rear today?"

"He was somewhere, señor."

"Where is the gang's headquarters?"

"We haven't one——"

The swinging foot brought an agonized gasp from the bandit. "Where?"

"I swear, by the Virgin Mary, señor."

"Dog!" The leader's kick was vicious. "Where?"

The bandit shook his head. "It was always being changed," he gasped painfully. "Ask the others . . ."

The other prisoners confirmed that neither La Pantera nor his gang had a permanent headquarters. They met, it seemed, only when a hold-up was contemplated the following day or so; and on those occasions the meeting-place was passed on from member to member, by word of mouth.

When it was apparent that no more information was to be

obtained from the prisoners, the convoy leader waved his hand at the jungle walls.

"String 'em up," he ordered. "We haven't time to waste. . . ."

II

Abigail's welcome perplexed Henry. He had been absent from Chagres little longer than his normal work periods in the Black Swamp; but this time her greeting kiss was deeper, and more lingering. She seemed reluctant to take her arms away from him, and when he showed her the Christmas present he had brought back for her she looked at him with eyes that, had they been another's, he would have believed were nigh to tears.

"Is that why you insisted upon going to Panama?"

He nodded. "There was nothing here."

"And I believed . . ." She looked away. "Did you see Mr. Fox? How is he doing? What . . ." She asked many questions.

So Henry gave her an account of everything that had happened since he had left Chagres; and when he had finished she kissed him again, and gazed at him with an expression which puzzled him for hours afterwards. If he had not believed such an explanation impossible in her case he would have identified it as uneasiness—nervousness—fear. . . .

This mysterious, tantalizing quirk persisted, but there was something else strange about her of which he first became aware the following morning: a slight sharpness in her voice which was not in conformity with her outward attitude towards him. He felt certain that some inner worry was troubling her, the existence of which she was resolutely trying to ignore. It did not take him too long to solve that particular mystery. A word here . . . a vague hint there. . . . In spite of good intentions not to, she resented his defiance of her wishes, even though his principal reason for doing so had been indirectly on her account.

The barrier between them which his going to Panama had raised did not disappear with time. It persisted, even as her strange fear persisted; but both were too slight to spoil their companionship to any great extent. It was just that they were there in the background; a warning to them both, perhaps, that their liaison was vulnerable. . . .

III

Cliff Armstrong had taken over James McCollum's job. Cliff was all right in his own way, but Henry missed Jimmy's sense of dry humour, his patient explanations of difficult or tricky problems, his quick decisions. More than anything else he missed Jimmy's easy companionship. Cliff was the boss, first and foremost.

He welcomed Henry with a quick nod of his head. "Morning, Malley. Received your letter—just! The man who brought it was screwed to his back teeth by the time he reached the hotel."

"He was the only man I felt like trusting——"

"All right! All right! I received it. That's all that matters. But it's not a habit of mine to grant extra leave without being given the option to refu—to discuss the suggestion."

Henry grinned. Armstrong had been quick to choke back the word 'refuse'. However much he might have 'discussed' the suggestion of extra leave, given the opportunity to do so beforehand, he wouldn't have dared to refuse the wish. One didn't take chances of having an employee walk out on one. Employees, especially on the executive staff, were too scarce. Too many of them, after a week's tryout, hadn't the guts to carry on. The extra pay didn't make up for the discomfort and risk.

Armstrong continued, "Anyway, you justified the leave. That was a fancy piece of shooting you did. Are you sorry it wasn't La Pantera himself?"

Henry gazed at the surveyor. "Who told you about the shooting, Mr. Armstrong? And about La Pantera?"

The other man laughed shortly. "You don't expect anything to remain secret in this country, do you? It was all round Chagres and Manzanillo, the morning after you shot that Chilean bandit, that you were gunning for La Pantera. Guess he knows it himself by now."

"The morning after——"

"Sure. The news reached here quicker than any man could have brought it. But ask me how, and your guess is as good as mine."

Armstrong eyed Henry's guns. "Now that you've blooded those guns of yours, Malley, don't get over confident and dive for them at the slightest provocation."

The same advice that Jim Braddock had given him; this time given with less trust and more condescension.

"Are you giving me that warning because I have red hair?"

"Well, haven't you?" Armstrong asked drily. "I haven't noticed that you're an angel when things don't go the way you like."

"Is my face that expressive, Mr. Armstrong?"

"It is." Armstrong grew more friendly, and clapped Henry on the shoulder. "Let's get going. We've got to check that gradient by the cemetery."

As the two men left the surveyor's office Henry was astonished to see how much the settlement had increased in size even during the short while he had been in Panama. More storehouses had been erected near the pier already built. Another pier was in the making. New machine shops had been built; a boat-building slip. Two Chinese had set up businesses near the saloon; one, a store, the other a laundry. Outside another building that was nearly finished a hand-lettered bill announced that Mr. Cy. Hawkins would shortly be opening a first-class barbering establishment for the convenience of gentlemen; at cheapest rates for best and reliable workmanship; open at all hours from sun-up to sun-down.

Right next to the future barber was a future saloon, 'Jake's Liquor Saloon, from Little Bend, Mo., Home from Home, Famous throughout the Civilized World for Hard Liquors served Soft. Come to Jake's next week, and tell him about your Home Town. Jake will know it. There ain't Nowhere Jake hasn't Visited. Home from Home. Hard Liquors served Soft. Only Your Favourite Brands Stocked.'

Farther afield, following the shore-line, more and more shacks, built on stilts, had gone up to house the ever-increasing labour force. Already there were enough dwellings to taint the air with the stench of the slops and refuse which were daily flung out of them into the morass which separated the buildings.

They reached the pile-driver, but its progress did not match the growth of the settlement. It had moved forward along the

routed line no more than a matter of yards. Just far enough for
mule-drawn carts to be substituted for the barrows which had been
used originally for the cartage of the filling material. The Irish foreman was still supervising the fill, but there was an expression of
resignation on his face as he sucked at his old pipe and swore good-
naturedly at the labourers. Once upon a time there had been a
bottomless pit . . . And faith! To think he'd once misbelaved
them fairy tales, to be shure!

One day was very much like another, and Henry fell quickly
into the old routine. Work was now proceeding simultaneously in
three places: on Manzanillo Island, on the mainland opposite, and
at Gatún. Moreover, with the end of the rainy season the sickness
cases had fallen to more normal levels. To work hour after hour in
broiling, continuous sunshine was trying enough, but preferable to
alternate sun and rain.

With the end of the rains Henry congratulated himself on
having been one of the few foreigners to work the season through
without falling sick. He rejoiced too soon. One morning, on rising
from the truckle bed he occupied in one of the executives' sleeping
huts, his head began to throb with agonizing intensity; and his
teeth chattered in a paroxysm of shivering. With a groan of misery
he relaxed back on to the palliasse, and scrabbled the thin bed-
clothing round his shoulders in an effort to get warm.

Armstrong shared the hut. When he heard the groan he crossed
the floor in his stockinged feet, and laid his hand on the fevered
forehead. He made a gesture of resignation. There was not a man
on the railroad pay-roll who, by now, could not recognize at a
glance the symptoms of the scourge which persistently ravaged all
those not born in the tropics.

"Malaria!" he grunted.

As if the word were a cue, Henry weakly raised himself on one
elbow and vomited. Armstrong soaked a handkerchief in a bowl of
water, and cleaned away the yellow froth which dribbled from the
pallid, trembling lips. No sooner had he done this than Henry's
helpless bowels evacuated and stained the bedding.

The surveyor hastily lighted a cigar. "It's the hospital for you,
old man," he added, with a casualness that had as its source familiarity rather than lack of sympathy; for similar scenes were a daily

occurrence, and inevitable. Besides, had he himself not been a victim not four months ago?

Henry felt as if his body were stiffening. "Home . . ." he gasped. "Not hospital—home——"

From behind a fog of spiralling blue smoke Armstrong nodded his head. "Leave it to me, old man. We'll see. . . ."

So Henry was taken home by a steamer that was on the point of leaving for Chagres. Within the hour he was in his own bed, being nursed by Abigail. When a tired-eyed doctor arrived he shook his head in doubt after examining the injected eyes, furred tongue, and yellow skin.

"It's a bad case," he warned Abigail. "Be ready for renewed vomiting and diarrhoea. And he may become light-headed for a time."

Henry clasped Abigail's hand in a hot grasp. "Jean—Jean . . . don't leave me. . . ."

The doctor glanced at Abigail. "Are you Jean?"

"No," she sharply denied. "He's wandering."

"I'll come back soon," the doctor promised. "He should begin to sweat in a few hours' time."

Henry's mind wandered far afield in between lucid periods. He wandered in a distorted world in which every man had the face of Al Simpson; and every woman, Jean's. He relived the past in a queer jumble of fact and fantasy. In company with Al he revisited gaming establishments, where his emotions were magnified ten-fold: he suffered torture in gambling away his father's home to a leering Al, but a moment later his heart was racing with jubilation at winning a fortune in gold bricks. Then he began to struggle furiously as disembodied memory entered into the saloon of the Californian Hotel, and he saw Al pushing dollar notes into Jean's bosom. Abigail had to exert all her unusual strength to hold him down, but her lips twitched with sadness when she heard the alarm in his voice as he called out to Jean to keep away: "Keep away from that man, Jean—he's a bandit and robber. . . ."

During those hours he often talked to Jean in rambling sentences that were mostly disconnected, but which laid bare his soul. Again and again he reproached himself for not knowing how much he loved her until it was too late. And every time Abigail cooled his forehead with a wet handkerchief it was Jean he thanked. "Thank you, my darling. My lovely, lovely Jean. . . ."

Abigail discovered unsuspected traits in his character, which consciousness kept locked up. She had known that he was obstinate and wilful and proud, but not how obstinate, how wilful, or how proud. Beneath the veneer of his urban upbringing his soul was as rugged as the Scottish mountain crags which ringed the birthplace of countless Stewarts before him. Because this was so he would never return to Boston without proof of his innocence; nor would he allow any scruple to stand in the way of his obtaining it. For that scrap of paper, which alone would assuage his offended pride, there was no sacrifice he would not make.

Her discovery might have alarmed women of lesser calibre; but where his character was concerned she revelled in the knowledge. Was not her own, in its own way, equally indomitable, equally without minor scruples? It was the future she feared, not the present. When Greek meets Greek . . . Yesterday she had had no doubts about the outcome of any tussle between them. Today . . . she was less certain. For the advantage was now his. He was young and virile. He could afford to take chances. Whereas she . . . She touched the flesh beneath her eyes, where only two days ago she had detected a new line. She smoothed her hair with a nervous gesture; a subconscious desire to bury more deeply the first grey hair to show itself.

A few hours later he was quiet and sweating. As she gazed down at his rueful boyish grin she could scarcely associate it with the patient of an hour ago. Could that cheeky, diffident expression really belong to the granite-like man whose real soul had been bared to her in those hours of light-headed ramblings? She had always considered herself an acute observer of human nature. For the first time in many years she felt unsure of herself. The knowledge was chastening. . . .

IV

The fever waned and waxed, and waned again. At the end of the third week of convalescence Henry was fit for work. It so happened that the morning he reported back to Armstrong marked a milestone in the history of Manzanillo Island. . . .

By chance he was in the vicinity of the pier as a ship from Carthagena was being warped alongside. Baldwin and Armstrong were there, too; and the Irish foreman in charge of the pile-driver. It was he who drew the attention of his companions to the ship.

"Begod! A shipload of women! Or is me eyes desaving me?"

"Women!" Baldwin turned quickly. The other two men also. Looking at the ship from Cathagena they were astonished to see a row of smiling brown faces lining the rails. Young faces, with thick lips, white teeth, and saucy rolling eyes.

"What the heck . . ." Baldwin exclaimed.

"Women!" The Irishman yelled in a gleeful, wondering shout. "Women!" he repeated in a still louder voice.

The sound travelled far and wide. Work came to a faltering stop as every man within sight stared at the smiling faces and waving hands. As comprehension dawned, a cheer was started: loud, long, and hearty. . . .

"What are they doing here?" Baldwin went on.

Tobacco-tinted saliva dribbled down the foreman's stubbly beard. "Glory be to God!" he roared, slapping his thigh with a huge horny hand. " 'Tis the foinest sight me eyes has seen since the face of O'Toole after I bate him up. 'Tis meself that will be after seeking their company as soon as me work is finished tonight. Look at that one, now—the third from the right, sor," he continued ecstatically. "Whin did ye ever see the like? May the blessed Saints be praised that me old woman ain't here to clap eyes on them wenches."

"A boatload of whores!" Armstrong gasped. "I'll be damned!"

"Shure!" the foreman agreed. "A boatload of dusky belles. 'Tis civilization that's come to the island at last."

The girls landed, and established themselves in a row of recently-erected huts. Their coming proved a mixed blessing, for there were too few of them and too many impatient men. There was a series of savage fights that night which cost one life, three serious injuries, and several minor ones. On the credit side was the fact that there were more contented faces the next day; and some men worked with a better will.

A few days later another boatload of whores arrived, this time from Havana, who set up alongside their darker-skinned sisters from Carthagena.

As the Irish foreman said, with a lewd chuckle, "Manzanillo's growing up."

CHAPTER TWENTY-THREE

THE fill went on, day after day. In spite of the foreman's pessimism, the tens of thousands of tons of rock that were shot into the oozing mud finally produced results. By slow degrees there emerged from the surface of the island a solid road that would eventually be firm enough to carry rolling-stock.

By this time the growing settlement established on the north shore of Manzanillo Island had gotten itself the name of Otro Lado. The Other Side! Nobody was quite sure who was first responsible for the christening. Probably the Irish foreman, who had a morbid sense of humour. But it was equally hell for quite a number of other people, so it could quite well have been any one of a couple of hundred men.

By this time, few ports of the same size were anywhere busier. Except when weather conditions interfered, few were the days when there were not at least two ships discharging, and others anchored in the bay waiting for accommodation. Storehouses were filled to bursting-point. Dock-sides were crammed with materials which did not have to be kept under cover.

One day in February a ship arrived from Philadelphia with a locomotive, rails, and a small number of open cars. A red-letter day for Otro Lado. Not only was the locomotive a symbol, as it were, of the purpose for which the island was being transformed from a belt of miasmic swamp to a railroad terminal, but still more important was the fact that, with rolling-stock available, progress would be considerably speeded up. Within a matter of hours, track-laying crews were at work.

Before long a steel road connected the dock with the farther-most limit of the filling operations. The trucks were loaded with rock, the locomotive fired and coupled up with the trucks. To the accompaniment of its own shrill whistle, and the enthusiastic cheers of hundreds of labourers, the locomotive began to chuff-chuff-chuff along the track.

From that moment the speed of progress increased out of all proportion in comparison with that of the months before the arrival of the locomotive. As quickly as the road foundations rose above the mud the track crew laid another section for the train to go forward. When the track reached the far side of the island, work was begun on making and filling up a causeway to connect the island with the mainland.

Meanwhile, round the corner of Toro Point, Chagres was still as busy as ever. As more and more gold was shipped back to the United States from the gold-fields of California, more and more of the world's restless inhabitants flocked towards that fabulous Eldorado—tinkers, tailors, soldiers, sailors, rich men (yes, even rich men, whose object was to establish commercial concerns destined to make them even richer), poor men, beggar-men, thieves. Especially thieves. Never was the old nursery rhyme more in tune with modern days.

To cope with the ever-increasing number of emigrants the Howland and Aspinwall engineering works at Otro Lado designed and built a new, fast steamer. On 6th February the *William H. Aspinwall* joined the other steamers already engaged in ferrying passengers up and down the river. Although she carried four hundred passengers, and covered the double journey to Gorgona in one day, there was still too little accommodation for all those anxious to reach California in a hurry. Many still went by cayuca. But some of these travellers did not reach their destination. What bandits could do on a grand scale boatmen could do equally well in a more modest way. And more efficiently. It was too easy. A quick stab, and the job was done. After that it was a simple matter to drop the body overboard. The alligators would probably make a good job of disposing of it. And if not . . . well, there was nobody to ask awkward questions.

II

This time it was Henry who objected to the idea of a journey.

"Oh! Henry dear, would you mind staying at an hotel next time you return on leave?"

"Why?"

"I've arranged to go off on a journey next week with Pedro Romanos and Piérola."

"To Panama?"

"No, to the source of the Chagres."

He dropped the old copy of the *New York Herald* he had been reading on the floor. "Are you mad?"

"Don't be insulting, Henry."

"I'm sorry," he apologized ungraciously. "But that's 'way back in the interior."

She nodded. "I know."

"You can't go there, Abigail."

"Why not?"

"Good God! Why not! You know why not as well as I do, Abigail. That part of the country has probably never been explored—at any rate, not since Spanish days——"

"That's why I'm going. You forget that I'm an explorer, Henry."

"You can't go so deep into the interior, Abigail," he argued obstinately. "Apart from the fact that you'd just as easily get lost as not. . . . Anyway, what the hell does Piérola know of the interior? I'll bet he's never been there——"

"Go on," she said frostily.

"It's not safe for any white person to enter the Cuna-Cuna country. The Indians there are killers."

"I haven't studied this country for the past year without learning something about the different tribes of Indian inhabitants, their homes, and their habits. I doubt whether I should find the journey any more dangerous than one to Panama."

"Abigail——"

"Should I?" she demanded angrily. "How many travellers on their way to Panama have been murdered during the past few weeks? How many trains have been held up by bandits lately?"

"There have been one or two minor hold-ups, I know.
But I don't know any white man who would dare to risk going
into the interior without a damn' powerful escort, still less a
woman. . . ."

He knew, by her expression, that he had said the wrong thing.
He cursed silently for having dragged her sex into the matter. He
should have remembered her fear of being thought feminine. . . .

"Why should you want to go there, anyway? The source of
one river is much the same as any other, I guess."

"How ridiculously you argue. No two places in this world are
ever the same—to one who has the wit to appreciate the difference,"
she scornfully told him. "I am no arm-chair writer, Henry. I write
only of what I personally experience. Second-hand accounts are of
no use to me."

"It wouldn't be safe, Abigail."

"But I'm going all the same," she informed him.

Thanks to her icy manner and rigorous self-control the argument did not develop into a quarrel, but it spoiled the remainder of
his leave. When he said good-bye to her, as he left for the Black
Swamp, his kiss was little more than a dutiful peck.

In spite of work, during the next few days he was not able to
forget his disagreement with Abigail. It was all very well for her
to point out that she had spent half a lifetime exploring some of the
danger-spots of the world, he reflected, but none of them had as
bad a reputation as those jungles and mountains of New Granada,
which lay far from the established routes and trails. He had come
into contact with the San Blas Indians and was aware that they
tolerated the white man only so long as he remained in that part
of the country that was now tacitly his by right, as it were, of
Spanish conquest. But that same white man strayed across the
border-line at his peril, especially after nightfall. Yet these
coastal Indians, who would cheerfully accept the possible consequences of killing a white man, were themselves in awe of the
fiercer mountainous tribes.

He had no faith in her companion's capabilities as escort. The
Panamanians were probably reliable, and conscientious, but that
wouldn't be enough to bring the party safely back from a trek into
the Cuna-Cuna country. Only a full-blooded Indian, whose

instincts and intuition might to some extent compensate for lack of topography, could hope to do that. Such a man would doubtless divine the ultimate destination of doubtful crosstrails; and would be able to smell danger ahead in time to avoid it.

It was not as if the hostile attitude of the Indians towards the white man was the only danger. Besides the risk of being killed by Indian arrows or spears, they might all-too-easily get lost in the jungle and starve to death. Or killed by a jaguar, an alligator, a poisonous reptile, a poisonous berry—there were a score of ways of dying in the jungle—to say nothing of the ubiquitous fevers. . . .

Now that it was too late he regretted not having obtained leave of absence from the company so that he might have accompanied her. Not that he would have been of much help in guarding against the many dangers, but—he would have been one extra. And, well, he could shoot, couldn't he? Better than most men. Or at any rate, quicker. Constant practice at drawing his guns had tightened his reflexes, even developed in him a warning sense of physical danger. Already this sense, and first-class shooting, had saved one man's life. Something had made him turn, without reason, in the direction of a Negro labourer who had been carrying one of the five-inch theodolites. He fired just as the fer-de-lance drew back its pitted head for a strike. . . . He chilled at the thought of Abigail's fate should she chance to approach too close to one of these vicious reptiles. They weren't like some snakes, afraid of noise and movement. The damned things were quite as likely to attack first. . . .

This constant worry soon began to affect his work, and eventually brought him into conflict with Armstrong. Neither man was in the best of health; no foreigner was, after a first attack of fever; a periodic recurrence of which could only be avoided by constant dosing with quinine, and the taking of immediate precautions upon the first warning symptom. Unfortunately, too, her departure coincided with a long period of almost continuous dry weather, during which the day temperatures had not once fallen below 90 degrees. The unbroken spell had frayed the nerves of most of the workers. Quarrels and fights had become a constant menace. In less than a week more than ten bodies had been carried to the Mount Hope cemetery as a direct result of fights or mêlées. Even in Chagres the latent antagonism between Americans and

Panamanians had flared up, and developed into a riot which had cost three lives, including one by lynching.

"For Christ's sake, Malley, did you check for curvature and refraction in your figures for the Mindi observation?"

Henry tried to remember, but his mind worked slowly: he had slept badly the night before, twice awaking from terrifying dreams about Abigail.

"I can't remember, sir——"

"Well, you didn't," Armstrong snapped. "Minus four over three kd cubed be damned! Kd squared is the correction for refraction——"

"I'm sorry——"

"It's not good enough, Malley. Ever since Miss Vandusen went off on that bloody stupid exploration of hers, you've mooned around."

Red hair plus frayed nerves, "You'll take that back, Armstrong ——about Miss Vandusen's exploration being bloody stupid——"

"Take back nothing!" the surveyor barked. "Who cares whether the Indians have one wife or two? She needs her god-damned brains tested——"

Henry aimed for the sneering mouth. He split the lower lip and caused blood to trickle down the unshaven cheek. Armstrong gasped, then made a wild uppercut. . . .

They were evenly matched. Henry's quicker reflexes and raging fury compensated for his lighter weight. For some minutes it was hammer and tongs; but when they drew apart, exhausted and panting heavily, Armstrong gasped unexpectedly.

"Hold it, Malley. We oughtn't to be fighting like this."

"You said——"

"Hell! I didn't mean it. I shouldn't have said it. It's the god-damned sun. It never stops shining. . . . If I apologize . . ."

Henry nodded. He knew Armstrong wasn't yellow, and could have carried on. "You don't have to, sir. I knew you didn't really mean what you said about her. I think I was spoiling for something, too."

They solemnly shook hands, and, up-ending the chairs they had knocked over, sat down.

"I'm glad nobody else was about to see us make fools of ourselves, Malley," Armstrong said, wiping the blood and sweat from his face. "You really are worried, aren't you?"

"Yes."

"I'm not sure that you have to be. Miss Vandusen is a seasoned traveller. I'm sure she can look after herself. Besides, the Indians may respect a woman."

"There are other dangers." Henry realized that his head was throbbing. He must have banged it harder than he had thought at the time, when he cannoned off the wall at one moment. "I did my best to persuade her," he explained wearily.

Armstrong nodded sagely. "You can't argue with a woman once she's made up her mind. Especially with Miss Vandusen, of all people." His voice turned formal. "Of course, we forget this ever happened, Malley?"

"Of course."

Thus the incident passed off, and was never referred to again. Both men acknowledged privately that the weather was chiefly to blame. Nevertheless, although their relations continued on a more-or-less pleasant basis, thereafter there was an undercurrent of wariness in their behaviour to each other.

III

Henry did not go to the hotel during his leave. When he tried to book a room he found out that the place was more crowded than ever. There was not a foot of space to spare for any sort of sleeping accommodation. Not even a hammock. So he went on to the house, deciding en route that he was glad that the hotel was too full to take him in. Even if the house should prove lonely without Abigail, the privacy of its silent emptiness would be preferable to the overcrowded hotel. As for meals, they were to be had at any of the restaurants.

To his surprise, when he went to bed that night, he felt less lonely than he had expected. Of course, the fact that Abigail and he always occupied separate beds made him less sensitive to her absence, but still . . . Well, it was her own fault, he comforted himself. If she would insist upon keeping him out of her bed except on the few occasions when she was moved by desire, she couldn't expect him to be too dismally aware that she was away, could she?

This reflection, he convinced himself, was not made in a spirit of annoyance. He had missed her earlier on in the evening; and would have gone along to some place for a little gaiety but for feeling too tired. No, he missed her as an intellectual and always interesting companion, he decided. But not as a wife. Somehow the physical side of life had come to mean less and less to him during the past few months. This worried him exceedingly. The prospect of losing interest at his age was alarming. And incomprehensible —unless the fever had done something to him—or the conditions of work, perhaps: the weakening effects of sun and rain; the miasmic swamp vapours. . . . Or perhaps he was suffering the after-effects of having his blood sucked by a vampire. Two nights before McCollum had left Manzanillo he had knocked a vampire from Henry's toe. Perhaps, he reflected, as he remembered the incident, the vampire had injected some sort of sterilizing poison into his system when first sinking its sharp incisors into his flesh.

After further reflection had disposed of this horrible thought, he decided that the blame for his own lack of enthusiasm was not initially his, but hers. Of late he had sensed in her connubial partnership a growing suggestion of hesitation; of scorn with herself for not rising superior to the call of the flesh. This mood had had its inevitable reaction. Every succeeding surrender had become less impulsive, more resistant. And therefore, from his point of view, less satisfying. Just lately, instead of happy relaxation, intercourse had induced a feeling of frustration.

Loyalty and respect soon made him feel disgusted with the trend of his thoughts, which had been no more than the rambling reflections of a physically-exhausted man. He turned over on his side, resolutely determined not to dwell upon such matters again. He was soon asleep.

The next night, while he was dining at a Chinese restaurant that had opened some months previously, his thoughts turned to Lucy. He felt in a mood for dancing, and had the money to buy her time. So why not? He hadn't danced in months. Not since the one and only time he had danced with her, in fact. Abigail did not like dancing. That was possibly because she was a bad dancer. She held herself too stiffly, subconsciously averse to being led by her male partner. Besides, she looked upon dancing as a waste of time.

So he went along to the Californian, and entered the saloon. There had been little change during the past year. The room was more crowded, and there was a hole in one of the gilded mirrors which looked as if it had been made by a bullet. Otherwise he might have been there the night before, for all the difference he could see. Even some of the women on the dance-floor he recognized, especially one who always danced with an inch of her tongue protruding from her thick lips. And the men dancing with the women were doing all the things the men of that other night had done—hugging them, slobbering down their necks, fumbling in their bosoms.

He looked eagerly for Lucy, but she was nowhere to be seen. Maybe she would return in a few minutes, he thought. He went over to the bar and ordered a drink. He made the drink last some while, but still she had not returned. Another reflection occurred to him. Perhaps she was upstairs with a man. He ordered another drink, which he gulped down. He knew he was a fool living in a dream-world when he tried to delude himself that she was not like the other bold-faced, hard-eyed women; that *she* was a dancing hostess only. All the same he boggled at the idea of associating her mischievous mouth and limpid eyes with the beastly, filthy sale of her shapely little body to drunken, leering, lecherous passers-by. No, no, no!

But she did not return, although he stayed for another hour.

Nor was she there the next night, or the night after. He concluded that she had gone back to the United States.

The week passed more pleasantly than, a few months ago, he would have expected. He did nothing but laze in the shade of the verandah at the back of the house. He had bought a rocking-chair some months back, and hour after hour he rocked and rocked and rocked, while his thoughts ambled dreamily.

On the last day of his leave he wandered along the street to the Chinese restaurant. He felt unusually refreshed, and ready for another week's work in the swamp. He had nearly reached his destination when he heard someone hailing him.

"Hey there, stranger!"

He turned and looked into a pair of melting eyes.

"Lucy! I've been looking for you all week."

"Where?"

"At the Californian."

"I left there some months ago."

"Where are you? I thought you must have gone back to the States."

"Me! The States!" She laughed scornfully. "Not for Lucy. I'm enjoying myself."

"But where?"

Her laughter changed to mischief. "The House of All Nations," she replied, waving her hand at a building on the other side of the street.

CHAPTER TWENTY-FOUR

Lucy—The House of All Nations. . . . He didn't want to believe . . . No, no, *no*!

As always, his expressive face betrayed him.

"It's true, honey." She frowned with perplexity, adding, "Are you really disgusted?"

"No-n-no—not really."

He was a bad liar. The melting eyes opened wider in surprise. "What's different between that and the Californian? 'Cept it's high-class stuff. The Frenchies certainly know how to run a house."

"Frenchies?"

"Sure, Red. Man and wife." Her face grew eager. "You're looking more prosperous than the last time I seen you."

He nodded.

"You must've struck it rich in California. I thought you weren't going there to dig gold."

"I didn't go. I haven't left the country, Lucy. I'm working on the railroad."

"Gee! You one of that tough bunch? But you ain't been coming to Chagres, have you?"

"Yes."

"How come I ain't run across you then, all the time we've been about?"

"Perhaps you're not about much when I am."

"That's true enough." She laughed merrily. "I ain't much of a daytime girl. This is the first time I seen daylight in weeks." She looked up at his face. "Where you off to, Red?"

"The Chinese Restaurant." He added on impulse, "Care to join me?"

"What you doing after eating?"

"Nothing."

"If I come with you will you come back with me to The House?"

"I——"

"Just for a look-see and a dance," she added scornfully, after a glance at his face. "You don't have to sleep with anyone."

Why not? he thought. He had heard enough stories of The House of All Nations to make him curious. He had nothing better to do. Why not take advantage of the opportunity?

"All right."

She slipped her tiny hand into the crook of his arm. "Let's go," she said gaily.

He enjoyed the meal. In fact, they both did. But half-way through the meal she surprised a smile on his lips at the wrong moment.

She stopped speaking, and pouted. "Why are you laughing, Red?" she demanded with suspicion. "What have I said?"

He mollified her with a lie. He dared not tell her the truth, for the reflection that had brought the smile to his lips was the contrast between her light-hearted, inconsequential chatter, and Abigail's invariably interesting conversation. Lucy's unceasing monologue consisted mainly of a commentary on the people and places of Chagres, told with a puckish sense of humour that added zest to her words. But so trivial was it all that, five minutes later, he found himself unable to recollect a word of what she had told him.

However, at one point he did manage to slip in a discreet question about herself. Why had she taken to that way of life? Money, no doubt. . . .

To his surprise, money—an easy way of making money—had not been her motive. Nor had she had an illegitimate child, committed a legal offence, nor had an unhappy childhood. She was quite frank. She was a prostitute solely and simply because she enjoyed a prostitute's life. She loved men, and more particularly the excitement of change. She wouldn't have been happy living most of her life with one man, she stated emphatically. She thrilled at the variety of male approach; and collected experiences with the avidity of a miser collecting gold.

At first her answer gave him strange pleasure. It comforted him to know that she liked men for their own sake, and not for what she could induce them to give her. But this mood passed when he inspected her tiny impish face, because her admission finally and irrevocably destroyed any belief in her innocence.

Damn her melting eyes! he thought in anger. Damn her ingenuous, wistful face! Nothing but devices of the Devil, calculated to deceive.

His anger passed away almost as quickly as his previous satisfaction. What the hell! It really didn't concern him whether or no she was a whore; whether she looked like one or not; whether she sold herself merely for money, or for erotic excitation.

After the meal they walked down the street towards The House of All Nations. Because of the darkness he could not see the building, but he had seen it often enough in the past for its exterior to be clear enough in his imagination. A square frame-building, little different from its neighbours save in having many more windows on the upper floor. These suggested the existence of more, but smaller, rooms—bedrooms, he did not doubt! There was one other minor difference, however. The main entrance to The House was discreetly at the side, instead of facing the road, as did the majority of the buildings in Chagres.

They reached the house and walked down a hard-core path to the entrance. All windows were curtained, but there was plenty of noise: music and the loud hum of conversation.

"Good evening, monsieur." A man bowed to Henry as they entered the house: he was an expansive bow-fronted man, and had a pasty face with a moustache and a half-imperial which vaguely reminded Henry of pictures of the Prince-President of the French

Republic, Louis Bonaparte. He had dark Latin eyes, under which the flesh was pouchy and black. His black hair was oiled, but incongruously curly. He looked like a satyr in French clothes.

"Oh! So there you are, *chèrie*," the Frenchman continued, after an appraising glance at her companion. He chucked her under the chin, and added, with a leering chuckle, "Madame and I were nearly thinking of sending out the search-party, no!" Henry had a feeling that the Frenchman's greeting would have been very different had she not been accompanied by a prospective client.

"Monsieur Duchamp." Lucy waved a careless hand in his direction. "This is Mr.—Mr——" She looked up at him from under drooping eyelids, and smiled mischievously. "What's your name, Red?"

"Malley."

"Enchanted, Monsieur Malley. We have not seen you here before, no?"

"No."

"Then I hope this visit will not be your only one to The House of All Nations. We try hard to please our clients *n'cest-ce pas, chèrie?*"

"Sure." She pulled at Henry's arm. "Come on, Red. I'm mad to dance."

"What about a drink first, while I look round?"

She nodded. "A quick one, then. My feet are itchy."

As they turned away from the door he realized that they were in a large room, which probably occupied half the total area of the ground floor. Of this space in turn nearly half, in the centre of the room, comprised the dance-floor. The remainder, except for one corner into which three instrumentalists had been squeezed, was filled with tables and chairs. Most of the tables were already occupied: a few by men who had already chosen their companions for the evening. But as the evening was still early, most of the men were content, meanwhile, to drink and take their time about selecting the particular woman each one wanted from among those who sat on sofas against the wall, or danced with one another.

Drinks were being served by brown-skinned waiters; local Panamanians. When Henry looked for the bar he could not see one.

Lucy laughed when he spoke about this.

"That is to prevent too much drinking, which might lead to a rough-house. Madame likes to keep the house refined, and Monsieur doesn't like to pay out for damage done during a brawl. And between you and me, Red—" she lowered her voice—"if the men aren't standing up at a bar they can't see what is poured into their glasses. So, no bar!"

Henry looked about him once more, this time with perplexed eyes. There was something about the room which made it different from any saloon he had seen in the United States, or even in Panama. For a time he could not see what caused the difference, but it became plain when he glanced at the walls. Instead of showing the bare timbers, relieved only by an occasional gaudy oleograph, and perhaps a wall clock, the walls were concealed by hangings of local folk-weave, with panels of oriental silk. The timbered ceiling had been painted a deep sapphire blue, with half a dozen silver stars scattered about to give the suggestion of approaching dusk. The oil-lamps, suspended from the ceiling, were concealed by silk tinted a sunset shade. Against the wall at frequent intervals were sofas upholstered in gay colours.

The atmosphere of voluptuousness was heightened by the contrast between the superficial appearance of exotic luxury and the primitive simplicity of all the other buildings in Chagres. Henry realized that only a man with ice-water in his veins would be able to remain in the room for long without becoming a victim of its pernicious influence. Even the smoky atmosphere seemed impregnated with the crude fragrance of native scents distilled from Khuskhus grass, or the leaves of the tobacco plant. He felt so completely relaxed, so utterly at peace with the world, that he leaned back in his chair and chided himself for not having visited the place earlier in the week. God! What a spot to come to after a week in the Black Swamp!

His mood changed as he glanced dreamily at some of the women who were occupying the sofas, patiently waiting to be claimed. They were all shades of colour, from the yellow pallor of an unhealthy white complexion to the ebony black of a Negress.

"Good Lord!"

"What's the matter, Red?"

"Those women—some of them coloured."

She laughed. "Madame believes in catering for all tastes."

"But pure-blooded Negresses——"

"Coloured women have a reputation, Red. Some men prefer them. Others prefer mestizas. I can't blame them. Look at that honey nearest the door."

The girl pointed out by Lucy was light chocolate and had the delicate beauty of a Greuze shepherdess. Before he could comment, Lucy went on:

"There's Madame, just come in."

Madame was even plumper than her husband. Her round face glistened in the soft reflected light as if her staple diet were butter or olive oil, and the flesh was dark above her sensual mouth. Her hair was black, and gleamed with a raven's sheen. Her bosom was ample, and as outstanding as a pouter pigeon's breast. Her waist was buxom, and her posture somehow suggested that she was standing with her legs astraddle beneath the black silk dress.

Henry shifted restlessly as her gaze embraced the entire room. The dark-shadowed eyes were hawk-like in their intensity. He felt as if in that one flashing glance her eyes had stripped every vestige of clothing from his body.

"Thunder!" he muttered. "What an old bitch! I'll bet her eyes don't miss much. Let's dance."

He tried to forget Madame as Lucy and he danced to the uneven music of the trio in the corner, but he couldn't: his glance was irresistibly attracted to her. He felt quite relieved when she presently turned and disappeared behind the door through which the waiters brought the drinks.

Lucy was aware of the change in his mood by his sudden abandon. She reacted in sympathy.

"Why so light-hearted?"

"Madame's gone out."

"Why worry about *her*?" she asked with genuine astonishment.

"She looks like something out of a cesspool."

She laughed carelessly. "She's all right so long as we keep busy. Let's not talk about her."

They danced for nearly an hour. In between times they sipped their drinks.

"Having fun?" she asked, laying her hand gently on his.

"Sure," he admitted with truth. "More fun than I've had for months."

"I wish we could carry on for the rest of the evening," she told him wistfully.

"Can't we?"

"Not unless . . ." She sighed. "Perhaps you are right. She is an old bitch."

He followed the direction of her glance, and saw Madame surveying the room again.

"I don't understand."

"If we don't, Red, she will blame me for wasting too much time on you."

"It's your own time, isn't it?"

"Yes and no. She gets her cut." She looked up at him from under her lashes. "Unless you'd like to, honey. I wouldn't disappoint."

He looked into her melting eyes, at her half-open mouth, at the lovely line of her neck, at the shapely swell of her small bosom— and realized that he oughtn't to have stayed so long. *He* hadn't ice-water in his veins.

"Where?" he asked thickly. "Upstairs?"

She nodded. He noticed for the first time that there were fires deep, deep down in her eyes. Well, he challenged himself, was that so surprising? Didn't she like men for their own sake?

II

She did. She had neither exaggerated, nor made a false promise. She first tormented him into a state of delirium, then sated him with ecstasy until at last he relaxed in blissful exhaustion. As he listened to the sound of her deep breathing he thought wistfully of Abigail. . . .

III

More locomotives arrived; more open cars; more rails; more of everything. The momentum of progress increased. The causeway to the mainland was completed. Rails were laid. A locomotive crossed, and with it went the pile-driver, and tons of rock ballast. The railroad began to move forward into the Black Swamp. Meanwhile, other locomotives and trucks were tipping ballast into what was left of the black mud which for countless centuries had comprised Manzanillo Island. The area of remaining swamp-land grew steadily less: soon it was no longer necessary to keep to well-defined paths. More buildings of all kinds were erected.

One day Baldwin saw Henry passing by the office.

"Hey there, Malley!"

Henry stopped and turned. "Hullo, Mr. Baldwin!" He liked Baldwin.

"You're good at mathematics, aren't you?"

"Supposed to be."

"Got a few minutes to spare?"

"Yes, sir."

"Come inside, will you?"

He entered the office. Baldwin was alone there. He waved to his companion to sit down, then sat himself down and mopped a face that was running with sweat.

"I've some figures I want you to check—the Colonel wants them right away, but I just can't believe them. And—er—Malley, they're strictly confidential, you understand——"

"I understand, sir."

Baldwin passed over a sheaf of papers. "Check all additions, multiplications, etc."

The task took Henry nearly an hour to complete. He looked up, and surprised the engineer looking at him with worried eyes.

"Finished?" Baldwin snapped.

"Yes, sir."

"Do you agree the final figures?"

"Yes, sir."

"Almighty God! I was afraid so." Baldwin mopped his face again. Nothing seemed to stop it sweating.

"Shall I go, sir?"

Baldwin hesitated. "Do you realize the significance of that last figure?"

"Is it the constructional cost to date?"

"It is. And it's staggering. It means that, by the time we reach Gatún, the first seven miles of the railroad will have cost more than one million dollars!"

Henry nodded.

"And that's the whole of the capital of the railroad," Baldwin explained.

"But—but—that means construction will come to a stop?"

"You can't build railroads without money."

"Can't more money be raised in New York, Mr. Baldwin? Won't one of the banks grant a loan . . . ?"

Baldwin laughed with caustic humour. "With Panama Railroad stock being hawked at ten cents in the dollar! Those Wall Street bankers aren't philanthropists."

"Then what . . ."

"God knows! But meanwhile there's still some money in the kitty, so I suppose the directors will order us to carry on. Perhaps the Colonel will think of some way out of our difficulties. He's a fighter, that man. He won't give up easily."

"I think I'd fight, too, if I were he, sir."

Baldwin nodded. "It makes one proud, to see what we have done. Thanks a lot, Malley."

So far as Henry could judge no hint of the coming financial difficulties leaked out. The road pushed on past the three-mile post, the four-mile post, the five-mile post. . . .

But at that point progress was slowed down for want of further capital. A fresh loan was floated on Wall Street; but as Baldwin had forecast, it was a dismal failure. But Aspinwall and Stephens still had faith in their project. They used their own capital to keep the work going to some extent.

Then came the return of the rainy season. At first the labourers welcomed a change from the months of almost uninterrupted sunshine, and worked with greater energy. They were in the jungle now; but the road crept forward, more quickly for being on harder ground. No longer was there need to tip tens of thousands of tons of rock before a rail could be laid. Unfortunately the rainy season brought with it a recurrence of fever. More white crosses had to be erected on Mount Hope cemetery; more men deserted to California Transit. There were racial riots, individual quarrels.

Men died as a result. More white crosses appeared at Mount Hope.

One day in July, a fine day for a change, Jim Braddock appeared before Henry's astonished eyes.

CHAPTER TWENTY-FIVE

"Mr. Braddock!"

"Red, you son of a gun!"

Their hand-clasp was warm with welcome. They gazed at each other with critical inspection.

"You haven't changed, Mr. Braddock."

"Hum! Kaint say the same fer you, Red. You don't have to tell me you've had fever. I kain see that. You've a face like a death's head, like the rest." Braddock shook his head. "This climate ain't no good fer a white man. It's poison."

"It's that all right."

"But you've changed in other ways. You've toughened plenty. You've got character." He waved his hand at Henry's guns. "So you've blooded them irons."

"Who told you?"

He laughed boisterously. "The old Fox, of course. He's as proud of what you did as I am myself. I sure wish I could've seen you shoot that critter down, Red. By all 'counts it was the quickest, prettiest bit of gun-play seen south of the Rio Grande. Well, it's nice seeing you again."

"How did you come to be out here in the swamp?"

"On purpose to see you, my boy. Fox told me you would be somewheres about here, if you wasn't on leave, so I got off the steamer at Gatún and made enquiries from the fellows building the railroad station there."

"I thought you were still in California."

Braddock chuckled. "Don't have to be no more. I was dealt all the aces in my last hand." He looked about him, and his gaze crossed Armstrong's frowning glance. "That your boss?" he asked, indicating Armstrong.

"Yes."

"He don't seem to like me none."

"That's Armstrong. He doesn't believe men should even breathe during working hours. In any case, he and I don't hit it off too well."

"Ef I hang around till you knock off, kain we spend the evening together?"

"I'd like nothing better."

So the rancher wandered slowly off, his keen eyes missing nothing of the work that was in progress.

They met later, and had a meal together in the canteen.

"I ain't been lazing all the afternoon," Braddock said presently. "I've been having a good look-see at thisyere railroad. It's been a tough job, ain't it?"

"Couldn't have been much tougher."

"Well, it's a mighty fine job somebody's doing, and makes me proud that it's Yankee grit that's doing it. When is it likely to be finished?"

"Oh! About then."

The keen eyes hadn't missed his companion's expression.

"Something going wrong?"

Henry hesitated. Baldwin had pledged him to secrecy. But Braddock was to be trusted. He leaned forward so that he should not be overheard.

"I'm going to tell you something that isn't known to more than a handful of people. The railroad company is almost bankrupt."

Braddock was astonished. "Are you sure, boy? They have a capital of a million dollars——"

"Which is approximately the cost of the road to date."

The rancher whistled. "A million dollars to build less than seven miles of railroad! *Madre de Dios!* Either there are some mighty sticky fingers about, or somebody doesn't know his job. A million dollars! That sure makes it the most expensive stretch of railroad in history."

"Shouldn't wonder. But I don't think sticky fingers or miscalculation are to blame. California's the culprit. And the fever."

"California?"

"Every time we import labourers they desert to join California Transit for higher wages. Or else to go to California itself."

"Raise your wages. That'll get them back."

"That's what we've had to keep on doing ever since work started. Besides, they won't work for us unless we give them danger money. You can't blame them. At one time they were dying like flies. It's the labour costs that have been mostly responsible for estimates being upset—plus the cost of the fill for Manzanillo Island and the Black Swamp."

The rancher pursed his lips. "It'll be a god-damned shame if the road shouldn't never get finished."

"It'll be worse than that."

He glanced sympathetically at the brooding face. "It'll mean something to you ef it's never finished, won't it, boy?"

"Well, you know how it is. I'm only one of a thousand, but when one's sweated blood at a job——"

"Sure do. You're proud of your part in it. And why not, by heck? Why doesn't the company raise more capital?"

"They tried. But with the original certificates being offered at one-tenth of their face value——"

"What's going to happen?"

"For the time being Mr. Aspinwall and Mr. Stephens are carrying it through on their own money, but how long can that last? I guess they're just playing for time."

"And praying for something to turn up, eh?"

"Maybe."

"Well, it has, Red."

Henry glanced quickly at his companion, and saw a broadening smile.

"You mean Wall Street——"

"Wall Street nothing! I told you I'd been dealt four aces, didn't I? Well, I meant four. The first was when I struck the richest placer ever. None of your penny-ante dirt, but the real McCoy. In one month it yielded seventy-five thousand dollars. The second ace was the sum I made from selling the placer to a mining company fer one hundred thousand dollars' worth of script."

He laughed at the expression on Henry's face. "Money comes easy in California in theseyere days. I ain't finished yet. The seventy-five thousand dollars gold I invested in real estate at San Francisco, buying one parcel of land fer twenty thousand, another fer thirty-five thousand, and two more fer ten thousand each. Six months later I sold the twenty thousand parcel for two hundred thousand, and it was cheap at the price. The following month I sold the thirty-five thousand lot fer three hundred thousand plus. The profit on the real estate is the third ace, Red—the two small parcels I'm keeping fer good luck."

"And the fourth ace?"

"Selling the script I'd had fer the placer fer one hundred per cent profit, which I reinvested in the Comstock lode. Boy, ef I ain't worth a million dollars at thisyere moment, may I be struck dead as a god-damned liar."

One million dollars! All that money in less than eighteen months! It wasn't credible! No wonder emigrants were flocking to California in tens of thousands.

He did not realize that he had spoken aloud until Braddock said.

"Sure that's why, Red. I'm only one of hundreds who's made a fortune overnight. One hundred per cent profit is jest chicken feed. What's more, it's not going to rest at that. Do you know what I'm going to do with them million dollars?"

"Reinvest them?"

"Yes, son. Fust I'm going to your Mr. Aspinwall and lend him half a million fer thisyere road to be finished——"

"Mr. Braddock!"

The rancher frowned. "Well, Red, why not? The money come easy enough. Why shouldn't I do some good with it, eh? You and Aspinwall and Stephens and the rest of the boys ain't the only ones to have faith in good old Yankee enterprise and grit. You, and what I seen today, has given me faith in the road, and I'm going to back it to the tune of half a million."

"But—but—suppose——"

"I ain't supposin' nothing. The other half-million I'm going to take up to New York and buy all the Panama Railroad stock I kain lay me hands on. Then I'm going to sit back and wait to make the biggest killin' Wall Street's seen in years." He chuckled. "And when I've made me another cool million I'm going back to Panama, to challenge that old Fox to a real game."

"Didn't you play this time?"

The rancher looked embarrassed. "Wal, I kinda chipped in fer a few rounds for old times' sake."

Henry grinned. "Considering the lucky breaks you've had in the past year I suppose you won for a change."

Braddock hit the table top with his fist. "That's just it," he roared. "I didn't. That god-damned son of Satan took a thousand dollars off of me." But when Henry's bubbling laughter was not to be contained, he joined in.

"By the way," he continued, when they had quietened down, "seen anything of Miss Vandusen lately?"

Henry's glance wavered in resentment of the form of the question, believing that it implied censure by the other man of something that was none of his business. But Henry changed his opinion after further reflection, for there was nothing censorious in the shyly-embarrassed scrutiny of the light blue eyes.

Braddock didn't know, he realized unhappily. Zachary Fox, who appeared to have primed the rancher on most of the other local news, had deliberately withheld that one item. If no other act of Fox's had ever proved the sincerity of his friendship for Henry, that of withholding information of the liaison did so. Yet Henry bitterly regretted the gambler's delicacy. It wasn't going to be easy to explain to Braddock. The rancher wasn't the sort of man, he believed, who was likely to regard with tolerance any excuse for a liaison with a woman of Abigail's breeding. With Lucy, yes. That would be understandable from his point of view. If a whore was willing to prostitute her body for gain, then any man who wanted to buy an hour's fleeting pleasure would be a fool not to take advantage of the offer. But Abigail . . .

Braddock was puzzled by the long silence. "She hasn't gone back, has she? Fox didn't say so."

"No. She is living in Chagres. She—she has a house there."

"Then you must see her sometimes, Red. You go to Chagres fairly often, don't you?"

"Every other week," he answered in a flat voice. "We can't

work in the jungle longer than one week in two," he explained.
Anything to postpone the inevitable explanation.

"Don't you call upon her sometimes?" Braddock persisted,
puzzled by Henry's manner. "You and she seemed to hit it off
together."

Henry swallowed. "I—I don't have to call on her, Mr. Braddock.
I live there when I'm in Chagres."

"Wal now! That's dandy," Braddock began genially. "You and
she can talk . . ." He came to a faltering stop as the significance of
Henry's words became apparent to him. "You *live* there? In her
house——"

"Ours," Henry corrected. "I earn good money."

After a long silence, "I see!" he exclaimed, in a toneless voice.
His bleak eyes avoided Henry's challenge. Again, silence. At last
his shoulders moved in the subconscious shrug of resignation.
Henry became aware that the rancher's eyes were fixed upon him
with a challenging intensity.

"Are you both happy, Red?"

"It means a hell of a lot to me, when I'm working up to my
waist in mud and slime, scorched by a hundred degrees of sunshine
and shivering with fever at the same time, to know that I shall be
going back to her in two or three days' time."

"Sure!" Braddock exclaimed drily. "You wouldn't be human
if it didn't. That's not what I asked, son. I said: were you both
happy?"

The question distressed Henry. He could answer quite truth-
fully that they were both happy. That is to say, both were content
with living together. But he knew that that was not the kind of
happiness Braddock had in mind.

They were certainly not so happy together as they had been
six months previously. Something had gone from their mutual
happiness on the day Abigail had announced her intention of
exploring the source of the Chagres. She had returned safely from
the journey; and had brought back a mass of notes, the elaboration
of which was still occupying her. But the arduous journey had tired
her, and her appearance had shocked him. For the first time he had
realized how much older than he she was. He had compared her
with Lucy, whose image was still fresh in his mind. The result had

been depressing. Lucy was young, vivacious, attractively petite, and shapely. Above all, she was wholly feminine; and made no attempt to challenge his sex by an assumption of equality—even superiority.

Yet they were not unhappy, he and Abigail. He still preferred her company to that of any other man or woman he knew; and he was convinced that he meant even more than that to her. He had only to look into her eyes when she welcomed him home to realize what his companionship meant to her. For one thing, it flattered her ego and smoothed away some of her extra years. . . .

"I think she's as happy as she could be living with any man, Mr. Braddock," he answered at last. "I don't take easily to having my life organized. Very occasionally our wills clash."

The elder man considered this reply before he commented on it.

"I think I get your meaning, Red, but what about yourself? Marriage ain't jest a matter of who rules the roost."

The bleak gaze held Henry's. He knew that prevarication would destroy the rancher's trust in him.

"If she were nearer my own age . . ."

Braddock looked sad. "But she's a fine woman, son," he muttered. "They don't come finer."

II

John Lloyd Stephens, President of the Panama Railroad Company, was himself a traveller and author of repute. As soon as he had heard of Abigail's presence in Chagres he had made himself known to her, and thereafter they had spent many pleasant evenings discussing the different lands they had visited.

Henry had no difficulty in arranging for Stephens to receive him and Braddock one day. The President of the company inspected Braddock with tired eyes as the two men shook hands.

"Sit down, sir. You, too, Malley." Stephens himself sat down. "I understand you have a matter of some importance to discuss with me."

"Yes, sir, I have. But first may I ask you a question?"

Stephens looked surprised, but he nodded. "By all means, sir —if it is one I can answer."

"None kaint answer thisyere question better. Am I right in thinking that the company has come to the end of its financial resources?"

The President started. "I don't know how that information reached you, sir——"

"News travels, Mr. Stephens."

"It seems so." Stephens shrugged. "Unhappily, you have correctly stated the facts. As soon as the railroad is completed as far as Gatún, which should be towards the end of September, we shall have spent not only the whole of the original capital of the company, but also certain private resources."

"What will happen then?"

Stephens hesitated. "I take it, sir, that you have a reason for these questions?"

"Sure, I have. I'm prepared to lend the company half a million dollars."

"Half a million . . ." The President's mouth tightened. "This is not a joke, sir, in bad taste . . ."

Braddock passed some papers across the desk.

After a careful inspection of them Stephens nodded. "Please accept my sincere apologies, sir, but I am sure you can appreciate the reason for my—er—doubts. To answer your question. The directors of the company have been discussing the problem of what is to happen when we reach Gatún, and have come to the very regretful—and regretted—decision to stop all further work unless Wall Street comes to our help."

"Would half a million help? If so it's yours."

The President patted the corners of his mouth with his handkerchief. "Your offer, your princely offer, leaves me almost breathless. If I may say so without offence, you are a very precipitate person, sir."

Braddock laughed. "Sure, I was born thataway and I mean to die thataway, too. Sometimes I have money in my pockets, sometimes I haven't. But it's all the same to me whether I have or I hasn't. Life don't seem no different either way."

"Then you must be as happy as you are generous. Of course

the money would be useful, but I must advise you that it would not be enough to complete the railroad."

"I kain work that out fer myself. But it would encourage Wall Street, wouldn't it?"

"I think it would. And it would encourage me to add more of my own resources. And Mr. Aspinwall as well, no doubt." Stephens's voice sharpened. "On what conditions, sir, would you lend the half a million dollars?"

"Conditions! Doggone it, I'm no damned moneylender. I ain't given no thought to conditions. All I want is to see the road finished as a monument to Yankee enterprise."

"You are a very extraordinary person, Mr.—er—Braddock, if that is your chief reason."

"Thank Red here. He made me realize what it would mean to a few million people to have thisyere road finished." Braddock leaned forward. "Lookee here, sir. I jest left California less than three weeks ago. I seen with my own eyes something nobody couldn't believe who wasn't there. Towns springing up overnight. Emigrants arriving in tens of thousands. Trade booming sky-high. A million people screaming fer goods which only the East kain give them. If thisyere railroad don't pay a hundred per cent dividend the first year it runs, then I'm a god-damned Dutchman." Braddock pounded the desk with his fist. "This isn't a question of dollars and cents. The world needs the road, and the world's going to have the road ef I have to go back to California and make another million dollars. Check, sir?"

"Check," Stephens echoed.

III

So the rails moved steadily forward in the direction of Gatún. A few days before the last tie was laid outside the new station, startling news reached Chagres.

La Pantera had struck again.

CHAPTER TWENTY-SIX

HENRY stretched out his legs, clasped his hands behind his neck, and leaned back against the chair in complete relaxation. A most inelegant attitude, and one that would be frowned on by Abigail should she enter the room. But that was unlikely to happen for the time being. She was in the kitchen, preparing dishes and cookies for a party. A farewell party for Jim Braddock, who was sailing for New York the next day.

He felt tired, and so damnably hot that he wondered how Abigail could stand the heat of the cooking. But then Abigail seemed to be able to stand heat more easily than most people. Phew! Until an hour ago the temperature hadn't dropped below 81.8 degrees for eight hours. And with a humidity of 89 degrees that temperature made one's body sweat with the least movement. He had changed his shirt not an hour ago, but the clean one was already wet where his back pressed against the chair.

Besides looking wan, his face was unusually reflective. He was wishing he could change identities with Braddock. Not on account of the money, but because the rancher was going back to the United States. God! How marvellous to have a chance of seeing his father and mother again. And sister Peggy. And all his old friends in Boston. And Jean.

He had been thinking a lot of Jean during the past few months. Why? He didn't know. Couldn't put his finger on any particular reason. Just one of those things, he supposed. But there it was. He would try resolutely not to think about her because the consequences were too damned disturbing, but his thoughts seemed cursed contrary; the more he tried to shut the memory out of his thoughts, the more it persisted in intruding.

Although he was not aware of the fact his mouth drooped in bitterness. To begin with, those consequences! To think too much of Jean was to become emotional. Too much emotion nearly always resulted in a restlessness that Abigail could no longer cure even when it coincided with her own feelings. That happened seldom. Even when it did, the sequel was never of the happiest.

Lucy was indirectly responsible. When one has tasted and enjoyed champagne, lemonade is apt to taste insipid.

As he liked champagne, there were times when his longing to taste it again was too intense to be resisted. To meet Lucy without Abigail's becoming suspicious called for considerable ingenuity, but he succeeded. Still, he saw Lucy never oftener than once in three weeks or so. Then he did so with a nagging feeling of guilt, because it was disloyal to Abigail; and her liking and respect—and gratitude!—were too sincere to enable him to be disloyal with an easy conscience, even though it was indirectly her fault. If only she would sometimes realize there was more in love than mere companionship. God knows! that was important, perhaps the most important part of marriage, but one shouldn't ignore Nature too much, especially in a tropical climate.

Thus, by a roundabout route, too prolonged meditation about Jean had the effect of throwing him into Lucy's willing, plump little arms. Whereupon, shortly afterwards, when the sharp spur of self-disgust had become blunted by time, the tingling recollection of Lucy's caresses would start him thinking of Jean, and how ten times, twenty times, a hundred times more sublime, more reverential everything would be if she, not Lucy, were the partner of those ecstatic moments—the married partner naturally: anything else in her case was unthinkable.

This comparison always angered him. The idea of associating sweet, lovely Jean, however indirectly, with the illicit embraces of a whore was as obscene as throwing dung at the Winged Victory of Thrace. But the vicious circle invariably completed itself.

An unexpected sound from the kitchen made Henry straighten up with guilty embarrassment, but the alarm was a false one. He looked in that direction with softening eyes. He knew now beyond any possibility of doubt that Jean was his true, spiritual love: and that he was attracted, in a solely physical sense, to Lucy. Yet, he still liked Abigail: more than very, very much. Dear Abigail! If only she were not quite so old.

II

Jim Braddock and Stephens arrived together. They had not heard the news. Baldwin brought it with him, when he arrived with Armstrong.

"Heard the news? La Pantera's struck again. In a big way. Quarter of a million dollars."

"Good God!" Stephens exclaimed. "Quarter of a million! You're sure?"

"There doesn't seem to be any doubt about the figure. I've had it confirmed two or three times."

"The usual place?" Henry questioned. His limbs were tingling.

Baldwin nodded. "The Gorgona fork. Two of the muleteers were killed."

"It's monstrous that nothing should be done to check such banditry," Abigail protested. "Has no protest been made to the Government?"

Stephens answered the question. "Again and again, Miss Vandusen. The British, French and our own Consuls have all reported the seriousness of the situation to their respective governments, and asked for marines to guard the route. Diplomatic representatives have been made in Bogotá, but without result."

Braddock turned to him. "If them brigands are still about when the railroad is finished, it's a dollar to a dime they'll ambush your trains."

The President gravely nodded. "We have not overlooked that possibility. I confess that we are worried. In fact, we have been discussing the idea of policing the railroad ourselves. In the light of this latest hold-up I shall press the New Granada Government for an immediate grant of those powers."

"And ef you get them I'd import a few Texas rangers ef I was you."

"It is an admirable suggestion, sir."

Braddock turned to Henry. "It looks like your spies ain't having much luck, son." He saw the surprised expression which passed across the President's face. "Red here has his own personal reasons fer wantin' to ketch up with thisyere La Pantera."

"Indeed! But, of course, I remember now that it was you, Malley, who saved the *Northerner* convoy."

"Pity you didn't shoot the right leader," commented Armstrong caustically, speaking for the first time. "It might have saved quarter of a million gold for Uncle Sam's coffers."

"Shucks! That ain't so," Braddock protested. "Once a bandit has pulled off a hold-up there ain't nothin' going to stop him carrying on till he's dangling at the end of a rope. I seen too many of them out West to believe in them mean critters. Even if Red here had shot both leaders the band would have carried on."

"But without the brains of La Pantera, perhaps with less effect," Stephens suggested.

III

So Braddock sailed for New Orleans, and, thanks to his assistance, work on the railroad continued. The gap between gangs pushing northwards from Gatún, and those moving southward, slowly lessened. One day the last tie in the gap was laid. A few hours later a loaded freight train completed the journey between Otro Lado and the station at Gatún—and passed on. The road was already heading for the next station, Ahorca Lagarto, another seven miles on.

Some days later two side-wheelers, the *Georgia* and the *Philadelphia*, with more than a thousand emigrants aboard, plunged and floundered off Chagres in a heavy sea. A stiff norther was blowing, and the captains eyed the vicious rocks off their port bows with an anxiety that was intensified by the knowledge that their anchors were dragging.

In spite of conditions, a few boatmen had the courage to sail their canoes out to the two steamers. The worse the storm, the higher the price they could exact for immediate transport. They found takers. They also found victims. Two of the canoes were swamped and overturned on the way back.

Frantic signals were exchanged between the two steamers as they drifted towards the rocks. The bargaining canoes were waved off, anchors were raised, and the two vessels turned their bows to the east in the direction of Navy Bay.

As the passengers saw their destination receding from the stern they raised a storm of angry protests. The skippers explained that their actions were for the safety of the people aboard. Hadn't they seen, with their own eyes, several of their fellow passengers drown as a consequence of trying to land in adverse conditions? The argument was howled down. The storm would die down soon, wouldn't it? And if it didn't, if anyone wanted to take the risk of drowning, it was his own life, wasn't it? So what the hell. . . .

The captains remained adamant. The storm wasn't likely to blow itself out for a couple of days yet, and the anchors wouldn't hold that long. The passengers could do what they god-damned liked with their ruddy lives once they got ashore, but they weren't going to risk their steamers. What was the hurry, anyway? No doubt the question was asked tongue in cheek, but it produced a howl of rage from many. Hurry! Of course there was hurry to land and continue the journey to California. Jesus! What a hurry!

The steamers rounded Toro Point into the comparatively calmer water of Navy Bay. As they cautiously approached Otro Lado a sharp-eyed passenger on the *Georgia* noticed moving tell-tale puffs of smoke flurrying above the roofs of the buildings. As his gaze travelled forward he saw, through a gap in the buildings, the outline of a locomotive lumbering southwards and pulling a line of open wagons behind it.

"Almighty God!" he bellowed. "Look! A railroad!"

He was quick-witted, that man. As the excited passengers made a concerted rush to the rails he yelled to a nearby seamen, "Hey, sailor! Where's the railroad go to?"

"Nowheres, chum, it ain't built yet."

"What the hell is that locomotive doing if it ain't going some place?"

The seaman shielded his eyes as he stared landwards. "Guess that's one of the construction trains. Looks like the wagons is full of ties and rails."

"How far does the line go, sailor?"

"Gatún, I guess. The track was almost finished as far as there last time we was in."

"Where's Gatún? Near the river?"

"Everywhere is near the river in this god-damned country."

The questioner turned to some of the passengers nearby. "What say we land here, and take the train to Gatún? It would save us a coupla days——"

The remainder of his words was lost in the storm of approving shouts which greeted his suggestion.

IV

Armstrong and Henry were closeted with Colonel Totten in his office.

"You sent for us, Colonel?" Armstrong asked.

Totten nodded. "I want a check on the grade between Tiger Hill and Lion Hill. Take the next construction train out, and let me have your figures by tomorrow night. When I was there last night it seemed to me——" He paused. "Can you hear anything out of the ordinary?"

His companions would have had to be deaf not to hear. The sound had a humming background to it, and resembled the angry buzz of a bee-swarm, magnified a hundred times. Even as the three men looked at one another in puzzled enquiry, the noise increased: they were able to identify human shouts, and the booming tramp of heavily shod feet.

Totten frowned in anger. "If another racial riot has broken out——"

Before he could finish they heard more footsteps; nearer this time, and running. The door was flung open, and a man hurried in. He was gasping heavily.

"Colonel——"

"What is it?"

"They want to—to see you. Mr. Baldwin . . . said for you . . . to be told——"

"Told what? Who are they? What do they want?"

"Passengers, sir, ex *Georgia* and *Philadelphia*."

"Don't know anything of the two ships. What are they doing here, in God's name?"

"The storm, sir. It was driving them ashore at Chagres, so the captains brought them here for shelter." The man was recovering his breath by this time. "When the passengers saw the construction train that's just pulled out they demanded to be landed."

"What for?"

"They want to go to Gatún by rail."

"Absurd!" Totten snapped. "Didn't Baldwin explain——"

"He tried to, sir. They won't listen to reason. They're crazy. They demanded to see you. Here they come——"

There was little time to say more. The hum became thunderous. Heavy footsteps approached, half running.

"I'd best go out before they wreck us." Totten glanced at Henry. "You'd better come with me, Malley. If it looks like trouble you'd better draw before they get out of hand. Armstrong, there's a gun in the top drawer of my desk——" He hurried into the street, followed by Henry.

The vanguard of the passengers surged towards him, were followed by the slower movers behind. There was soon a compact mass, pushing and swaying in a semi-circle.

"You in charge of this here railroad?" one of the men in the forefront asked.

"I am."

"Well, the track's laid as far as Gatún, isn't it?"

The Colonel thrust out a defiant chin. "What of it?"

"We've just landed here, and wants to get there by the quickest route. We're on our way to California——"

"Don't make a speech, chum," another man in the crowd shouted. "Tell him what we want."

The first speaker nodded. "Look, mister, what we wants is to go to Gatún by rail."

"Impossible——"

The word produced a resentful growl from those who were nearest the speaker, and could hear what he had said.

"Look, mister, there's a track, isn't there, and there's a bloody locomotive over there, isn't there?" He waved his hand behind him where a locomotive stood in a branch line with steam up, ready to shunt a line of ballast wagons.

"I tell you we can't take you. Go back to Chagres——"

The growl turned menacing. One or two hotheads shouted threats. "Tell the bastard what!" "Kick him in the guts!" "Anyone here drive a loco?" "If you don't give orders, mister, you'll see who will. We ain't too patient——"

"Malley!" Totten warned sharply.

The growling threats travelled way back, but the men in the forefront of the crowd grew tensely silent. Nobody was conscious of having seen Henry's hands move, but they were acutely aware of the two guns which threatened their guts with fire and lead at the first move.

The Colonel lost control of his always uncertain temper. "Get back there, you damned sons of mongrel bitches. Get back before we blow a few holes through your filthy carcases."

There was something belligerent about the Colonel's face.

"Get back, will you?" The spokesman of the passengers gave the man behind him a jab in the stomach with a vicious backward swing on his pointed elbow. "How d'you expect me to talk, crowding me? Tell them shut their traps back there."

The example was followed by others nearest to Henry's guns, and the moments of commotion were followed by an uneasy, shuffling silence.

"Look, mister——" the spokesman began in a surly, but more respectful voice.

"The track's not settled down yet," Totten interrupted sharply. "We've no stock for passengers."

"You've flatcars, haven't you? We seen some on our way here."

"That doesn't change the track. It isn't safe."

"Safe! It's as safe as being landed at Chagres. We already seen six men drown there today." His voice turned wheedling. "Look, mister, we're in a hurry. We'll take risks if you'll take us."

"No rates have been fixed——"

"What the hell does that matter? We'll pay what you want, mister. We'll pay double what you want."

Totten shrugged. There was still one way of getting rid of the unwelcome passengers.

"All right. Fifty cents per head per mile, and three dollars per hundred pounds of baggage——"

Q

An excited shout of assent greeted his words. "We're in, boys.
Pile your gear aboard. . . ."

There was a rush in the direction of the flatcars. Totten watched
them go as he mopped his forehead. There was an amazed expression
in his eyes.

"Fifty cents a mile," he gasped. "Three dollars fifty per head.
Multiply that by a thousand—no, more than a thousand—three
thousand five hundred dollars—maybe as much again for baggage——" He laughed uproariously. "Of all the bloody fools!
Seven thousand dollars for one short journey!"

He stepped back into the office. Henry waited outside; for one
of the travellers had not joined the rush for the empty flatcars,
but was leaning in lazy fashion against the wall of Totten's office.
He was dressed in Western clothes, and smoked a cigar which
seemed so securely anchored by thin colourless lips that it might
have been a permanent fixture. His ten-gallon hat was pushed well
back on his head, exposing hair that was chestnut in shade and as
unruly as Henry's. One hand was thrust deep in his trouser pocket,
but the other, Henry observed with interest, was so small and
delicate that it would have fitted quite easily into a lady's glove. He
was of slight build; but in spite of this his wiry limbs looked sinewy
and strong. His complexion was deeply sun-burnt, but this fact did
not detract from the delicacy of his features. Or their boyishness.
He looked no more than twenty-two or twenty-three years of age.
Altogether, Henry thought, an unobtrusive character. One from
whom no harm was to be expected. He relaxed.

The other man continued to eye Henry with a quizzical
air.

"Howdy, stranger," he drawled.

Henry nodded. "Hello," he replied in a curt voice.

"Saw you draw them guns just now."

"Well?"

"You pulled them mighty slick."

"I've practised."

"You don't talk like a Westerner."

"I'm not. New England."

The stranger laughed softly. "You don't say. Shouldn't
have believed it," he went on in a drawling voice, "if I hadn't

seen it. I'm from Texas," he added. "Name of Runnels. Ran Runnels."

"I'm Henry Malley. Red to my friends."

"Glad to meet you, Red." Runnels extended his small, delicate hand.

Henry shook it. "Me, too, Ran."

"You working on the railroad?"

"Yes."

"Surveying?"

"Assistant."

"Busy?"

Henry resented the questioning, but he knew it was not intended to be offensive, but just curious.

"Enough."

"Care to change it?"

This was going too far. "Look, brother, isn't it time you took your place in the train?"

The Texan shook his head. "I ain't taking the train. I'm here to see Colonel Totten." He inclined his head towards the office. "That him?"

"Yes."

"Good! I'll go see him. Just one more thing, Red. Jim Braddock says to be remembered to you and Miss Vandusen."

"Jim——"

"Sure. He said to be sure to look you up," Runnels drawled. "He kinda thought you might be open to a proposition."

"Jim Braddock thought that? What sort of a proposition?" Henry demanded bluntly.

"Helping me."

"Doing what?"

Runnels chuckled softly. "Smoking out La Pantera and his boys, Red. You see, I'm an ex-Texas Ranger...."

CHAPTER TWENTY-SEVEN

RUNNELS a Texas Ranger! This slightly built, boyish looking man with the hands of a woman, this man a Texas Ranger! The man was joking. The mere idea was laughable. Henry began to smile.

Because he was watching the Texan with a condescending gaze he was a witness of the change in the man's face. It was not so much the expression which altered, but the man behind; the being, the spirit, the soul, call it what you will. It was as if something had exploded into fire inside him; something that was savage, primeval.

"Don't laugh, Red," Runnels drawled. "You don't draw *that* fast."

Henry knew that he didn't. He knew intuitively that the Texan's guns would be roaring long before his own were half-way out of their holsters. He knew that death lurked in the Texan's soul. And Henry was afraid. More afraid than he had ever been in his life. More afraid than on the occasion when he had stared in terror at a runaway horse that had been bearing down upon him.

"I'm not laughing," he asserted with truth.

Runnels relaxed. "I don't like being laughed at," he explained naïvely. "Guess you thought I was too young to be an ex-Ranger?"

Henry had a feeling that the other man would prefer frankness to prevarication.

"Yes."

"How old do you reckon me?"

He inspected the Ranger's face. In the steady eyes—which in their bleakness vaguely reminded him of Jim Braddock's—was the wisdom and experience of several decades, but apart from being weathered the rest of the face was so obviously young that Henry hesitated to revise his original estimate.

"Twenty-three or four."

Runnels looked amused. "Twenty-one, brother."

An ex-Texas Ranger—a killer—at twenty-one!

"Looks like Texas breeds them tough," Henry muttered.

"Sure!" Runnels shifted the cigar from one corner of his mouth to the other with a dexterous flick of his tongue. "How about my proposition? Interested?"

"If you've talked to Braddock, you know how much."

"Sure. I do. Look, Red, you know the company are establishing their own police force?"

"I knew they contemplated asking for powers."

"Well, they got them. And I'm the man Mr. Stephens hired to get things moving. Seems like Jim Braddock suggested my name. He and Stephens met me in New Orleans. I got full powers to handle the job my own way. And first thing I'm going to do is to go after this here La Pantera and his gang."

"Go on."

"I could do with a lieutenant. Especially one who can draw fast. Seems like you're hand-picked for the job. Care to cut in?"

"How about the railroad?"

"Look, Red, if I got full powers, I got full powers. If I tell this here Colonel Totten to lend you to me for a time, then he lends you to me, see? Or I goes back to Texas, pronto."

"Where are you going to start? Panama?"

"Is that the best place?"

"I'd say so."

"Panama it is."

It did not take Henry many seconds to reach a decision. Hadn't he come to the Isthmus for no other reason than to find Al Simpson? Besides, it would be fun to see Zachary Fox again.

"You can count me in, Ran, if—you leave La Pantera to me."

A lazy smile passed across the Ranger's face. "Jim Braddock's no mean judge of men," he drawled. "Let's go meet the Colonel."

II

That evening Henry told Abigail that he had been seconded to help Ran Runnels round up La Pantera's gang, and was leaving Chagres for a time. She listened to his explanation without interrupting, but when he had finished she said quietly:

"Is that the only reason for your going to Panama, my dear?"

He looked at her in bewilderment. "What other reason should there be?" He added, after a pause, "Unless it's getting away from Armstrong. But you didn't mean that?"

"No, Henry, I did not." A sad expression revealed itself. "I meant, will you be glad to—to get away from me?"

"For Pete's sake, what put that damn' silly thought——"

She raised a protesting hand. "Let me finish——"

"But, Abigail——"

"Please!" When she saw that he intended to remain silent, she continued, "You know that you are free to leave for ever, whenever you wish. That was our bargain, Henry. Don't let your loyalty make you unhappy."

"For God's sake!" He was growing angry. "What's all this leading up to? I'm going to Panama in the hope of obtaining Al's confession, and for no other reason—unless you call rounding up the brigands a separate reason. What makes you think I want to leave you?"

"Don't you, Henry?"

"I've never given the idea a single damned thought," he stated in blustering anger.

"But you're no longer happy with me, my dear."

"Damned nonsense, Abigail. I swear I am——"

"No, don't swear. You see, I know about your visits to The House of All Nations."

"You know. Oh Christ!" he exclaimed miserably, after a long interval. "I'm sorry——"

"Please don't apologize, Henry. That makes the matter even more painful for me. Besides, I am not hurt. Not too hurt."

Not hurt! That was the most surprising fact of all. That her proud, intolerant nature could accept his unfaithfulness so calmly.

She went on, "You cannot believe it, can you, my dear? You see, I can read your face so well. But it is true, because I had prepared myself for the discovery some time back—soon after my return from the interior. That was the first time, wasn't it?"

He nodded miserably. "How did you know?"

A suggestion of her old scorn and intolerance showed itself. "Any woman would have guessed as much. The way you kissed me. The way you touched me. Your dissatisfaction with my embraces which you tried so hard to hide from me. I knew you had been—taking lessons."

He could not think what to say, and felt horribly foolish.

"I suppose I should be more hurt if I had not been expecting this to happen. Age is one barrier which a man and a woman cannot overcome, however hard they try. You have been very sweet to me, and I shall always be grateful——"

"*You* grateful!" Her unexpected humility embarrassed him. It was so unlike her. Besides, if either one had reason to be grateful to the other, surely his was the principal claim. "You mean I—to you."

"No," she denied, surprisingly. "You gave me something that I would not have dared to have asked from any other man. But what I gave you——" She became scornful again. "Any one of those women down the road would have given—far more generously, perhaps, which is what most men want——"

"You gave me a home, Abigail."

"Thank you for the nicest thing you've ever said, my dear."

"It wasn't said to be nice. I meant every word——"

"I know." She smiled wistfully.

"Then why can't it continue that way? I won't go to that damned House again. That's a promise."

"One that you would inevitably break."

"No," he exclaimed in anger. "That's not fair."

"You wouldn't be able to resist."

"Yes, I would. Especially if——"

"If, Henry?"

"You were sometimes a little more—more tolerant, more co-operative at times when I—— You were, at first——"

"I am nearly two years older than I was then."

"Two years! What's two years?"

"Nothing, at your age. At mine——" She sat on the arm of his chair and played with his hair, which she sometimes liked to do when she was in one of her rare tender moods. "At my age sex doesn't mean to a woman all it does to a man. Although I have mixed with men all my life I didn't really get to know them. I realize that now. Two years ago I believed that desire was bilateral. Now I know it's too often unilateral."

Her fingers twisted his hair so tightly that she pulled at his scalp and made him grimace. Convinced that she did not realize what she was doing, and sensing that she had something important to say, he kept silent.

"Don't you think, my dear," she continued in a low, flat voice, "that this might be a good moment to—to part——"

"Abigail!" The distress in his voice was sincere. His stomach felt as if it were turning over and making a vacuum. "You can't mean you want us to part——"

"Not want to. I feel it might be fairer to you. I have no claim on your exclusive love, especially as I'm too old, too dried up to satisfy it——"

"For God's sake! You're making me feel like a despicable cad."

"That's the last thing I want to do, my dear. But you don't *love* me, do you?"

"I—I—I like you more than any woman I've ever met."

"Liking is not loving, Henry. And that one at the House— is there a particular one, by the way?"

He shifted restlessly. "I've only slept with one particular one, if that's what you mean. But I don't *love* her. God! Love!" He wanted to spit. "She's attractive in her way. She's small, but not skinny. She has eyes that make you think of the moon and the stars and—and—oh! all those things. And a kiss that blisters. But I couldn't love her, Abigail, ever."

"Then whom do you love, my dear? For there is someone, isn't there? Sometimes, when you touch me . . . Is it someone back home? Perhaps the Jean whom you're often talking about?" She saw by his face that her guess was correct. She sighed, and unravelling his hair from her fingers she patted the unruly curls into some sort of order.

"Go to your Panama, Henry, and think on what we've talked about. When you return——"

"May we discuss it again?" he asked with sudden, eager hope. "I shall have had a chance to find out what I really want."

She nodded, then quickly turned her head away so that he should not see the sad doubt in her eyes.

III

During the journey across the Isthmus he gave considerable thought to what Abigail had said. Once away from the atmosphere of the house, and more particularly from the influence of Abigail's own masterful personality, he had to allow that she had been justified in everything she said.

For one thing, now that she had admitted the fact he realized that during the months they had lived together—and their total was not far short of two years—she had become progressively less interested in the sexual side of marriage. Whereas, in his case, the reverse applied. Lucy was mostly responsible. But the climate, too, was not blameless. It even changed the habits of the local fauna. Unlike their species of colder climes the birds and the beasts were not seasonal in their wooing: they mated the year round. It was scarcely to be expected of men that they would be more abstemious.

On the other hand, it was not pleasant to contemplate the loneliness of nights spent in an unshared bedroom. It was comforting to have someone to talk to while taking one's time to undress. It was even nicer to be awakened in the morning by a light kiss on the brow, and the familiar, "Time to get up, dear."

Which did he want more? The excitement of Lucy's voluptuous all-embracing caresses, or the more gentle comfort of a butterfly kiss on the forehead? "Time to get up, dear." He could no longer have both. Now that the secret of his meetings with Lucy had been shared with Abigail, it would be too embarrassing for them both to know they were continuing. Imagine, "Just going out for an hour or two, darling. Have to check over some grading figures with Armstrong," knowing all the time that she knew that what he really meant was, "Going along to The House of All Nations for an hour or two, darling. Don't wait up for me——"

IV

The first man in Panama Henry took Runnels to see was Zachary Fox.

As usual, the gambler was surrounded by animals. The same old dog still thumped the floor with his heavy tail, for he recognized Henry and wagged a special greeting. But for Ran Runnels there was a slight warning growl.

"Meet Ran Runnels," Henry introduced.

"Texas Ranger?" Fox asked, as he offered his hand. If he was surprised that the other's hand was even slighter than his own his white face did not reveal his thoughts.

"Ex," Runnels told him. He turned, frowning, to Henry. "News travels too fast for my liking. Who's been leaking?"·

"Nobody," Fox interrupted. "Where I came from in the States your name was well known. If you didn't want your fame known, then you must be here on business."

"Yes. Express Agency," the Ranger promptly answered. His expression relaxed into a boyish grin. "Red tells me you are to be trusted, Fox. La Pantera and his gang brought me here."

"Ah!"

"Bogotá has given the Railroad Company absolute police power on the Isthmus, with the right of imposing the death penalty without trial or subsequent accountability."

"Somebody must have a persuasive tongue," Fox murmured.

"I'm here to organize a police force. Red, here, is my deputy."

Fox's reaction to this news astonished Henry, who had expected approval and congratulation. The exclamation made both hearers start.

"No, Runnels. You mustn't accept the boy's offer."

"Mustn't!" The thin lips twitched. "Look, mister, that's a word I don't much care for when it's said to me," Runnels drawled.

Fox was not alarmed. "You'll agree when you hear what I have to say. La Pantera is gunning for Red."

"That's different." The Ranger relaxed.

But Henry laughed. "Al gunning for me! I won't lose any sleep."

The pale eyes did not respond. "You've learned to draw fast, lad. What one man from Boston can do, so can another."

Runnels broke into the conversation. "How do you know all this, Fox?"

"There's a Negro I'm in touch with——"

"I told you about Juan," Henry explained to the Ranger.

Runnels did not move his head: he watched Fox with a snake-like stare. "Juan tell you about La Pantera gunning for Red here?"

"Yes."

"How did he find out?"

"You'll hear. A drink?"

"Sure. I'm always ready to drink with friends."

So drinks were poured out, and tasted. The dog continued to watch the Ranger with wary eyes, some mysterious instinct warning him that the new visitor was a dangerous man to cross.

"About this here Juan——" Runnels prompted at last.

"Red told you about him and Al Simpson—La Pantera?"

"He told me. And about Juan."

"Well, a week ago Juan was in a saloon when he overheard two men talking. One was a Mexican, the other a Frenchman. They had been drinking hard, so perhaps they were more careless than usual. The Mexican asked the Frenchman if he had heard that La Pantera was taking lessons with the guns." Fox paused.

"Go on."

"Between them the two men let out that La Pantera had heard that Red Malley was gunning for him, so he meant to get Malley first—in the back!"

"The rat! That's what comes of letting people out East play with guns." The thin lips tightened. "This man Juan useful?"

"Few more so."

"Think he'd join my police?"

"Couldn't say. He is a hill man, and doesn't take kindly to towns. You can try next time he comes to Panama. But I haven't finished yet."

"Sorry, Fox."

"Juan was convinced that the two men were bandits, so he made enquiries about them, and found out their names. The Mex is Lagasca; the Frenchman, Edouard Perrigot."

"Dandy! That gives us a lead. Two leads. Know where they live?"

"No. But it shouldn't be hard to find out. They're often in one or other of the saloons."

"Thanks a lot, Fox. I'll rustle round after those addresses first thing in the morning."

"There's another you might find worth while. A few months ago another gentleman of uncertain reputation was playing penny-ante outside the walls. Now he plays at my tables, and the sky's the limit. He lost more than a thousand dollars last week, and a hundred already this week, but he's still coming back for more punishment."

"What is he? Panamanian?"

"American."

"What's he staking? Eagles?"

"Gold-dust."

"And he's not from California?"

"Not this side of last Christmas. His name's Holmes, by the way. Jim Holmes."

The Ranger's thin lips parted in a gratified smile. Not so his eyes. Their expression sent a shiver down Henry's spine. God! he thought. It's Runnels, not Al, who should be nicknamed La Pantera. He's a killer. . . .

CHAPTER TWENTY-EIGHT

FOX continued to urge Henry to leave the policing of the Isthmus to the ex-Texas Ranger, whom past experience had equipped for the job, and return to his work with the construction gangs. Runnels, too, added half-hearted arguments to this effect. But Henry remained obdurate, and insisted upon retaining the job of Runnel's lieutenant. As he pointed out to his companions, the work might, by leading him to the bandit's hide-out, provide him with an opportunity of confronting Al, which was the purpose of his coming to the Isthmus. What he did not add was that, even if there had been no question of a personal grudge against La Pantera, he would have refused to return to the construction work until the bandits had been rounded up. He had smelled blood, as it were, and the hazard, the fascination of restoring law and order, appealed to the streak of recklessness in him, to his taste for high adventure, and perhaps also to the Stewart obstinacy, the Stewart pride in completing a job once started.

So the argument finished when Fox indicated that he had nothing more to say on the subject. But Runnels had the last word.

"Seeing that's settled, Fox, just you quit worrying about Red. He can take care of himself. I seen him draw."

"It's his back I'm worried about, not his front."

Runnels laughed softly. "Nobody ain't going to work his way round to Red's back while I'm around," he drawled. And somehow his confidence reassured Fox in spite of commonsense reasoning that no man could be that infallible.

Thereafter, the rest of the time his visitor remained in Fox's rooms passed most pleasantly. Though Fox and Runnels eyed each other with the circumspection of two men not in the habit of making snap judgments, they had enough mutual respect to relax and enjoy their first meeting.

Presently gambling was mentioned.

"Guess business is good, Fox, with all the gold about?" Runnels asked.

"Good enough."

"Red tells me, sky's the limit in your establishment?"

"Yes."

"Play pretty high?"

"At times."

"Ever have trouble with losers?"

"Sometimes."

"Suppose you're pretty slick with a gun yourself? You gamblers have to be."

"Fox never carries a gun," Henry explained.

"No!" The steady eyes surveyed Fox with surprise. "Is that safe?"

"It always has been."

The Ranger frowned. "That don't mean to say it always will

be. There are hotheads in this country same as others. One of these days, after you've emptied a man's pockets, you're going to find him threatening you as a cheat, and demanding the return of his losses."

"It's a risk one takes. There's usually somebody about to stop anyone drawing on an unarmed man."

"I still don't like it," Runnels bluntly stated. "But it's your life."

"By the way, speaking of gambling, I've been thinking lately, Ranger, about the hold-ups."

Runnels stiffened. "Well?"

"During the past twelve months there's been well over half a million dollars' worth of gold stolen. That's a heap of money."

"Sure."

"Well, for Red's benefit I've been keeping an eye open for anyone possessing more gold than you might expect him to have. And I made friends with some of the whores living in the red light district just outside the walls; reckoning that any money come by that easy is most likely spent at gaming tables, on women, or in the saloons."

" 'Easy come, easy go,' eh?"

"That's how I see life."

"You're probably right. What of it?"

"It's strange but, with the exception of Jim Holmes, every stranger who's gambled with gold Nelson has checked in from California."

"Who's Nelson?"

"Shipping agent for the steamship companies, and American Consul."

"What's on your mind?"

"If the gold hasn't been spent, it must still be some place."

"So?"

"Maybe it will be worth looking for it where you find La Pantera."

"Yeah," Runnels drawled. "Yeah."

II

Henry and Runnels booked rooms in a small hotel off Plaza San Francisco. The following morning they went hunting for a stables and a string of mules. When Henry asked him why he wanted mules he merely answered briefly:

"You'll see."

After a long search they found a local Panamanian who was willing to sell mules and stables for a price that was not more than two and a half times their value. Long haggling brought the sum down to double the proper price, so Runnels accepted and completed the sale. Then he established Henry in a tumbledown room at the rear of the stables.

"This is it, Red."

Henry didn't quite follow. "What is what?"

"The office. Our headquarters."

Henry glanced behind him. "I'm glad you didn't buy goats," he murmured.

The Ranger chuckled. "You'll get used to it. Can you do hand printing? With pen and ink, I mean."

"Of a kind."

"Then print a notice we can nail up on the door."

"Saying what?"

Runnels reflected. "Something like this. 'Runnels Express Service. Panama—Gorgona or Ocean-to-Ocean.' Think you can do that and make it look genuine?"

Henry was puzzled. "What's the idea, Ran? I thought you were going to organize a police force, not an Express Agency."

"Want me to put them in uniform, so that everyone will recognize them a mile off?"

Henry grinned. "You tell me, so I needn't ask fool questions."

"Right. In three days we'll advertise in the local press for muleteers. Among those who will answer will be some good men we'll enroll secretly as guards. Afterwards I'll turn them loose in Panama, and one or two other towns; officially to tout for business, but in fact to pick up information. Like your friend Juan," he concluded.

Little happened for three days. Runnels was rarely in the office. He spent most of his time visiting the foreign consuls, and consulting the local agents of the different transportation companies. He also visited the markets and the saloons, often stopping to chat idly with any loiterer whose appearance he liked. Henry, meanwhile, printed several notices for distribution around the town, and wrote out an advertisement for the press.

On the morning the first advertisement appeared the fun began. Soon after 7 a.m. there was a nervous tap at the door of the office.

"Come in," Runnels called out, at the same time giving the thumbs down signal to Henry.

A man entered. His complexion was coffee-coloured. His clothes were threadbare. He looked nervously at the two seated men.

"Good morning, señores," he began in Spanish. "You advertised for muleteers. I do not read, but the good priest told me."

"Panamanian?"

"Yes, señor. Born at Matachin."

A few more questions asked and answered. Runnels shook his head. The man left, more relieved than disappointed that he was not being offered work.

"How did you know you didn't want that man even before you had seen him?" Henry asked.

"By the sound of his footsteps approaching the door, and the nervous way he knocked on it. The kind of man we want must be bold and decisive; ready to shoot first and ask questions afterwards."

Shortly afterwards two more men arrived. The Ranger interviewed them separately, and dismissed them both. A fourth man arrived, and entered with the suggestion of a swagger. This man was broad-shouldered, and stocky; there was a raffish expression on his face which Henry mistrusted on sight. His manner was aggressive, almost insolent.

"You're wanting muleteers," he began. "I'm one. Been one all my life. None better than me on the Isthmus. What wages you offering?"

"You call me señor when you speak to me," Runnels barked.

The man grinned. "Time enough to be polite when you're employing me."

"What chance of that, the way you're talking?"

He shrugged. "Other people will be wanting muleteers." He turned to leave.

"Wait! Name?"

"Francisco Garcia."

"Where from?"

"Peru."

"Why are you living in this country?"

"That's my business. Do you want me or don't you?"

"Leave Peru in a hurry?"

"Maybe. What of it?"

"We want muleteers we can trust."

"You can trust me so long as you employ me."

"Suppose I offer you double the pay you'd get as muleteer?"

"Doing what?"

"Convoying mule-trains against bandits."

"Me! A guard! That's funny."

"Funny because you were chased out of your own country and are now being asked to do the chasing?"

"Maybe."

"Double pay. Are you interested or not? Yes or no?"

The Peruvian stared between narrowed lids at the Ranger. "You going to be Captain?"

"Look!" Almost more quickly than the other man could blink, a pair of guns appeared in Runnel's hands.

The man stepped back in alarm, but the guns disappeared into their respective holsters.

"Jesucristo!"

"Do you want to become a guard?"

"Armed?" the Peruvian eagerly enquired.

"At the right time."

"I'm your man, Señor Capitán."

"Starting from now?"

"As you say, Señor Capitán."

"Right. Then you're officially a muleteer, in the employ of Runnels Express Service. First, you will go out into the town, and

R

pick up all the information you can about La Pantera and his gang. Try and bring me names and addresses of members of it. Report here every morning for orders."

The dark raffish face broke into a pleased grin.

"Understood, Señor Capitán."

"Do you go regularly to Mass?"

For the first time Garcia looked nervous. "Of course, Señor Capitán. I should go to Hell if I did not."

"Then swear on this Bible to serve the Isthmian Guard faithfully; to obey all orders of your superior officers without question, even at the risk of your life; and never to betray the Guard."

The oath was sworn.

"Now get out on your job." Garcia moved towards the door. "And Garcia——" He turned.

"If you should ever risk eternal damnation by breaking your oath, I send you there, pronto——"

For the second time he saw the guns appear miraculously in the Ranger's hands. Then the magnetic attraction of the light blue eyes held his own, which were dark pools of murky brown. He swallowed. "Don't fear, Señor Capitán," he muttered. "I won't break the oath."

As soon as the sound of Garcia's feet had died away Runnels glanced at Henry's face, and grinned.

"You don't have to ask it, Red. Your face does it for you. Why did I enrol Francisco Garcia?"

Henry nodded. "He looks like a brigand himself."

"So much the better. If other people think as you do they'll more likely open their mouths to him. He acts like one, too, which is even more to the point. La Pantera's gang are getting bolder every day. We must fight recklessness with recklessness. To bring an end to the bandit gangs we need many more men like Garcia. Men without scruples or conscience."

"Without scruples, Ran?"

"That's what I said, Red. We'll not bring safety to the Isthmus without spilling blood." He stiffened as the tiger in him showed in his eyes. "And I'm going to see that it's bandit blood that's spilt, not ours."

III

All that day men were going in and out of the small room at the back of the stables. The majority of them Runnels quickly dismissed, but some of them he swore in as members of the Isthmian Guard. Among them were men from Mexico, Costa Rica, Chile, and from Garcia's country, Peru. There were also several Panamanians. Nor were they all of one colour. Three of the enrolled men were pure Negro; four others could have passed as white except on close inspection.

Juan was among the Negroes. Henry liked the look of him. He was sturdily built; and there was an expression in his dark eyes which suggested a high degree of intelligence. Although his manner towards the white men was thoroughly respectful, there was never any doubt about his independence.

"That man is going to be useful to us," Runnels stated with confidence.

His words proved prophetic within twenty-four hours. The following morning Juan brought a local man along.

"Do you want any more recruits for the Isthmian Guard, Señor Capitán?"

"At least ten."

"Then I have one outside. Brother of one of the muleteers who was killed in the last hold-up."

"Show him in," Runnels snapped.

Sosa's grief was a little too obvious to be completely sincere, but Runnels was satisfied that the Panamanian was sufficiently vindictive to make a good recruit. So Sosa, too, was enrolled. Then Sosa said he could bring three cousins along, if the Señor Capitán wanted them. The Señor Capitán did so want; and, shortly afterwards, enrolled the three cousins. Then Juan remembered that he had a cousin who was out of work.

Before the end of the third day after the appearance of the advertisement Runnels had enrolled the maximum number he wanted, forty.

"Now what?" Henry asked him.

"We sit and wait."

The days passed. Fresh bandit raids of a minor character were reported. Runnels did nothing. He sat in the room behind the stables, and waited. A letter reached him from Mr. Stephens to ask what was happening. He replied briefly that nothing was happening.

Two more weeks passed. News of two more hold-ups reached Chagres. Mr. Stephens wrote a testy letter. What about some results, please? The Ranger replied even more briefly, and continued to sit happily in his little office, with a local cigar anchored in his lips and his feet up on an upturned box. He and Henry played pinochle for hours on end. In the evenings they drifted aimlessly from one saloon to the next; from one gaming table to another; watching, listening, and asking innocuous questions.

But appearances were deceptive. Something was happening in that dingy office with its pungent effluvia of urine and dung and cigar smoke, the reek of garlic from a nearby kitchen, the overall stink of a city lacking all but the most primitive form of sanitation.

Names and addresses were beginning to drift in from individual members of the Isthmian Guard. Odd, disconnected scraps of information from many different sources were adding up to something. Item by item the list of names grew longer. Six, ten, fourteen, twenty, twenty-three.

As Runnels' boyish grin of satisfaction grew ever broader, Henry, on the contrary, became doleful. No identification, yet, of La Pantera. No mention of Al Simpson. Nor did any further evidence reach the office that Jim Holmes was a member of the gang. Juan was certain that he was. So was Runnels, but he hesitated to add the name to the list he was compiling with such care. As he said to Henry, suspicion was not evidence.

The name of Perrigot, on the other hand, came in again and again. From Garcia, from Juan once again, from one of Sosa's three cousins, from Sosa himself.

Runnels milled over the scraps of information all of one afternoon, and smoked five cigars in that time.

"If he's not La Pantera himself, then he's La Pantera's deputy," he told Henry.

"He is not La Pantera," Henry obstinately denied.

"You can't know."

"Maybe I can't know—but I just do. Everything about La Pantera smells of Al."

"So you know!" Runnels said without rancour. He nodded his head. "Same as I know this hombre Jim Holmes is mixed up with the gang somehow."

The list grew. Twenty-eight names. Thirty-one. Thirty-five. Thirty-seven.

Runnels buckled up his belt.

"This is it, Red. Tell the boys to meet here tonight."

"But——" Henry was puzzled. "What for? There's no gold train due out, Ran. The next steamer, which has nearly two hundred thousand in gold aboard, doesn't arrive for another two days."

"That's why we move tonight," Runnels drawled.

CHAPTER TWENTY-NINE

THE streets of Panama were silent and mysterious with shadow as the members of the Isthmian Guard walked through them to their first destination. Few people were about, for the hour was nearly 2 a.m.; and only bold citizens, revellers from the saloons, and lovers dared to move about after dark in a city where there was a minimum of public lighting, and no police. But there were some mangy dogs slinking about; a few cats; and many rats; they all fed on garbage.

A warning hiss from Runnels brought the company to a halt before one of the small stone-built houses in the vicinity of Plaza Independencia. It stood in its own courtyard, in which the stone storage cistern occupied a prominent place. The cistern was surrounded by potted ferns and palms, and the effect was charming even in the darkness of a night that was lighted by uncountable stars. A three-foot stone wall, surmounted by an iron railing, separated the courtyard from the street; and the only means of entry, a gate of wrought-iron tracery, was bolted.

At a signal from the Ranger, some of the Guard formed themselves into a human ladder by which Runnels and Henry could climb to the top of the railing and drop into the courtyard beyond. The house, too, was locked, and all windows barred and fastened; but as almost every building of consequence in the city was similarly protected against uninvited intruders, Runnels had made preparations accordingly. He went to the door and pulled the bell chain. The house echoed with a loud jangle.

After a time they saw through the small square grille in the door, which was of heavy timber decorated with iron nails, the figure of a man shuffling along the narrow stone passage. He carried a lighted candle, was dishevelled, and looked alarmed. He peered through the grille at the dark shadows on the far side of the door.

"What do you want, señores?"

"Señor Mendoza?"

"Yes."

"Open the door. We want to speak to you."

"Who are you?"

"Never mind who we are. Open up."

"Certainly not. Go away. . . ."

Runnels had anticipated argument. He drew his gun and thrust it through the grille.

"Open up."

The door was opened. An alarmed man peered at the Ranger.

"What do you want?"

"You. You're coming with us. Dress, and make it pronto."

"But, señor . . ." The voice was growing very frightened. "I do not understand. What right——"

"You'll learn. You and the rest of the hold-up men."

"*Madre de Dios!*" Mendoza swallowed. "I do not understand, señor. I am a merchant, a dealer in goods from China. . . ."

"Sure, sure!" Runnels was becoming impatient. "With a spot of banditry on the side. Dress."

Henry watched one of Runnels' men escort Mendoza down the street. The prisoner had his arms tied behind his back, and another rope was bound round his ankles so that he could only shuffle along. There was to be no chance of escape.

"Where are they taking him, Ran?"

"The ramparts."

"Why. . . ."

"You'll see, Red. All in good time. Now for that stableman, Rasina. . . ."

One by one the members of La Pantera's gang were arrested, fettered with ropes and marched off to the ramparts. The first three came from a neighbourhood of moderate substance; the remainder from a warren of narrow stinking streets which bordered each side of the old wall. Ten, twenty, thirty, thirty-five, thirty-six, and finally the thirty-seventh, Perrigot, the Frenchman. Perrigot was less amenable than the others. He fought like a trapped rat when two of Runnels' men tried to bind his arms. He used his feet, his teeth, his arms. He was not subdued until he had been knocked half unconscious by the butt of Runnels' revolver.

"Just what do you propose doing with them, Ran?" Henry persisted, as the two men made their own way towards the ramparts.

"What would *you* do with them?"

"It wouldn't do any good to send them out of the country, I suppose. . . ."

"It sure wouldn't," Runnels drawled. "They would be back here before you could turn around."

"That leaves the dungeons beneath the Sea Wall. A few years in those damp, stinking vaults ought to discourage future bandits. Or a flogging," Henry added as an afterthought.

"There's an alternative fate," the Ranger pointed out in an unusually sombre voice.

Henry puzzled over this alternative. "Almighty God!" he exclaimed suddenly. "Ran . . ."

"It's the only way, Red."

"But, Ran . . . thirty-seven of them . . . and you can't even be certain that every damned one of them is a bandit. . . ."

"Aren't you certain, in your own mind?"

"In . . . in my mind, I suppose, but there's no legal proof. . . ."

"We don't need legal proof, 'cause there ain't going to be no legal trial. If we let them free, for want of legal proof, them bandits would multiply quicker than rabbits. It's my job to restore law and order to the Isthmus, and I'm going to do it *my* way. . . ."

II

As the rising sun quickly dispelled the grey mists of night, Panama stirred from its slumbers. The rats had already vanished into their befouled warrens: now the many mangy dogs and the few cats slunk away into the shadows to escape the quickening heat, and digest their scavenging. Now people began to move about in the streets, for the fisherfolk and the farmers were bringing their produce to the markets. They were followed by slippered women with shopping baskets, often carried on their heads.

The noise of a waking city grew slowly louder; but as it worked up in its daily crescendo, there was an unexpected pause, followed by an even more unexpected hiatus; for the news travelled in ever widening circles and spread with the rapidity of flooding waters. A mysterious hush descended upon the city, and its citizens shuffled towards the ramparts in eerie silence.

And being good Catholics, most of them crossed themselves as they stared with fascinated horror at the thirty-seven corpses which hung there; horribly limp and still, for there wasn't even a breath of wind to ruffle their dark hair or make their dangling limbs shiver.

In silence the onlookers departed, having seen their fill of the grisly spectacle. No need to ask what the bodies were doing there, or why. Retribution had struck the bandit gangs which had preyed upon the gold trains of the fabulous Yanqui people. And if one chose to accept what had happened in the nature of a gruesome warning, well. . . .

The silence gave way to the usual hubbub of noise. One had seen the corpses, one had prayed for the soul of the departed sinners. But one had to eat. Especially had one's husband to eat. . . .

III

After four hours' sleep Henry woke up as usual at the first light of a new day. Fatigue had brought about a dreamless sleep, and he was grateful though surprised: he had expected to dream for many nights afterwards of the gruesome scene duty had compelled him to witness. In his imagination he re-enacted the events of the previous night, and the horror of it was not less vivid than the reality had been. To have seen one man hoisted to a strangling death would have been horrible, but thirty-seven . . . and not one had died easily. . . .

To distract his thoughts from that picture of kicking limbs and contorted faces, he concentrated on Ran Runnels. In the light of what had happened a few hours previously, the Ranger's character became more than ever a fascinating problem. To realize that a man of his age, a man who was barely yet a man in a legal sense, could have given orders for the hanging of thirty-seven human beings without a tremor of indecision in his voice was something that was still not easy for a city-born man to assimilate. Especially when this fact was considered in conjunction with Runnels' physical appearance: the slightness of his build, his small, delicate hands, the almost feminine quality in his boyish face.

Not for the first time did Henry reflect upon the strange coincidence of Al Simpson's being known as La Pantera. Of course, one could appreciate the reason for the nickname: the silent approach, the sudden spring, the killing . . . all that was true of the panther's physical characteristics. But the spirit of the panther, the ruthlessness and daring of that silent-footed killer, belonged more to the Texas Ranger than to the Al Simpson of Boston days.

On the other hand, a sense of justice compelled Henry to admit that there had been nothing of the panther about Runnels when he gave the order to hang the thirty-seven suspected bandits. Neither voice nor expression had been vindictive or sadistic. On the contrary, both had been solemnly judicial. These men had robbed the gold trains; they were bandits, and the punishment for banditry was death. It was the law of the jungle; and the law of the Western State from which Ran Runnels had come. It was the law of the newest of the States, California; it was the law of any community lacking the administration of statute law, and a proper police force. Runnels had been employed to restore security to the Isthmus. If summary justice and swift execution were the only means of doing this, then it was his duty to hang bandits.

As the bedroom flooded with light Henry realized, in a moment of self-revelation, that it would not take him long to adjust himself to arbitrary justice. Calmer reflection was already making him regard the mass execution with some degree of equanimity. Time might even make him callous of the death sentence. Feeling that he needed exercise to restore his thoughts to normalcy, he dressed and went out into the streets.

He failed to achieve his purpose. The hanging obsessed his thoughts, even though it no longer made him feel sick. Because he had no destination, he turned left or right without conscious volition. He was shocked when he came-to and saw that he was close to the courtyard from which the Frenchman Perrigot had been dragged not many hours previously. He realized, then, that he had been thinking of Perrigot for the past five minutes. That death had left him with a particularly unpleasant taste. Possibly because of the way Perrigot had fought; first when three men of the Isthmian Guard had tried to bind his limbs, again as the noose was being adjusted round his neck. He had kicked at Runnels, spat at him. Even as he was being hoisted into the air he had cursed Runnels, damning the Ranger's soul to eternity in a strange medley of three languages, French, Spanish, and English. His last movement was defiant, as, gasping for air and swallowing his tongue, he had again kicked weakly at Runnels, this time at the head. One of the guard had jeered at the Frenchman's feeble effort, whereupon the Ranger had kicked the Guard's backside, and called the man a goddamned bastard. No, the memory of Perrigot's death was a particularly unhappy one.

As Henry stood by the entrance to the courtyard he assured himself that the Frenchman was as deserving of death as the rest of the gang . . . perhaps more so. His might well have been the gun which had killed the muleteers in the last big hold-up. A strong desire to confirm the possibility tempted Henry to enter the small room above a mule stable which the dead man had occupied; apparently on his own, for he had been alone in bed, and there had been no visible evidence that he shared it with a woman. No weapon had been found on Perrigot's person; but if there were one somewhere in the room, this, Henry reflected, might be construed as evidence of a kind.

Impelled by this vague hope he entered the dingy courtyard,

turned right and made towards the flight of rickety wooden stairs which led up to an equally unreliable balcony. This was built round three sides of the courtyard, and was the only means of reaching the series of small rooms which overlooked the stable yard.

He reached the door of Perrigot's room, but as he lifted his hand to push it open he heard a sound which arrested the movement: the noise of muffled sobbing. Deep, shuddering sobs which brought about a return of Henry's bitter conscience. So there had been a woman, after all. . . .

He paused, feeling that it was his duty to enter, but reluctant to do so because he would not know how to comfort her sorrow. Besides, the irony of the situation alarmed him. That he, of all people, should be the first one to find her! He cursed the impulse which had tempted him to search Perrigot's room, but knew he could not retrace his steps. He could not leave this woman alone in her misery whoever, and whatever, she might be. To desert her would not only be cowardly, but cruel.

He swallowed, wondering why his mouth should be dry; then pushed open the door, and entered. There was no window in the room; the door alone afforded light and ventilation. But the room was on the shady side of the courtyard, and was in semi-darkness. His eyes took time to become accustomed to it. Meanwhile, his entrance interrupted the sobbing. He could hear her gasping in an effort to restrain her grief.

Then he saw how mistaken he had been. No woman lay on the truckle bed, but a boy. No, a young man in his late teens.

The momentary silence was broken by a cry of anguish from the youth.

"Please don't take me, too, señor. Please, please, please! I don't want to hang." The terrified voice spoke in Spanish.

"God!" Henry exclaimed, this time aloud.

The voice rose in terror. "I haven't done anything, señor. I don't want to die. Please let me live."

Henry realized that his silence was probably torturing the unhappy youth.

"Nobody is going to hurt you, son," he said in the same language. "I didn't come here for you. I didn't know you were here even. Do you understand? You won't be hanged. You won't even be hurt."

The boy did not even listen. He shrank against the wall. "Please, please, please," he whimpered. "Don't hang me. Please don't hang me."

Henry felt disgusted. How old was the youth? Seventeen, eighteen? Only three or four years younger than Ran Runnels. He ought to have more spunk than that. But a moment later Henry was annoyed with his own intolerance. After all, if the boy had seen Perrigot hanging among the rest. . . .

"Be quiet, son, and listen to me," he began, with as much sternness in his manner as he could simulate. "Nobody wants to touch you. So be quiet, and answer my questions. What's your name?"

"Félix Perrigot, señor."

"Perrigot!" No oath followed this time, for Henry was shocked into stupefaction. Félix must be the son of Edouard, and the knowledge that he had helped rob the boy of his father made Henry feel sick.

"Edouard Perrigot was—your father?"

The youth began to sob again. "Yes, señor."

"You know he is . . . is dead?"

"I saw him . . ." Félix gulped. "Just now. . . ."

The poor kid! To see that contorted *thing* suspended in mid-air, and know it was . . . it had been your father. . . .

He moved across to the bed and sat down, but Félix crouched away and stared at him in fear. What a puling brat the boy was. It was hard to think of him as a son of the man who had fought, courageous and defiant, to his last gasp.

"Your father was a bandit, wasn't he?"

No answer.

Henry persisted. He had to have reassurance that there had been no miscarriage of justice.

"He was, wasn't he? You knew . . ." he demanded.

His voice must have been harsher than he intended.

"Yes, señor," Félix gasped in terror.

Henry sighed with relief. Thank God! he thought. In a calmer voice:

"Then you know he deserved death? Your father knew he was risking death when he became one."

"Yes, señor."

"You weren't here last night when your father was taken away?"

"No, señor. I was staying the night with Señor Holmes."

Henry started. "Jim Holmes, the American?"

"Yes, señor."

"Wasn't he a friend of your father?"

"Yes, señor."

"You are French, aren't you?"

"Yes, señor."

"How long have you been in Panama?"

"Nearly two years."

"Did you both come here from France?"

"From Calais."

"Why did you come?" The boy's hesitation gave him a clue. "Was your father in trouble with the police?"

Félix gulped. "Yes, señor."

"Have you ever been in trouble with the police?"

"No, I swear I haven't."

Henry believed the denial. "Have you a mother, Félix?"

"She died when I was only two years old."

"Have you any relations in Panama?"

"None, señor."

"Or—friends?"

"No, señor, none. Except Señor Holmes."

Henry sighed. This was the answer he had feared even while asking it. He rose, and placed his hand on one thin shoulder.

"Come, Félix."

"Where, señor——" the boy began in alarm.

"To live with me for a time," Henry reassured him. It was the least he could do for Perrigot's son, he thought.

CHAPTER THIRTY

HENRY had expected scorn from Ran Runnels when he took Perrigot's son to live with him. But he had misjudged the Ranger.

"That's dandy of you, Red," Runnels said in a quiet voice, as his tongue transferred his cigar from one corner of his mouth to the other, with that deft flick which Henry had vainly tried to imitate. "Sort of thing I'd have expected of you."

"I'm a damned fool."

"Of course you are, but I'm glad you and not me found the boy."

"Why?"

"Because I should have done just what you did." The intense gaze rested on Henry's face, which was inclined to be moody at that moment. "You know, Red, I could just as soon been sick as not, seeing those men dangling."

"But . . ." Henry did not know quite what to say.

"But I ordered the hanging!" Runnels nodded. "I had to. It is what we would have done in Texas. That doesn't make all Texans natural born killers. I don't take pleasure in killing. I don't eat food for days after I've killed a man." Back went the cigar to its original corner.

"There's something the boy said you ought to know, Ran."

"Shoot."

"We didn't see him last night because he was with Jim Holmes."

"The hell he was!" Runnels snapped. "That's the first real tie-up between Holmes and the gang."

Henry nodded. "Might be worth-while questioning him later on, when he's had a chance of calming down."

"You betcha! But now you've got the boy what are you going to do with him?"

"I don't properly know. I was wondering just what."

"Care for a suggestion?"

"Sure."

"Let's take him round to Zachary Fox. I kinda have faith in that man's judgment."

Henry nodded his enthusiastic agreement. "As soon as he's likely to be up."

Some hours later the two men took Félix Perrigot round to Fox's rooms. They found the gambler having breakfast. The cat sat on his shoulders, and stared solemnly at every mouthful he ate, waiting with cat-like patience for the moment when the remains of the meal would be divided between it and the dog. Rover, meanwhile, sat with his chin on Fox's knee, and gazed adoringly at his master with upturned eyes.

"Hello!" Fox greeted his visitors. "Pick yourself a chair. Mind if I finish?" Undoubtedly he must have been surprised to see a youth accompanying them, but nothing in his face or manner revealed this.

The dog did not share its master's impassiveness. A deep growl rumbled as the sad eyes regarded the visitors with hostility. Henry was astonished. Usually Rover welcomed him with a thumping tail; and even Runnels had lately been accepted. Must be young Perrigot, he reflected.

"Rover!"

The dog ignored his master's admonition. The growling took on a still deeper, uneasy note.

"Can the boy go into another room?" Runnels asked.

Fox nodded. "Take him, Red, will you? Give him a book. You'll find one about."

Henry installed Félix in Fox's bedroom, and returned to the sitting-room. To his astonishment the animal was still growling. He snapped his fingers. "Hey! Rover boy! You know me." But Rover made no response, which was strange.

"What's the matter with him, Fox?" the Ranger demanded irritably.

"I don't know. I thought it was the boy. Rover!"

Although neither of the other two men detected any variation in Fox's voice, the dog must have done so, for the growling reluctantly died away.

"What's now?" he questioned.

"Plenty. There are thirty-seven corpses hanging from the ramparts. . . ."

"Ah! I should have known."

"Known what?" Runnels asked sharply.

"Bandits?"

"Yes."

"You and Henry?"

"Sure. Who else?" The episode of the dog seemed to have upset the Ranger.

Fox nodded at Roger. "He knew. He smelled death."

"Goddam!" Runnels rubbed his fingers through his chestnut hair. "What d'you know!" He frowned, and added, " 'Taint as if there was any blood spilt. He might have smelled that."

"They just seem to know, dogs." Fox leaned down and patted the dog's head. "It's all right, old boy. Nothing to worry about." The tail began to thump for the first time. "Go to Red now, and say you're sorry."

Rover rose to his feet, crossed over to Henry's side, sat down and put one paw on his knee.

"Goddam!" exclaimed Runnels for the second time.

Fox looked at his visitors in turn. "Well?" he prompted.

So Runnels told the story of the massed hangings, and oι Henry's visit to Perrigot's room.

"What do you reckon should be done with the boy?" he finished. "Red says he is willing to sort of adopt him for the time being."

"Are you also proposing to adopt the widows and children of the other thirty-six?" Fox questioned drily.

Henry grimaced. "Félix is different," he protested. "He hasn't a relative this side of the Atlantic, or anyone likely to be responsible for him."

"He's old enough to look after himself. Many other boys have to do so."

"Maybe, but . . . if you had heard him weeping . . ."

Fox nodded, understandingly. "He must have spent a terrible night."

"That's just what he didn't. He didn't know until this morning. He spent the night with Jim Holmes."

"Holmes!" There was almost a note of self-congratulation in his voice. "Have you questioned the boy yet?"

Runnels answered the question. "We thought we'd give him a

chance to recover. But you haven't answered what you would do with him, Fox, if you was Red."

"Take him to Chagres, and see that he gets work on the railroad," Fox answered. "It might help to make a man of him."

The reply confirmed Henry's opinion of Fox's quick perception: the gambler had scarcely given Félix more than a passing glance, but it had been sufficient to dissect the boy's character, as Henry himself saw it. He could not make himself like the lad. There was a furtive expression in the dark eyes; and the set of the mouth was sullen. The chin was inclined to be weak; but in a hesitant way, as if it were in a state of indecision: it might firm up in the right circumstances, Henry believed.

"Sure," Runnels added quickly. "Just what the little bastard wants."

So the Ranger didn't think much of him, either! Henry was worried lest all of them were prejudiced by the fact that Félix was a Frenchman, lately from Europe.

"I wouldn't trust him farther than I could see him," Runnels continued. "A chip off the old block, I'd say."

"The father had guts," Henry pointed out. "He fought to his last gasp; which makes me think, in spite of every indication to the contrary, that Félix isn't quite the weakling we think."

"Suppose we have him in," Runnels suggested.

Félix returned to the room at Henry's call. He gazed at each man in turn with suspicion, and ignored the dog; it was obvious that he knew they had been talking about him.

"You got anyone in the Isthmus who cares a damn what happens to you, Félix?" Runnels asked him.

"Only Señor Holmes."

"Who is he? A friend of your father's?"

"Yes." Félix added quickly, "But he wasn't a bandit."

"How do you know?"

The boy glanced with sullen eyes at each man in turn, then pressed his lips in obstinate determination.

"You heard what I say . . ." Runnels began.

Fox turned. "May I, Runnels?"

"Sure."

S

Fox faced the young Frenchman. "You like Señor Holmes very much, don't you, Félix?" he asked in a friendly voice.

Félix's furtive upward glance at Fox was suspicious, but at last he nodded.

"You wouldn't like to see him hang, too, would you?"

The boy shuddered. "No, señor."

"Then do your best to save him, by telling Señor Runnels all you know about Jim Holmes."

After a few moments' reflection Félix turned his sullen face towards the Texas Ranger.

"What do you want to know?"

"How do you know that Holmes wasn't a bandit?"

"Because every time Papa went out with the bandits I spent the night with Señor Holmes."

The three men glanced at one another. Runnels appeared disconcerted. He had been so certain that Holmes was one of La Pantera's gang.

"Besides," Félix continued with spiteful scorn, "I heard Papa try to make Señor Holmes go out with him on the hold-ups."

"He did, eh? And what used Señor Holmes to say to that?"

" 'You, Perrigot, you got the brawn. But me, I got the brains, see.' "

Runnels' cigar danced a jig. "Sure, son," he drawled, "that lets Holmes out. He'd got too many brains to take risks in riding with the bandits. Had your father any other friends 'sides Holmes?"

"Only one or two. Papa didn't make friends easily."

Runnels took a knife from his pocket and began to trim his nails. "Any other American friends?"

"Papa had no time for Americans."

"So he hadn't! What about Holmes? He's American."

"Señor Holmes is different."

"Yeah! I guess he is, son. But I'll bet Holmes had American friends, hadn't he?"

"Yes, many."

"Know any of them by name, son? You see, they will be able to help you prove Holmes ain't no bandit."

Félix mentioned five names, all strange to Runnels and Henry. But Fox knew two of them.

"I know Canfield and Karl Muller. Canfield runs a saloon. Muller has something to do with the *Star and Herald.*"

The Ranger grunted, and continued with his nail paring. "Ever heard him speak of Al Simpson as one of his American friends?"

"The one that lives in the mountains?"

"Sure," Runnels drawled. "Some place way back of beyond. 'Course, I ain't suggesting he's a bandit. I just want to know the names of everyone so's I can check up. Where does this here Simpson live?"

"Señor Holmes doesn't know. I think he wants to find out."

"Why?"

"I don't know."

"How come Holmes knew Simpson?"

"They do business. Señor Holmes sells the food to Señor Simpson which he buys in Panama."

"Why not, son?" Runnels laughed. "He sounds a good business man, your Señor Holmes."

For the first time since entering the room the face of the French youth lost something of the sullen expression which had clouded it. It was apparent to the three men that he regarded Jim Holmes with the eyes of a hero-worshipper. In this enthusiasm to extol the virtues of his hero he began talking in French.

"Mais oui, monsieur, celui-là est homme d'affaires, et très riche. . . ."

"Hey! Hold it, son!" Runnels interrupted. "Say it in Spanish. I don't speak French that good. Do you speak English?"

"A little," Félix answered in that language.

"Do you, now!" The Ranger also spoke in English. "You people in Europe sure know plenty. What about Holmes?"

The youth answered slowly, picking his words with care. "Mr. Holmes is very good business man. He makes plenty money, taking food and goods to the American, Mr. Simpson. I think Mr. Holmes is going to be rich man soon."

"Is he, now! But if Holmes doesn't know where Simpson lives, where does he take the food to?"

"To a different place every time. Mr. Simpson sends message where to meet. I went once."

Runnels snapped his fingers. "Where did you go?"

Félix looked unhappy: the others had the impression that the information about his going with Holmes had slipped out by mistake. For some seconds he remained silent. He appeared to be thinking. Then, at last:

"Up into the mountains behind Obispo."

"Did you see this Mr. Al Simpson?"

Félix nodded.

Runnels flicked the cigar over to the other corner. "Take over, Red."

Three questions were enough to satisfy Henry that the Al Simpson to whom Jim Holmes had taken food and goods was the Al Simpson of Boston days. He leaned back against the chair, breathing deeply with satisfaction.

The mountains behind Obispo, Félix Perrigot had said. . . .

II

The following day Ran Runnels organized a party to search for the spot where, at least once, Jim Holmes had delivered supplies to La Pantera. Besides Henry, Félix and the Negro Juan as guide, he took a dozen members of the Isthmian Guard.

But once they had reached the small hamlet, inhabited almost solely by bush people, Félix completely lost his sense of direction. He indicated trails which made Juan look doubtful even before the party began to explore them; and having done so he was unable subsequently to recognize a single feature. Finally Juan refused to go any farther.

"It is no use continuing, señores. It would not be safe."

"Not safe? With you, Juan?"

"Even I could lose myself in country which I do not know, señor, and I do not know the country beyond this point. I have talked with the other men. None of us knows it."

"Where La Pantera can go, we can."

"I do not think La Pantera has ever come along here. Look for yourself." Juan waved his hand at the thick jungle growth which blocked the trail ahead. "Nobody been there for a year."

"Is that young devil playing us up?" Runnels asked angrily.

Said Juan, "I have thought so from the first."

So had Runnels; but when he questioned Félix, the youth swore that Holmes had certainly brought the supplies to a place somewhere in the vicinity. Was it his fault that he could not remember precisely which trail he had taken the previous time? All trails looked alike to him. The search continued until it was obvious to Henry that further efforts were useless. Deeply disappointed by the failure to meet up with Al, he agreed with Runnels to give it up.

So Runnels took the members of the Isthmian Guard back to Panama, but Henry and Félix turned north along the trail for Gorgona. There they caught the steamer for Otro Lado.

The first person Henry saw upon arrival was Baldwin.

"I thought you were in Panama, Malley."

"I'm back for one night only, sir." He indicated Félix. "Can you do with a recruit for the labour force?"

"Can we do with recruits!" Baldwin laughed, a trifle bitterly. "When can't we?"

"He's young. . . ."

"He can still be useful. Take him along to Briggs. By the way, you've come back at the right moment. Today is an important day."

He answered Henry's look of enquiry. "His Excellency, Victoriano de Diego Paredes, minister to the United States, is laying the cornerstone of the first brick building to be erected on Manzanillo Island. When you remember the swamp as it was when you and I first jumped ashore from the canoe. . . . And those damned hulks we lived on. . . ." He waved his hand. "We've progressed, eh, Malley?"

Henry nodded as his glance travelled along the rows of buildings which faced him. Two years ago, jungle and mud and alligators and mosquitoes and fever! And now . . . a thriving township with a population of more than three thousand souls, docks, a railroad terminal, sidings, a hospital, many stores, even more saloons, brothels, a dozen hotels . . . and undertakers, of course. No end of undertakers. . . .

Henry went along to the grand ceremony. Everyone who was

anyone was there; and on the outskirts were all the everybodies who were nobodies, and who had time to spare.

The mutual admiration society was in great form. New Granada was a small country, but great-hearted. She was proud to have the friendship of that great country, her sister republic, the United States of America. She was privileged to have the co-operation of the greatest race of engineers in the world in building a railroad across the Isthmus of Panama. One day the world would have reason to be grateful to the mutual trust, the friendship, and the co-operation of two such great-hearted republics in building the Panama Railroad. And let the doubters, the scoffers, and the faint-hearted take note. There had been, and there still would be, difficulties to be overcome in completing the railroad. But it would be completed. Claps and cheers. . . .

Finally—His Excellency was almost breathless with enthusiasm for the brilliance of his rhetoric—finally, the time had come to name this town which the magic alloy of American industry, American engineering, American capital (New Granadian applause), and New Granadian acumen, New Granadian generosity, New Granadian co-operation (American applause) had fashioned from a dismal and miasmic morass; this marvellous town, this, he might say, this miraculous town . . . His Excellency faltered: Where was he? Ah yes! . . . he therefore proposed that this example of nine-teenth-century enterprise and progress should be named—another pause, this time for the sake of drama—should be named after that genius, that visionary of empire, that great American who was virtually the founder of the town, William H. Aspinwall!

Aspinwall! Why not? As good a name as any other. Weren't there a dozen, a hundred towns back home named after their founder, or some famous person: Houston, Nashville, Montgomery, Trenton. . . . If anyone deserved a memorial, that man was William H. Aspinwall. So Aspinwall it was. Approving claps and cheers. . . .

After the ceremony was over Henry wandered along the streets of Aspinwall, and examined the town with fresh eyes. Here and there the surface had settled and left dangerous potholes of varying sizes, but ultimately they would be filled in: one gang of men was kept permanently engaged in filling settlements. Here and there a frame-building wore a drunken, lop-sided appearance from the same cause. But if one shut one's eyes to these trifling imperfections, one found a town, bustling, crowded.

He passed by the three big hotels, the Aspinwall, the Howard and the City, and marvelled. Two years. . . . He walked along street after street of labourers' homes, hundreds of them. Two years. . . . He looked up at the catch basins on the roofs of the buildings, the only source of water supply until the pipe from Gatún should be completed. What if they were filled with enough wriggling and still life to ensure that no resident could hope to escape intestinal disease? Conception and planning alike were an achievement. Two years . . . no, less than two years; for he and Baldwin and McCollum and Trautwine had felled the first coconut palm in May, 1850, and the present month was February, 1852. Come to think of it, the excitable little Minister hadn't really exaggerated. . . .

Having circled the town Henry was at last compelled to face the real problem which had kept him restlessly moving, but which he had weakly tried to postpone considering. Where should he spend the night? In the circumstances, it was hardly decent for him to go on to Chagres, and Abigail. On the other hand, suppose during the past weeks she had relented, or seen reason. . . . What would she think of him if he ignored her, failed to give her an opportunity of reconsidering her decision?

Did he want to go back to Abigail? Yes—no? God! How was one to make up one's mind? How to balance desire against pride?

As he drifted aimlessly, deep in thought, a tiny mittened hand was slipped into the crook of his arm.

"Hello, Red," welcomed Lucy's lilting voice.

CHAPTER THIRTY-ONE

"HELLO, Lucy," he exclaimed, embarrassed, and glancing quickly in all directions. Suppose news of the encounter should reach Abigail! She would think . . . oh hell! Of all people to run into. For want of anything better to say he went on:

"Come here for the celebrations?"

She laughed. "No, Madame's transferred the House here. More custom."

Henry remembered the two boatloads of women from Cartha-gena and Havana who had arrived at Aspinwall. "Also more competition," he commented.

"Madame isn't afraid of competition. Besides, it wouldn't have been much use us staying on at Chagres any longer."

"Why not?"

The question surprised her. "Don't you know?"

"Know what?"

"Where have you been since I last saw you, Red?"

"Panama."

"Lucky man!" She sighed. "I wish I was there instead of here. Panama sounds *so* romantic."

"There's something about the old quarter," he admitted. "Especially in comparison with Aspinwall or Chagres. What don't I know about Chagres?"

"Ever since those people from the *Georgia* and *Philadelphia* were taken to Gatún by train all the steamers have been landing their passengers here instead of Chagres."

He whistled. "So Madame brought you all here, did she? She doesn't miss a chance."

"She's not the only one. All the express agencies and business people have done the same. Now everyone else is, too. Soon there won't be anyone left in Chagres."

Abigail! Had she transferred her home to Aspinwall? he wondered. No, he decided a few moments later. She wouldn't do that without letting him know. She would do nothing to interrupt their *friendship*. She wasn't one to bear rancour.

Lucy shook his arm. "What's the matter, Red? What are you thinking about?"

"Just things!" he answered vaguely. "Chagres . . . Aspin-wall . . ."

"Red?" she exclaimed after another long pause, this time of her making. "You coming back with me tonight?"

His first reaction to her invitation was to refuse it. Unfortu-nately, he was overlong in replying: and with every passing second the suggestion became more attractive. For three months he had been living almost a monastic life: the only woman to whom he had spoken more than a few words had been the coloured señora at the pension in Panama. For some days past he had been aware of a growing desire to relax in a woman's company but had resolutely refused to pander to it, feeling that, when the time arrived to discuss the future with Abigail, he should do so with a clear conscience.

His resolution had not been easy to keep, for there were streets just outside the old walls of New Panama where a man might purchase all that he could desire for a few silver coins. Lovely women, too, some of them, with sensuous mouths, melting eyes, and lithe, sinuous bodies to tempt St. Anthony himself. On several occasions he had lain awake at night wishing he had the cool detachment of Zachary Fox to the inviting charms of the other sex. How did Fox manage never to want a woman? he wondered. It was not as though Fox were only half a man. He was as much a man as the next, often more so; yet he could cheerfully let the years go by without ever desiring to experience life's most devastating emotional experience.

Then there was Ran Runnels. Another who was, apparently, not particularly interested in women. Yet Henry was less sure of Ran than he was of Zachary Fox. There were at least three occasions he could remember when Ran's eyes at breakfast had been slumberous and self-satisfied.

Lucy tugged at his arm. "C'mon, Red, and give a girl a break, will you? I haven't talked with a man I liked since the last time you and me were together." Her melting eyes glanced up at him from under her long lashes. "We can dance, can't we? If you don't want anything else that's all right by me . . . though I don't know why you shouldn't, unless——" Her voice became tart. "You ain't wore out, making up to some of them Panama señoritas, are you?"

He grinned. Lucy jealous of other women! That was amusing. Still, it was true what she had said. There was no reason why he shouldn't dance with her. That would give him plenty of time to make up his mind where to spend the night. Having made this decision, he grimaced. So much for earlier resolutions.

They made their way towards the new House of All Nations. He let Lucy act as guide, so she took him first to the docks. At one point, where the placid sea lapped lazily around the wooden piles on which a landing pier had been constructed, she brought him to a standstill and made him slip an arm round her tiny waist. Then she leaned back against him, snuggled the back of her head into his shoulder, and stared out to sea. The sun was somewhere behind Toro Point, sinking fast.

"I often come here about sundown," she murmured in a dreamy voice.

"Why?"

"Don't quite know. Guess it gives me a nice feeling inside to watch the sea, and steamers, and things."

His gaze lazily travelled round the Bay. The sea was so smooth and blue and peaceful it seemed impossible that it could ever be otherwise; but incontrovertible proof that underneath its present benevolence it had a tigerish spirit was offered by two or three wrecks of ships which had piled up on the rocks. If the Bay is to offer a safe anchorage, he thought, one of these days somebody will have to build a breakwater.

Her mood made him feel curious to find out the reason for it.

"Does the sight of the ships make you want to leave?"

"Not really. I'm quite happy."

Was there a false note in her voice? "Is that a hundred per cent true, baby?"

"Well . . ." After a pause. "There are times when I feel that it would be nice to be married, but . . . anyway, it's too late. . . ."

She had reason to feel bitter. What man would take, and install in his home as the future mother of his children, a whore from The House of All Nations? Not such a man as she would choose: on the one hand, decent, hard-working and respectable; on the other, sufficiently man-of-the-world to hold and maintain her interest. Henry felt sorry for her until he recollected that, on her own admission, she had deliberately chosen her present life.

Yet for any man who could possibly forget her past . . . was there such a man? . . . she was still provokingly attractive with her winsome expression, and melting eyes, and tiny, well-formed body. Lord! he reflected, if it weren't for her past life . . . and Jean.

The thought, desultory and fleeting, disgusted him, and he stiffened.

"What's the matter, Red?"

"Nothing," he answered harshly.

But he had betrayed his thoughts to her. "Aw! Let's go, I've seen enough," she told him in a high-pitched voice as she freed herself from his arm.

They wandered back through the area of the docks, with its piles of tar, beer and wine barrels, its storehouses, its criss-crossing pattern of railroad lines, its sunken pot-holes, its untidy litter of rusted scrap-iron, broken packing-cases, filling material, and the like.

When they reached the boundary of the docks area Lucy led her companion into a long narrow street. Like the majority of the streets in Aspinwall, the surface of the roadway was covered inches deep with black fetid mud. It was also littered with hundreds of empty bottles, and masses of broken glass. On either side of the stinking, glass-impregnated mess was a narrow strip of concrete on which two rows of small stall-like buildings, with swinging doors, had been erected. Various methods of exterior lighting— for it was now dark—from flares to guttering candles in cracked glass funnels cast a fitful yellow glow upon the scene.

Outside many of the swinging doors stood a coloured man, often barefoot with ill-fitting clothes and a battered hat of local straw, who called out in an unceasing and competitive sing-song, meanwhile beckoning to every man who passed by; often seizing him by his arm or his coat in an attempt to attract or push him through to the farther side of the swinging doors. In this pande-monium it was impossible to distinguish what the barkers were shouting, but Henry could see, from the grinning faces of the men who perambulated up and down the street, that it was evidently very amusing.

"What the heck——"

"Bottle Alley," Lucy interrupted with a mischievous laugh.

Henry was no wiser. "What's happening? What are the men calling out?"

"You'll hear. C'mon on, Red." She tugged at his arm in her excitement.

He followed her into the flickering glow of light, and as they neared the first of the barkers he was able to distinguish the gist of the man's announcement.

"Go no further, señores, but stop here to spend an hour with Carmen, the Queen of the Caribbean Coast. Take a look at no cost to yourselves, señores, and see the succulent body that connoisseurs have fought and died for. See the firm breasts that artists have paid a hundred *reals* to paint. Look for yourselves upon charms that will make your heart beat faster."

The man's words were lost in the high-pitched, labial shouts of the next barker. "Here is Dolores from Havana, señores, the most beautiful, the most passionate woman north of the equator. Dolores' kisses will delight you, her lovely fingers will excite you. . . ."

"Señores! Señores! Señores! Take your turn here for Lola, the Cleopatra of Chagres; Lola, the woman of your dreams; Lola, the only woman in Bottle Alley who is all things to all men. Wait here. Señores! Señores! Señores! Wait here for Lola. . . ."

"Look, señores, I swing the door . . . so . . . and what do you see . . . ?" And what the amused eyes of Lucy and Henry saw was the naked figure of a slim, young Negress who stood inside the bare, stall-like room, and kissed her fingers to the row of black, grinning faces that ringed the door. "You see a Jamaican girl, señores, who left Jamaica for Jamaica's good——"

So it continued down the length of the street. The Jamaican girl was not the only one to be revealed by a swinging door, for there were other barkers who sought to whet the appetite of the passers-by with a provocative glimpse of the woman whose charms he advertised with merry quips and innuendos. But a few of the barkers leaned up against their own particular swinging door, and smoked a cigar. And sometimes an empty bottle came hurtling out of a swinging door. . . .

Bottle Alley!

II

Perhaps he was unduly influenced by the scene which he had just witnessed; but it seemed to Henry that, in contrast to squalid

Bottle Alley, the new House of All Nations was even more ostenta-
tiously exotic than the one at Chagres. Profits at the old House must
have been prodigious, he thought, for the new House bore evidence
of lavish expenditure.

To step inside was to enter another world; the world of the
Arabian Nights. The scheme of decoration was Oriental, and
every device had been used to give *les clients*, as Madame called
visitors to the House, an impression of entering the harem of a
Turkish Caliph. The door was opened by a smiling, turbaned
Negro whose shining black body was naked to the waist; he wore a
pair of baggy trousers, secured at the waist by a flowing white
sash and bound at the ankles with heavy silver bangles. Henry's
hat was taken by a cheeky Negro lad, dressed in a white tunic and
scarlet turban, who vanished with it behind a green velvet drape
which hung from an elaborate ogee-arched doorway on their
left.

All three doorways in the small entrance-hall were of similar
design, and similarly hung. The walls were concealed by carved
latticework, the polished floor was of parquetry.

Lucy smiled up at Henry, and pointed to the doorway on their
right. "You go on in. I'll join you in a few minutes." She passed
behind the draped doorway in front of them.

The Negro doorkeeper held the curtain open for Henry to
pass through. He found himself in a large room, nearly half as
large again as the one in the Chagres House. He stood there for
many seconds as with startled eyes he surveyed the fantastic
scene before him. Only in one particular did this room resemble the
one he remembered; a sizable part of it was set aside for dancing.
But the painted ceiling, the colourful drapes, the tables and chairs,
and the Panamanian waiters had gone. Here the ceiling was hidden
by soft blue fabric draped in graceful folds. The walls had been
painted to reveal, behind a lattice screen, a panorama of an Eastern
city with minarets, cupolas, and towers, a fig-tree-bordered market-
square and fountains, with desert beyond. Ottomans upholstered
in rich fabrics, and littered with large cushions, had displaced the
chairs of Chagres days; tables were of Eastern design; inlaid, and
hexagonal in shape.

The most striking change of all was in the service, for girls now brought in the drinks; they wore white diaphanous trousers and gilded slippers, but were naked above the bright sashes which encircled their slim waists; they wore a gauze veil, like a yashmak, which hung in concealing folds over their breasts and now concealed, now revealed a fleeting, provocative glimpse of taut, carmined nipples, and firm rounded breasts which made men's hands sweat to stroke or cup them.

There were only three vacant ottomans, so Henry made his way towards one of them and sat down. While he waited for Lucy he looked about, and fresh impressions of the place disturbed him. In the first place, the incongruity of modern clothes, which looked ridiculous against the unreal, quasi-Near Eastern background. Then there was the cloying smell of strong perfume which drowned even the heavy cigar smoke. He detested strong perfume.

There was a difference in the clients themselves. In contrast with the bearded, roughly dressed emigrants who had filled the Chagres House, here in Aspinwall the majority of the men were sallow-cheeked and smooth-chinned; their hair was oiled; their finger-nails clean and pared. Their clothes were formal, and often white. These men, he judged, belonged to the upper crust of Aspinwall society; men who worked in shipping offices, or consulates; wealthy Panamanians.

Then another, more insidious comparison between the two Houses disturbed him. For all its more obvious immorality, and its gaudy decoration, there had been something honest and forthright about the Chagres House that was missing from the Aspinwall House. The atmosphere in this imitation harem was vicious. It did more than offer welcome relief from Nature's restlessness; it deliberately pandered to extra-natural desires; in honeyed, titillating subtleties, it hinted at unsuspected and exquisite pleasures; at voluptuous rites known only to the initiated.

Before he could decide whether he was being disastrously affected by the place—and as he caught a flashing glimpse of the satin, rounded thighs of a perfectly proportioned Chinese half-caste girl he recognized how difficult it would be to remain unaffected—Lucy joined him. Like the other girls she was dressed in diaphanous clothes. For the first time he saw pink, shapely breasts which he had so often kissed in the darkness of a bedroom, and the lovely curve of her hips. And the provoking glimpse provided its own answer to the problem which had been worrying him.

"You're beautiful," he told her in a thick voice. "Goddam! You're beautiful!"

The heavily mascara'd eyes burned brilliantly as under the veil her carmined lips parted in a triumphant smile. She had waited so long for this whole-hearted surrender.

III

Henry started his return journey to Panama the following day, but, when he reached Gatún and saw the railroad stretching southward beyond the range of his vision, he almost regretted his promise to return to service in the Isthmian Guard. The track was moving forward at a far more satisfactory rate; an additional six miles or more had been laid since November, when he had been seconded to Runnels.

While he was awaiting the arrival of the *William H. Aspinwall* to take him on to Gorgona he encountered Armstrong.

"God, man!" the surveyor exclaimed. "Is the story of that massacre at Panama true?"

"Depends on the story."

"As I've heard it you and Runnels strung up forty-three bandits."

"Thirty-seven," Henry corrected.

"Even thirty-seven . . ." Armstrong mopped his forehead and gazed with incredulous eyes at Henry. "I wouldn't have credited you with that much———"

"Much what, Mr. Armstrong?"

"Well, hardihood, Malley, for want of a better word."

"Maybe you mean heartlessness."

"I'm not sure what I mean, except that I didn't see you helping to hang thirty-seven men without a trial."

"We had proof of their guilt; every one of them."

"I damn' well hope so for their sake."

"Runnels acted under powers given to him from the New Grenadian government."

"I don't doubt he did, but it still needed guts, didn't it, to string up thirty-seven?"

Henry shrugged. "How is the road going, Mr. Armstrong?"

"Well, thanks. We should reach Bohio Soldado some time next month. And Barbacoas by July, I should think. When will you be coming back to your old job?"

"As soon as we're satisfied we've put an end to the bandits."

Armstrong laughed. "I should think you've all but wiped them out . . . thirty-seven, by thunder! Ah well! may be seeing you soon, Malley. So long."

But Armstrong was mistaken. Ran Runnels quickly disabused Henry.

"They're nothing like wiped out, Red," he drawled. "A bunch of three names came in this morning."

"Nothing fresh on La Pantera?" Henry questioned eagerly.

"Not a damn' thing. You know, he's smart, that Al Simpson of yours. Too smart—for a New Englander."

"You think someone is behind him? Jim Holmes?"

"He's my guess," Runnels spat. "It took a brain to think out that business of selling food and goods to your friend Al."

"I don't see——"

"Don't you, brother? I do. If anyone wants to know where Holmes is getting gold from, that's the answer. Selling food, etc., to Al Simpson."

"Where's Al supposed to get it from?"

"What does Holmes care where Al gets it from? That's Al's responsibility, to account for it. Besides, Holmes can't suspect that we know that Al is La Pantera. Therefore, he is doing legitimate business, selling goods to Al against gold. But I think there is more to it than that."

There was a restrained excitement about Runnels that puzzled Henry.

"Well?"

"Jim Holmes is friendly with most of the leading commercial men in Panama, and the Express Companies' agents. Suppose he's La Pantera's ears and eyes?"

"You mean, he could pass advance information of important trains on to Al whenever they meet in the mountains?"

"It's a possibility."

"Then I'll stay, Ran, as long as there's hope of meeting up with Al. . . ."

IV

Information trickled slowly into the little office behind the mule stables. Names of muleteers who had become rich overnight. Names of boatmen whose passengers had vanished in peculiar circumstances. Names of workless people who could get drunk almost every night.

On the other hand, no news of further hold-ups reached Runnels' office. Apparently the execution of thirty-seven bandits had been taken very much to heart. For the first time in many months it looked as though travellers could cross the Isthmus without fear of being robbed or murdered. The Express Agencies were particularly grateful for this security, for people continued to flock to California in their tens of thousands and the Agencies were trying to work out ways and means of shortening the total time of transit across the Isthmus. But in May news reached Panama that seven Americans on their way to Gorgona had been murdered.

V

Runnels, grim-faced and tight-lipped, strode into Henry's room at the pension. Henry was undressing after having spent a couple of hours at Fox's gaming-room.

"On with them things, Red."

Henry tightened his belt. "What's up?"

"Another hanging party. Seven Americans murdered. The Gorgona trail again."

Henry flinched. "How many this time, Ran? A tooth for a tooth. . . ."

"Every bloody tooth we can find."

"That might mean as many as before. . . ."

T

"More. I've one short of fifty on the list."

"Fifty . . . for seven?"

"Suppose Fox had been one of the seven, Red? Or Miss Vandusen?"

Henry nodded. "You're right. It could be . . . next time."

"There ain't going to be any next time," Ran stated harshly. "Get a move on."

So the Isthmian Guard rode again. The next morning forty-one corpses dangled from the Sea Wall.

VI

More weeks passed, but no more names trickled into Runnels' office. The eight men whom the Rangers had failed to pick up vanished from Panama. None saw their going, none knew whither they had gone. Runnels was well satisfied. His warning had not gone unnoticed.

Only La Pantera and Jim Holmes remained: Holmes, in his usual haunts; La Pantera, God knows where.

"I don't think there will be much more trouble from organized bandits, Red," Runnels said one morning. "Like to go back to the railroad?"

"Well——"

"Worrying about friend Al?"

"The years are passing, Ran. My parents aren't getting younger." And Jean is getting older, Henry thought with despair. Suppose she meets someone. . . .

"Leave him to me. Guess I'll have more time to spare."

Henry temporized. "I'll write."

So he wrote to Baldwin, who replied, "Stay where you are for the time being, and take care of yourself. Cholera has broken out. . . ."

CHAPTER THIRTY-TWO

HENRY tried to divert his thoughts from the subject of cholera, but without success. Each day brought news of the havoc the disease was causing among the labourers on the railroad.

"I feel like a rat," he moodily confided to Fox one afternoon. "Skulking here in comparative safety while those poor devils up north are dying like flies."

"We are no safer here, Red. It will spread."

"I know, but . . . I hear the executive staff haven't escaped. Eight American executives have died. I'm needed."

Fox's steady gaze rested on Henry's unhappy face. "There's another reason, too, isn't there?"

"I—I suppose so."

"You are worrying about Miss Vandusen?"

Henry nodded. "I don't like her being there on her own, perhaps ill. What should I do, Zachary?"

"You mustn't ask me. It is a question you should decide for yourself."

"You think I ought to go. I can see that."

"No," Fox sharply denied. "I don't permit myself the luxury of acting as the conscience of others. On the one hand, I realize that you might be going to your death: on the other, I should admire your courage in going."

"I'm going," Henry announced abruptly. "To hell with the risk."

"Good boy!" Fox murmured. "I'll get my good friend the priest to pray for your safety, Red. But there's one word of warning —keep the time of your departure secret from everyone except Runnels."

"Why?"

"I spoke to Juan an hour ago. He says that he has fresh evidence that La Pantera has sworn to kill you and Runnels."

"Juan didn't say anything to us."

"Probably didn't want to cause you alarm. So watch out for yourself, Red, and be wary of an ambush."

"If he has anyone left to help him set up an ambush. God! I wish I knew where he is."

Zachary Fox stroked the dog's head, but his colourless eyes were directed towards the window. He appeared to be thinking deeply.

"I can't understand why he never visits Panama," Henry went on. "It just isn't like Al not to."

"Perhaps he doesn't trust himself to do so. He may realize that he couldn't come here without spending gold, which might make people curious about where it came from."

"It isn't like Al to be cautious."

"It may be the result of Holmes' advice. No information yet about the whereabouts of the gold, by the way?"

"No. Ran is working on that angle now."

"*If* Al is hiding it some place he must be a rich man, since his gang can't share in the proceeds of the robberies."

"*If?* Is there any doubt? Surely, as La Pantera——"

"Jim Holmes must make vast profits from selling food to Al Simpson," Fox murmured. "But he's that type of man. . . ."

II

Wherever the Gorgona trail touched human habitation there was evidence of burial and mourning rites. White foreigners and Panamanians alike eyed fellow humans with fearful, hostile eyes, and wherever possible avoided any contact which might help to spread the scourge. The Indians alone were stoical and resigned to whatever was to be their fate.

It was not Henry's first experience of cholera, for his arrival on the Isthmus had coincided with the end of an epidemic which had bereaved many families. But the present one was more severe; and fear stalked the land. Those men who wore guns, he noticed, held themselves alert, as if ready in the cause of personal safety to threaten with death anyone who might pass on the disease.

In spite of Fox's warning he was travelling alone, mounted on the best of Runnels' mules. But although he defied the warning he did not disdain it. He remained constantly on the alert, listening and watching for any movement which might prelude an ambush. There was a grim smile on his face. In the event of trouble he intended to fire first and ask questions afterwards. He felt confident of being able to give a good account of himself.

He had reached the foothills and was moving towards the pass over the Divide when he heard the echo of sounds ahead which brought his free hand swiftly on to the butt of his Colt. Precisely what was strange about the noise he was not, at first, sure; but he knew, instantly, that it was unusual and unexpected . . . and anything unusual was cause for alarm. He brought his animal to a halt and listened.

Presently he heard the sounds again; an agonized groan, followed by a low murmuring of voices.

Ahead of him the trail curved in a sharp U-bend. The inside corner of this bend was composed of bare volcanic rock, beyond which were other rocks behind which a man might well conceal himself. An admirable place for an ambush! The only doubt in his mind that he might be running into danger was the groan. It seemed scarcely likely that La Pantera would set his trap with that particular bait. Al was not that subtle, Henry considered.

He shrugged. If he were to reach Gorgona on time he must go forward. He booted his mule into movement, and continued his ascent towards the bend. But every muscle was tensed for immediate action. As he neared the bend the noises beyond it ceased. They've heard the mule's hoofs, he told himself. Ready for action, Henry. . . .

So round the bend, but not into an ambush. Some twenty yards farther on four men were grouped about a fifth who, dressed only in undershirt, stockings and boots, lay on the ground doubled up in a contorted attitude. The rest of the man's clothes had been roughly folded to make a pillow for his head.

Henry was surprised to notice that the other four men were in the uniform of the United States Army. He halted his mule, and called out:

"What's the trouble, soldiers?"

The faces of all four men betrayed uneasiness. After they had looked at one another in doubt, one of them said:

"It's Charlie, here. He's been taken bad, coughing his guts out ever since we left the river. Now look at him." The man's chest was heaving as he vomited pale liquid in a spurting stream.

One glance at the sunken eyes and pinched cheeks told Henry the whole story.

"Cholera," he explained brusquely.

The men's first instinctive act was to draw away from their companion. Their fear grew more marked.

"Christ!" one of them gasped.

The first speaker swallowed. "What're we to do with him, mister?" he asked in a husky voice.

"What are you doing here?"

"Vanguard of the Fourth Regiment of Infantry, on our way to California. We was landed at Gorgona and ordered to march in single file along this here trail for Panama."

"Where is the surgeon? Behind?"

The soldier nodded his head. "He stayed behind with the women and children. What about Charlie?"

"He needs medicine to check the diarrhoea, hot baths or packs to ease the cramps."

"How the bloody hell can we do anything like that?"

"All you can do is to get him to Panama as quick as you can. If you don't——"

"Jesus Christ! Poor old Charlie!"

"What about us, mister?" one of the others asked. "Ain't we likely to catch it?"

"You can leave him to die, if you prefer. He won't be the only one," Henry added bitterly as he urged his mule forward.

"Hey, mister. . . ."

But Henry ignored the call and made the mule trot. There was nothing he or anyone else could do for the poor devil. Besides, there would probably be others along the trail.

There were. The long line of soldiers stretched for many miles, in groups of varying numbers; among them, as he pressed quickly on, he saw many casualties from the scourge. To all he gave the same advice. "Get to Panama as quickly as you can." Wherever he saw an officer he stopped, and impressed upon him that nothing could be done for the sufferers while they were on the trail. They must be hurried to Panama where astringents and sedatives could be given to arrest the diarrhoea in its premonitory stage; or in the later stages, mustard in warm water, or calomel to stop vomiting, and warmth to ease the cramps.

At Gorgona he met the surgeon, Captain Charles Tripler, and the Supply Officer, Captain Ulysses Grant. They were desperate from their inability to move the women, children, and invalids; red-eyed from want of sleep, and unsteady from liquor.

"Good God, man, what's the use your urging me to move the people to Panama? Don't you think everyone else has been saying the same thing to me for the past three days?"

"Hire mules——" Henry began.

"Damnation to all muleteers!" Grant stormed. "I've contracted for mules at eleven cents per pound, but blasted civilians are over-bidding me; they're offering sixteen to twenty cents."

"At least you could give the patients emetics. . . ."

The surgeon caught hold of Henry's jacket with both hands and thrust his drawn face to within a few inches of Henry's.

"I've used up every ounce of medical supplies on hand, and still they're coming sick. I've been promised fresh supplies from Aspin-wall, but where are they, sir? I ask you, where are they?"

"Something must have gone wrong. . . ."

"Of course, something's gone wrong." The surgeon laughed unsteadily. "The whole world's gone wrong. I see women and children dying for want of supplies from Aspinwall, but does anyone there care what happens to the Fourth Infantry? No, sir, not a damn' soul."

"Why not go to Aspinwall yourself, sir? A train would get you there in little more than an hour. . . ."

"There are no trains running."

"No trains! Impossible, Captain! Construction trains run frequently."

The surgeon laughed scornfully. "My dear young man, you are living in the past. Work on the railroad has stopped."

"What!" Henry's face turned grim. "I'm on my way to Aspinwall, Captain. I'll get you there even if we have to borrow a handcar. Will you come?"

Captain Tripler steadied himself. "By God! That's talk I like. I'm ready, sir, as soon as you are."

The two men paddled down the Chagres to Barbacoas. The

river was in flood after the heavy rainfalls of the past few days, and the strong current carried them downstream at some eight knots. As the canoe neared Barbacoas, where the track was to pass over the river, Henry saw that the rails had almost reached the water's edge; an advance of nine miles in a little more than three months. That was the best rate of progress to date, and his first reaction was one of regret that he had been away from the job. Then he realized that the doctor had not exaggerated: no work was being done on the track. As far as one could see from the river, the track was deserted. In all directions the scene was one of dismal neglect.

They landed, walked to the end of the track, and after a search found a handcar. They each took a bar and set to work. Soon the small wagon was moving along the rails at a fair pace. But they were glad to reach Aspinwall. Twenty-two miles was far enough. . . .

"I hope I manage to get back," said the surgeon, rubbing his arms. "Thanks a million, Malley, for your help. Ask for this day's work to be taken into consideration come Judgment Day."

"Where will you be when you've traced your medical supplies?"

"Why?"

"To wish you god-speed. . . ."

This was not Henry's reason. He went in search of Colonel Totten.

The Colonel was in his office. His face was drawn. He looked ill. For a moment he did not recognize Henry.

"Yes, yes, what do you want?"

"This is Malley, Colonel . . ."

"Malley . . . Malley . . . I ought to know your face. You've been helping that Ranger fellow string up bandits. Sit down, and tell me what happened. Have a cigar—good for you. Help to keep that bloody disease at bay. By God! It's a killer."

"There's something else first, Colonel."

"Well, what is it?"

"You know the Fourth Infantry are crossing the Isthmus. . . ."

Totten nodded. "We transported them and their families by special train. Their Supply Officer has some damfool name . . . Homer Grant . . . Achilles Grant. . . ."

"Ulysses Grant, sir."

"I knew it was something to do with Homer. What about the Fourth?"

"The epidemic's spread to them. There are dozens ill at Cruces, and along the Gorgona trail."

"God pity them!" Totten wiped his forehead. "This blasted country is only fit for alligators to live in. Why anyone should want a bloody railroad——"

"They're dying for want of medical supplies, Colonel."

"They are, by God! Whose fault——"

"Captain Tripler and I pumped in by handcar. He's collecting supplies; wants to get back quickly."

Totten thrust out his bearded chin. "Stop beating round the bush, Malley. What are you hinting at?"

"A special train could save lives, Colonel."

The Colonel stood up, thrusting papers aside in a disorderly mess.

"I don't quite know why God let you live, Malley. You're too good to be true. A few weeks ago you were hanging people by the dozen. Now you're trying to save 'em. Damned inconsistent, if you ask me."

Henry chuckled as he saw the Colonel stamping out into the hot sunshine. He knew that a special train would set off for the railhead as soon as steam was raised. He followed the Colonel out, and went to look for Armstrong.

But Armstrong had died two days previously.

III

"He just went out like a snuffed candle," Baldwin explained. Underneath the sun-burned bronze his flesh was ashen-grey: his face was so gaunt that every bone stood out in relief. Had he been a skeleton, covered with thin parchment, he could not have looked very different.

"Bauer's dead, too, and Fratelli, Johnstone, Freeman, Richardson, Miller, Krautz, young Henderson, after only a month on the job, Reisner, Amory. . . ."

Henry was appalled. "Good God!"

"There are others," Baldwin went on wearily. "And more are ill. They won't all live. Have you seen Monkey Hill lately?"

"No."

"The carpenters can't make crosses quickly enough to keep pace with the demand. God-damned stinking country! We nursed them through the fever, we nursed them through Yellow Jack; and now, by thunder, along comes cholera. Twenty-four executives dead already, Malley, and many more to die, as sure as the sun will rise tomorrow. Perhaps me among them. Mr. Stephens, too, I guess."

"Is that why work's practically stopped, sir?"

"Only partly. It would have stopped anyway."

"Why?"

"Money. Same as last time. Unless you have another Mr. Braddock up your sleeve?"

"Not this time."

"No, I guess miracles don't happen twice in a lifetime. This railroad swallows capital like Manzanillo swallowed rock."

"I thought it was already earning substantial money."

"So it is. But not enough to balance the construction account. The latest estimate is that it will cost another three and a half million to build Barbacoas bridge and carry the line on to Panama."

"So what's to happen, sir?"

Baldwin shrugged. "I think all of us executives that are left would vote for carrying on, even if it meant earning less money; but trouble is, there are not enough of us left. God-damned guts are not enough on their own to build a railroad."

"I hate to think of the jungle beating the railroad."

"Oh, the company isn't licked that much. Idea is, to finish the line by contract."

"Totten and Trautwine?"

The engineer's grin was wry. "Not on your life! They've taken a beating once. Some other company, not so wise. . . ."

IV

As Henry walked along the Chagres road towards Abigail he was astounded by the changes which had taken place since his last visit. The abandoned buildings were already so derelict that the town had the appearance not of being merely dead but in the last stages of morbid decay. With the reckless prodigality of easily acquired wealth many of the late owners had not troubled to secure windows or close doors. High winds and rains had soon played havoc with these buildings: doors had been wrenched off their hinges, windows blown in. Insect and animal life had taken advantage of easy entrance, and now inhabited the rooms where human beings had worked or dwelt not many months ago. Most ominous sign of all, the greedy jungle was already reclaiming its own: vines had covered much of the cleared ground with a green and brown carpet, and in some cases had begun to curtain the weather-stained walls. Soon the voracious timber-eating ants would complete the work of destruction. The buildings would collapse, and disintegrate; trees would force their heads up through the tangle of thorny creepers; lianas would grow, entangle, and become a thick wall which only a machete would destroy. . . .

How could Abigail bear to live amid such desolation, he wondered. Surely she was too vital, too intolerant of weakness and defeat. Rather than not conquer, or at least repel, surely she would move away; perhaps to Aspinwall, perhaps to Panama. She had told him that she intended staying awhile in Panama before leaving the country. But she must still be in her home: she would not leave Chagres without letting him know and giving him her new address. Unless the cholera . . . but he refused to let his thoughts dwell on that ghastly possibility.

His pace slackened as he neared the end of the road. He was not looking forward to the few first minutes of their meeting. He knew he would feel embarrassed at having to meet her steady, discerning glance, and admit that he was willing to leave her. He no longer deluded himself. He liked her as much as ever, respected her as much as ever . . . but as a woman, not as a mistress. The last night he had spent with Lucy had crystallized his nebulous desires.

He knew that he wanted youth; the exuberance and the passionate generosity of youth; the fragrant breath of youth. He wanted the quintessence of all those qualities. . . . Jean!

Meanwhile, Abigail. It seemed she had not yet deserted. There were drapes in the windows. And he heard laughter. The sound made him warm inwardly with relief on two counts. The fact meant that she was not yet a victim of the scourge . . . and the dreaded moment of decision could be postponed.

His knock was quite gay.

The door was opened by Jim Braddock.

CHAPTER THIRTY-THREE

"WHY, Red . . ." Braddock began.

"Henry!" Abigail had stepped forward to Braddock's side. Her gaze rested on his face. Then, "So it's true?" she asked, in a low, tremulous voice.

"What is, Abigail?"

"You did help to hang those bandits at Panama?"

"Yes, but——"

"Oh, my dear!" She pulled him into the house, and ran her hand over his hair. "Your expression! It is grim and hard. You look so much older."

He glanced into a girandole which she had imported from New York. His face looked no different to him. But then he changed his opinion. Yes, one could see what she meant. It had lost its boyishness; also the last vestige of a northern complexion. It was stern, humourless . . . yes, as she said, grim. Grim, and older than his years warranted.

"Sit down, my dear," she went on.

He did so; worried by a fleeting impression that something somewhere was different, not as it should be. Not the furniture. It was mostly where he remembered it as having been. The drapes? The same. Then . . .

Abigail herself! That was it. The expression in her eyes, her manner towards him, were maternal. Ye gods! Maternal! But a second inspection confirmed his first impression.

He glanced at Braddock, and decided there was something unusual about him, too. He appeared uneasy; a state in which one would never have expected to find the forthright rancher. But Henry amended the word. Embarrassed was a truer description.

"Didn't expect to find you in Panama, Mr. Braddock. Thought you were still whipping Wall Street to heel."

Braddock chuckled. "Son, I'm that ashamed of the money I've made outer them wolves, I hadn't the heart to carry on."

"You made a killing?"

"I massacred 'em. As soon as I landed in New Orleans I sent orders to New York to buy every god-damned P.R.R. share on the market. By the time I reached New York I was near being a majority stockholder."

"Have they risen?" Henry was still conscious that the rancher was not his normal self. He was a little too boisterous.

"Have they riz! When them city slickers heard what happened to the passengers from the *Georgia* and *Philadelphia* they jest went mad trying to buy the shares back. They rocketed them to more than three hundred dollars. Son, me and you is rich men."

"Me!"

"Sure, you. It was you got me all het up about thisyere railroad, wasn't it? So I says to myself, why shouldn't Red have a cut? And bought a block of shares in your name."

While Henry was struggling to find words to express his gratitude, Abigail saw his embarrassment and came to his rescue.

"You can thank Jim some other time, Henry. Just now you said you didn't expect to find him here. Didn't you get our letter?"

Our letter! Henry's puzzled glance rested alternately on each of his companions. What lay behind their embarrassed glances?

"No."

"Oh!" exclaimed Abigail.

Braddock loudly cleared his throat.

"Henry dear!" Abigail continued gently. "I'm sorry the letter did not reach you." She sat on the arm of the chair, and twisted his hair round her fingers. "After you had left here for Panama I wrote to Jim in New York and told him that you and I were parting. A week ago he returned to Aspinwall——"

"You see, son, I'd heard about the cholera. I was god-damned scairt of Miss Vandusen catching it."

Henry nodded his head understandingly, but he did not really comprehend.

"As soon as he heard that our break was irrevocable . . . which we both knew, in our hearts, it was, my dear . . . he asked me to marry him."

"I kinda fell for her, son, that first day she joined our party. . . ."

Henry swallowed. The simple declaration made him feel a damned swine. If it hadn't been for his cursed eagerness, that night in the cave——

" 'Course, I knew it weren't no use expectin' her to love an old bush-whacker like me, but I aimed to try and make her a tol'able good husband. . . ."

"So I accepted him, Henry dear."

A long silence followed. He stared, grim-eyed, at the opposite wall, and became consciously aware that her fingers were tugging at his hair. He resisted an impulse to push her away with his arm; but his thoughts were angry. God! He had always respected Abigail; looked upon her as being on a higher level than most other women: incapable of deceit, lies, inconstancy. . . . Damn his own judgment! Apparently she was as much a deceiver as the next woman . . . as all women! The countless times she had implied that he was the only man she could ever care two bits about! But he only had to leave her for a few months to have her find someone to supplant him! Constancy! Bah!

For a while his hurt pride raged; but by degrees he calmed down. His natural sense of justice was able to reason, and consider the situation in perspective. To begin with, he was not himself blameless. Those hours he had spent with Lucy. . . . Had they never happened, maybe Abigail would not have considered Jim Braddock's proposition. Moreover, it had been understood, from the first, that either was free to bring the partnership to an end. And then, hadn't he already decided to end the affair? Lastly, if any man deserved happiness, Jim Braddock, the old scout, was he. And he and Abigail had seemed to like each other from their first meeting. So maybe Abigail would be the woman to give him that happiness. God knows! The two were as ill-assorted as could be, but so were cement and sand. Yet few amalgams were more lasting. So . . .

He jumped to his feet and seized Braddock's hand.

II

Three weeks later, Abigail and Braddock were quietly married in the little wooden church, not far from the railroad employees' eating-house, which had recently been erected by one of the missionary societies. After the ceremony and reception, which had been fixed to coincide with a scheduled sailing for Havana, they left to spend their honeymoon in Cuba.

As soon as he had seen their ship thrust its bows into the bay, Henry made for The House of All Nations. Although he was a little unsteady from the effects of too much champagne, he felt depressed. He tried not to be 'dog-in-the-manger' about the wedding, but it was no use: something had gone from his life; a solace on which he had come to depend. He realized that he was going to miss Abigail; and although she and Jim Braddock were returning to the Isthmus, for another year at least, he had no longer a home to return to.

Monsieur and Madame received him with obsequious flattery. It was a pleasure to receive Monsieur Malley. It was a matter for regret that all their clients were not so charming as Monsieur Malley. Monsieur had no idea how jealous the other girls were of Lucy. Lucy was a lucky girl to enjoy the exclusive custom of Monsieur Malley.

Lucy kissed him. With a tender caress which did nothing to relieve his depression. That was how Abigail had sometimes kissed him. Damnation! He wasn't a boy, to be fussed over.

"Give me a real kiss," he ordered, grasping her tiny waist and pressing his mouth against hers. She tried to resist, but she was powerless in his arms: they weren't the flabby muscled arms of the man who had left Boston nearly three years ago; they were like whipcord, immensely strong. So she kissed him the way he wanted it, but without pleasure. It gave her the clue to his unusual behaviour.

"You've been drinking," she reproached, when her mouth was freed.

That's a good one, he thought, in a bemused way. You've been drinking! That reproach from a girl who spent her life trying to get men to drink. Funny, that!

"I've been to a wedding!"

"Oh!" Understandingly. Forgivingly, too. Then, "Hers?"

Abigail was always Her to Lucy. Just Her, without particular significance.

"I'm glad," she added, when he nodded. "Sorry for you, honey, but glad for myself."

"Why?"

"Might see more of you now."

He gave the idea thought. "There's something to it," he agreed. Then, wonderingly, "But what's it mean to you if you do, Lucy? You don't get more from me than you do from other men."

"Don't I?" After a pause, "Why the frown?"

"Thinking. God! When I think of you with other men. . . ."

"Don't think!" She glanced up at the waiter who was standing by, waiting to take an order. "Two Blue Moons," she told him.

"*Two!* But the señor——"

"Has had enough to drink already. A glass of coloured water will do him less harm than rye. That's right, isn't it, Henry? You shouldn't order anything at all, but if you didn't Madame would be after me. If you want to dance——"

"A woman always knows what's best for a man," he agreed, looking about the room with a benevolent gaze. It was quite a place, this new House of All Nations, he reflected. Much better than the one at Chagres. Ostentatious, of course, in the matter of gilt and colour and exotic hangings. But maybe Madame was right. He remembered Bottle Alley; the crude stalls, the indifferent lighting, the hoarse voices of the barkers, the vulgar postures of the women. . . . That scene would have been enough to disgust all save the most desperate, or the drunken, or the degenerate. Whereas, this place! Well, it sort of put one in the right mood. Madame was right. If one had to have vice, at least let it be gilded. . . .

"Still thinking?" she questioned. "What about? You look smug."

"It's the champagne. I feel smug."

She rested her elbows on the table, locked her fingers together, rested her chin on her knuckles, and gazed at him with her melting eyes. Her expression had rarely been more whimsical.

"D'you know, Red, most men are more bearable when they're liquored. They're still nasty, most of them, but the liquor makes 'em softer, and easier to deal with. I don't mean really liquored up, mind you. That makes them brutes. Filthy, beastly brutes. Just so-so, I mean. But you. You're different."

"How come? I'm not liquored up," he protested. "Only just— just smug," he added with a chuckle.

"I mean, you're different because you're nicest when you're dead, cold sober. Then you're so gentle, in spite of your grim face, and courteous and—and—and—what the hell! Madame likes you so much she'd give you the pick of us girls for nothing, and you can't say more than that."

"You're a sweet girl, Lucy."

Her eyes filled with tears. "See what I mean?" she choked. "You say the nicest things. Aw! Let's dance before I make a fool of myself." She dashed the tears away with the back of her hand, and jumped to her feet.

III

News reached Aspinwall from New York that the Panama Railroad had signed a contract with Minor C. Story to bridge the Chagres at Barbacoas, and complete the track to Panama. The period of the contract was limited to twelve months.

So Mr. Story came to Aspinwall and sat at Stephens' desk. He brought a small executive staff with him, because more than fifty Americans on Stephens' executive staff had died from cholera, and most of the remainder chose to follow Mr. Stephens back to the United States: they had had enough of the tropics to last them a lifetime.

When Stephens heard that Henry did not propose to leave, he offered Henry the opportunity of staying on at Aspinwall as one

U

of the railroad staff responsible for keeping a regular service running as far as Barbacoas. There was still no diminution in the
number of emigrants travelling to California. On the contrary, the
volume of traffic had induced other transport agencies to compete
with the Isthmus Transportation Company. These agencies worked
in conjunction with the railroad, and organized an ocean-to-ocean
schedule which undertook to take a passenger off a ship at Aspinwall
and put him on the connecting ship at Panama.

Henry accepted the position and installed himself at the Howard
Hotel. But in between times he went to Barbacoas to see how the
bridge was progressing. Mr. Story had taken over the labour gangs
from the railroad, but after the loss of hundreds from cholera, and
a still greater number from desertion, their numbers had again
dropped to an unworkable minimum. A fresh recruiting drive was
launched, and several hundred Irishmen were attracted to the
Isthmus by the promise of generous wages.

The bridge, constructed on the trestle principle, grew by
degrees. It had to be a long bridge, and a steep one; the river was
deep at that point, and its maximum width was three hundred feet.
Meanwhile work was proceeding at several points on the other side
of the river. Henry believed that the time period before the first
train ran from Aspinwall to Panama was at last measurable.

The bridge had reached half-way across the river when Mr. and
Mrs. Braddock returned to the Isthmus. Henry met them, and was
astonished by the difference in Abigail. The weeks she had been
away from the pernicious climate of the Isthmus had restored a
more healthy shade to her flesh. But the expression in her eyes was
the most noticeable. It took him some time to realize what it was:
contentment. The discovery nettled him at first. With the utmost
respect to dear old Jim Braddock, why should she have found the
contentment with Braddock which she had been unable to find
with a younger man? It was not until a chance remark about age
gave him a clue. She was not afraid of losing Braddock. He was hers
for keeps.

In the following week Abigail and Jim moved to Aspinwall.
They settled in a small bungalow to the left of the railroad hospital.
It was set in a grove of coconut palms, and faced the sea across a
fifty-yards strip of beach. In the rear was a small garden, shaded by

two banana trees. Altogether a pleasant spot. His first glimpse made Henry envious. He wished he could have been living in it. Not with Abigail, of course. That episode in his life was finished: already he could look back upon it and wonder if it had really happened. No, Jean was the woman he had in mind. Jean. . . .

One day there was a cloudburst over the Chagres watershed. It followed two days of intermittent rain, and lasted more than four hours. The rain turned rivulets into rivers, rivers into raging torrents, and the Chagres into a destructive monster which thundered inexorably seawards. En route it hurled its mass against the nearly-completed bridge. One span crumpled like matchwood.

The partial destruction of Barbacoas bridge was the straw which broke the back of the constructional camel. When the Irish labourers fell ill and died, or deserted, they were not replaced. When men of other nationalities and shades died or deserted, they, too, were not replaced. Once again in the history of the railroad the employment line in the constructional graphs took a steep downward plunge. Less and less new work was done. Like the Chagres in reverse, the flood of work became a river, the river a rivulet, the rivulet a trickle. . . .

As far as it could go—that is, as far as the unfinished bridge at Barbacoas—the railroad maintained a regular service, and paid handsome dividends. The high mileage rate, which Colonel Totten had originally fixed as a means of discouraging travellers, was maintained. Gold was still being produced in phenomenal quantities in California, so the fortune-seekers paid whatever was demanded of them.

The higher the railroad income the more Jim Braddock enjoyed, in retrospect, the whipping he had given Wall Street.

"Goddam, son, even ef I'd lost every cent later I wouldn't have missed the faces of them Wall Street coyotes! First, when I bought the shares at ten cents. Here's another sucker, they thought, when the smoothies tolt me I was buying good. You could see it in their sneering eyes, feel it in their flabby hands.

"And then, when they wanted to buy back at three hundred dollars! Ef I'd been Emperor of Japan himself they couldn't have been more respectful. It was Mister Braddock this an' Mister Braddock that. How did you know, Mister Braddock? Kain you foresee the future, Mister Braddock? You *must* meet my wife, Mister Braddock. You must visit us at our home one week-end, Mister Braddock. No party would be complete without you, Mister Braddock. Bah! I'm disgusted!" Braddock absentmindedly looked about him for a spittoon, but meeting his wife's warning gaze he hastily swallowed.

A shy knock on the door checked his jovial laughter. "Come," he bellowed.

Pedro Romanos entered. He removed his hat with a nervous gesture. "Please, señor y señora, excuse."

"What is it, Romanos? You want me?" Braddock asked.

"Not you, señor. Señor Malley, if you please, señor."

"Well, he's before you, man. . . ."

"Jim," Abigail reproved. "Señor Romanos may want to speak in private."

Braddock chuckled. "Hadn't thought of that, son. Shows you how a woman thinks different, don't it?"

Henry stiffened. "Is it about La Pantera?" he asked sharply.

"No, señor." Romanos hesitated. He looked decidedly uneasy. "Madame sent me."

"Madame?"

"Of—of The—The House of All Nations, señor. Excuse, señor."

Braddock exploded into chuckles. Abigail pressed her lips together. Henry reddened, and gestured his annoyance.

"What the devil——"

"It's about Señorita Lucy, she say to tell you, señor."

"Oh!" Henry glared angrily at the Panamanian. The man should have known better than to have mentioned Lucy's name in front of Abigail, of all people! But the damage was done, and with that thought he became anxious. Why, in God's name, should Madame be sending a message to him about Lucy? Was the poor kid ill?

"Well?"

"Madame say to tell you that the señorita has gone into the mountains with Garcia——"

"Garcia?"

"One of Piérola's Negro boatmen . . . you remember, señor?"

"Lucy's gone with a Negro, a Cimarrone? In God's name . . ." His muscles tensed; and the veins in his forehead began to throb with fury.

"Not that," Romanos hastily corrected. "The señorita persuaded Garcia to take her to a *bocor*."

"Isn't a *bocor* one of them bloody witch-doctors?" Braddock barked.

The Panamanian sucked at his dark lips. "Yes, señor."

"What the hell for? The girl must be mad. Will she be safe?"

"Maybe not, señor, that's why Madame she ask me to let Señor Malley know."

"But what's she gone for?" Braddock persisted. "Does your madame know? Answer, man. Does she know?"

"Madame thinks she gone buy love charm from *bocor*, señor."

"A love charm! For God's sake——"

"The girl must be mad," Abigail interrupted scornfully. "What does her sort know of love?" Her gaze rested for a moment on Henry's troubled face. "Hasn't she done enough harm?" Turning back to Romanos, "When did she go?"

"Sometime in the night, señora."

Abigail pressed her lips together in exasperation. "The stupid girl! She must be pursued before it's too late. Go get your guns, Henry, and anything else you need. Quickly. And come back here."

"I'll not do that, Abigail. It will save time if I go straight——"

Braddock's booming voice halted Henry as he began to move off.

"Hey, there, Red. You come back here like Abby says. I'm going with you."

Henry stopped, turned. "No, Jim. This is my affair."

The Westerner chuckled. "Try and keep me away. I'm going."

"We're both going," Abigail amended quietly.

"Abigail!" Henry protested. "That's madness. I won't let you go. To risk . . . God knows what! And for Lucy of all people——"

"I'm going," she asserted, with the authority he knew so well. "Not for her sake. She doesn't deserve to be helped. But she's a white woman, Henry. Whatever she may be, she mustn't be allowed to suffer in the hands of Cimarrones. It could start a race riot. There have been too many here already." She faced Romanos. "Do you know which way she went?"

"I could find out."

"Would you guide us?"

The man's eyes showed white. He began to tremble. "No, señora. I don't know country. I've never left Chagres valley."

"Then who? Piérola?"

"I don't know, señora. He might for many dollars. He know Trinidad River. He not done so well since steam-boats and railroad come here. Cayuca prices not so high."

"Go get him, then. You'll be paid well for your trouble."

"Yes, señora. I get him soonest possible." Romanos disappeared with speed.

CHAPTER THIRTY-FOUR

ALL three were ready, equipped for a long journey into the mountains, by the time Romanos returned to the bungalow with Piérola. Both men were uneasy, and it was evident to the Americans that they would have to pay a high price to secure Piérola's services.

The boatman paid his respects to each one in turn. "Señora Braddock, Señor Braddock, Señor Malley."

Abigail's marriage had not changed her character. She took immediate charge of the situation.

"Señor Romanos has told you what we want?"

"To follow Garcia and the American señorita, señora."

"Do you know where they have gone?"

"I know where Garcia's family live, señora. I cannot say they have gone there."

"Could you guide us there?"

"It is different from poling passengers up the river to Gorgona or Cruces——"

"I asked whether you could guide us to the home of Garcia's family; and if you can, whether you will?"

"I could, señor . . ." Piérola began to twist his hat round and round between his fingers. "But it is well away from the Chagres valley, and might be dangerous."

"From Indians or Negroes?"

"From both, señora. We should have to go through Indian country to reach the district where the Cimarrones live."

"Is it a question of price?"

"Yes, señora. If I took you where you want to go, I must risk dying from many causes. It is more dangerous than following the Chagres to its source."

"How much?"

Piérola hesitated. The Americans could see that the man was wondering how much he dare ask.

"A thousand dollars," Romanos said quickly.

"I was not asking you, Señor Romanos."

"I'm his agent, señora."

"Oh! I see. Then it's too much——"

"We'll pay a thousand, my dear," Braddock interrupted. "By thunder, the girl is in danger!"

"It is still too much," Abigail snapped. "However! How soon can you start? At once?"

"Money down before he starts, señora," said Romanos.

"Pay him, Jim. At once?" she asked again.

"Yes, señora. Have you food, weapons, ammunition——?"

"I am used to organizing exploration parties. We'll start in fifteen minutes' time. Which way do we go?"

"By cayuca up the Chagres to the rio Trinidad, then along the Trinidad until we reach a spot which I shall recognize when we reach it. From there we shall have to find a trail that will take us to the village."

"How about that other Negro of yours, Garcia's brother, wasn't he? Wouldn't he know the way? Will you bring him?"

"It might not be safe if there should be trouble, señora. He might help his people."

"Will you take anyone else, to help pole?"

"It would be safer not to, señora, if the señores will help pole. He might be too frightened to come with us, and if we left him in charge of the cayuca that would not be safe."

"He might use it to get back to Chagres and leave us stranded?"

"Yes, señora."

"Very well, we start in fifteen minutes from now."

From Aspinwall the three Americans, with Romanos and their mestizo guide, sailed to Chagres, where they transferred to Piérola's cayuca. Romanos pushed them off and waved them good-bye, as they moved slowly upstream. Piérola sat in his usual place in the bow, Henry took the stern, Braddock sat amidships. The Americans tried to take their time from the mestizo, but their action was clumsy; they often smacked the water with their paddles instead of dipping them in with a deft flick of the wrist; each time they did this they showered the canoe with water; soon they were all wet through.

After a while they fell into a more even rhythm, and made better progress. Even so, as Braddock pointed out in a breathless chuckle, "You won't win no races on thisyere trip, Piérola."

"No, señor." His voice sounded resigned.

Braddock was in one of his talkative moods. "Say, Abby, do you know anything of thisyere love-charm business that Romanos was gabbling about?"

"A little from personal experience, and more from reading. It seems to me that Negroes are rarely able to shed the old superstitions inherited from generations of African ancestors. Except, perhaps, in the United States, there are few Negro communities whose lives are not controlled by tribal ritual, and the secret worship of ancient African gods, even though many of them are at the same time practising Catholics.

"This cult goes under different names . . . in Haiti it is known as voodoo; in Jamaica, obeah. Naturally it varies, but two of the rituals that are invariable are dancing and subjection to the tribal or local witch-doctors.

"Beside their other duties, the witch-doctors, or *bocors*, are responsible for the preparation of secret formulas—or potions, charms, ouangas, fetishes as they are variously known—for almost every imaginable purpose . . . to protect a man from death, make a woman fertile or prolific, guard against the evil eye, make a man or woman love you, make a woman hate her husband, cure venereal disease, get rid of worms. . . ."

"By thunder! It's sure bad enough to think of Negroes going in for sich nonsense, but a white girl. . . . Is she mad or somethin'?"

"She's in love, Jim dear. So desperately in love that, well, perhaps she is a little mad. Desperate enough to risk everything; her life . . . perhaps worse . . . in the hope of winning the love of the man she wants. You don't *love* her, do you, Henry?"

"No," he denied emphatically. "I'm not in love with her, Abigail. I suppose I like her. She's a far nicer kid than probably you give her credit for. Darned attractive in a clinging-ivy kind of way. First she looks at you with melting eyes that make you feel all paternal, then she kisses you in a way that makes you darn pleased not to be her father. I wouldn't ask for a better date. But love!" He shook his head.

Didn't Abigail comprehend that a man could thoroughly enjoy anything a girl offered him, without necessarily being in love with her? Love was more than just a matter of sleeping with a girl. Love was—was—well, wiser men than he had tried to define it without success. He loved Jean, whose image never deserted him for long. He had only to relax for memories of her to crowd in upon him; bitter-sweet memories that tantalized and tormented him. Sometimes, especially since Abigail's marriage to Jim, he had turned to Lucy in sheer desperation, to soothe a nagging ache to see Jean again; to see her sweet smile, to look into her serious eyes, and hear the lilting music in her voice. But that didn't mean he *loved* Lucy. Not in a thousand years, it didn't.

"Hey there, Abby!" Braddock had been trying to get a word in. "What did you mean jest now when you said somethin' about worse'n death? Like Red says, she's jest a whore, ain't she, so why should she worry?"

"With Negroes, Jim?"

"Hell! I wasn't thinking. . . . Yeah! I suppose——"

"She might have to suffer that; and then, afterwards . . . if the *bocor* should be needing a sacrifice——"

"Jesus! No!" Braddock shouted.

"Ask Piérola."

"Don't ask me, señor," the boatman wailed. "Please, señor——"

"He's answered you," Abigail said.

"Stark, raving mad!" Braddock muttered.

They slept the night at the old village of Gatún . . . for a new village had grown up about the railroad station on the opposite side of the river. After they had eaten, Piérola went round the village to find out whether Lucy and Garcia were there, for there was just a chance that they might have rested there for the night.

The boatman returned with bad news. Garcia had been seen poling up-river soon after one o'clock in the afternoon.

At daybreak they started off again. The river was more crowded than any of them had ever seen it. Early on in the morning the *William H. Aspinwall* passed them doing a steady four knots on her way up to Gorgona. Later, the *Raphael Rivas* went by them at double that speed, on the return journey downstream. Cayucas with emigrants, and several of the Isthmus Transportation Company's lifeboats, their passengers protected by canvas canopies, kept pace with them. Empty cayucas and lifeboats, returning from Gorgona or Cruces, sped downstream with the impetus of the swift-moving current. In addition to all these craft there were many cayucas, piled high with produce from the cultivated lands round about Bohio and Buena Vistita, which were being poled down to the market at Aspinwall.

Soon after midday they reached the confluence of the Chagres and Trinidad rivers. After some hard paddling on the part of the three men they nosed into the Trinidad river, and entered a quieter, wilder, less-frequented world. No more side-wheelers or lifeboats, no more shouting Americans, no more vistas of distant country. The silence was, in their present mood, ominous and depressing.

Although the jungle had closed in upon the Trinidad even more than upon the Chagres, at first there were still signs of human life. Cayucas floated downstream, guided by impassive Indians who ignored them except to respond brusquely to Piérola's greeting. At intervals, clearings had been hacked out of the greedy jungle to house and feed small communities of Indians. But these grew less frequent as they proceeded steadily upstream, and towards late afternoon they passed a small settlement which Piérola said was the last of the river folk.

"How much farther do we have to go before we land?" Abigail asked.

"Another two hours' paddling, señora."

"It will be dusk by then."

"There will be moon enough to see by if the clouds move away." He sniffed the air. "I think they will. There's wind in the air."

"How far have we to walk after landing?"

"Two hours, señora. If the moon is right, I suggest we land and sleep until daybreak."

The boatman's forecast proved correct. With the coming of darkness the clouds moved off, and a first-quarter moon lit up the river and gave them the illusion that they were moving along a winding silver ribbon. So clear was the surface that it was possible to distinguish dark objects afloat on it; driftwood, a small tree, floating clumps of water hyacinths, and the scaly back of a disturbed alligator.

By then the two Americans were so weary from the labour of many hours hard paddling they were almost falling asleep, so accustomed had their bodies come to the automatic rhythm of in-pull-out, in-pull-out, in-pull-out. . . . Even the cold beauty of the scene was, in a way, soporific, for it was like something from a dream: everything was either black or silver; there was no mean. The silence, too, was soothing and conducive to sleep, for nobody spoke, and the only loud noises were far away in the jungle and made an obligato to the eerie swish of the water stirred up by their paddles.

For Henry this state of near-sleep was presently disturbed by a distant sound no louder than a whispering throb, like the echo in a pillow of a heart beating with excitement. Titty-titty-titty-tom-tom. Titty-titty-titty-tom-tom. Titty-tom-tom-tom. Titty-tom-tom-tom. Titty-tom-tom-tom. Boom. Boom. Boom. Titty-titty-titty-tom-tom. . . .

"Good God! Listen . . ."

After a few moments, "I can't hear nothin'——"

"Santissima Maria!" Piérola exploded in a frightened gasp.

"Quiet!" Abigail hissed. Then, "Drums!"

"Drums! I kaint hear. . . . Yes, by thunder, I kain. Away over this to the west. . . . Hey there! What the hell . . ." for the canoe was rocking as Piérola tried to turn it too quickly.

"We must turn back, señora, señores. We must not go on."

"Why not?" Abigail demanded.

"You hear those drums. I know what it means. I've heard them before."

"Hold that there paddle still," Braddock roared at him, and the Panamanian was still. "What are you planning?"

"Get back to the last village. We could sleep there——"

"What them drums do to change your plans?"

"I think I can tell you, Jim. Those drums are calling the Negroes for a Petro dance, aren't they, Piérola?"

"Yes, señora. It isn't safe——"

"It wasn't safe before, you damned coyote," Braddock bellowed.

"You don't understand, señor. The Negroes might talk to you during the day, but it would be death to let them find you when they were holding a Petro sacrifice."

"Sacrifice . . . Jesus! Not the girl, Piérola? Not Lucy?"

"I don't know," Piérola sounded as if he were weeping with fear. "Perhaps yes, perhaps no. Who can say? But even if they aren't sacrificing a human, they would kill us if they found us near. They become mad with liquor——"

"He's probably right," Henry confirmed. "I remember my father telling me about the Petro dances in Haiti. Oh, my God! When I think of that girl. . . ."

"You want to turn back, Red?"

"We must, Jim. There's Abigail. . . . You take Abigail back. I go on with Piérola——"

"*No lo quiera Dios.* I won't take you. Not to a Petro dance. . . ."

"No?" Henry freed his left hand from the paddle. The unhappy boatman saw the moonlight reflected as a thin silver streak on the barrel of Henry's Colt.

"*Madre de Dios!* Why did I come?" the man whimpered.

"Don't be stupid, Henry," Abigail snapped. "Leaving me behind——"

"It's my fault. All my fault. If it hadn't been for me——"

"If it weren't for Adam, none of us would be in danger," she pointed out in a calm voice. "We're all going."

"Not you, Abby——" her husband began.

"All of us, I said," she asserted. "I've faced risks more times than you have fingers on your two hands, Jim Braddock. Turn the canoe up-river again."

The boatman made no move.

"You heard what the señora said," Braddock roared. He in turn drew a Colt. "Get going, you god-damned yeller-belly. Turn thisyere craft upstream."

After a moment's hesitation Piérola did as he was told. The Americans replaced the guns in their holsters and began paddling once more.

The sound of the drums grew louder. *TOM*-tom-tom-tom. *TOM*-tom-tom-tom. *TOM*-tom-tom-tom. One deep boom, followed by three staccato notes. The same rhythm now, repeated again and again and again until every nerve in their bodies was jumping in time to the muffled, pounding beat. *TOM*-tom-tom-tom. *TOM*-tom-tom-tom. Subconsciously Piérola set his time by the beat; the stroke became shorter and quicker. The two Americans behind were compelled to keep time with him, but they would have done so in any event. There was a hypnotic quality about the beat which was irresistible. *TOM*-tom-tom-tom. *TOM*-tom-tom-tom. No awareness of weariness, now. The canoe skimmed along the silver ribbon as the three paddles struck the water in perfect unison.

Amidships, between Braddock and Henry, Abigail kept time with her feet. BANG-tap-tap-tap. BANG-tap-tap-tap.

The noise grew fainter. Braddock turned round. "We've gone past, you double-crossing rat."

"No, señor. Another two, three miles."

"The drums aren't so loud——"

"That's not strange, Jim dear," Abigail interrupted. "One of the mysteries connected with African drums is that it is difficult to locate them. Sometimes the nearer you are to them the quieter they sound. Perhaps the lie of the land affects the echo."

"Huh!" Braddock turned back to his paddling. "I think I kain live without the noise of god-damned drums in my ears all night long."

TOM-tom-tom-tom. *TOM*-tom-tom-tom. *TOM*-tom-tom-tom.

"Señora," Piérola began. "I don't think the sacrifice has started yet. The drums are calling the people."

"Thank God!" she murmured.

Another mile. The sound of the drums increased, and the rhythm increased.

Boom. Tom. Boom. Tom. Tomitty-tomitty-tomitty.

"Hurry!" Piérola called out. "Quicker, señores, quicker."

The paddles scattered silver rain as the blades dipped in and out of the water. No more talking. The sense of urgency communicated to them by the threatening rhythm of the drums was too intense for useless words. Henry thought of the river as one immense black belly, and thrust his paddle into it with a vicious jab that took all Piérola's skill to counteract. Then he pictured Lucy's trim little body as he had last seen it, so tiny and yet so rounded and smooth. God! he gasped, as he saw its loveliness exposed to lustful eyes, and its uttermost intimacies explored by black fingers. God!

Tomitty-tomitty-tomitty-tom. Tomitty-tomitty-tomitty-tom. Louder and faster now. Tomitty-tomitty-tomitty-tom.

Piérola gave a warning shout. "We're reaching the place, señores. Careful. . . ."

They slid gently broadside on against the bank. Before them they saw a small clearing. They clambered out, Piérola at the point of Henry's gun . . . he had made as though to thrust off again. He stepped ashore a very frightened man. The others did not blame him. They were no less frightened. The night was frightening. The noise of the drums was frightening. The black jungle ahead of them was frightening. It was as well not to think too much. . . .

"Get a move on, Piérola," Henry ordered. His voice was unrecognizable, even to himself; it was more of a croak than a voice.

The boatman made one last appeal. "In the name of the Blessed Virgin and the Infant Jesus, let us wait here until morning. I don't want to die, señores. I would not have come for ten times a thousand dollars if I'd known there was a Petro dance——"

"Get moving," Henry snarled. "Or, by God . . ."

Piérola sobbed and led the way across the clearing into the black and silver-laced jungle. The trail was just visible.

Somewhere in the distance the biggest of the three drums pounded out its call to the Cimarrones.

Boom. Boom. Boom. Boom. Boom. Boom. Boom. Boom. Boom . . .

CHAPTER THIRTY-FIVE

As they moved steadily forward into the jungle Henry thanked God for the wind which had swept the sky clear of cloud formations. Without moonlight it would have been impossible to follow the trail. Even so, it was not easy, for the wall of jungle threw a black shadow across the narrow pathway.

Henry led, for the terrified boatman refused to do so even at the point of Braddock's Colt. So he followed in second place, giving directions from there whenever they came upon a cross-trail. Abigail followed Piérola, with Braddock in the rear.

In spite of difficulties they made fair progress for half an hour, for the going was on level ground. Later the land began to rise; at first in a moderate gradient, but later on more steeply. After a time the breathing of the boatman alone remained normal; for the three Americans were gasping. Their limbs ached, and Henry wondered whether Braddock would last out their journey. As a rancher he had gone everywhere on horse-back, and was not used to excessive walking. But he made no complaint.

Up, up, and still up. At one moment they emerged in a clearing large enough for them to see the moon-bathed countryside in all directions; to the north, east and south, the land fell away from them; particularly towards the east, where the Trinidad river looked more than ever like a long length of silver ribbon that had no beginning and no ending. But in front of them, to the west, the land sloped sharply upwards to an undulating line of jungle-capped peaks of varying heights.

Piérola placed a hand placatingly on Henry's arm. "This is as far as I can guide you with certainty," he began in an unsteady voice. "This is as far as I came the last time."

"By thunder! What's the good of bringing us this far?"

Abigail interrupted her husband's angry reproaches. "This was all that was promised, Jim." Then, to Piérola, "Have you any idea which direction to take from here?"

He nodded at the black outlines of the mountains ahead of them. "Only . . . forward, señora."

"See if the drums tell us," she suggested.

They listened. Tomitty-tomitty-titty-titty-tom-tom. Tomitty-tomitty-titty-titty-tom-tom.

"From there," Henry said, pointing.

"No, there," contradicted Braddock, indicating several points north of Henry's direction.

She turned to the boatman. "What do you say?"

"Anywhere between the two."

"I would have agreed with you, Henry. Suppose we make for some place between the two, as Piérola says? When we get nearer, maybe the direction will be clearer."

This seemed the only sensible course to take, but as they made their way across the clearing Braddock muttered, "What about when there won't be no god-damned drums to guide us back to here again?" But nobody answered him. They searched for a trail; and, finding it, re-entered the jungle.

As they descended the valley which separated them from the next height, Henry listened to the sound of the drums. Rather to his surprise it was about the only sound to be heard. He had, without having had time to give much thought to the matter, expected to hear more of the night beasts; the guttural bellowing of black howler monkeys, perhaps; the roar of a jaguar, the eerie swish of bats' wings, the hoot of an owl. But the only noises he heard were the dull crash of decayed vegetation falling to the ground, and the scamper of swiftly-moving feet; a peccary on the move, no doubt. Perhaps, he reflected, the pounding boom of the drums had hushed the usual noises. Down in the valley they reached a cross-trail.

"Which way?" Henry asked.

They listened carefully. The echo of the drums seemed to come, as they faced the trail they were on, from their half right.

"It could be either," Braddock despairingly answered.

Abigail turned to Piérola. "Which do you say?"

After a moment's hesitation the man replied, "The cross-trail, señora."

"If you're trying to lead us away——" Braddock threatened.

"Listen, Piérola," Abigail went on. "You're with us now whether you like it or not."

"Yes, señora, you don't have to tell me that." There was enough pathos in the man's voice to bring a smile to her lips.

"Very well. If we reach home safely *after* rescuing the girl we'll add another thousand dollars to what we've already given you."

Piérola gulped. "I'll do my best, señora. Another thousand dollars——"

"Do you still say . . . the trail on our right?"

"Yes, señora." For once his voice was almost eager. "Then perhaps the next cross-trail to the left, or one after that, according to how far off, and the sound of the drums."

"All right, Henry."

They turned to the right, along the valley bottom. The trail was knee deep in mud and water, and the going was atrocious. Then, unexpectedly, neither mud nor water were there and they found themselves bending forward with each step. They were evidently rising again.

At the next cross-trail they listened. This time the Americans felt that they should go to the left, as Piérola had originally suggested, but the Panamanian was doubtful.

"I think it will be the next after all, señores." He added, sensibly, "If it isn't we can come back to this point."

"We hope!" added Braddock, who was growing more pessimistic with every step forward into the heart of the jungle. One shouldn't be surprised at that, Henry reflected. The rancher was a man of open spaces, illimitless horizons: the narrow, jungle-walled trail would make him feel shut in, a prisoner.

The trail they were on continued along high-level ground. As the echo of the drums began to bear a sharper note they were encouraged to think that they must be approaching the dancers. The sound came from their left, and when they reached the next cross-trail Piérola had no hesitation in pointing towards it.

"I'm sure it's that way, señores." He was less frightened, more anxious to help; perhaps the extra thousand dollars had made the risk of dying worth while. Or perhaps, Henry reflected, the quickening tempo of the pounding drums was beginning to fire the man's blood. And no wonder, for it was impossible to deny there was a deeply-exciting quality about the staccato rhythm with its deeper, slower obbligato. The unceasing vibrations of sound reacted on one both physically and mentally: they destroyed one's moral inhibitions, and started one's limbs swaying to the beat of the drums. It

x

made one impatient for that beat to grow louder, louder, louder, and quicker, quicker, quicker. God! he thought. For five cents I'd join in their dance. Tomitty-tom-tom-tom-tom-tom. Tomitty-tom-tom-tom-tom-tom. Swing your arms, shuffle your feet. Swing your arms, shuffle your feet. Tom-tom-tom-tom. No need for a Master of Ceremonies. The drums beat out the movements, and you make them. Anyone can dance to the beat. Anyone would be compelled to dance to the beat. Tomitty-tom-tom-tom-tom-tom.

"*Madre de Dios!*" the boatman gasped with slobbering excitement, and Henry knew that the Panamanian was equally affected.

They quickened their steps. There was a hysterical note in the beat now that convinced them the dance had begun, and was working up to its climax. The sky was still unclouded. The sound of the drums grew louder. Louder . . . louder . . . louder. . . . As loud and as quick now as Henry had earlier desired.

"Jesus!" Braddock shouted, and Henry realized that the rancher was standing by his side instead of guarding the rear. Then he saw Abigail and Piérola in front instead of behind him. He didn't remember seeing them brush by him, or remember stopping. But how could anyone remember anything? Tomitty-tom-tom-tomitty-tom-tom-tomitty-tom-tom. The pounding beat drugged one's conscious reflections. . . .

And suddenly, round a bend in the trail, they saw the red glowing heart of a huge brushwood fire, and flames which leaped higher than the trees, and a circle of shining black bodies revolving round the fire, and three sweating Negroes pounding on three drums, and . . . Lucy. . . .

"Dear God!" Abigail murmured.

II

She was on the far side of the clearing, seated on the trunk of a dead tree. Her face looked terribly white, but perhaps this was in contrast with the black faces which shone even blacker in the reflection of the fire, for she did not appear terrified. On the contrary, there was something about her attitude which was more suggestive of interest than fear.

Freed from his anxiety for her, if only for a few moments, Henry glanced quickly about the clearing. It was hard to think clearly, for more than ever the waves of sound seemed to atrophy the power of thought. But with an effort of will he kept his twitching limbs still, and concentrated upon the scene before him. Thus his first reaction to the fantastic spectacle of posturing, whirling black bodies was, that he was undergoing a horrible nightmare. The next moment, his impression was completely changed by a trick of the imagination. No longer something out of a dream, the dance was something very real to him because he had seen it before, knew exactly what would happen next. Several seconds passed before he realized that he had only seen it through the eyes of his father. How often had he heard him tell the story of that night in Haiti, many decades ago, when Duncan Stewart, Toussaint, L'Ouverture, and Henry Christophe had watched ·the runaway slave Bouckman inflame the slaves with rebellion against their French masters.

That scene of primeval savagery had been such a one as this: a clearing in the undergrowth of the Choiseul le Marquis plantation, reddened by the flames from a cone of burning brushwood; three half-naked, frenzied Negroes beating the drums of hatred, murder, and rapine; the circle of several hundred Negroes and Negresses squatting on their haunches, swaying in unison to the drums and chanting a dirge to Damballa Ouedo, the Serpent-God.

Yet there was this difference, Henry presently saw. There was no black boar pawing the ground in its terror; no bleating, rearing white goats, no wooden case of white cockerels waiting to be sacrificed to Ogoun Badagris. Nor was there yet any chanting to the gods of Africa. Perhaps it was not time for that.

Also here there were two circles; for, within the outer circle of black people who squatted on their haunches, there was an inner circle of shuffling dancers. They were moving round and round the perimeter of the fire; so near to it were some of them that Henry could not understand why their flesh was not scorched. And their postures were obscene to gentle eyes, for their movements were orgiastic, frenziedly imitative of the copulative act, while their white-rimmed eyes were wild; and saliva dribbled from their thick, black lips.

Tom-tom-tom-tom-tom-tom-tom-tom-tom-tom.

Quicker, quicker, quicker moved the shuffling dancers: below their white trousers their naked feet stirred up clouds of dust which hung about their legs from the knees downwards like a remnant of fog that was not allowed to disperse. Wilder, wilder, wilder. Suggestive postures which dried Henry's mouth, and set his own limbs jiggling . . . for some of the dancers were young women naked to the waist: their firm breasts were outlined against the flames, which their sweating flesh reflected; an eerie effect, for they seemed to glow with an inward fire.

Piérola had said it was to be a Petro dance. Not a Legba service which is a community dance. But this was what the Africans called a Petro dance, wasn't it? Petro, the name given to a Voodoo ceremony in which a blood sacrifice is made. Then where was the sacrificial victim? Not Lucy. No, not Lucy. She wasn't bound. Perhaps a monkey, then. But where was the monkey? Henry glanced beyond the circle of squatters, looking for a monkey or some such animal. So it was that he saw her . . . no, *it* . . . standing to the left of the spot where the Americans stood hidden. The fire was between her—it, and Lucy, so perhaps she didn't realize. . . .

It stood unmoving, although all limbs were free. It was dressed in a one-piece cotton garment, with elbow-length sleeves. The frock had, no doubt, once been white. Its feet were shod in a pair of old slippers. It had the black, frizzy hair of a Negress, and a developed figure which was probably more than thirty years of age.

But its face was the empty, expressionless mask of a dead woman. Even the flesh seemed lifeless, for it neither absorbed the glow of the flames as the breasts of the dancers did, nor reflected it, as did the sweating, glistening torsos of the men. Light and colour seemed to shun it; even its blackness seemed ashy-grey rather than black: the shade of decayed flesh. The eyelids were half-closed, but he could distinguish the eyeballs: like the face, they were dead eyes; more dead than coloured glass.

He stared at the thing with the fascination of horror; this thing, this travesty, this monstrosity of humanity; and presently the explanation grew clear in his mind as he remembered the discussion with Abigail on the subject of zombies. That thing which stood in the clearing and stared unblinking, unseeing at the stamping dancers was a zombie—a woman dead in all but fact, a soulless body snatched from decay by the ungodly black magic of a native *bocor*.

Tomitty-tomitty-tom-tom. Tomitty-tomitty-tom-tom.

The ever-quickening tempo grew wilder, madder. Henry felt a hand grip his wrist. The hold was vice-like. He turned, startled, and saw that the hand belonged to Abigail. Impossible to believe that her slender arm could possess so much strength. Impossible to believe that the pounding drums could possibly affect her unimpulsive, inhibited nature. But the impossible was unmistakably happening. She was staring at the dancers with lusting eyes. Her mouth was half-open, and he heard her breath hiss in palpitating gasps. She swayed her hips to the staccato boom which pounded against the eardrums of them all; and with her free hand stroked her right breast, a circular movement which made its small, shapely roundness stiffen beneath her shirt.

Abigail, of all people! Of many lewd spectacles he had witnessed in The House of All Nations, this was by far the lewdest. On the instant he abominated the drums as things profane. If that frenzied rhythm could do this to Abigail, what might it not do to others less inhibited?

The answer was before his eyes. Jim Braddock . . . Piérola. . . . And the three score Negroes in the clearing. They were no longer human beings, but black-skinned, lusting satyrs, some in the first stages of a cataleptic trance induced by the abnormal exhaustion of both physical and mental powers. Others were leaping over the fire. Others, led by a painted *bocor*, were advancing with high, frenzied leaps upon the zombie . . . the first destined victim of the devilish saturnalia which was rapidly working up to its climax. They ripped every stitch of clothing from the zombie, then lifted the unflinching body into the air, carried it to a tree and tied its ankles together with a rope of liana, the other end of which they threw over a high bough. Before Henry could realize what was happening the shouting, maddened executioners had hoisted the zombie into the air, head downwards, so that the witch-doctor could perform his devilish operation.

The drums beat louder, louder, louder. . . .

"God Almighty!" Henry found himself shouting, but the booming drums drowned his voice. How much more could he stand?

How much longer could he restrain himself? How much longer could any of them remain sane?

He had his answer a few moments later.

The zombie screamed . . . the high-pitched terror rose above the boom of the drums. The *bocor* had brought the dead to life, had returned the woman's soul to its living shell. For the Voodoo cult of the Cimarrones demanded the victim's awareness of the sacrifice. . . .

A second scream, but this time from Lucy. The sound of it was a counter-irritant to the spell of the drums, and restored sanity to Abigail and Jim Braddock.

"Henry . . . Jim . . . quick, before it's too late."

Both men knew what she meant. Their hands went automatically to their guns.

CHAPTER THIRTY-SIX

PIÉROLA moved even more quickly than they. He stepped in front of them, arms outstretched. His body shook with fear, his teeth chattered.

"You mustn't let them see you, señores," he shouted, to make himself heard above the throbbing waves of sound. "They will kill you. . . ."

"Four guns kain do a helluva lot of harm and put the fear of God into these bastards. Come on, Red."

"Wait, wait! The Negroes are not themselves. They're mad with drink; and under the influence of the *bocor* they have no fear."

"We'll risk that. . . ."

"If you are killed, señores, what about the señora and me?"

"Yes, by God! Abby!" Braddock muttered, shaken by his own thoughtlessness. "Those god-damned drums! A man can't think——"

"Nor a woman," Abigail admitted. "But we must do something for that poor girl."

Both the women in the clearing had stopped screaming, but for the moment neither was visible to the four people hidden behind the fringe of jungle, because surging dancers were obstructing the view. Lucy's silence was more alarming than her screams.

Braddock voiced the apprehension they all felt. "Why has she stopped yelling?" he shouted in Henry's ear. "I don't like it."

The dancers swayed once more, by chance leaving a clear path between the jungle and the zombie. For no more than a few seconds the Americans were able to see what was happening before a surging mass of black celebrants closed the path again; but the time had been long enough for horrified eyes to see a stream of blood spurting from the zombie's throat into a bowl held by the *bocor*.

"I'm going to get her," Henry shouted back in Braddock's ear. "Can't stand much more——"

"How?"

"I'll creep round, behind the trees."

"You've no machete——"

"I'll manage."

As Henry moved off to his right Braddock lifted an arm in restraint, but only to lower it slowly with a gesture of resignation. Somebody had to do something about rescuing the girl. Besides, there *was* a chance. It was in Henry's favour that the drums were making too much noise for the Negroes to hear him forcing a way through the thick undergrowth.

He dared go no deeper into the jungle than one tree's breadth from the clearing, for he needed the light from the fire to help him see; the upper branches of the trees were too thick to let enough moonlight through. In normal circumstances he could not have hoped to remain unseen, or even unheard, but he felt safe in taking a chance; for the Negroes, already made frenzied by liquor and the beat of the drums, were quickly reaching a state of delirium.

After he had progressed a short distance he could see the tree trunk on which Lucy had been sitting. To his relief he saw that she was still there, but much changed. Her attitude was now one of terror, an emotion that was reflected on her face. It was apparent that she realized at last her own danger. Close by her side stood a tall, square-built Negro.

The sight of the guard made Henry's expression even grimmer. He had hoped to reach a point from which he could remain under cover while shouting directions to her what to do. The presence of the Negro made that impossible.

He paused to look across the clearing in the direction of the zombie. Horror was succeeding horror: he saw the Negroes pass the *bocor's* bowl from one to another, each man taking a deep draught of the zombie's blood before doing so. Meanwhile, the *bocor*, having sliced open the zombie's stomach, had extracted the entrails from the corpse, and was chopping them into small portions, of which the remaining Negroes partook.

The increasing tempo of the drums warned Henry that the crisis could not long be deferred. Already some of the maddened dancers were wrestling with women no less inflamed with lust and passion; but others, not yet having reached the stage when restraint was no longer possible, were now and again turning towards the white woman in their midst with jeering cries and obscene gestures. Soon these men might demand a second sacrifice. . . .

Using even less caution, Henry continued to work his way round the clearing. The vegetation tore his clothes and flesh; he was soon smeared with blood. He reached the nearest point to Lucy. If it were not for that damned guard . . . He wondered whether he dared risk shooting the man in the back: with luck the roar of the explosion might be drowned by the drums. But after that . . .

He listened to the crude chanting of the Negroes who made up the outer ring of celebrants. He could only distinguish a word here and there, which seemed to be a form of bastard Spanish. This gave him an idea. It was not likely that many, if any, of the Cimarrones would know English. He cupped his hands round his mouth, and, keeping time to the chant, called out:

"Lu-cy! Lu-cy! Lu-cy!"

Neither Lucy nor her guard made any move, so he was sure that he had not been heard. He tried again, raising his voice slightly.

"Lu-cy! Lu-cy! Lu-cy!"

This time she heard. He saw her start, then raise and half-turn her head as if to listen more acutely.

He called again. "Lu-cy! Red . . . here! Red . . . here!"

Again she heard and turned impulsively towards the jungle. The movement attracted the attention of the Negro by her side.

He, too, turned. Henry dodged behind a royal palm. He sheltered there for what seemed many minutes before he dared to peer round it. Then he saw that both Lucy and the guard were staring at the weaving, swaying, surging mass of dancers again.

He started shouting again. "Lu-cy! Don't turn! Don't turn! Do you hear me? Signal!"

She lifted her hand above her shoulder and waved it to and fro. Thank God! he thought. She can hear me.

"Lu-cy! Step backwards slow-ly! Step by step. Don't let guard see. Do you un-der-stand? Signal!"

She signalled, so he did not shout again. No need to take needless risks. He watched her with anxious eyes. Quickly, quickly! he commanded in his thoughts. Then he grinned wryly. Hadn't he just told her to move slowly? It was a case of make haste slowly. . . .

She rose to her feet as if to watch more easily what was happening. The guard seemed to have no objection. For nearly a minute she stood still . . . at least that was Henry's impression. Then he realized that she had not stood still, but had actually shuffled backwards several inches. Good girl! he thought. Good girl!

She moved more inches towards the fringe of the jungle . . . more and more . . . until she was less than twenty-five feet from him. At this rate, he reflected with sudden optimism . . . He concentrated on watching her, willing her in his thoughts not to panic; and praying that she would avoid a rotten branch that was in the way: it might easily snap under her weight, and cause alarm.

An unexpected discovery shocked him out of his mood of hope. In spite of the not-inconsiderable distance she had shuffled backwards, the space between her and the Negro guard had barely altered. The man was keeping pace with her; playing with her like a cat with a mouse. At the last moment, no doubt, he would pounce. . . . Henry drew his right-hand Colt.

Tomitty-tomitty-tomitty-tomitty-tomitty-tomitty-tomitty-tomitty-tomitty. . . .

Earlier, it had not seemed possible that the tempo of the drums could increase, but it had quickened so much that the rhythm resembled one loud and unceasing peal of thunder. In the manner of idle thoughts which occur even in the most critical of moments, Henry wondered how much colossal energy was needed to maintain such a stupendous feat of endurance as the three drummers had maintained. Fingers, wrists, and arms seemed tireless as they pounded out their unholy beat on the cowhide heads of the tree-trunk drums. Their flesh ran with sweat; their white-rimmed eyes had the fixed stare of an epileptic. Quick, Lucy! he thought, desperate that she should reach comparative safety before the drummers, by physical collapse, brought an end to their spell. Quick, in the name of God. . . .

And then she was close enough for him to touch her. As he pulled her beside him, the Negro began to turn. He fired, but Lucy jogged his arm, and the bullet grazed the man's shoulder. The force of the blow made the Negro stumble to his knees.

"Señor Malley . . ." he gasped in reproach.

"Red . . . it's Juan . . ."

"Almighty God," Henry exclaimed.

Juan clambered to his feet. He did not trouble even to staunch the bleeding. "Quick, señor," he shouted, the note of urgency loud in his throat. "Before the drums stop. This way . . ." He began to force a way through the undergrowth.

"Wait. . . . Juan . . . I have friends near——"

"Good!" Juan exclaimed. "Where?"

"Near the trail from the river. This way." Henry pointed.

"I see your track, señor. Follow." He turned and hurried along the precise route Henry had made on his way round: even in the uncertain light from the fire his skilled eyes could detect the bent ends of green twigs and torn-off leaves on the muddy ground.

Before they reached the spot where Henry had left his companions he called upon Juan to stop.

Juan turned: his shining black face looked anxious. "There's no time to stop, señor. At any moment——"

"Señor Braddock may shoot first, as I did——"

"Ah!" The argument appealed to the Negro. "You go first."

So Henry led, and presently slowed down. "Jim . . . Jim," he called out.

Braddock appeared mysteriously from behind a tree. "Hullo . . . ." he began. Then, "Who the devil——" His gun flashed out.

"Stop, Jim. . . . Juan is a friend, an Isthmian Guard. . . . I've already shot him. . . ."

"Goddam!"

"Where are the others?"

"Farther down the trail."

Juan broke in. "Hurry, hurry, señores, at any moment——"

The drumming stopped with an abruptness that made Lucy gasp. Juan wasted no more time in words. He caught hold of her hand and pulled her after him, running. Henry and Braddock followed. Behind them, in the clearing, an angry roaring succeeded the sound of the drums. It was obvious that Lucy's escape had been discovered.

They pounded on down the trail. A short way down Abigail and Piérola came out of the blackness of the jungle wall.

"Follow them two!" Braddock gasped. "Red and me will hold the other bastards back with a shot or two."

For a brief while the noise of shouting grew fainter. Henry guessed that the Cimarrones had automatically entered the jungle at the nearest point to the trunk on which Lucy had been seated; but reckoned that it would take no longer for them to see the trails he had made than it had Juan.

Sure enough, in a short while the shouting grew louder again as the maddened Negroes followed the track round to the normal trail.

"Won't be long now," he shouted to Braddock, who nodded agreement.

It wasn't. A louder yell from behind warned them they had been seen.

"Now," Braddock ordered.

The two men stopped, turned round and fired. An agonized howl advised them that at least one bullet had found its mark. The noise of shouting grew less. Several minutes elapsed before the pursuit was resumed. But those minutes had gained the fleeing party valuable distance.

Henry and Braddock waited until the last possible moment before turning and firing again. This time they slowed down and took deliberate aim. Two Cimarrones pitched forward into the mud, and their companions slowed down, halted. The Americans gained more ground.

"Thank God they've no weapons with them!" Braddock panted. "Guess we caught them napping."

They ran on, but for the third time the drunken, blood-lust-

demented Negroes continued after them. There could be no hope
of parley. So the Americans fired for the third time, and again their
bullets halted their pursuers.

This time the lesson was not lost upon the Cimarrones. The
instinct to live was stronger than the desire for revenge. Even their
muddled thinking could reason that with no weapons, and no room
along the narrow winding trail to manœuvre, they could not hope
to catch or kill the few white people who had robbed them of their
most exciting sacrificial victim for years.

The echo of their shouting grew fainter, then died away
altogether. Yet none of the pursued party breathed freely until their
cayuca was moving swiftly downstream on a river which changed
from silver to black velvet as the moon sank behind the mountains.

II

The following afternoon Henry was lazily rocking on the porch
of the Braddock home. Braddock was with him. It was coolest
there; in addition to the protection of the roof, the two palm trees
shaded the porch from the glare of the sun. It had rained all the
morning and the air was still fresh.

Abigail joined them. Her lips were pressed firmly together;
there was a hurt expression in her eyes. As soon as they had all
settled, Henry asked:

"Is she awake yet, Abigail?"

She nodded. "About half an hour ago. She is still resting
quietly."

"How is she?"

A dry smile. "Perfectly well. Why should she be otherwise?"

"The shock——"

"Wasn't long enough to have a lasting effect. She is young,
resilient, and on the whole, healthy. Besides, you had rescued her
almost as soon as she had realized her danger."

"Good."

"Have you found out why she really went on that damnfool
trip?" Braddock asked. "Love charm . . ." He snorted his disbelief.

"If you mean have I questioned her, the answer is that I have not, my dear. I should not dream of prying into her private affairs, but it is not difficult to guess." She turned to Henry. "What are you going to do with her?"

Braddock protested. "Hey! Old girl——"

"Please don't call me old girl, Jim. You know how I dislike the words."

"Sorry, honey. I have the darnedest memory! But what's the girl to do with Red anyway? Just because he's visited her some-times that doesn't make her his responsibility. There were—er—others——"

"Not directly, perhaps, but he visited her too often. She has fallen in love with him."

Henry fidgeted. "Nonsense, Abigail. There was never any question of love on either side. I'm sure I did nothing—that is, I had no idea. . . . Besides—well, that is her job. Maybe she didn't chose it in the first place, but——"

Abigail's smile was ironic. "You have nothing to blame your-self for, Henry, but I think you should help her. As a kindly action, with no tags attached."

"I suppose I should, but what can I do to help?"

"In spite of everything, she's possibly still a decent girl at heart. Somewhat nicer than I had imagined. Absolutely unmoral, of course, but she's young. If her energies could be diverted——"

"Marriage?" her husband demanded. "Goddam! Abby, you're not suggesting that Henry——"

"Of course not. Don't be ridiculous."

"All right then, but what decent fellow is going to marry a—to marry her now?" he asked forthrightly.

"Not here, but back home perhaps, where she could start a new life. If she stays in this country the usual fate of worn-out prosti-tutes is inevitable for her. Especially after what has happened."

"Why especially?" asked her puzzled husband.

"Because she has failed to get what she wants so desperately. She'll probably persuade herself that she owes the world a grudge. If once that happens there will be no more hope of saving her."

Henry shook his head. "I don't think she would settle down to marriage. She's frankly voluptuous, and once she was over the initial stages she found it an easy life. She told me so."

"When?"

"Oh!" Henry gestured vaguely. "When I first met her, I guess."

Abigail nodded. "I thought so. Since then she's discovered that she thinks she's in love. That makes quite a difference." Her gaze rested for a moment on her husband's rugged face, and she smiled affectionately.

"If you think so, Abigail," Henry conceded. "That's good enough for me. I'll send her." After a pause, "But why are you specially suggesting that *I* should speak to her?"

"Because you are the only person she is likely to listen to, my dear. She's a wilful young woman. Go, talk to her, Henry."

Henry rose, and entered the bedroom. The blind had been lowered, and the room was in semi-darkness. When his eyes had accustomed themselves to the twilight he saw that her tiny head had sunk into the pillow, and that the white sheet had been modestly arranged under her chin so that only her small winsome face was visible. She looked sad and forlorn.

Abigail had left a chair beside the bed, so he sat down on it.

"Hello!" he greeted awkwardly.

"Hello!"

"Abigail says you are almost all right again."

"Yes." She spoke in a whisper.

"Lucy . . ." he began, but stopped short. How was he to begin? He was not helped by the knowledge that her gaze was fixed on him with a wistful pleading that was easy to interpret: she did not want him to talk about what had happened.

He forced himself to be firm. "I've got to talk with you, my girl," he began primly. "You know now, I suppose, what sort of a mad prank you got up to last night?"

"Please don't scold me. I don't think I could bear that." There were tears in her voice.

He took a handkerchief out of his pocket and wiped the sweat from his face. A few moments before he had thought it cool in the bedroom.

"Look, Lucy," he began gently, "I haven't come here to scold. Let's forget the past and talk of the future."

"Yes," she exclaimed with eagerness.

"We've been talking, Mr. and Mrs. Braddock and I, and we don't want you to stay at the House any more."

"I don't want to stay there either, Red. That's why I—I did what I did. I won't go back there ever . . . I'll kill myself first."

He felt confused. "I don't understand. I thought you were happy there—well, happy enough——"

"I was, but everything's changed now. It's beastly, horrible."

"Is it that woman?" he asked harshly. "If it is——"

"It's nothing to do with Madame," she hurriedly interrupted. "It's me, Red. I've changed, I tell you." There was a note of urgency behind her tears now. "I can't stand the life any more. Having men stare at me with dirty eyes, feeling their hands pawing me all over, lying with me in bed——"

The threatening tears overflowed. She turned her face away from him, but he saw them well out of the corner of her eye and roll slowly down the white cheek.

He had never had to deal with woman's tears since he had become a man. He was embarrassed, and uncertain what to do. So he did nothing.

"All the more reason for sending you away, Lucy," he said at last.

"Away!" She sat up abruptly, so that the sheet fell away from her. He saw that she wore one of Abigail's cambric nightdresses, lace-frilled at neck and wrists. "You can't do that, Red. Please, please."

"But, Lucy . . ." He stared at her with astonishment. "I thought that's what you wanted."

"To leave the House, but not to go away. I want to stay."

"Stay where? Doing what?" he asked irritably.

A long pause. And then, "With you, Red," she whispered. "Let me come and live with you." At last the words came easily, so quickly they were scarcely intelligible. "I'll housekeep for you. I'll do your mending and cooking. I've never done any, but I could learn. I'll nurse you when you have fever. I'll do anything you want. Everything. Only let me live with you. Please, please, please. You don't know how much I love you. . . ."

The incoherent words ceased as abruptly as they had started. She sank back against the head of the bed, exhausted and breathless, and stared at him through a mist of tears that seemed to enlarge her dark eyes and magnify their pathos.

He dared not look too long at her, for he knew that it would be all too easy to fall a willing victim. Equally, he knew that it was essential to maintain rigid self-control; that he must not allow himself to be influenced by impulse; that he must dispassionately consider the idea from every angle. Abigail had taught him to appreciate what it meant to have a home and a woman's companionship. Taught him too well; for he hated living alone at the Howard Hotel, and although he enjoyed his visits to The House of All Nations his present mode of life did not begin to compare with that blissful period when he had lived with Abigail. To repeat that experience with Lucy substituting for Abigail was a chance that he longed to seize. But to do so would be, in effect, an insult to Abigail which he knew she would never be able to forgive, and he would never offer. To set up a household with Lucy as his mistress would be to reduce Abigail to the level of a strumpet. For it would make her liaison with him, in retrospect, a sordid affair as though he had been merely making use of her until he found another, younger, woman to take her place.

"No," he gruffly told Lucy. "No."

Her lips quivered with disappointment. "Why shouldn't we? I love you, and you—you don't dislike me, do you? You enjoy all I can give you, don't you?"

"Of course. More than."

"Well, then. . . . And if I keep house for you at the same time——"

"No," he answered brusquely. "With Mr. and Mrs. Braddock living in the same town? Don't forget, my girl, they did as much as I in rescuing you last night. Would that be your idea of gratitude to them . . . to flaunt ourselves before their eyes?"

Her expression grew hopeless, and she turned away. "I wouldn't want to hurt them," she whispered. "Not ever." After a pause. "But I won't go back to the House——"

He leaned forward and pushed back one sleeve of her nightdress so as to expose her hand, which he took in his own.

"Let me send you back to the States," he pleaded gently. "Some place where nobody will know you or your past, where you can start a new life. Memphis, maybe? My old nurse lives there; the dearest old soul in the world. She would soon grow to love you; and you, her."

"Do you want me to do that?" she asked in a flat voice.

"I want you to be happy, my dear. I want you to have a chance of making something of your life."

"Do you *want* me to go?" she persisted.

"I—I——" He could not lie to her. "Not for my own sake, perhaps——"

Before he could finish she had turned to him. Her eyes were wide with hope and excitement.

"Suppose we didn't live here but some place else?" she questioned breathlessly. "Gatún, or Barbacoas? I would promise never, never, never to come back to Aspinwall."

It was his turn to glance away so that she should not see the hot desire in his eyes. To have a home of one's own to return to, even if it were only a native hut! And a woman to give one companionship and love, even profane love! It was asking too much of a man to refuse.

He pulled her into his arms, and kissed the puckish little mouth with a passion that made her body stiffen in response.

CHAPTER THIRTY-SEVEN

THROUGHOUT the months which followed Henry's decision to accept Lucy's offer, he never had reason to regret it. The first crisis, when he announced to Abigail and Jim his intention of setting up a home with Lucy as his mistress, was the worst. At first Abigail's face had stiffened with resentment; but her sense of justice soon asserted itself and she accepted the decision with more graciousness than he had anticipated, especially when she was told of Lucy's promise not to enter Aspinwall so long as the Braddocks continued to live there. Perhaps her own contentment was mainly responsible for her tolerance.

There were times, of course, when he grew irritable with Lucy;

for she loved to talk to him, and her prattle was as unceasing as it was artless. But in so many other ways her company more than compensated for her inability to let him relax after a long spell of absence. Her solicitude for his comfort embarrassed him. Sometimes her love touched his conscience so that he considered marriage.

But he was haunted by too many spectres for the vague idea to progress beyond the stage of troubled contemplation. Jean was occupying his thoughts more than ever. Perhaps the letters from his mother were responsible: not one arrived that did not mention Jean at some length. Jean was going to New York next week. Jean was knitting a shawl for Elizabeth Webb's baby. Jean would be twenty-two next Fall, and still not affianced! Jean . . . Jean . . . Jean. . . .

He spent Christmas with Abigail and Braddock. The following day he left for Panama, to spend a while there.

Zachary Fox was still the same: impassive, white-faced, immaculate. His menagerie had increased. A cheeky little marmoset had joined the family: the cat had kittens. Rover still thumped his tail whenever his master looked in his direction, or else sat with his chin on Fox's knee.

In spite of two substantial losses to lucky gamblers, he was still making money. Some of his winnings he had invested in local commercial undertakings, which in turn were paying him handsome dividends. Like Braddock, he seemed unable to do anything wrong.

Ran Runnels welcomed Henry with a warm handclasp.

"Good to see you again, Red. Sit down. What's yours?"

They toasted each other. "Anything new?" Henry asked the Ranger.

"No. A few individual hold-ups, but nothing organized. You know we've come out into the open?"

Henry nodded. "Everyone knows the Isthmian Guard, Ran. I hear you've started policing the trails."

"Sure we have. We've hung five men in the past two months."

"And La Pantera?"

"Like I wrote you in November, nothing new. Guess he's retired and living some place on his spoils. Say, that was a queer story Juan brought back with him from furlough."

Henry gave Runnels an account of the Petro sacrifice, and its sequel.

Runnels nodded thoughtfully. "Lucky for you all that Juan had chosen that week to visit his people."

"Did he choose it purposely?"

"Don't think so. He swears it's the first human sacrifice he's ever seen. They usually sacrifice a monkey. I believe him. I kinda trust that feller. You know, he thinks a hell of a lot of you, Red."

"Why?"

"Because of the way you rescued the girl, I guess. If anyone finds La Pantera it will be him." Runnels frowned. "Jim Holmes ain't taking no more stores out to La Pantera."

"Why not?"

"Guess he don't want to be trailed."

"How does he know?"

"Easy. Young Perrigot told him."

"Perrigot! But——"

"He's back in Panama, living with Holmes."

"I didn't know. He was still on the payroll three weeks ago, when I made enquiries. One of the few that are left on it."

"Well, he's here now, so I guess he spilled enough for Holmes to sort of put two and two together."

"Then that may force Al into the town. . . ."

The Ranger chuckled. "I shouldn't get het up yet, Red. There are other ways for Holmes to get food out to La Pantera besides taking the stuff himself. Sending some other trusted party, f'rinstance. We can't keep tabs on everyone in Panama."

"I can't understand Al keeping away from the town all this time. It isn't like him."

Runnels transferred his cigar to the other corner of his mouth with a quick flick. " 'Taint like most anybody to stay away so long from civilization, Red. I reckon he's got the gold from them robberies cached away some place, and is sitting on it to see that nobody don't help himself."

"What for? What's the use of gold if you don't spend it?"

The Ranger chuckled. "Maybe he's waiting for me to die so's he can take it back to the States without any questions asked."

II

Another dry season began and ended, with Henry wondering gloomily whether he would ever be able to return to Boston. He spent a large proportion of his generous salary in employing spies to find the whereabouts of the elusive La Pantera, but without useful result. Now and again he received news that an American named Simpson had been seen here, and there, and some place else, but as he never stayed in any place more than a few hours the reports served no useful purpose, other than to reassure Henry that Al was still in the country. There was one other item: Simpson was usually accompanied by a woman. Illuminating, but otherwise useless: it explained why Al was apparently content not to visit Panama, but it did nothing to help solve the mystery of how he could remain hidden so long in such a small country. The only possible solution was that he lived in a small village tucked away in the interior in so remote a spot that no one was likely to visit it by accident. However, the knowledge that Al was still in Panama was enough to keep the flicker of hope alive in Henry, and prevent his thoughts from dwelling too often on the question of time. Time which was aging his parents. Time which might allow some young fellow in Boston to win Jean's heart. Time meant everything to him, but in the country of Mañana, where time meant nothing to the majority of its inhabitants, he was powerless to hurry along the day when he could meet Al face to face, and wrest a confession of theft from him.

Time was likewise the enemy of the railroad. The bridge at Barbacoas remained precisely as it had been the day after the flooding waters of the Chagres had smashed one of its spans. Elsewhere, at various points between Barbacoas and Panama, desultory work was being done by a handful of labourers, but it meant little. Henry began to despair that the road ever would be finished. He settled down unwillingly to a life of monotony, which was all the more appalling when he considered how much drama had been packed into the previous four years. Only four years! It seemed more like a decade to him, in retrospect.

But one day in May something happened to shift him out of

the peaceful rut along which he was drifting. A man entered his office.

"Hello, Red," he greeted casually.

Henry looked up, and leaped to his feet. "Jimmy, you old so-and-so! Jimmy McCollum, by all that's wonderful!" He wrung the other man's bony hand. "You're looking fine; a thousand per cent better than when you left. . . ."

"Not so surprising, Red."

"I'll say not. And the family, Jimmy? All well?" A happy nod from McCollum. "Good. But what are you doing back here? Not on your way to California? You've not fallen for this gold fever?"

"Can you see me?"

Henry couldn't. Not dry, unadventurous James McCollum grubbing for gold in California.

McCollum went on, "You know the year's contract with the contractors is due to expire soon?"

"In July, or thereabouts?"

"Yes. Well, the contractors are through. So the railroad's going to resume work on it."

"No!" Henry laughed. The history of the railroad had too many tragic pages, especially for contractors, but there were humorous pages, too. He pretended to pick petals off an imaginary flower. "I'll do the work. You'll do the work. I'll do the work." He stopped. "Where's the money coming from?"

"Wall Street. The financiers reckon that the road will pay for itself in a few years if the present rates are maintained." He glanced quizzically at a chair. "Aren't you going to ask me to sit down, Red?"

Henry grinned apologetically. The two men sat down, and lit cigars. "Colonel Totten is starting another of his labour-recruiting campaigns. He wants to have a big enough force here to start work as soon as the existing contract with Mr. Story expires. That's why I've come back, to organize the survey staff."

"But, Jimmy . . . your family. . . ."

"Look, Red," McCollum explained in a flat voice. "My conscience hasn't given me a moment's peace from the time I left here . . . especially when I heard about Armstrong. He wouldn't be dead now if it weren't for my damned cowardice."

"But you probably would be. And Armstrong didn't have a wife and family."

"I know, but . . ." McCollum looked unhappy. "I can't bring the poor devil back to life, but I can finish his work. And that's that." He changed the subject with a snap to warn Henry not to reopen it.

"We'd better finish the road pronto before it's too late," he went on. "Did you know that our Government is reopening the idea of a canal? In a few months' time they are sending out a naval party to survey the route from Caledonia Bay to the Gulf of San Miguel."

"Why that one?"

"Because an Irishman by the name of Cullen has given a glowing report of it."

"There won't be much use for the railroad if a canal is ever opened."

"Oh! I don't know." McCollum studied the smoke of his cigar as it spiralled up to the ceiling. "Depends where it's located."

"Why?"

"Suppose the Chagres valley were used, the railroad would be invaluable."

"If! But a canal couldn't be built here, Jimmy. What about the Continental Divide? We are using the lowest point, and that's more than two hundred and fifty feet above. How could anyone surmount two hundred and fifty feet of solid mountain?"

"Several ways, Red. One, by tunnelling through."

Henry whistled.

"It's possible," the surveyor said sharply. "But probably too damned expensive. A second method would be to cut through the mountain."

"All two hundred and fifty feet of it, Jimmy?"

"It would be quite a job," McCollum admitted. "But possible. And, like the tunnel, expensive. Lastly, one might have a smaller cut, and lock up to it. Anyway, that isn't my job. The railroad's my business. Want your old job back, Red?"

"You mean, with you?"

"Sure, sure."

"Count me in," Henry replied with the emphasis of eagerness.

III

Back to the Isthmus came Colonel Totten. Later, he was followed by boatloads of labourers from many countries. First came those who had sailed from the nearest ports; Kingston, Jamaica; Havana, Cuba; and from other West Indian ports; and of course from Totten's favoured Carthagena. Next arrived a ship from New Orleans which brought a number of American coloured people, and a sprinkling of whites as well.

Later came ships from the United Kingdom, France, Germany, Spain, bringing not only nationals of those countries, but a fair number of peasants from countries farther east. Then came workers from India and the Middle East. The number of employees leaped upwards: from a few hundreds to two thousand, three, four, five and more. Work was resumed simultaneously at several points.

Ships arrived from Georgia with cargoes of pine poles and timber for the completion of the bridge at Barbacoas. By the end of October the Chagres had been spanned at a height of fifty feet above its average level by a trestle bridge more than 600 feet long. The bridge builders were quickly followed by the track-laying gangs. On the 26th November the first engine noisily chuffed its way across the bridge. There was rejoicing at Aspinwall. The last great obstacle to the completion of the road had been surmounted. What still remained was more or less straightforward work.

But the Isthmus was not to be conquered so easily. It still fought back. Black clouds of mosquitoes swarmed upon the newly arrived labourers, and their deadly bite completed the work already begun by tropical heat and torrential rains. One by one, ten by ten, score by score the labourers sickened and fell ill. Irishmen and Frenchmen were particularly susceptible. Many died, and were buried at Monkey Hill. Others had to be shipped back to their native lands. The old, old story was retold. Send a message to the recruiting agents. More labourers wanted. More labourers wanted. More labourers wanted. So the agents busied themselves once more. They went into the highways and by-ways of India, Malaya, and

China where there were inexhaustible wells of starving labour to draw on.

Hindus arrived, Malayans arrived, one thousand Chinese arrived. Nearly one thousand Chinese, that is to say, for sixteen died on the way across the Pacific; bland-faced, almond-eyed, pig-tailed Chinese, complete with stocks of tea, hill-rice, and opium.

Opium! The idea of their employees' drugging themselves with opium was offensive to the white employers. They mustn't be allowed to bring obnoxious Eastern habits into contact with Western civilization. Especially a habit that cost 15 cents per man per day. So the order went forward—no opium.

Within a few days thirty-two of the Chinese were prostrate. A week later, eighty more were taken ill. Life without the drug which gave them such beautiful dreams was intolerable to the unhappy emigrants. Surely that celestial paradise of unlimited opium, lovely flowers, much rice, and the companionship of one's honourable and illustrious ancestors was a preferable world to that in which one's body craved the unobtainable, and one was desperately home-sick for the paddy-fields and temples of one's own country. So those bland-faced, almond-eyed, pig-tailed Chinese labourers proceeded to despatch themselves to that other, lovelier world by the quickest possible route. Some drowned by tying heavy rocks to themselves and jumping into the swollen Chagres. Others sharpened wooden stakes which they thrust into their throats. Others bribed Malayan workers to shoot them. Others strangled themselves with their own queues. Others waded out into the ocean and waited for the tide to drown them. Others starved themselves to death. When all but two hundred had died the company took pity on them, and shipped them off to Jamaica.

But the road must be completed. What was a matter of a thousand deaths more or less? Just a question of adding a zero at the wrong end of the already large total of deaths. So the cry went forth again. More labourers wanted . . . more labourers wanted . . . more labourers wanted. . . .

CHAPTER THIRTY-EIGHT

RUMOURS of the mounting death-roll among the labourers and the mass suicide of the Chinese naturally reached Henry, but he paid scant attention to them; mainly because gruelling work occupied every waking hour at that time, and partly because familiarity with death had come to breed contempt for it; as Zachary Fox had forecast. From bitter experience, railroad construction across the Isthmus and mortality were by now accepted as synonymous terms. So many had to die. Pray God you were not one of 'em. As for the poor devils, the unlucky ones, well . . .

From Obispo onwards the track ascended a gradient of sixty feet per mile to the summit gap through the mountains which had been discovered by Baldwin as late as 1849. Here, by Summit, as the spot became known, the line was routed through a winding pass which had long been called Culebra, or Snake. Even here a forty-foot cut, almost a third of a mile long, had to be excavated through the peak.

In January 1854 the track reached Summit. By then it really seemed as though no further set-backs could prevent the completion of the railroad. Less than twelve miles to Panama. Not easy miles, maybe, for the ground on the far side of Summit was precipitous, and the road would have to cross rocky spurs, deep ravines. High embanking had to be done; and some heavy cutting. A mile on from Summit the road would have to skirt a basaltic cliff; its perpendicular formation gave a terrifying picture of the natural forces which had thrown it up. Farther on the Rio Grande would have to be bridged; and the Rio Grande was a narrow, turbulent torrent whose destructive propensities would have to be allowed for. Then, once level ground was reached, much of it was swampy and more filling would be required. Nevertheless, in comparison with the obstacles which had faced the constructors on the other side of the Isthmus, such difficulties were of little consequence: time, and sufficient labour, should see the line completed.

Meanwhile, trains ran to Summit, which at once became the temporary terminus of the railroad. Within a matter of days a small hamlet of a few native huts, set amidst groves of wild mango and guava, grew in importance. Three pre-fabricated hotels, imported from the United States, were erected; and often had to house overnight the larger part of the ship-load of passengers discharged at Aspinwall earlier that day, men, women and children being herded in every available room. The less fortunate had to make do in native huts. In addition to the hotels, stores and warehouses were built; and stabling for the hundreds of pack-animals which carried the passengers the remaining twelve miles to Panama.

From Summit onwards the Pacific could often be glimpsed, gleaming like a vast sapphire set in an emerald ring. Everyone worked with a better will. After so many years of heartbreak, merely to see the end of the track was encouraging: it made everything that had gone before worth while—especially since it meant that one was still living. A reverential thought, for rumour said every tie had cost a man's life. As with all rumours, the figure was grossly exaggerated: only ten to twelve thousand had died to date, countered the wiseacres, who could calculate how many ties went to one mile of track, and knew that many, many more ties than that had been used.

Only ten thousand. . . .

II

In spite of somewhat easier conditions, spells of leave were still necessary to help men recover from the enervating effects of tropical sunshine, torrential rain, and bouts of malaria. Henry spent some short leaves with the Braddocks at Aspinwall; and as all three had by now entirely recovered from embarrassment, they enjoyed his company no less than he did theirs.

But one day, after he had settled in his favourite rocker on the porch, Abigail said to him, "Henry dear, we've bad news for you. The book's finished."

"*Bad* news!" He looked at her in surprise. She was seated on the arm of his chair, making a mess of his hair. "But that's wonderful news, Abigail," he went on warmly. "I'm just crazy to read it."

"I think it is my best," she agreed absently. "But don't you realize what it means, Henry dear? Jim and I will be returning home."

"Oh!" Bad news, Abigail had said. It was worse than that. The Isthmus without Abigail and Jim. . . . "Does that mean soon?" he asked in a flat voice.

"In about three weeks' time, my dear." Abigail glanced quickly away from the misery in his face. "Of course, you have Lucy, but you'll be lonely——"

"Damnably."

"Jim and I were wondering—wouldn't you care to risk coming back with us? The firm couldn't wish to prosecute after all these years."

A long silence followed which neither she nor Braddock cared to break. The rancher puffed at his cigar, and watched Henry with quizzical eyes. He was quite sure he knew what Henry's reply would be, but he was not unaware of the mental struggle that was plainly revealed on the younger man's face.

Henry's expression did not lie. Abigail's suggestion tempted him even more than she had thought it would. He had never been more homesick than at that moment.

Home . . . his parents . . . Peggy . . . Jean. . . .

Besides, there was probably something in what Abigail said, about his old firm's not wanting to prosecute for the loss of the week's wages. After so many years, the partners—were they still both alive?—might well consider that he had been sufficiently punished. And even if they didn't, well, he would go home financially sound enough to employ the best attorney in Massachusetts to defend him. Surely a good lawyer would be able to prove his innocence to the Court?

He almost opened his mouth to say Yes to Abigail's proposition, but for no conscious reason he thought of James McCollum. McCollum loved his wife and children with a deep, abiding love all too rare; but had left them to come back to Panama. Why? To finish the job he had begun. To do his small share towards glorifying American engineering, and helping world commerce. Pride had brought him back; pride in his work and countrymen alike.

Henry felt that he could do no less than McCollum and others who were forgoing the amenities of their homeland to help build the railroad. In fact, the railroad had an even greater call on him than on the others, for it had made him financially sound, and set him up in several ways: he was never likely to want for a job in future. Besides, he, too, was proud of the railroad, and did not feel inclined to relinquish, at this late date, the satisfaction of being on the first train to complete the through journey from Aspinwall to Panama.

Lastly—and here again pride played a prominent part in his reflections—to leave the Isthmus before he had fulfilled the objective which had brought him to the country would, he felt, be the equivalent of admitting defeat, and he was in no mood to do that. Sooner or later he would catch up with Al. However elusive Al might be, the law of averages must sooner or later betray him. He would be seen and recognized, his whereabouts reported, and then——

Henry shook his head. "I'm not leaving here before the railroad's finished, Abigail . . . and perhaps not then unless I've settled with Al."

Braddock chuckled loudly. "What did I tell you, Abby? Red ain't no quitter." He grinned at Henry. "There's only one thing wrong with you, son."

Henry played. "What's that, Jim?"

"You and the East ain't gotten a thing in common. You oughter been born a Westerner. . . ."

III

Although his visits to Abigail and Jim had been more infrequent since he had gone with Lucy to Gatún, Henry missed his friends even more than he had anticipated. Their going seemed to have snapped another precious link with his own country. So pessimistic did his mood become that he was tempted anew to break the last link of all; marry Lucy, and settle down to a lifetime in the Isthmus. Other white men were living out their lives there, and seemed quite content: there seemed no valid reason why he shouldn't be equally happy. Hadn't he his own father as an example of a white man who was content to live in a tropical land? Duncan had lived more than thirty years in Haiti, and had left there only because circumstances had forced him to do so,

Marriage with Lucy? Why not? In so many ways she was worth marrying. She had taught herself to cook, and could turn out an enjoyable meal. Maybe not one in the best traditions of French *haute cuisine*, but still remarkably good considering the lack of amenities. She was a neat little needlewoman, and kept his clothes clean and in a sound state of repair. As a physical mate, no man could ask more of any woman. The emotion which she had once dispersed among many she now concentrated on him alone. He knew she adored him with a deep passion: she expressed it in the way she looked at him, in lingering kisses, in the tenderness with which she would gently stroke his hands. The backs of his hands held a strange fascination for her: they were hairy, and muscular. For her they represented the epitome of masculinity and strength. Because she was weak, mentally and physically, she idolized and idealized strength.

She would make as good a wife as many: better than most. Two factors alone prevented his speaking the words that would condemn him to perpetual banishment. In Panama he need have no shame in making her his wife. The people of Panama were—broad-minded. But who in New England would receive an ex-prostitute?

Apart from a reluctance to become a permanent emigré, his secondary reason for not marrying Lucy concerned children. He wanted children. It was possible that the years of prostitution had made her incapable of bearing children; but even if that were not so, he did not want to have children by her: the idea was too horrible. She was a sweet woman in so many ways, but the life she had led must be paid for. . . .

So Henry remained silent; while Lucy, as if trying to make up to him for the loss of the Braddocks, became still more loving. She was a slave to his slightest wish. He was sincerely grateful to her. Although he could not give her love in return, he tried to make her life happy; and succeeded. Often he planned pleasant surprises for her.

One day, "Like to come for a trip into the jungle next Friday?"

If he had suggested a trip to Hades she would have said Yes. So she clapped her hands in joy, said, "Yes," and added, "What for, Red dear?"

"Juan has told me where to find some Lady of the Night for your birthday."

"Oh!" she exclaimed. She had a passion for orchids, and had created a little paradise of them round about their hut. And Lady of the Night was one of the rarest; so called because its fragrance was only to be smelled at night.

"Dear, dear Red," she continued happily, and wrapping her tiny arms about his broad shoulders she nibbled the lobe of his ear. "You couldn't have offered me a nicer birthday present," she assured him.

IV

The two mules plodded along the jungle trail at an easy pace: though each carried a rider, neither was being prodded by impatient heels nor whacked on the rump by a heartless muleteer. The sky above was cloudless; the tropical sun shone whitely without obstruction, and scorched the parched mass of mountainous jungle. Fortunately the trail was lined with giant espevé and corato trees which cast welcome shade, so neither rider was unduly disturbed by the heat.

Though they were many miles from the nearest settlement, the jungle was noisy with sound: the chorus-like calls of the chachalaca; the grumbling chatter of troops of curious monkeys in the tree tops; the raucous paroquets as they fluffed gay plumage in anger at human intrusion; and occasionally the crashing progress of a peccary.

Presently the travellers reached a clearing, in the centre of which was a single espevé tree on which had been fixed a small shrine, a carved oak canopy over the figure of a saint whose face time had ravaged.

"Here's where Juan said to branch left," Henry told Lucy.

She stared doubtfully at the cross-trail. It was narrower than the one on which they had come, and less cared-for: the jungle was already trying to reclaim it, for thorny creepers and whippy branches were beginning to bridge the narrow track.

"I don't like the looks of it, Red," she said nervously.

"I'll go ahead and use my machete, honey. Juan's sharpened it so, I could shave with it."

"I wasn't thinking of the vegetation."

"Then what?"

"I don't know," she confessed. "Something's making me frightened, and sending cold shivers down my back."

He chuckled. "Lucky you, in this heat."

"Please, Red," she appealed. "Let's turn back."

"And give up the chance of taking home a Lady of the Night to add to your collection of orchids? Your birthday wouldn't be complete——" His face, gaunt and pale from recurrent attacks of malaria, crinkled with high spirits. "Another five miles, honey, and we'll be able to eat and take a siesta under the biggest mango tree between Panama City and Gatún."

She glanced at his rugged face, handsome in its strength and masculinity, and lost her fear of the unknown. Why should one feel afraid with Henry by one's side? Even if one didn't know he could draw a Colt quicker than anyone in Panama, there was something very dependable about the steady eyes, and square obstinate chin; in the tousled red hair which no comb could subdue; in the lithe swing of his fine, firm body; in the rippling muscles which his leanness made prominent.

"All right," she agreed. "I'm as hungry as a hunter."

They left the clearing and moved into the side trail. Before they had gone far she had a recurrence of the uncanny and disturbing premonition which had affected her back in the clearing. She felt that the jungle was closing in upon them, cutting off their retreat. She recollected stories she had heard of travellers who, being lost in the jungle, had died a horrible death from any one of a dozen different causes. Worse than that, she was conscious of an eerie sensation, a feeling that every movement was being watched by human eyes which lurked behind the green curtain of bamboos and gigantic ferns which lined the trail on either side. Once she thought she heard the sound of a movement. When she mentioned it to Henry, he laughed.

"Probably a tapir," he suggested. "Or, maybe, a boa-constrictor. Whichever it is, it is more frightened of us than we are of it."

So they carried on, along a trail that rose ever higher. In spite of this the heat steadily increased. Her head swam with the high humidity. Besides, her heart was thumping with a fear she could not control.

"Can't we stop——" she began.

Her words were interrupted by a shout.

"At last, Red Malley."

Henry's hands moved towards the Colts strapped at his thighs, but he was too late. The echo of a staccato shot was followed by the ghastly thud of a bullet's impact on flesh. A second shot resounded as Henry toppled off the back of his mule.

V

Because the haze of semi-consciousness made the face bending over him swim to and fro in an arc, Henry was unable clearly to distinguish its features; but he did not have to, everything about Jean was engraven on his memory: the soft hazel eyes that were so easily filled with a glow of compassion and sympathy; the mobile lips, so crimson and soft; the straight little nose; the tiny cleft in the chin which dimpled at the slightest excuse; and the chestnut curls which framed her face in long ringlets.

"Hello, Jean honey," he gasped. "I'm not hurt, thank Heaven. I shall be all right in a minute."

He tried to raise himself on one elbow, but the effort was too much for him. His head swam.

"Funny I didn't find out how much I loved you until after I'd left Boston," he mumbled.

Boston—Boston—but why was he thinking that he had left Boston? He was still in Boston, wasn't he? Al and he. . . . Hadn't they just had a drink together? In Murphy's Saloon? Al and he. . . .

VI

As his mind gradually cleared he saw that the face bending over him was not Jean's after all. Nor was it Lucy's, but Juan's. The Negro was forcing raw native liquor down his throat.

"I—I thought I was back in Boston," Henry muttered. "I've been dreaming of Al——"

"Holy Mother be praised!" Juan exclaimed when he saw consciousness return to Henry's eyes. "The señor is not badly hurt. The bullet struck your gun first, señor, then flew upwards, and grazed your forehead."

"And made me unconscious?"

"Yes, señor, for more than an hour."

"An hour!" He tried to remember what had happened: his thoughts were still confused. "Did somebody shoot me, Juan?"

"Yes, señor, but missed, thanks to the Blessed Virgin."

"But why, who——?"

"I think it was La Pantera, señor. I was on my way to warn you." Juan's face was concerned. "One of my spies sent me a message that he had seen a masked man along this trail. La Pantera must have heard that you were coming this way."

"It was La Pantera right enough. I recognized Al's voice."

Juan nodded. "I tried to catch up with you, but was too late. I heard two shots, and shouted. He must have thought I had a posse with me; he had gone by the time I arrived."

"*Two* shots!" Henry struggled to sit up.

"Lucy . . . Juan! Lucy was with me. Where is she?"

The Negro's expression was unhappy: the white-rimmed eyes filled with tears.

"The second shot was better aimed than the first. The poor señora is dead. . . ."

VII

Henry did not recover easily from the shock of Lucy's death: particularly the cold brutality of it, which was matched by previous shootings organized—and for all one knew, carried out—by La Pantera. He worked every hour of the daylight, and often into the night, in the hope of tiring himself into slumber. He practised and re-practised drawing his guns with a hatred which transcended any emotion he had previously experienced. He doubled, and a few days later trebled, the reward which he had offered for news of the whereabouts of either La Pantera or the American Al Simpson.

z

He pleaded with Juan to urge his fellow tribesmen, and other Negroes in the Isthmus, to search for the murderer.

Juan needed no encouragement. Since the episode of the Voodoo dance he had regarded Lucy with a paternal devotion, and his determination to revenge her death was little less vindictive than Henry's own.

"I'll find him one day, señor," he stated with confidence. "La Pantera is not the man to hide away in the mountains for the rest of his life."

Henry was even better aware of that assumption than Juan. The amazing thing was that Al could have remained so long hidden in the interior. Al, with his love of gaiety, of gambling, of women. The only possible explanation of the mystery must lie, as Zachary Fox had once suggested, in Al's hesitation to leave the gold stolen with such damnable effrontery.

Henry returned only once to the hut he had occupied with Lucy, and that was to collect his few belongings. Thereafter he camped on the job and tried to ignore the gap in his life which Lucy's passing had left.

In his sorrow Fate was for once kind to him. One day he was surprised to receive a letter from Boston in a handwriting that was strange to him. It was from Jean.

It began with prim formality:

Dear Mr. Stewart,

You will, I am sure, be surprised to receive a letter from me after all these years, but when I asked your dear Mother to give you some personal news about brother Duncan, Mrs. Stewart said she was sure you would welcome hearing the news from me.

The letter went on to tell simply and shortly of Duncan Martin's engagement—he was named after Duncan Stewart—to a Miss Amelia Tucker (Henry had never heard of her). Henry was glad to hear the news, for he and Duncan Martin had been buddies for as long as either could remember. Jean finished:

I often hear of you from your dear Mother, whom I love as much as ever; and am very happy to learn how well you are doing in that far-off, tropical country.

Dear Mama, whom I have told about this letter, sends you her
sincere regards, as do the rest of the family; especially Duncan, whom
I have never seen looking more happy. With good reason, for Amelia
is a delightful girl and will, I know, make Duncan a loving and dutiful
wife. So, with these words I will finish this letter by subscribing myself,

Your sincere friend,

Jean Martin.

Henry read the letter through many times during the next few
days; each time he did so the sight of the rounded, girlish writing
made him glow with joy. After what he hoped was a discreet
interval he wrote back a short letter of thanks, and indicated that he
would welcome hearing from her if she could occasionally spare a
few minutes from her household duties; he would like to have full
news of the entire family. . . .

The correspondence, once started, flourished in the months
which followed. Yet the happiness which her letters brought him
was not without a degree of bitterness; for her ingenuous prattle
of people and places he knew so well made him feel sick with
nostalgia. It also confirmed his love for her, and made him increasingly impatient for Fate to deal him a trump card for a change.
Al couldn't for ever remain hidden in the interior. It wasn't in
keeping with his character. He was no miser. Sooner or later he
would want to spend the gold he had stolen from the mule-trains.

Meanwhile, the track advanced slowly to its destination. But
one day a transient New Yorker asked Henry and James Mc-
Collum:

"What the hell you two wasting time for, driving a railroad
across the Isthmus?"

The question startled the two surveyors. They looked at each
other.

"Well, it's one way of earning a living," McCollum answered
drily.

"Sure, sure! But I wasn't talking personal. I mean, what's the
use of spending so many millions of dollars building a railroad
across the Isthmus which won't be no damn' use in a few years'
time?"

"Why not?" Henry asked shortly.

"Because the American Government is going to be building a canal soon, that's what! And what hope do you think your goddamn railroad will have then?"

The man had been drinking, he decided. "There's been talk of constructing a canal across the Isthmus ever since the time of Christopher Columbus."

"Yeah, yeah, I know, but this time Uncle Sam is really serious. Haven't you people heard yet that a naval party has landed at Caledonia Bay?"

He remembered McCollum speaking of the proposed survey on his return to Aspinwall.

"We heard they were on the way. How many——"

The New Yorker knew his facts, and answered the question before it was asked. "Twenty-seven men under Lieutenant Isaac Strain," he snapped. "And that party don't cost a dime! What they want to send twenty-seven men for, when three or four could do the job good?"

"You think so?" McCollum asked drily.

"Yeah! Me and two others."

"You a surveyor?"

"Sure am. And am I going to make good in California?"

"Know this country at all?"

"Panama, you mean?"

"Yes."

"I've never been here before, if that's what you mean."

"It sure is what I mean. Who would look after your back while you were taking sights, eh?"

"What's wrong with my back?" the man challenged belligerently.

McCollum grinned. "Nothing, brother, but it wouldn't look so good with an Indian arrow sticking in it."

"Indians!"

"Yes, brother; Indians. That part of the country's so full of mean Indians they would make three men on their own look like pin cushions. So just you talk about what you know, in future, and leave the Navy alone, see!"

The stranger saw. "Indians!" he repeated uncertainly.

During the next few days belated news of the naval expedition trickled along the railroad track—the New Yorker wasn't the only critic to comment acidly on the chance of a trans-Isthmian canal being started before the railroad was finished. The naval party, it seemed, anticipated crossing the Isthmus in something less than ten days, for they were carrying a supply of provisions calculated to last that long. And each man was armed with a rifle and forty rounds of ball cartridge.

With quizzical interest the people of the Chagres valley settled down to await further news of the survey party. For ten days nothing was heard of the expedition; but then nobody expected otherwise, for the surveyors were striking through country that was jungle from coast to coast, so that they would not encounter civilization until they emerged on the Pacific coast. Meanwhile, the constructors drove their labourers harder: there was a sting in the joke that the canal would be started before the track was finished, which didn't exactly raise a laugh.

The ten days expired, and then ten more—and the American population of the Isthmus was shocked to realize that there was still no news of the surveyors. Anxiety mounted day by day. Another week passed; by which time there was scarcely a soul in Panama who did not believe that disaster had overtaken the party. "Indians," murmured some. Others said, "The jungle!" Prayers were offered for the safety of the explorers—and if it were too late for that, then for their souls.

More days passed; then four scarecrows tottered out of the fringe of the jungle; haggard, unshaven, starving, and bloody. As soon as he was able to speak one of them identified himself as Lieutenant Strain. Later he told his story. The party had soon lost themselves in spite of their surveyors' instruments. They had picked their way through jungle, climbed and descended mountains, been bogged down in fetid swamps, had crossed and recrossed alligator-infested rivers until their food was exhausted, their clothes and flesh torn to shreds, their muscles pulled and their resistance sapped. They had been constantly aware of unseen, hostile Indians; and the knowledge had frayed their nerves as they awaited the attack which never came. It had not taken them long to realize that the Indians had more subtle ways of killing: the natives went before them, and swept their paths clear of food. Soon the men were compelled to live on a diet of nuts, a toad or so, and the few birds they succeeded in killing. This diet gave them dysentery and skin sores, and loosened their teeth: jiggers buried into their flesh and grew there, agonizing the unhappy men. At last, realizing the hopelessness, after twenty-three days of relentless battle with the jungle, of getting all his men back to safety, Lieutenant Strain had taken the risk of pushing on to the west ahead of his party, in the hope of reaching civilization and securing help.

A relief party was quickly organized, led by skilled guides. They vanished into the jungle. Weeks passed, but eventually news reached the anxious Americans that the survivors of the survey party had been located, thirty-nine days after Strain had left them. But alas! of the twenty-seven men who had landed at Caledonia Bay, nine died in the jungle: few of the remainder recovered complete health.

The possibility of canal competition ceased to worry the shareholders of the Panama Railroad Company. What had they to worry about? Just a dream. . . .

VIII

Mile by mile the track crept forward towards Panama City. Every day the spirits of the executive rose. They had seen an impossibility develop first into a possibility, then a probability, and now—a certainty. Only a handful of miles still to be completed, as many months would see the job done.

Henry was one of the happiest of men. Letters were arriving regularly from Jean. Not love letters in the true sense, but every prim, proper little word breathed unspoken and undeclared mutual love and confidence. Each knew that an understanding between them existed. One day, perhaps as soon as the railroad was finished, he would return to the United States: if not to Massachusetts, then certainly to New York; there to request her hand in marriage.

One night, as he leaned against a palm tree smoking a prebedtime cigar and dreaming of that happy day to come, he was disturbed by a hissing.

"Señor."

He turned, but the darkness hid the speaker.

"Who is it?" he snapped, feeling for the guns which were not with him. He tensed his muscles. Al was not going to shoot him a second time without some sort of a struggle. . . .

"Juan, señor. I have news for you."

"Well?"

"La Pantera is in Panama City. Come quickly, señor. . . ."

CHAPTER THIRTY-NINE

HENRY went in search of McCollum.

"I want a few days' leave, Jimmy," he announced brusquely. "I've just had news La Pantera's in Panama."

The surveyor inspected Henry's set face. "Sure, Red . . . and good luck." He extended a bony hand.

"Thanks, Jimmy."

Henry took Juan along to the frame-building which he was sharing with McCollum and two other members of the executive staff. It took him only a few minutes to pack a few toilet articles and change of underwear into a small haversack. Juan watched him with a dog-like devotion.

"Now to hire me a mule, and I'll be with you, Juan."

"You do not want a mule, señor. I brought one for you from Panama, the best in the city, in case you couldn't get one here."

"I mayn't at that. Thanks a million. Let's get moving."

The two men were soon moving down the Panama trail. As soon as they were clear of the village Henry took the risk of a spill on the precipitous slope they were descending, and began to spur his animal. Juan remonstrated.

"It is not safe to spur your animal, señor. There is no hurry."

"No hurry be damned! I haven't waited all these years to meet that man to let him escape for the sake of a possible spill."

"He won't leave Panama before you get there," Juan said with confidence. "Señor Runnels is seeing to that."

"He knows——"

"I let him know at once. La Pantera will not move a step without one of the Isthmian Guard."

"Juan, you're a treasure!" Henry let the animal select its own pace. "What happened?"

"One of my tribe was returning home after having taken bananas to Matachin, for transport to Aspinwall, when he passed an American apparently on his way towards that place, señor. Knowing that you had offered a reward for news of La Pantera he turned and followed the man. At Matachin the American met another American, and a young Frenchman——"

"Young Perrigot?"

"Yes, señor, as I found out later on. Young Perrigot and Señor Holmes."

Henry snapped finger and thumb together. "Go on, man," he barked.

"Antonio—the name of my tribesman, señor—found out that the three people were starting off right away for Panama, so he sent me a message to watch out for them. . . ."

"A message! How could you get a message before they reached Panama?"

Juan regarded Henry with sombre eyes. "That is a tribal secret, señor. . . ."

But Henry was sure he knew. "By drums?"

"Perhaps, señor," the Negro agreed non-committally. "As soon as I received the message I made arrangements to hide by the trail. They passed by me soon after three o'clock."

"And you recognized Holmes and Perrigot?"

"At once, señor, and also their companion, from your description of him. I am sure it was the man you call Señor Simpson. Besides, señor, I overheard Señor Holmes call him Al.'"

Henry stared into the darkness. Light clouds covered most of the sky, but the white reflection of the moon through the clouds dispersed the darkness enough to make travelling easy. But he was not conscious of darkness, lightness, or the wind which, at that height, made the night almost chill; he was conscious of nothing save the fact that God willing! he might, before many more hours had passed, have achieved the objective for which he had waited with such patience these past few days.

He tried to control his feeling of excited exaltation, but it was not easy. Don't count your chickens until they're hatched, he kept on telling himself. Don't count your chickens . . . But he was deaf to common sense. He did count them, not once but a hundred times. The knowledge that Al was in Panama brought Boston, New England, the United States, so much nearer: in his imagination the lush tropical scenery rolled away from either side of him and was replaced by the frost-spangled, leafless woods, the grey, slabby rocks, the fields and farmhouses of Massachusetts. He smelled the incense of smouldering logs, and listened to the creaking rumble of wagon wheels, the slow clop-clop-clop of hooves, and the drawling, "Gid along, thar, gid along."

Home! The prospect of returning home after long years of exile obsessed him; he could not concentrate on the present, because there was room in his thoughts only for the future. Frosty nights, snowy mornings, sleigh bells, a Christmas tree in the window, parties, American voices—and his parents, God bless them. Older, but not too much older than when he last saw them, he hoped, although one could scarcely expect time to stand still for people at that age.

Unconscious of what he was doing he heeled his animal and made it buck in anger, and back towards the edge of the trail which thereabouts fell away in a steep slope.

"Señor——" Juan called out in warning, but Henry did not have to be reminded of the danger he was in. He quietened the animal, and gently enticed it back on to the trail. It soon settled down when it sensed that its rider was composed again.

"Guess I let my excitement get ahead of me, Juan. I didn't think what I was doing."

"No, señor."

Juan did not sound very understanding. He couldn't very well be, Henry reflected. The man didn't know what it meant to glimpse home, even in one's imagination, after being virtually exiled for more than five years.

Five years! Not too long a period in terms of a man's normal life, but then years of exile were not normal years. They were twice, thrice as long. . . .

He kept a rigid control on himself for the rest of the journey.

2A

There was no knowing what might have happened had his animal backed another foot or so. Death, as likely as not! To die just when one was on the threshold of return would have been a cruel jest on Fate's part: a jest that would have hurt him least of all.

They reached the outskirts of Panama just after 1 a.m.

"What now, Juan?"

"Señor Runnels will be waiting for you——"

"Not at this time. He will be in bed."

"He said for me to take you to him whatever the time."

"All right."

They clattered along a series of dark, quiet streets, the hooves of their animals echoing loudly as the high buildings on either side of them first magnified the noise then flung it back at them—Henry thought that nobody could hope to sleep through such a racket. He grinned drily. How different present conditions were from those on the night Ran Runnels' Isthmian Guard had walked silently through the streets on their way for the first time to round up La Pantera's bandit gang. God! That was already three years ago. And now, at last, he was on his way to round up La Pantera himself, but noisily, without special precautions.

"Red!" Runnels looked sleepy, but his handshake was firm enough. "Glad you were able to get here."

"He hasn't left——"

"Left! Of course not! He's not likely to leave. I'll see to that."

"Where is he now?"

Runnels' blue eyes twinkled. "In a hurry to meet him, Red?"

"Can't be too soon. Is he back at Holmes' place?"

"Not yet. He's gambling."

"Gambling!" A quick smile of anticipation passed across Henry's face; relieving, for a moment, the stern expression which had settled there upon hearing Juan's news. "Not—not Fox?"

The Ranger's boyish grin was its own answer, but he went on, "Yeah. He went to Holmes' rooms first of all, as I s'pose Juan told you——"

Henry nodded.

"Soon after dark he and Holmes and young Perrigot went out to Henri's French Restaurant for a meal. They stayed there 'bout an hour or a little more, I reckon. When they came out they sent the French boy home—by which I mean Holmes' rooms, if you can call them home. Then they went on to Fox's gambling joint."

"So early? That's Al right enough. Couldn't wait to start flinging his money about."

"Sure he couldn't. Anyway, as soon as I heard where they'd gone I went round to Fox, and sent a message up to him—I didn't want Holmes to see me, you understand: he's smart, that feller——"

"Damnably."

"You should have seen Fox's face when I told him Al Simpson was in his rooms—in a manner of speaking, that is, Red, for nobody don't ever get nothing from Fox's face. But I was sort of certain that the news meant something to him—I kinda sensed his nerves go stiff, you might say——"

Henry nodded. "Like you, before you reach for your guns?"

"Exactly it, Red. Then Fox, he thinks for a few minutes then says, 'Come with me, Ran,' and takes me to a small room next the gaming-room. It was all dark, but Fox guides me past the furniture, moves something on the wall, and I finds myself looking through a small round window straight into the gaming-room."

"A peep-hole?"

"Sure. Fox likes to use it when he's eating, to keep an eye on what's happening when he ain't there," Runnels explained in his lazy drawl. "Wal, I looks through and sees Holmes and a stranger, an American, playing faro. It was your Al Simpson, or my name ain't Runnels."

"Go on."

Runnels inspected Henry's grim face. "Take it easy, Red. Simpson's wearin' guns."

"Well?"

"You ain't forgetting he's still gunning for you," the Ranger warned. "With as pretty a brace of Colts as I've seen in years—ever since I left the States."

"I haven't forgotten."

"Listen, Red," Runnels continued earnestly, "if you challenge him in your present mood you're liable to be dead before you know what's hit you. Calm down, man——"

"How in God's name do you expect me to remain calm? I've waited five years for this minute——"

"Then wait five minutes till I finish telling you what I saw. Then start thinking of Jean and your Ma and Pa, and how they want to see you again."

Henry swallowed. "All right. So you saw them playing faro?"

"Yeah. Holmes looked like he was enjoying himself, but your Al didn't seem none too interested——"

"Poker used to be his game."

"Ah! Fox know that?"

"I told him."

"That explains what. For while I'm looking through this here peep-hole I sees Fox come into the room, and after wandering round casual-like he sits him down at a spare table and starts shuffling a deck of cards. Soon one or two other fellers sit themselves at his table an' he starts a school of poker. Before you can say Jack Robinson, your pal Al chips in."

Henry's eyes glowed. "And he's still there?"

"I ain't heard different."

"Then I'm off there, Ran. Thanks a million——" He made for the door.

"Hey there! I'm coming, too."

"But Ran, what about your sleep?"

"Do you think I'd miss what's coming to that critter?" A boyish grin appeared—then vanished. The Ranger laid a hand on Henry's shoulder. "Remember what I said about keeping cool, pardner. Them as remains cool lives the longest."

Henry turned. "Right now, Ran, I'm icy-cold with hate."

The blue eyes inspected Henry's forbidding face, then warmed with approval. "Sure you are," Ran said with relief. "Just you remain that way."

They walked round to Fox's gaming-rooms; Juan accompanied them. To all Runnels' orders to take himself off to bed he had remained obstinately deaf. His black eyes had scarcely blinked while the two white men had been talking: they had rested on Henry with a devotion that made the Ranger believe there would be little hope of Simpson's remaining alive for long if chance should protect him from Henry's avenging bullet. Not that Juan was likely to get *his* chance at killing Simpson, Runnels reflected grimly. For after Red there was himself to reckon with—and he was neither hot with desire nor ice-cold with hatred. He was the Law in this strange, lawless country; and the Law knew no emotion, only Justice. He had no doubts about his own ability to deal adequately with La Pantera. So he let Juan accompany them as Henry's shadow, because he thought that the man who had been mainly responsible for bringing about the meeting should have the reward of witnessing it.

Henry's thoughts were sombre. Overhead the clouds had cleared away, leaving the black-blue velvet sky a scintillating mass of stars: it seemed to his sharpened imagination that he had rarely seen the sky quite so studded: that he might never see so many again. Or any again! Death was in his heart and thoughts—but whose death? His or Al's? If rumour were correct, Al, too, had been preparing for this meeting. Perhaps his journey into Panama was his challenge to Red Malley. If you want me come and get me. I'm ready for you. My skill against yours.

Within the next few hours you may be dead, Henry told himself—and the thought made his heart flutter. He did not want to die. He wanted to kill Al, and would kill Al if no confession was forthcoming, but he did not want to die. Life was still very sweet in spite of its grey moments. He wanted desperately to see the stars tomorrow night, and for many, many nights after that. He wanted to live so that he could return to Boston and squarely face the people there with a fearless, easy conscience. He wanted to see his parents again. He wanted to make Jean a worthy husband. He wanted a family, a silver wedding; maybe a golden wedding. God! He wanted so much. Never so much as at this moment when life itself might be denied him if Al were that fractional part of a second quicker on the draw.

The fluttering grew worse. He despised himself for it, but it continued. He wanted to pray to God for success; but when he tried to piece words together, another part of him boggled at the idea. Don't drag God into the business, Henry. Man against man: leave it at that. Don't ask God to interfere in an affair of hate. God is love.

From time to time as they passed an occasional lighted window

Ran Runnels glanced with curiosity at his companion; and noted with satisfaction the even pace at which Henry walked, the flung-back head, and squared shoulders. He also noted the strained expression, and guessed what thoughts were passing through the mind of the man beside him. And Ran Runnels, the ex-Texas Ranger, Ran Runnels, the killer, Ran Runnels, the executioner, both sympathized and rejoiced. He, too, in the past had squared his shoulders and stiffened his neck to disguise his fear of never seeing the sun rise again. He also knew that fear would make Henry the better marksman. That is why he rejoiced.

Upon reaching the stairs which led up to Fox's gaming-room they found a man stationed there; a burly Irishman whom Fox employed as chucker-out. Would they be after going into the little private room instead of the main room, for Mr. Fox would be wishing to speak to them first?

Runnels nodded. "Sure. How are we to let Mr. Fox know we'll be there?"

"It's meself that will be giving him the sign, sor. It's all fixed between us."

"Then the Americans are still there? Still playing?"

"Begod! an' they look like they'll never be stopping this side of tomorrow morn," the man reassured them.

Runnels led the way into the little private room, Henry and Juan followed. The Ranger moved a curtain which concealed a door with a peep-hole in it.

"Look, Red."

The man facing Zachary Fox was Al. Unmistakably, undeniably Al. He had changed. He was more handsome, in a raffish sort of way, for his face was weathered, and lean and reckless. Less dissolute, maybe: the years he had spent in the mountains had tightened the skin under his eyes, and firmed up his once loose mouth. But there was no mistaking the blond hair, the high cheekbones, the defiant, challenging chin. Al! Al at last, after five years of patient waiting.

"Thank You, God," he murmured. "Thank You—thank You—thank You. . . ."

CHAPTER FORTY

As soon as Henry was able to think with some degree of coherence and regard the scene before him as a whole, he became aware of several unusual features. In the first place gambling had stopped at the other tables; and the handful of bankers and backers, who had stayed on after the normal closing time, had for once found the excitement of watching others gamble more fascinating than the lure of easy money; just now they were gathered in a circle round Fox's poker table; silenced by the drama of the duel that was taking place there. Henry had never known the gaming-room so quiet: so still was it that he could hear quite plainly the clink of coins, the soft shu-shu-shu of the cards as they were shuffled, and the flat voices of the players when they asked for cards, or made their bids.

Five players sat round the table. Two were strangers to Henry. Transients, perhaps. They were American in appearance. The third was a rich Panamanian whose only interest in life other than women was gambling: night after night Henry had seen him in Fox's gaming-room; he appeared to have no liking for one game more than another; he joined in any that promised to be exciting, or where the stakes were higher. He was a good player, Henry remembered, with average luck. At that moment he had a pile of coins before him big enough to suggest that he was a moderate winner: in addition he had won a few bags of gold-dust. Of the two Americans, one had only a few coins before him; his scowling expression suggested that he was a loser. The second American still had money on the table, but if his face were any indication, he was less interested in the game than in watching the two chief protagonists, Al and Fox. Both he and the other American wore Western clothes.

Last of all—he felt like a child, saving the tastiest morsel for the end of the meal—Henry looked at the two men in whom he was interested. Fox first. But not for long. Fox was always Fox. Impassive, imperturbable, immaculate, and pale-faced. From his appearance he might have sat down only five minutes previously. His pile of money proved otherwise. Henry did not remember ever having seen so much money before him; not even on that still-remembered first night in Chagres, when Braddock had had to draw his Colt. The coins were stacked before him in irregular piles. Ten, twenty, thirty piles. . . . Henry stopped counting. There were also gold nuggets, and bags of gold-dust. He could not begin to compute how much Fox must have won during many hours of play.

Lastly, Al. Although he still had as much money before him as the two Westerners combined, there were several indications that he was a loser. His oiled hair was untidy, and looked as if he had frequently brushed his fingers through it, his mouth was sulky, and behind his raffish expression of defiance Henry believed he detected anger and frustration, and an obstinate determination to defeat the unsmiling gambler who sat opposite him.

One of the Westerners, the loser, dealt the cards. All save himself doubled Al's original ante, and drew cards. Al, on the Westerner's left, drew three; the Panamanian, one; Fox, one; the winning Westerner, two.

The Panamanian (Henry could not remember the man's name) opened the betting.

"Five," he said, pushing the money towards the centre of the table.

"I'll see that and raise it five." This from Fox, on the Panamanian's left.

The winning Westerner pushed some coins forward. "Another five."

Al sneered. "Chicken feed! I'll make it thirty dollars."

The Panamanian thoughtfully studied his hand, and threw in.

Fox said, in his emotionless voice, "And another ten."

The Westerner grinned at a private joke of his own. "You two again, eh? You don't frighten me this time, mister. I'm staying with you. Show!" He added more coins to his original bet.

"Another twenty," snapped Al.

"I'll see, and raise fifty." This from Fox.

"Guess you've frightened me, after all," said the Westerner, throwing his cards in.

"You're bluffing," Al snarled. "I'll see you, Fox."

Fox exposed a small straight. Al threw in his hand with an

angry gesture. Fox added his winnings to the pile of money in front of him.

"I suggest a ten-minute break, gentlemen," he said in his slow, soft voice. "You wish to continue afterwards?"

Holmes touched Al on the shoulder. "Let's get going?"

Al glared at him. "Hell! If you think I'd stop now before one of us two is cleaned up! His luck can't last for ever. It will be my turn soon."

"I am at your service for as long as you wish, gentlemen," Fox assured the players.

The losing Westerner rose to his feet. "So long as we're stopping, then I've had enough. A drink first, and then it's bed for me."

"A drink certainly, señores," the Panamanian agreed, likewise rising. "But I am not sleepy."

"Nor me," joined in the more cheerful of the two Westerners.

Henry closed the peep-hole, and was not astonished when Fox entered the ante-room by way of the communicating door. He gripped Henry's hand.

"The end of the trail, Red."

"Thanks, Zachary!" Henry muttered. "Now for Al——"

"Wait," Fox ordered sharply.

"For what? This is my moment. . . ."

"I ask you to wait, Red. Your friend Al is in a dangerous mood. . . ." He saw Henry's expression. "It is not cowardice to wait for the right moment, Red. Ask Ran."

"Of course it ain't," Runnels confirmed. "It's policy. What's on your mind, Fox?"

"The more he loses the angrier he will become."

"Sure, and the less cautious. Ain't that just what I've been telling you, Red, you mustn't let your heart control your head?"

"Suppose he wins," Henry objected.

"He will be flushed with victory, and equally off-guard. If you want his confession you must manœuvre him into a position where he can't have a chance to draw and fight it out."

"Fox is right," Runnels urged. "There's no time lost by waiting."

"All right," Henry agreed with reluctance.

Fox returned to the main room. After a few minutes the game continued, but Al had had a couple of drinks in that time, and was more reckless than ever.

For a time it seemed as if his forecast that Fox's luck could not last was justified. The gambler lost several highly backed bluffs; he also found better hands against him, and lost even more. His pile of money shrank appreciably, much of it going to Al. But his expression did not change.

The same could not be said of the other three men. The dark, almost sloe-eyed, face of the Panamanian looked pleased; the Westerner waxed still more cheerful; Al smirked with triumph. Time passed. The session seemed as if it could last for ever. Then, slowly, the tide turned. The gold coins began to mount up again before Fox. He won a big jack-pot on a pair of jacks; he won several large bets on high threes; and also won several hands without having to reveal his. Bluffing? Henry could not decide. The impassive face was as changeless as time.

An hour passed. Another. The game went on. Three of the onlookers left, but the rest remained, too intent on the game to care whether they slept or not that night. At last the Westerner's pile was exhausted. He shrugged his shoulders.

"I'm through," he announced good-humouredly. "You three play on."

The Panamanian's luck continued even: his pile of money remained much the same. But Al began to lose steadily, though occasional handsome wins made the process a slow one.

To Henry, the long wait for action was beneficial. His nerves were steady, his emotions neutral. With the patience that five years' delay had developed, he waited for an opportunity to confront Al Simpson and force a written confession from him. When and how were questions which he did not allow to bother him. Fate, he decided, must determine the circumstances of that meeting. As long as he remained on the alert . . .

Play continued. The onlookers drifted out one by one until only Holmes and two employees remained. Even the players were jaded—all save Fox, whose waxen face looked as cool and fresh as an iced pear, and as inexpressive.

The climax was fast approaching. Al had little more than one hundred dollars left on the table. His forehead was beaded with sweat, and his eyes bloodshot. Instinctively Henry adjusted his holster belt, and made sure that his guns were free. As soon as Al rose from his chair . . .

Fox dealt, and when all three had staked, he looked at Al.

"One," Al answered.

The Panamanian took three.

Fox said, "Dealer takes one."

The Panamanian bet first. "Two dollars," he began modestly.

"I'll see and raise one," Fox said.

Al reflected. "I'll make it ten."

"Fifteen," said the Panamanian.

Fox raised the bet to twenty.

"I'll double that," Al said: there was a faint note of desperation in his voice.

With an expressive shrug the Panamanian threw in, and lit a cigar.

"I'll see forty, and raise it twenty-five," Fox murmured.

Al peered at his cards, then pushed all that remained of his money towards the centre of the table. "Make it . . ." he counted. "Ninety-three dollars," he finished.

"See and raise another twenty-five."

"Damn you!" Al shouted. "You can see I've nothing left."

"Then you must throw in, sir," Fox reproved.

"God! On this hand? It's worth double. Will you take an I.O.U., Fox?"

"I'm sorry, sir, I do not take I.O.U.s. Cash only."

Al turned to the Panamanian. "What about you, señor?"

The Panamanian shook his head. "With the greatest respect, señor, I make a rule never to lend money. Alas! it makes too many enemies."

"Curse the whole damned crowd of you," Al mouthed. "You took advantage of me, Fox. You're bluffing. You only raised me because you could see I had no more money left."

Fox placed his cards down on the table, face downwards. "I did not wish to take advantage of you, sir. For all I knew you might have had a reserve of money in your pocket."

"Señor Fox was justified in thinking so, señor," the Panamanian interrupted. "I thought so. Most gamblers keep a hidden reserve."

"I will make you a proposition, sir," Fox went on. "A chance to carry on playing for as many more hours as you wish—if you have the cards to win this hand." He glanced at Al's hand.

Henry swore. "What's he playing at, just when he has Al where he wants him?" he asked angrily. "I'm going in."

"No," Runnels ordered sharply. "Al's facing this way. He could shoot you as you opened the door. Leave it to Fox."

Al leaned across the table. "Make your damned proposition, Fox. I'm listening."

"If you will be content with one bet, I'll wager everything I have on the table against a little piece of signed paper from you, sir."

"*Madre de Dios*," the Panamanian gasped. "All that money——"

Al looked startled. "An I.O.U., a bill——"

"Something even less valuable, and less negotiable. If you lose the piece of paper will cost you nothing. If you win you win—this——" Fox pushed some of the heaps over with a flick of his fingers.

Al stared with avarice at the gold. All his own money back, plus Fox's original capital, plus the winnings from the two Westerners. A small fortune. . . .

"Give me paper and pen," he gasped hoarsely.

At a signal from Fox one of the two remaining employees placed paper and pen on the table before Al Simpson. He took up the pen, dipped it in the ink.

"What do you want me to write?"

"A confession exonerating your friend Henry Stewart."

Al dropped the pen back in the inkwell. His hands hovered out his guns.

"What do you know of Henry Stewart?" he demanded. His ? and manner were dangerously cool.

?nry curled his fingers round the handle of the door, but ?he could turn it Runnels' hand had covered his with a steel-

" he hissed in Henry's ear. "Trust Fox——"

Fox was already answering. "Does it matter to you that he is a friend of mine? You never wished him harm. You only wanted the money, didn't you?"

"Well?" The hands did not move away from the guns.

"Do you hope ever to return to Boston?"

"No."

"Then—this money, with a chance to make as much again, against something that can never harm you—isn't the stake worth the risk?"

"By God! it is. Where's that pen?"

He wrote for half a minute, then passed the paper across the table to Fox. The gambler read it through, nodded, tossed it on top of the money already in the pool, then added all his own money to the total stake. Al's eyes glistened in anticipation. He leaned forward.

"What you got, Fox?"

"A pair of deuces," the gambler murmured.

"A pair——" Al laughed. "By God! Bluffing!" And laughed again. "Of all the cock-eyed times to bluff! Look!" He threw his hand down before Fox. "Against four kings." He laughed again, till he was gasping for breath. "So the money's mine, and the paper, too." He stretched an arm towards it.

Henry kicked open the door and stepped into the gaming-room. "Hold it, Al."

Al stiffened, looked up. "Henry Stewart!"

"Red Malley to you, La Pantera," Fox mocked.

"Malley——"

Two guns roared. Henry felt something strike his left shoulder with a force that spun him half round. But for Runnels he would have fallen. He wasn't conscious of pain, but tears of mortification welled from his eyes. So much for years of practice, for an overwhelming egotistical confidence in his own quickness. So much for his hopes of proving his innocence. . . .

He heard a thump as Runnels straightened him up, and turned him back towards the centre of the room. Al was lying on the ground, still and crumpled. . . .

"Not so bad," Runnels drawled. "Right through the heart. . . ."

II

Another Christmas. The sixth he had spent in Panama. And the last, for he and McCollum had booked passages in a ship scheduled to leave Aspinwall for New York during the second week in February. By then the track would be finished, and a regular service established. Both men could have spent that Christmas at home had they wished, for their job was virtually finished, and there were other surveyors prepared to stay on and cope with routine, and the renewal work which local conditions had already made necessary—the wooden trestle bridge at Barbacoas, for instance, which would shortly have to be replaced by an iron bridge; that part of the track across the Black Swamp, where the foundation would persist in collapsing at frequent intervals; and the relaying of the track on account of slides: a constant menace in the neighbourhood of the Culebra cut near Summit.

Neither man took advantage of the opportunity of an early return. They felt they owed it to themselves to ride in the first train to complete the trip from Aspinwall to Panama City. So they stayed at Panama City, and spent Christmas Day in the company of Zachary Fox and Ran Runnels. It was Henry's happiest day.

Towards the end of the meal Fox rapped on a plate for silence. When he had obtained this he fingered his glass.

"Fill your glasses, gentlemen. I want to propose a toast."

The bottle circulated—they were drinking champagne; which, for a change, was without its usual dose of quinine.

"I give you Henry Stewart, alias Red Malley. Here's to his triumphant return home to rehabilitation. . . ."

"Jees!" Runnels interrupted with astonishment. "Words like that after all the likker we've downed. . . . What's it mean, anyway?"

"Rehabilitation," Fox explained, "means—means . . . ask me some other day, Ran. Anyway, it's what he's returning to; and to loving parents who never lost their trust in him; and to a sweet girl whose likeness tells me she will make a loving wife and mother—in short, friends, to our Henry."

"To Henry," McCollum echoed with a far-away expression in

his eyes. "And to Phyllis," he whispered aloud to himself, "an' Susan, an' Maggie, an' Junior. . . ."

"Sure!" exclaimed Runnels loudly. "To Henry, a good scout." He grimaced at the bubbling liquid. A toast like that called for a man's drink. For Bourbon. . . .

"To you," concluded Zachary Fox, and drained his glass.

One toast called for another; they were all good scouts. But they were drunk quickly, in embarrassment, and soon they were at ease again, and cheerful.

"By the way, Red," presently commented Runnels, "your two friends have vamoosed."

"Friends?"

The boyish face twisted in a mischievous grin. "Holmes and Perrigot. They left for 'Frisco last week on the *Golden Gate*."

"That's strange!"

"What's so strange about them skipping? I told them to go or else . . . You thinking about La Pantera's loot?"

"Yes."

Runnels shrugged. "Fox there may be right in thinking La Pantera cached it some place, but if so it ain't going to be found that easy."

"But when it is, somebody's going to be in the money, Ran, I'm certain of that," said Fox.

"I shouldn't wonder."

"How much do you think he may have hidden away?" McCollum asked.

"Quarter to half a million dollars' worth, maybe. What do you think, Fox?"

Fox nodded. "Quite a quarter of a million, Ran."

McCollum joined in. "Wasn't he supposed to be living with some woman?"

"That was the story. But!" Runnels turned to Henry. "What was on your mind, Red?"

"That Holmes probably considers himself heir apparent to the old. I couldn't understand his being willing to leave the country without trying to find the cache."

"That's what I figgered!" Runnels' eyes gleamed with mischief. "And he wasn't exactly willing. But he won't return. If anyone's going to find that money it's me, see, not hoodlums like him. The gold belongs to the express companies."

"Forget it, fellers," urged McCollum. "This is Christmas Day, isn't it——"

III

Just before midnight, on the 27th January, 1855, the last rail was laid. The rain teemed down, and the night was dark: the labourers had to work by the light of oil flares. But the weather did not damp the spirits of the men present. They cheered in many languages; they sang, they danced, and they drank hard liquor and soft; and celebrated the occasion. Their work had been done at great cost in human lives and American dollars. But it *was* done, so they rejoiced—Colonel Totten, McCollum and Henry particularly; three of the few to survive from the beginning. Occasionally they thought of the ten thousand men who had given their lives to see 48 miles of railroad track constructed through some of the most difficult terrain in the world. Presently they piled into the train that waited to take them back to Aspinwall for a few hours' sleep.

Tomorrow was dedicated to the first ocean to ocean train, and their places on it were reserved.

THE END